Praise for *New York Times* bestselling author

Lori Foster

"A sexy, believable roller coaster of action and romance."
—*Kirkus Reviews* on *Run the Risk*

"Bestseller Foster…has an amazing ability to capture a man's emotions and lust with sizzling sex scenes and meld it with a strong woman's point of view."
—*Publishers Weekly* on *A Perfect Storm*

"Foster rounds out her searing trilogy with a story that tilts toward the sizzling and sexy side of the genre."
—*RT Book Reviews* on *Savor the Danger*

"The fast-paced thriller keeps these well-developed characters moving.… Foster's series will continue to garner fans with this exciting installment."
—*Publishers Weekly* on *Trace of Fever*

"Steamy, edgy and taut."
—*Library Journal* on *When You Dare*

"Intense, edgy and hot. Lori Foster delivers everything you're looking for in a romance."
—*New York Times* bestselling author Jayne Ann Krentz on *Hard to Handle*

"Lori Foster delivers the goods."
—*Publishers Weekly*

"Tension, temptation, hot action and hotter romance—Lori Foster has it all! *Hard to Handle* is a knockout!"
—*New York Times* bestselling author Elizabeth Lowell

Dear Reader,

I often get asked if I have a favorite book or favorite character that I've written. The truth is, I wouldn't write a character I didn't enjoy, or a plot that didn't excite me. So all my stories are favorites in one way or another.

BUT... *Bare It All,* the second in my new Love Undercover series, does include a very special heroine. Alice was originally meant to be strictly a secondary character in *Trace of Fever,* a book from my previous Men Who Walk the Edge of Honor series. Alice had a pivotal role in wrapping up the plot of that story, but she was so quiet, so withdrawn that some readers might have overlooked her. I could not.

Because of her strength and courage, because of what she'd endured, Alice stayed in my mind. When Reese Bareden showed up in the first Love Undercover book, *Run the Risk,* I knew he was exactly what Alice needed. The characters agreed, and a plot was born.

I hope you enjoy Alice's "happy ever after" as much as I enjoyed writing it.

Lori Foster

LORI FOSTER

BARE IT ALL

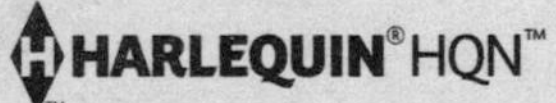

ISBN-13: 978-0-373-77761-7

BARE IT ALL

This edition published by arrangement with Harlequin Books S.A.

For questions and comments about the quality of this book, please contact us at CustomerService@Harlequin.com.

Printed in U.S.A.

Also available from
LORI FOSTER
and Harlequin HQN

Love Undercover

Run the Risk

Men Who Walk the Edge of Honor

"What Chris Wants" (ebook novella)
A Perfect Storm
Savor the Danger
Trace of Fever
When You Dare
The Guy Next Door
"Ready, Set, Jett"

Other must-reads

Love Bites
(anthology with Brenda Jackson, Catherine Mann, Jules Bennett and Virna DePaul)
All Riled Up
The Buckhorn Legacy
Forever Buckhorn
Buckhorn Beginnings
Bewitched
Unbelievable
Tempted
Bodyguard
Caught!
Heartbreakers
Fallen Angels
Enticing

Coming soon, three classic tales in one sizzling volume

Hot in Here

And don't miss an all-new tale of Love Undercover, also coming soon

Getting Rowdy

BARE IT ALL

CHAPTER ONE

As she came toward him, Alice's baby-soft hair hung loose, silky tendrils drifting over her shoulders. Her big brown eyes, so innocent and yet so aware, watched him intently, the way she always watched him. She smiled, and that smile did remarkable things to him. Made him ravenous, when he'd never quite experienced anything like that before. Lust, sure. But such a powerful need? No, never.

Only with Alice.

Very close now, so close the warmth of her touched all over him, she brushed her nose against his jaw, his neck, his ear.

He groaned. Out loud. He heard it but could barely credit that the sound came from him.

From a gentle nuzzle.

Against his *ear.*

It was insane, but it took very little from her to get him painfully aroused.

"Reese?"

He wanted her mouth on him. He turned his face toward her, and he felt her breath. Hot. Then her tongue. *Wet.*

"Oh…um, Reese?"

She sounded so tentative that he smiled as he reached for her and opened his eyes. His hand encountered dense fur, and the expressive brown eyes staring back at him weren't Alice's.

They weren't even human.

His dog, Cash, panted at the sign of life. Delighted to have him awake, he barked, turned a quick circle and…licked Reese's face.

Again.

"Shit." Reese dodged the dog's sloppy fondness while trying to get his bearings. The dream had felt so incredibly real. And so welcome. He shifted—and found himself cramped from head to toes…on a sofa.

Alice's sofa.

Lifting his head, he looked down at himself. He wore only boxers, and as was usually the case when he first awakened, they were tented. Hmm…

Where had the sheet gone? Ah, over the side of the couch to the floor.

Levering up to one arm, Reese attempted to orient himself—and there stood Alice at the foot of the couch, fully dressed in summer slacks and a sleeveless blouse, her hands locked together in front of her and, yes, her soft brown hair hanging loose.

But now, with him wide awake, her hair looked tidy, like Alice, not sexily rumpled as it had been in his dream.

She watched him, but those soul-sucking brown eyes weren't on his face.

They stared with absorbing attention at his morning wood.

Great. Playing kissy-face with his dog was bad enough. Scrambling for the sheet now would only make him look more foolish. He wasn't used to finding himself in tricky, uncomfortable situations. At least, not with women.

As a police detective, sure, he'd often found himself discomfited by perps, though not in boxers while sporting mahogany.

Alice was many things—a neighbor, an enigma, an irritant and a subtle bombshell.

And obviously, based on that ramped-up dream, she was also the current focus of his fantasies.

He cleared his throat. "Up here, Alice." Her curious gaze rose to his face. "Thank you. Now if you don't mind, you could turn around a moment. My modesty is beyond compromised, so it doesn't really matter to me, but with your face already going pink, I'm not sure—"

"Of course." Turning, she gave him her back. Posture stiff. Air uncertain.

That lovely fawn-colored hair fell just beyond her shoulders.

"Sorry about that." She strode, fast and unsteady, to the patio doors that led to her small deck. She'd left the door open, allowing in a muggy, late-August breeze that teased her beautiful hair.

Given the heat of his interest, air-conditioning would have been nice, but since this was Alice's apartment, and she'd been generous enough to let him crash on her couch, he wouldn't complain. Much.

"What time is it, anyway?" Sitting up, Reese reached for the sheet, but Cash sat on it. The dog watched Reese, his furry ears perked up, his expression hopeful. Reese grinned. After tugging out the sheet and covering himself, he patted the couch beside his thigh. "C'mere, boy."

The dog bounded up with over-the-moon enthusiasm. Because of the undercover sting they'd just wrapped up, he'd spent as much time away from Cash as with him—and still he and the dog had bonded.

"It's a little after one o'clock."

And she hadn't awakened him? How long had she been sneaking around the apartment?

How long had he lain there without even a sheet?

He was generally a light sleeper, so either he'd been really out of it, or she was…stealthy.

That thought bothered him and meshed with other concerns he had about Alice. Her keen observance of everything around her, combined with her cautious air, planted awful background possibilities into his head.

Then there was the way she'd come onto the scene yesterday, a big, *loaded* gun in her hand….

"Cash hasn't been out for a few hours. I was trying to lead him through without waking you, but he saw you there on the couch, and then you made…a sound."

"A sound, huh?" Given the erotic dream, he could just imagine.

"Cash sidetracked to you and—"

"I thought he was you." When her shoulders stiffened more, Reese felt devilish enough to say, "And I was having this rather sexual dream."

Wide-eyed with something akin to astonishment, she faced him, stole a peek at his lap and, when she saw he'd bunched the sheet there, she met his gaze. "What do you mean?"

"You and me." He gestured between them. "And damn, but the dream felt real." Reese scratched under Cash's furry chin. "You were near me. Breathing on me."

Indignation brought her brows together. "Breathing on you?"

Wondering when she'd catch on, he gave a sage, serious nod. "You nuzzled my ear, and I felt your hot tongue—"

Backing up fast, she bumped into the screen on

the patio door and almost fell through it. After an accusatory scowl at Reese for making her stumble, she checked the screen, saw that it remained in the track and cleared her throat. "I would never—" She searched for a word and came up empty.

"Lick me?"

To his surprise, she kept quiet, but her mouth—and her expression—softened.

"No? What a shame." He gave the dog a few pats, which encouraged him to shower Reese with more affection. "But apparently Cash would."

Realization dawned. "Oh." A smile twitched. "You felt Cash trying to wake you, and you thought…?"

"Yeah. Helluva way to start my day. I mean, I'm fond of him, but…" Reese looked her over. "Not that fond."

"He's adorable!"

"Sure he is." Reese had only recently gotten the dog, and while he'd never considered himself a pet-lover, he and Cash were getting acclimated—with Alice's help. "I just don't want you mistaking my…" He nodded at his lap. "Reaction."

Though she covered her mouth, a short laugh escaped, anyway.

That laugh was as mesmerizing as her smile, and his sheet-covered boner twitched. "Keep it up, and I'll never get it under control."

Rather than backing up or blushing again, she chastised him. "Really, Reese. It's not something to talk about."

"Not something to be embarrassed over either." But he sort of was, anyway. What was it about Alice that affected him so profoundly—and so physically? "Not to minimize your appeal, but it happens to most guys in the morning."

"When they awaken, you mean?"

"Yeah. It's called morning wood, or in this case, afternoon wood, I guess."

"I see." She tipped her head to study him. "But when you knocked on my door this morning, you were wide awake, fully dressed and had just finished working."

He'd also been aroused over the possibility of spending more intimate time with her. Knowing he shouldn't tell her that—yet—he scrubbed a hand over his tired eyes.

"Yet even then," she continued, her tone mischievous and teasing, "you had a…um…"

Having her talk about it wasn't helping. Reese trapped her gaze with his own. "An erection."

"Yes." A little too matter-of-factly, she nodded. "You had one then, also." Though the color in her fair skin intensified, she didn't look away. "You told me not to worry about it."

"I know what I said." God, he wanted to kiss her. If she'd been any other woman, he would have.

But he hadn't known Alice that long, and what he did know of her kept him from pushing things. Already, thanks to the fiasco the day before, she'd seen the hazards of his job.

Wasn't every day that murderers and hoods, the very criminals he investigated, showed up on his doorstep. It was even more uncommon for those offenders to get the drop on him. Usually he was great at his job. But yesterday…yeah, he'd suffered a first-class cluster fuck—and Alice had managed to get right in the middle of it.

Maybe that's why he'd been dreaming of her. She'd been helping out by watching his dog while he and his partner closed in on their quarry, and then when shit went sideways yesterday, she'd recognized the deadly situation and sent in reinforcements.

He eyed her understated, prim facade that hid so much intuition, bravery and cunning. "You will never have reason to worry about anything with me."

"Okay."

She was the most curious woman, and that, too, could explain his unaccountable reaction to her. "Just like that, huh?"

"I know you're honorable."

Sensible Alice. Of course she was right—he *was* honorable, most especially where women were concerned. But in the short time they'd known each other, how could she possibly be that confident about his intentions?

She couldn't.

So he'd taken in a stray dog—a dog she now adored. So what? He was polite, mannerly, dressed well and had his own proper persona. It meant nothing, and she should realize that.

Yet from what he'd seen so far she had great instincts.

The type of instincts usually honed in the field.

When she'd agreed to let him sleep on her couch, he'd thought to use the time alone with her in her apartment to do some in-depth talking. His curiosity about her was extreme, almost as sharp as his attraction.

But once she'd made up the couch for him, he'd sat down and exhaustion had all but pulled him under. Their talk had stalled.

Then.

Now he had all the time in the world. Or at least for the rest of the day. "Alice—"

"I should take Cash out. *Again.*" She smiled at the

dog with consuming love. "We both know he'll only hold it for so long."

She had the prettiest, sweetest smile—when she smiled. Not that she seemed to know it. Hell, if it wasn't for his dog, or the carnage in his apartment…

Remembering the carnage, the very reason for being on Alice's too-small couch instead of his own spacious bed, Reese groaned.

Alice paused in her attentions to Cash. "Are you okay?" She inched closer. "Did you get hurt yesterday?"

"I'm fine." But frustrated. Yesterday, in the culmination of a lengthy investigation, a damn parade had trooped through his apartment. Friends, suspects and heinous thugs. *Murderous* thugs. Thugs so ugly, their souls were surely black and decrepit.

Rowdy Yates, a "witness"—what a joke that had turned out to be—who should have been in protective custody, instead had gone to Reese's apartment to snoop. Alice had recognized that Rowdy was up to no good and had called Reese. He'd gotten to his apartment only minutes before his lieutenant also showed up.

They'd all been taken unawares by the lowlifes, and while a gun stayed on Rowdy, Reese and the lieutenant had been handcuffed to the headboard of his bed. That he and the female lieutenant butted heads more often than not made it an especially unpropitious situation. Lieutenant Peterson hadn't taken it well, and his efforts to shield her had been met with much resistance.

Instead of getting the protection afforded all witnesses, Rowdy had ended up a target for death. He had abilities, which included breaking into Reese's apartment to snoop, but against two gunmen set on executing him? The odds had not been with him. If they'd killed Rowdy, they would have next turned those guns on Reese and the lieutenant.

Without Alice's help, there would have been several dead bodies in his apartment, instead of just one.

And hell, one was bad enough. It wasn't easy to get *death* out of the carpet, curtains and off the walls.

Fortunately, sensible Alice had assessed the situation and sent in Reese's good friend Detective Logan Riske as backup. Because Logan possessed a lethal skill set unique to only a select few, he'd gotten the upper hand—but not before taking a bullet to the arm.

Chaos had reigned for a couple of minutes, all but destroying Reese's bedroom. In the end, they'd apprehended one gunman and another man who'd played lookout at the front of the apartment building.

The worst villain Reese had ever known had died from a broken neck. Never again would he threaten anyone.

Reese eyed Alice with renewed interest. At the tail end of the bloody melee, not long after Reese had been freed from the cuffs, Alice had shown up in his apartment with a big gun held in her slender, delicate hand.

She was a good judge of character, but then, so was he. And in his gut, Reese knew his straitlaced, often silent, skittish, timid and sexy-as-hell neighbor would have used that gun with fatal precision.

It made his blood run cold and ramped up his interest in her and her past. So many unanswered questions. He knew Alice was good with his dog and that he liked her. He definitely knew he wanted to get her under him.

But so far their relationship had been so odd, he didn't even know her last name yet. Alice…something or other.

Insane.

She inched closer still—*just as she had in his dream.* "You have some dark bruising."

Reese followed her concerned gaze to his wrist and saw the ugly marks there, testament to how he'd tried to free himself from the key-lock metal cuffs—*his own friggin' handcuffs*—that had been used against him.

"It's fine." Never had he felt more helpless than when he'd been in those restraints, knowing that his own failure could facilitate the murder of others. Never again would he be caught unawares.

Once was more than enough.

Alice hesitated. "Are you hurt anywhere else?"

Other than his pride at being taken off guard in his own apartment… "No." He wanted nothing more than to move past it all.

She accepted that without an excess of coddling. "Your friend will be all right?"

"Logan? He's a detective, like me."

"I thought so. When I saw him yesterday, I knew he was safe."

Safe? The things she said always had double meanings. "Just as you knew the others were dangerous?" Alice had seen people come into the apartment building, and somehow she'd known they weren't friends. Not only was she astute, but she also wasn't afraid to react—thank God.

"Yes." She gave him a level stare. "I can usually tell."

How? Reese wanted to know. It wasn't as if criminals walked around with a damn sign on their foreheads. God knew, if they did, his job would be a hell of a lot easier.

As a detective, he'd dealt with enough shady characters that he'd gained something of a sixth sense about them. He noticed things, slight nuances that others missed.

But what had happened in Alice's life to give her that edge? "Logan is fine. You met Pepper?"

"Yes. She stayed in my apartment with me while Detective Riske went to your aid."

"Call him Logan—I'm sure he'd insist." Reese thought of the moment when he'd realized Logan had been shot. He hadn't let the wound slow him down, until blood loss had done that for him. "He's home with Pepper now, healing and no doubt being pampered."

Because of Alice's quick thinking, Reese and his friends were all alive, and a very bad character dealing in every aspect of corruption, including new ventures into human trafficking, was dead.

Reese had a lot of regrets for how things had gone down yesterday, but he didn't feel even a smidge of remorse over that.

Alice tipped her head. "Logan and Pepper are in love?"

"He is for sure." It wasn't like him to talk out of turn, but he heard himself say, "And that added to the craziness of the sting. Cops going undercover do *not* fall in love with key witnesses."

"Why not?"

"Complications, for one thing. Hard to think rationally when you're emotionally involved."

"He didn't seem emotional to me. As soon as I related my suspicions, he took over. He stuffed Pepper into my apartment, prepared himself the best he could and warned us—unnecessarily, I might add—to keep the doors locked."

"Knowing Pepper, that had to be a laugh a minute."

She smiled at his sarcasm. "She was mostly silent,

and very worried. You do realize that Pepper is also in love with your friend?"

Alice sounded so sure about that, Reese shrugged. "Okay."

"Rowdy is her brother?"

"Yes." Reese stretched, felt too many kinks in his shoulders, and winced while rubbing a hand over the back of his neck.

He saw Alice gaze in awe at his biceps, and it warmed him. He left his arm up a few seconds longer—until he realized how absurd that was.

Damn it, she seduced him without trying, and in totally unconventional ways. "You met Rowdy?" Reese couldn't recall any introductions, but then, he'd had his hands full dealing with everything else.

"Briefly." Alice's attention coasted over his chest, then down to his abdomen.

His muscles constricted in reaction.

"I wasn't so sure about Rowdy. He worried me at first. That's why I called you when he showed up. But he's not as ruthless as the others. I have a feeling he walks a very fine line between what's lawful and what fits his own moral code."

Since that described Rowdy perfectly, Reese felt his own share of awe. "Probably."

"The lieutenant?"

Though Alice had entered the scene in the midst of pandemonium, she had all the key players down. "When last I left her, she was running roughshod over anyone who stood in her way, issuing orders like a general." He shook his head. "For such a petite woman, she rules with an iron fist."

"I liked her." Alice stared at his lap again.

"I figured you would." Reese sat forward. "I need

some caffeine to kick-start my brain. How about I take Cash out and you put on a pot of coffee?"

The dog, who had almost been asleep, bounded up in agreement.

"If that's what you want."

That wasn't even close to what he wanted, but for now it'd have to do. "Thank you." He waited, but when she continued to stand there watching him, he shrugged and tossed the sheet aside to stand.

AT THE SIGHT of Reese's big strong body, Alice sucked in a breath and all but fled to the kitchen. Reese thought he'd embarrassed her, and yes, he had. A little.

But it was so much more than that, more complex than mere embarrassment. It was…something she hadn't felt in far too long.

And she relished it.

After two deep breaths, she called out to him, "I'll have this ready in ten minutes."

When he finally replied, his voice came from close behind her. "That works."

Startled, she turned to see him and almost dropped the carafe.

Shirtless and barefoot, he leaned in the kitchen doorway, only a few feet away. He'd pulled on rumpled slacks, zipped but unbuttoned so that they hung low, showing off his taut abdomen and that silky line of dark blond hair that disappeared into his boxers.

Boy. The pants helped a little, but not much. He still looked indescribably awesome.

Sighing in resignation at her distraction, Reese said again, "Up here, Alice."

Mute, she performed the near-impossible feat of lifting her attention to his face. She had a feeling that with

Reese so uninhibited, his reminders were going to come fast and furious.

Really, how could any woman *not* stare at him?

The very first time she'd seen him, she'd recognized him as a prime physical specimen. Her past had damaged her, sure, but she wasn't blind or stupid.

It had taken a lot of effort to remember her need for privacy, to look past him, to ignore his friendly smiles and polite greetings.

Then, seeing him with the dog…well, that had sealed her fate. Alice knew she'd lost a small part of her heart to him the moment she'd seen his patience with Cash. Reese stood over six and a half feet tall, but he wasn't lanky. He had a honed body that drew everyone's attention. No one could mistake his strength. Yet he'd been so gentle with Cash.

And yesterday, watching him in hero mode as he'd not only taken charge of the deadly situation but also tended to his injured friend… How could *anyone* be immune to him?

Fully dressed, Detective Reese Bareden was a heart-stopper. Half-naked, he was enough to turn her stupid with lust.

Amusement showed in the glitter of his green eyes. "I like it strong."

"What?" Oh, Lord, she'd been visually devouring him again. She swallowed and tried to get it together.

"The coffee."

"Oh." How could she have forgotten? She held the carafe with both hands and summoned a smile. "All right."

New concern eased his smile away. "What is it, Alice?"

"Nothing." She couldn't very well tell him that he was one of the most impressive males she'd ever known—and that was saying something, given that she'd met some truly remarkable men.

Men from her past. *Good* men…who'd been there to counter the depraved.

Even thinking about it caused her to tighten, to close in on herself protectively—

"Alice?"

That deep, gentle voice brought her out of dark memories. Her racing heart slowed, her muscles uncoiled. She let out a tense breath and tried to sound casual. "Yes?"

"You and I are going to have that talk today."

He made it sound almost like a threat, but she'd known real threats, and Reese didn't scare her. Not that way. Not in any way, really. "Yes, we will."

Her quick compliance seemed to surprise him. Had he expected her to refuse him? To get defensive?

Truthfully, there were times when even she didn't know how she'd react. Ugly memories had a way of surfacing when she least expected them.

When it came to men, most of the time she steered clear of them. She definitely hadn't planned on being drawn to Reese. But she enjoyed talking with him, so why avoid it? He wouldn't get the information he wanted because it was information she couldn't share, but she'd tell him enough to keep him satisfied.

For a little while, anyway.

Cash strained the length of the leash, impatient with the delay. The adorable dog, still more a puppy than not, was notorious for piddling on the floor when he got excited, curious, when he had to go…pretty much for any reason at all, really.

Luckily both of their apartments had hardwood floors, which made cleanups easier.

After another long look, Reese nodded at her and led the dog away. Moving out of the kitchen, warm with admiration, Alice watched him go. His disheveled blond hair and darker beard shadow only made him more gorgeous. Sleek muscles flexed…everywhere. Over his very wide shoulders, his back, down the length of those thick arms and thicker thighs…

He pulled the door open.

Breath strangled in her chest. "You're going outside like *that?*"

He glanced down at himself and shrugged as if he didn't have a body that could stop traffic and hearts alike. "Why not?"

The man was all but naked! He hadn't even buttoned his pants. "You're…indecent."

"I won't be long." He checked that the door wouldn't lock when he closed it, and out he went.

CHAPTER TWO

ALICE STOOD THERE lost in thought for far too long before she remembered that she had coffee to make.

Never had she thought to have a man in her apartment. Certainly not a hunky police detective and most definitely not overnight. It made sense for her to be off-kilter.

She'd no sooner finished preparing the coffee than she decided Reese might also like something to eat. It was lunchtime for her, but he hadn't even had breakfast yet.

Maybe he hadn't had dinner the night before either. His work as a detective had literally landed on his doorstep, and she doubted he'd had time to relax, much less enjoy a real meal. A man his size likely required a lot of sustenance.

Yesterday had consisted of bad guys coming and going, good guys sneaking in, gunshots and arrests, deaths and ambulances.... Shivering, Alice wrapped her arms around herself.

The life-or-death scenario had been unsettling for her, too. Having Reese on her couch, near at hand, gave her a sense of security that no weapon could. Even having Cash underfoot was reassuring. People still left her ill at ease, but animals were so nonjudgmental, so welcoming, she naturally took comfort from them.

Reese didn't know it, but being Cash's dog-sitter was

the greatest gift. Until he'd proposed the arrangement a few days ago, she hadn't realized what a difference it made to have another living, breathing creature nearby.

She sighed, noticed several minutes had passed, and decided she'd ask Reese what he'd like to eat.

Picking up her keys, Alice locked the door behind her. Never again would she take chances when it came to security. On her way out, she glanced up the steps at Reese's apartment door. Unlike in the movies, there was no dramatic caution tape draping it, but yesterday Reese had said his colleagues preferred for him to stay out until they'd finished gathering their forensics, or taking photos, or whatever they had to do. She really had no idea of police procedure. Other than Reese, she'd never known a good officer.

Sure, she'd been acquainted with a few shady men who claimed the badge but not the honor that should have been inherent in the job. Yesterday, she'd met good cops.

She'd learned the hard way to recognize the difference.

Remembering the day before made her palms sweat. Yes, Reese had only come to her because of the destruction in his place, but she was glad for any reason. While she hopefully put up a brave front, no way had she wanted to stay alone.

As she'd done so many times, she pushed the unpleasant memories to the back of her mind and went down the steps to the glass, double entry doors.

Before she stepped out, she saw Reese standing there in the shade, Cash's leash held loosely in his hand.

Two neighbor ladies, one a beautiful blonde with oversize breasts, the other a cute and petite brunette, stared at him adoringly while chatting.

They wore jogging shorts and sports bras and had a lot of skin showing. They stood far too close to him for mere conversation.

Alice didn't think about it, didn't even have time to process her reaction before she found herself striding out to the yard and right up to Reese and Cash. She snatched the dog's leash from his hand, startling him.

Lifting one eyebrow, he looked down at her. "Alice."

Her heart punched painfully against her breastbone. Unfair that a man with morning-rumpled hair and whiskers could still manage to look so good. "The coffee's done." She stared at the women while thrusting the keys out to him. "I can wait with Cash until he finishes up, if you'd like to go on in and get a cup."

Slowly his expression shifted from surprise to amusement. "Why, thank you, Alice." With a knowing grin, he accepted her key ring. "Your hospitality knows no bounds."

She had no idea how to reply to that.

With a pleased smile, Reese touched her cheek, bid good day to the others and headed inside. The bright sunshine gleamed on his shoulders and gilded his fair hair. Though barefoot, he didn't pick his way across the grounds; he strode like a confident man in control of himself and those around him.

When Alice realized that she wasn't the only one noticing, she cleared her throat, loudly.

The blonde laughed. "Sorry, honey, but you know, I just can't pull my eyes away. He's an awful lot of man."

The brunette agreed. Looking at Alice, she asked with palpable doubt, "So, you two have a thing?"

A thing? Understanding sank in. "What? No!" Alice looked down at herself, too. No, she wasn't cute and petite like the brunette, and she certainly didn't have the curves that the blonde flaunted. She was just herself, plain, understated, most times all but invisible.

Hadn't she been told that often enough?

And thank God for it.

"We're only neighbors."

"Uh-huh, sure you are." The friendly blonde continued to smile. "I wish I was that type of neighbor, too. I've suggested it, but I swear, Reese is a squirrely one, always dodging me."

"You've actually suggested…"

"That we hook up, sure. And believe me, I haven't been subtle!" She laughed. "I figured he turned me down because we're too close for comfort, being in the same apartment building and all that. But if he's spending the night with you, then that must not be an issue for him."

The women stared at her, waiting for an explanation. Why hadn't she left well enough alone? She had no claim on Reese, so she should have kept her nose out of it.

But she had butted in, behaving like a territorial girlfriend, giving them reason for speculation. Walking away now would be both rude and fodder for gossip.

"Do you both live here?" she asked, while trying to decide how to proceed.

"Upper floor," the brunette said. "She's on one side of Reese, and I'm on the other."

"Doesn't that sound naughty?" The blonde laughed again. "We've known Reese awhile now."

Alice's temples pounded. "How…nice."

The blonde performed introductions. "I heard Reese call you Alice. I'm Nikki, and she's Pam."

"Hello." Until Reese, Alice had managed to keep her

distance from all of her neighbors. Now she had Reese's admirers curious about her.

Knowing she'd just complicated her life, Alice turned her attention to Cash. Perhaps she could distract the women by playing with the dog?

But no, Cash flopped down in a ray of sunshine and looked so comfortable, she hated to disturb him. There was no help for it. She smiled at the women. "If you live that close to Reese, then you already know what happened yesterday."

Pam lifted both brows. "You mean between the two of you?"

"No!" Good grief. Such a suggestion. "Really, nothing happened between us."

Nikki grinned some more.

"I was talking about the police conflict that took place in his apartment."

"We were out late," Pam said.

"And much of the morning, too," Nikki added. "What happened?"

Hoping to extricate herself soon, Alice did her best to summarize. "Yesterday, I saw a person going into Reese's apartment, so I called him."

"You have his number?" Pam asked with disbelief.

"I… Yes." Alice wanted to groan. Pam and Nikki looked ready to pounce on her every word. She nodded toward Cash. "I watch his dog for him while he works, so it was necessary to exchange numbers."

The women peered at Cash with disdain. Nikki said, "He pees *everywhere*. I'd send him to the pound for that."

Feeling very protective of the dog, Alice scowled. "He's a puppy still. He's learning."

Pam couldn't quite uncurl her lip. "So he's actually

Reese's dog? I assumed he was yours since you're the one I usually see bringing him outside."

"I pet-sit for him. Reese only recently got him, but being a detective, his hours can be…unconventional. And right now Cash needs a lot of attention, not to mention structure."

"So yesterday, when you said someone went into his place?" Nikki dismissed the dog. "Reese was getting robbed?"

"Not exactly. It was just…" Unsure how much she should actually tell, Alice fudged the truth. "A conflict of sorts, that's all. It all ended well enough when another detective showed up. But Reese's apartment got a little…messy."

With bullet holes. Blood. A dead body on the floor.

She shook her head. "Reese had a lot to do once they made arrests, a lot of follow-up work, so he got in late." Or rather, early. "His apartment is still considered a crime scene."

Uncaring of all that, Pam asked in disbelief, "And so he came to *you?*"

Alice shrugged. "He slept on my couch."

"Your couch?" Nikki put a hand to her heart in dramatic fashion. "I would have *dragged* him into the bedroom."

"Or joined him on the couch." Pam grinned.

Through tight lips, Alice explained, "We don't have that type of relationship." In fact, she wasn't sure what type of relationship they had. A couple of times now Reese had hinted about an attraction, but was it just teasing?

And if it wasn't, what then?

"Oh, honey," Nikki commiserated. "That must've

been torturous for you, having a man like him so close but not getting the advantages."

"It's great news for us, though." Pam elbowed her friend. "He's still up for grabs."

Alice couldn't fathom their attitudes. "So you're both interested in Reese?" How would that work? Neither of the women felt possessive?

Pam shrugged. "I do my best to get his attention, but Reese is a master at being polite without encouraging too much."

Nikki agreed. "I'd be on him in a heartbeat if he'd give me a signal. He's so delectably big and brawny."

Big and brawny were not attributes that Alice generally admired. Not in a man who showed too much intimate interest in her.

But for whatever reason, Reese was different, and her heart raced every time he got near.

"He's very compassionate," Alice said, then suffered through some curious expressions from Nikki and Pam. "It's true. He saved Cash. Someone had put the dog in a cardboard box and left him in the middle of the street."

"Probably because he pees everywhere!" Nikki laughed.

Alice didn't find it at all funny. How could anyone be that heartless? Luckily, Reese had cared enough to investigate when he saw the box, and once he'd discovered Cash, he'd taken him to the vet, adopted him and loved him. True, Reese spent too much time away, but he made sure the dog had proper care.

With her.

She sighed. "Reese is one of the kindest men I've ever met."

Nikki grinned at her. "Yeah, and despite his big hard

body and that incredible face, I'm sure it was his *kindness* that you noticed first, right?"

No, that quality might not be what first drew her attention to Reese, but it was definitely what got past her defensive walls.

"He's also a police detective, honest and protective of others."

Pam snickered. "And with as long as we've been talking, the big, bad cop just might be in the shower right now." She gave Alice's shoulder a pat and started away with Nikki. "If I was you, I'd hurry in and join him."

"Have some fun for me, Alice." Nikki smiled as she followed Pam. "We want to hear all the juicy details tomorrow!"

Alice was too frozen to say her goodbyes. Until Pam's parting remark it hadn't sunk in that she'd left Reese Bareden, a *detective,* alone in her apartment.

Oh, good Lord.

There was no telling what he'd find if he decided to snoop. And for a detective, snooping no doubt came naturally.

"Cash, come on, boy. Let's go!"

Ears lifted, eyes bright, the dog jumped up, always ready for some excitement.

Good thing, because it seemed to Alice, wherever Reese Bareden went, excitement definitely followed.

WHILE ALICE LINGERED outside, saying God knew what, Reese did a quick surveillance of her apartment. Her bedroom was plain to the point of painful, not at all like most females' rooms. In lieu of a frilly comforter, she had a simple beige quilt over a full-size bed. Utilitarian curtains were pulled back to allow in the warm summer breeze. Not a single piece of clothing showed out of place. Other than one photograph sitting on her dresser, she kept her surfaces clutter-free. He approached the picture for a better look.

She'd had shorter hair when the photo was taken, and beside her sat a girl some years younger. A sister? They shared the same eyes, hair color and the same lush mouth. Alice looked happy in a way that Reese hadn't yet seen.

Carefree.

Relaxed.

The Alice he knew never looked quite that tranquil, and seeing the contrast in the photo bothered him.

He strode to her closet to look inside.

Her very basic wardrobe hung in neat array, with her shoes lined up side by side on the floor. A shoe box on top of a shelf drew his attention, and he lifted it down.

Inside he found the heavy Glock that she'd carried into his apartment yesterday. Again he remembered the weapon in her hand and the look in her eyes.

"Shit." He returned the box to the top of her closet and closed the door. He started to leave the room, hesitated, and instead looked under her bed.

Not a speck of dust, but he did find a lethal retractable baton. Scowling, he opened her nightstand and saw a Taser.

"Son of a bitch." How many people did she expect to fend off? And what the hell had happened to her to make her think all the weapons were necessary?

None of it gelled. Alice was a first-class introvert. Painfully solemn and withdrawn. Sort of…quietly dignified. She reminded him of his third grade teacher, minus the bun and support hose. He curled his lip, disliking that comparison a lot—especially given how she turned him on.

There had to be something twisted in that.

At first, Alice Something-or-other—he really needed to learn her last name—had felt like a challenge. He didn't want to think himself conceited, but women didn't ignore him, so her disregard had piqued his interest.

Then he'd noticed her odd intensity, the extreme way she focused whenever she ventured outside, almost as if she watched for the boogeyman. Why would a young, middle-class woman in a good neighborhood need to be so over-the-top cautious, even in broad daylight?

Her softness felt like a lure. Big dark eyes. Baby fine brown hair.

And that soft, full mouth…

The first time he saw her smile—*at his dog*—something had sparked. Reese couldn't explain it any more than he could dismiss it, but something about her turned him on at a gut level.

He saw that tempting smile of hers, and he got hard.

Knowing she could come back in any moment, Reese searched through her bathroom, but in his cursory exploration he found only the usual female products. No meds, other than a few OTCs like aspirin and cold pills.

In the spare bedroom set up as her office, he struck gold. With enough time to dig around, he could probably uncover all kinds of info on that elaborate computer network. Paper files occupied a rack on the corner of the desk. She had an external drive set up. Mail filled a basket, meaning he could learn her last name with a simple peek. Everything was so neatly organized that going through it would be a breeze.

But that would be such a huge invasion of her privacy.

Worse than peeking in closets and under beds.

God, it was tempting....

In a belated bid for integrity, Reese shut the door. He'd talk to Alice. He'd ask questions and hopefully get answers, and then he'd decide how to proceed.

Right now, after seeing the guns, Taser and baton, he really did need that coffee.

A few minutes later, he'd just sat down at the table with his second cup when the front door flew open and Alice charged in, Cash hot on her heels.

Reese half rose from his seat. "What's wrong?"

She halted comically, still breathing fast. Cash looked at her, looked at Reese, and twitched his ears as if awaiting further instruction.

"Alice?"

After blowing out a breath, Alice shook her head. "Nothing is wrong." She closed the door and simply... stood there.

"Just felt like taking a wind sprint, huh?" Would he ever understand her?

Damn straight he would.

"I had no idea you could move so quickly." Coffee in hand, he left the table. "I believe your temples are dewy. Did you run all the way in?"

She looked blank for only a moment, then visually searched the apartment as if seeking signs of his intrusion.

Let her look. He'd folded up his blankets. Put his clothes near the door. He'd even buttoned his slacks.

No way would he put on a shirt, though, not when he enjoyed her appreciation. And thinking of her appreciation...

He started toward her.

She locked her gaze to his. "What are you doing?"

Her uncertainty cut deep. "Greeting my dog." Gently,

Reese took the leash from her small hand and unhooked Cash. He knelt down. "Did you miss me, Cash? Did you?"

Alice stared down at him. "You talk to him like he's a baby."

"He likes it." And then, to drive home that point, he said in his most ridiculous voice, "Don't you, boy? Yes, you do."

Alice blurted, "I'm sorry I intruded."

Huh. What was that about? Slowly, so he wouldn't make her any jumpier, Reese stood. "Let's go to the kitchen. This is my second cup, but as foggy as I am today, I might need the whole pot."

"All right." She marched ahead of him. "I was going to offer you breakfast. Or lunch." At the sink, she pivoted to face him. "What do you feel like?"

Such a loaded question, and being male, so many inappropriate comments came to mind. But given all her weaponry and secrets, he got right to the point instead of teasing.

"I feel like an explanation." Or two or three. He helped himself to another cup of coffee, which put him within touching distance of her, and started with her last apology. "When did you intrude?"

"Outside. With your lady friends."

Ah. What justification would she give for that little display? "You wanted me to get my coffee." He saluted her with his cup. "Much appreciated."

"Actually…no." She rubbed her forehead. "I mean, yes, I did want you to have your coffee, of course. But I…I don't really understand what I was thinking. I saw you out there with those women and the next thing I knew, I was behaving like a jealous wife."

Wow. Reese stared at her, flabbergasted. She threw that out there like it was nothing. No reserve at all.

No sense of self-preservation either.

"Again," she said in that same no-nonsense tone, "I'm sorry."

Shaking off the surprise, Reese opened her refrigerator. "No problem." He withdrew her cartoon of eggs.

She frowned. "They're both very attractive."

"Nikki and Pam?"

The frown intensified. "Don't be deliberately obtuse."

"All right." If she wanted to dish it out, he could dish it right back. "They're both sexy as hell." He grinned like a sinner—or a man ready to provoke. "And they know it, too."

Alice reached around him and pulled out bacon. "This is awkward."

She didn't act uncomfortable. She acted like it was routine to have such an odd conversation. "Nothing with me should be awkward."

She eyed him, moved around to get out a pan. "I understand they were…trying to attract your interest?"

"With those two, always. They're relentless in their pursuits." He put just enough complaint in his tone to sound comically pitiful.

"Oh, poor you. How awful it must be to have *sexy-as-hell* women hitting on you."

The bite of her sarcasm was so totally unexpected, he loved it. "Since I don't want to get involved with either of them, even for a one-night stand, it gets tedious."

"So you really have turned them down?" She quickly added, "That's what they said. That they kept trying and you kept dodging them."

He crossed his heart.

"Is it the proximity? That was Nikki's guess."

Since proximity would also put Alice off limits, he denied it. "That might have factored in a little. But mainly they're both drinkers and heavy partiers."

"And you're not?"

"When was the last time you saw me head to a party?"

"I haven't kept track of your agenda, one way or the other."

Bull. Alice was far too aware of everyone and everything not to have noticed him. Even without her keen powers of observation, few would miss a man of his size. Thanks to a good draw from the family gene pool, he had both height and strength.

Men and women alike made note of him. But it wasn't until Cash that Alice had acknowledged his existence.

He turned on a burner to get the skillet hot. "I work too many hours, and when I get some downtime, I like to kick back with my friends, which usually means watching sports, fishing, that sort of thing." He opened a drawer and found an egg turner. "And I like to hit up the gym a couple of times a week just to unwind."

"You look—" she coughed lightly "—physically fit."

"Thanks." He was in prime condition, but if she wanted to understate it, he wouldn't debate it with her.

She got out bread for toast. It was interesting how easily they moved together to prepare breakfast.

"Another strike against Pam and Nikki—they're not dog people." He smiled at how Alice maneuvered around Cash without complaint, giving him the occasional pat or stroke without even thinking about it.

"That matters to you?"

"The dog and I are a package deal now." He began laying bacon in the skillet. "Love me, love my dog."

Silence filled the air. Had the *love* word thrown her when likening herself to a jealous wife hadn't? The mysteries added up. "So, Alice, while we prepare breakfast, why don't we have that talk?"

"All right." She took down glasses and poured orange juice. "Before we get into that, though, would you like to tell me what you found while snooping?"

He went still, unsure if she bluffed, or if—

"I know you did, Reese."

"You assume—"

"I *know*."

Giving up, he said, "You're loaded down with weapons. Want to tell me why?"

One shoulder lifted. "Self-protection."

"Most people cover that with one gun."

She avoided his gaze by turning the bacon with a fork. "So, what did you find?"

"Glock in bedroom closet, Taser in nightstand—"

"You got into my nightstand?"

Interesting reaction. "Long enough to see the Taser, yes." He studied her frown. "I also saw the baton under your bed."

Mouth tight, she asked, "Is that it?"

No fucking way. "There's more?"

With only the slightest hesitation, she lowered the heat under the bacon, took his hand and led him out of the kitchen and down the hall.

Reese was so astounded by her touch that he barely noticed Cash trotting along behind them. It seemed that wherever Alice went, the dog followed.

She veered into the bathroom, released him and gestured behind the toilet. Frowning, Reese leaned around her to see…a revolver strapped to the tank. It was hidden from view so that only someone who knew where to look would find it.

He started to say something, but Alice walked out, so he followed, as did Cash. She went into her office, pulled her chair out from her desk and tipped it back to show another Taser and a spare cell phone attached underneath.

"Jesus." Reese rubbed a hand over his head. "What else?" Because somehow, he just knew there was more.

She marched back into the kitchen, opened a cabinet drawer, and one by one, set out a flashlight, another spare cell phone, a big knife, mace and finally a stun gun. "I prefer a Taser so I won't have to get close, but the stun gun is here just in case."

Muscles knotted, tension mounting from her dispassionate explanation and overabundance of weapons, Reese growled out, *"Why?"* She had a damned fortress going on, and there must be a reason.

"I don't want to be hurt."

In contrast to his tone, hers was soft, and a little chilling because of it. It wrecked him, imagining what might have instilled so much caution.

His worst fears were confirmed when her big dark eyes lifted to his, and she said softly, "Again."

CHAPTER THREE

METHODICALLY, ALICE replaced each item in the drawer. She heard her own heartbeat, felt the rushing of her pulse, but outwardly, she showed nothing but calm resolve.

God, how good she'd gotten at that.

For the longest time, Reese said nothing. She wasn't sure what to expect, how he'd react.

But when he did finally move, it was just to turn the bacon.

She closed the drawer, searching for something to say. "You seem competent in the kitchen." He seemed competent at *everything*. "Would you like to do the eggs, too, or should I?"

"Why don't you take a seat, and I'll handle it."

Ooookay. He sounded almost indifferent—not what she'd expected, especially from a detective. She pulled out a chair, and Cash came to lay by her feet.

"Do you have permits for the guns?"

That stalled her but only for a moment. Surely she did. "Yes."

"That wasn't a very confident reply."

She repeated, more firmly, "Yes."

"Hmm."

"Stay, Cash. I'll be right back." She went into her office, checked that Reese hadn't followed her and got out her special paperwork hidden within the register vent on the floor, held in place by heavy magnets. Inside, she found several permits. She located what she needed, put the rest back and returned to Reese. "Here you go."

"If I check those, will they be legit?"

"I'm confident they will be."

He shook his head at her. "The things you say and the way you say it—"

"*Yes,*" she amended. "They will be." Not even for a second should she have doubted it. Everything she had, every resource, and yes, every weapon, would bear up under close scrutiny.

The bacon smelled delicious as Reese put it on a plate and got started on the eggs. "How many do you want?"

"One, please." Watching him work, she appreciated the view: Reese shirtless, his shoulders flexing as he cracked eggs, his big bare feet planted apart on her linoleum floor. She could so easily get used to the sight of him in her kitchen. "Most women would want to cook for you."

"Maybe." He lifted his coffee cup for another drink, then glanced back at her. "I appreciate it that you aren't being so clichéd."

No, she couldn't be. She was so unlike most women, any comparison would be hard to find.

He continued to watch her. "Does anyone else know about your cache of weapons?"

No one that he'd ever meet. She didn't like lying to him, but really, she had no choice. "No."

"You took far too long to answer."

"I'm sorry."

Reluctantly, he turned to flip the eggs. "So, why did you tell me?"

Alice shook her head. "I've been sitting here wondering the same thing myself. I'd appreciate it if you didn't repeat it to anyone else."

"Who would I tell?"

"Your friend Detective Riske. Or Lieutenant Peterson. I'd as soon not have to answer difficult questions."

"All right." He set the plates on the table. "Unless it becomes necessary to tell someone else, I'll keep your secret." The toast popped up. Reese put a pat of butter on each piece.

"It's not a secret as much as it's my private, personal business."

He handed her a napkin, touched her cheek and took his seat.

Though he ate without pressuring her, Alice knew he still waited for an answer.

"It's strange," she said after a bite of bacon. "But I think I trust you."

"That's a start."

"I'm a good judge of character," she said with a shrug. "You're trustworthy."

"You think that because I'm a cop?"

She laughed, realized how awful that sounded and covered her mouth with a hand. "No." She shook her head. "No, being in law enforcement has nothing to do with it."

"Unfortunately, you're right." Without seeming indelicate, he ate so heartily that his food quickly disappeared.

His statement made her curious. "Why do you say that?"

"All that stuff that happened—the shooting in my apartment, I mean. There are a handful of cops on the force right now that aren't honest, good cops. The lieutenant is doing her best to clear out the corruption, but it's not easy. One bad cop is catastrophic. You get several working together, and the entire department is compromised."

"Your friend Logan?"

"As trustworthy as they come."

"I thought so." Yesterday, while she'd fretted, waiting to see if Reese would be okay, Logan Riske had pulled up with his brother and Pepper Yates. Alice had studied him for a short time, long enough to recognize in him the same attitude that Reese had.

In a leap of faith, she'd explained to Detective Riske about the intruders with Reese in his apartment.

"More of your intuition, huh?" He drank half his orange juice. "I gotta say, Alice, I'd love to know how you do it. How do you sift the good from the bad with little more than a glance?"

It grew so quiet after that, they could hear Cash snoring under the table. Alice finished off a slice of bacon, wondered where to start and decided it didn't really matter when it all ended the same way.

"I was taken."

Everything about Reese sharpened; his attention, his posture. His warm concern. And something more, something like rage.

Because he's a good man, as well as a good cop, and he cares about others.

He set aside his utensils. "You were kidnapped?"

Oh, God, she hated hearing it said aloud. "And held captive."

"When?" He leaned toward her. "For how long?"

Unwilling—even unable—to elaborate, she shook her head. "The only important detail is that I got away. And now that I'm free, I don't take chances. That's all I can say."

"I need more."

"I'm sorry, no."

Abruptly, he sat back. "Stop apologizing, damn it!"

She smiled at his show of temper. "Honestly, Reese, I didn't expect to ever tell anyone any of it. I don't like to think about it. I definitely don't want to talk about it." Mired in confusion and conflicts, she reached a hand down to Cash and put her fingers in his fur. Contact with the dog always brought her composure. And oddly enough, exposure to Reese brought her that and other elusive emotions. Ones she'd feared she'd never again feel. That had to mean something, but what? Finding the right words wasn't easy. "The thing is, I like you, when for the longest time I didn't like anyone or anything, not even myself."

Reese held himself still and silent.

"I'd gotten used to feeling..." She didn't want to sound dramatic, but only one word would do. "Ugly." Inside and out.

With stark conviction, he stated, "You're not."

He was the type of nice guy that would do his best to reassure her, only she didn't need that from him. "Then I decided I was just plain."

Folding his brawny arms on the tabletop, he leaned closer again. "Far from it."

Her breath came faster, deeper. "The way you look at me, I know you must not think so."

"Tell me why *you* think it."

No, she couldn't go there. For many, many reasons, not all of them her own, elaborating was impossible. "I can't."

"Can't, or won't?"

"Both, I guess." Shoring up her courage, she met his piercing green eyes and saw the sympathy there. But she knew she didn't deserve sympathy. She didn't really deserve anything.

Not after what she'd done, what she'd let happen.

How cowardly she'd been. *But not anymore.*

She'd been given a second chance, and by God, she would grab it with both hands.

Reese had mentioned love. Love him, love his dog.

Easy enough, since she'd lost her heart to Cash the second she'd met him. That Reese came with the dog, or vice versa…well, that could be a wonderful bonus.

Her throat tightened. She'd come to accept that love was well out of reach. She hadn't been worthy of love.

Then.

But now?

She desperately wanted to explore the expanding emotions he inspired. Did she dare?

She would never again be a coward.

Clearing the constricting uncertainty from her throat, she forced herself to meet his gaze. He watched her so closely that she felt it right down to her heart. "When can you move back to your apartment?"

The seconds ticked by. "In a hurry to get rid of me?"

"Not at all." Alice admitted the truth. "I'm hoping you still need a place to stay. That is, I hope you'll want to stay here again." And just in case he wasn't getting it, she added, "With me."

He dropped back in his seat, his eyes closed, his expression frustrated. "You don't pull your punches, do you?"

When she'd so generously been offered a new lease on life, she'd vowed to be clear and concise in all things. She wanted Reese. For how much, she didn't yet know, but she wanted to find out. "I didn't mean to put you on the spot."

He half laughed and opened his eyes to watch her again.

"You shouldn't feel obligated to…do anything." That sounded terrible. "I mean, you're welcome to sleep here. On the couch." *Worse and worse, Alice.* She screwed up her flagging courage and put on a serious face. "I wasn't hitting on you, as Pam and Nikki do."

"I can tell the difference."

Of course he could. She felt like a fool.

Reese smiled at her. "I would have asked, you know."

Tension eased from her shoulders. "You want to stay?"

"For several reasons. First and foremost, after the excitement last night, you shouldn't be alone. Yes, you're coping well. And now that I know a hint of your past, I suppose being well-armed makes…sense."

Was he trying not to insult her? "You think I'm overdoing it."

"I think you're doing what you need to in order to feel safer."

Safer, but not *safe.* Reese understood the difference. Now that she knew how easy it was to become the victim, never again would she feel entirely safe. "Yes."

He toyed with his empty glass, turning it on the table. "I can only imagine how you were affected by the shooting and the death—"

She lifted her chin. "I would have helped."

"You did help. You sent Logan in with full knowledge of what was happening. Without you, he might have ended up in the same boat as the lieutenant and me."

She still didn't know everything that had happened, how or why. "Handcuffed to a bed?"

"Or dead." Reese pushed back from his chair and carried his empty plate to the sink.

Were all men so comfortable in a kitchen? So tidy?

Not that she could remember. Her dad was wonderful, but he'd left household chores to her mother.

The few relationships she'd had never went beyond casual dating, so she had no idea how those men had been in a kitchen.

As if merely curious, Reese asked, "You would have used that gun yesterday?"

"If necessary." That was one thing she'd proven to herself. She *could* pull the trigger. "I gave my other gun to your friend, since he'd left his with his brother—"

"Other gun?" He turned to face her again. "You have *more?*"

"Another revolver. Logan didn't tell you it was mine?"

"He got shot, and he was bleeding all over...." Reese looked at her face and cursed low. "So damn much confusion, and too many people involved." He cleared his plate and put it in the dishwasher. "The CST has your gun, so I hope you're right about that permit."

"I am." Curiosity got the better of her. "CST? Is that Crime Scene Tech?"

"Yes. They're responsible for taking photos of the scene and collecting evidence."

She scowled. "When will I get it back?" The idea of being short a gun didn't sit right. She'd gotten used to knowing exactly where to find each weapon.

"If everything checks out, it won't be long." He took her plate to the dishwasher, too, then came to stand right in front of her. He touched her chin, lifted her face. "Whenever an officer is involved in a shooting, he gets mandatory paid time off, usually three days."

Hope bloomed in her breast. "So you'll be off for the next three days?"

"Not if I can help it, but maybe."

Oh. Unlike her, he wasn't rattled by the violence. He was ready to get back to work, and she only worried about being alone with her thoughts.

And her memories.

It felt far too uncomfortable to be sitting while he towered over her. She eased out of her chair and stood behind it. "You don't want the time off?"

"I want to follow up some leads. One bastard died but not before telling us…"

When he trailed off, Alice filled in for him. "About his human trafficking venture." Her hands tightened on the back of the chair. "That's what you were going to say."

He rubbed the back of his neck. "It burned my ass to have divided loyalties yesterday."

How she would love to put her hands around his bulging biceps; the skin there looked so smooth and taut. She could maybe trail her fingers over the solid muscles in his shoulders, too, and down through his crisp chest hair….

"Alice," he warned.

"Divided how?"

He took a step closer but didn't touch her. "Logan was shot, Rowdy was in a fury and Pepper was all emotional."

Sorting out the people involved would take some doing. "You said Pepper and Rowdy are siblings."

"The reason Rowdy was so furious. The guy that died? He'd planned to give Pepper to the traffickers."

Sickness churned in her stomach, burned in her

throat. "That's why you and Detective Riske were after him?"

"Not entirely, no. Morton Andrews was guilty of many things, all of them worthy of death."

So many awful people in the world. Too many. She swallowed back the distaste of evil. "I'm glad he's dead."

Reese gave her a long look. "Pepper wasn't emotional over that, though, and it wasn't just fear for her brother."

"No?"

"Mostly it was Logan getting shot. She went all girly over it, which was a shocker because before that, she'd been stoic to the point of being stony. Especially around me."

"She didn't trust you?"

"Apparently not. But seeing her at the hospital…I think she softened some once she realized I wasn't in cahoots with the bad guys."

That ludicrous idea struck her funny. "She must not be very perceptive if she ever thought that."

"Actually, she's sharp as a tack, and since I'd been keeping secrets, she had her reasons for doubting me." He shook his head, averting her many questions. "No, don't ask. When you share, so will I."

Unfair. "I have valid reasons for keeping some things to myself."

"Yeah? Me, too." He went around her toward the living room. "Anyway, while I was at the hospital to check on Logan and keep an eye on Pepper, other detectives followed up our lead."

"You wanted to be there when that happened?"

"Damn straight. But policy is that any cop involved in a shooting has that mandatory time off I mentioned."

He shrugged. "Doesn't matter. They had it covered, and that meant I could stay at the hospital with Logan."

"You're a good friend." Cash walked away to lounge in the sunshine pouring through the patio doors.

"While I was otherwise involved, Lieutenant Peterson finagled a group bust, and last I heard officers were en route to intercept a transfer…of women."

Panic closed in on her, trying to suffocate her, compressing her lungs and stinging her eyes.

That sickness roiled again, but Alice swallowed several times and willed away the awfulness by focusing on Reese, watching him lift his clothes, dig out his keys…

His keys. New panic exploded. "You're leaving?"

He took one look at her and dropped the clothes again. In three long strides he reached her. "I'll only be gone long enough to shower and get clean clothes." He held her shoulders, hesitated then drew her in to his chest.

Warmth and Reese's unique scent enveloped her. He didn't wrap those thick arms around her, didn't crush her close. He merely held her.

Fascinated, curious in a way she hadn't experienced in far too long, Alice lifted her hands to his bare chest. That soft cushion of chest hair, a few shades darker than that on his head, teased her palms. She rested her cheek against him and inhaled deeply, wanting to eat him up.

The top of her head didn't reach his chin. She felt his heartbeat against her cheek. He smelled of man, sex and excitement, but at the same time, he filled her with peace and contentment, emotions so long absent from her life. "I'm sorry. I keep imposing when I don't mean to."

"I want you to."

That made no sense. "You want me to impose?"

He put one hand to the back of her head, tangled his fingers in her hair. "I want you to tell me what you think and feel. I want you to confide in me."

"Oh. Okay." She turned her face a little so that it was her nose touching his furry chest. "I wish I was as strong as you."

He made a gruff sound. "Honey, this wouldn't be happening right now if you looked like me."

Another smile. That was a special gift in itself, the humor he brought her. Humor was one more thing she'd never again take for granted. "I meant your courage. Not your physique."

"You were plenty brave yesterday."

"No." She owed him the truth about that, since she couldn't be truthful about everything else—much as she wished it otherwise. "I have tunnel vision in dangerous situations. Knowing armed men had come to hurt you and probably anyone else who got in the way…" Taking a step back, she put a hand to her stomach. "I trembled so badly inside, I felt queasy and weak all over."

He shocked her by covering her hand with his own, but since his was so much bigger, his fingertips pressed into her sensitive flesh. Even through her shirt, his touch felt far too intimate.

And stirring.

Gaze compelling, he spoke in a deep, hushed voice. "Come on, Alice. That's just a healthy respect for danger. You'd have to be an idiot to be indifferent to thugs with loaded weapons."

Yes… Wait. What were they talking about? She'd stopped hearing him the second he touched her.

"Alice?" He turned his hand to catch hers. "I'm going to leave Cash here with you."

"Thank you." The dog provided so much comfort,

and in the short time she'd been watching him, she'd grown accustomed to his presence. When he wasn't around, she missed the sound of his snores, his occasional bark.

Even the sound of him breathing.

"Before I go, there's one thing I need to know."

Dreading the inquisition, Alice nodded.

"I'd appreciate it if you'd tell me your last name."

REESE WATCHED HER eyes widen, saw her soft lips part with a husky laugh. "We've never been properly introduced, have we?"

Damn, she leveled him without even trying. The way she laughed, how her dark eyes all but devoured him. He'd let her off the hook with details of being kidnapped—but only until he had her more relaxed.

She might think she kept it together, but he looked at her and saw so much, all of it painful to witness. She was on the edge, and if she lost it, if she cried, it'd crush him.

Hearing about it would be even worse, so, yeah, maybe he needed a little more time to get it together, too.

"I was all right and proper and introduced myself, but you were determined to cut me cold." He liked holding her hand and that she hadn't yet pulled away. "If it wasn't for Cash, I'd never have gotten even a simple nod from you."

"I'm sor—"

"Do *not* apologize."

Her grin widened. "Okay." She did a silly curtsy. "Alice Appleton."

Why that tickled him, Reese couldn't say, but hearing her name, how melodic it sounded, left him smiling, too. And after she'd kept him at such a distance, getting a last name meant he was finally making strides.

"I like it. It suits you." He tugged her in close again, and when she didn't resist, he rested his chin on top of her head. "Involvement in a shooting is always difficult. Even for a cop, counseling is offered, and strongly advised. It'd make sense if you needed to talk to someone, too."

Giving away nothing, she said simply, "No."

Accepting that, because he felt the same, he asked, "Will you talk to me about it?"

"I already did. It was awful." She burrowed closer. "I was cowardly, but I would have done what needed to be done, and I'm proud of that."

Wow. He'd never known anyone, much less a woman, who spoke so candidly. In one respect it worried him, because she left herself so emotionally exposed, she could be easily hurt.

Her lack of artifice also humbled him, made him more determined than ever to know her and all her dark secrets. "You've done what had to be done before?"

Instead of answering, she snuggled closer still. "You smell incredible, Reese."

A diversion—but he got the message all the same. He *had* made strides, so he wouldn't get too greedy. Not right now, anyway. "If you say so, but I need a shower."

He put his nose to the crown of her head. She was the one who smelled good. Sort of warm and soft and uniquely…Alice.

Maybe because she wasn't ready to let him go, she asked, "What happens now? With your work, I mean?"

"The coroner already had the body transported for autopsy."

"I'm glad it's not still in your apartment."

He felt her shudder. "Yeah, me, too." He ran his hand up and down her spine, settling his palm low at the small of her back, close to where her backside started a gentle rise. The subtleties of her figure teased him, made him anxious to discover more. "Because the death was officer involved, IAD will send an investigator. The D.A.'s office, too."

"Internal affairs?"

He splayed his fingers, spanning the narrow width of her back. She was so small, so delicate. The contrasts between his large frame and her slender figure had him stirring again. Insane. He couldn't let that keep happening. Not with Alice.

Not while they discussed things so awful and real.

He told himself that he *would* have her.

When she was ready. When *he* got her ready.

At the moment, Alice didn't seem clear on what she wanted, but he wasn't inexperienced, and unlike her, he wasn't conflicted. He felt her nearly tactile interest every time she looked him over with those big, dark eyes.

Yes, she wanted his company so she wouldn't be alone.

And she wanted him—as a man. Thank God.

But now was not the time to seduce her…easy as it'd probably be.

"Both offices will want to interview Lieutenant Peterson, Logan and me, the sooner the better."

She pressed back to scowl up at him. "Are you in trouble?"

"It's just routine. We're not accused of any wrongdoing, but it's smart to cover all the bases. Don't worry about it." Mostly he just wanted to get past it so he could get back to work.

"Officers talked to me last night."

Damn. Of course they had. Feeling his way, he asked, "How did that go?"

"It was fine. I told them what I knew, but really, other than recognizing there was a problem and loaning a gun to your friend, I didn't know what had happened or why."

And yet, other than asking how everyone had fared, she didn't pry. "I can finish explaining everything to you later, okay?"

She nodded. "You still haven't told me how long it will be before you can return to your apartment."

"After a couple of days, we'll be through all the necessary tasks. Then I'll have a company come in that specializes in cleaning…crime scenes."

"Meaning blood and gore and such?"

He moved right past that. No reason to dwell on the nastiness. The cleaners would get done in a day, but because he figured he'd want to stay with her longer, she didn't need to know that yet. "So, Alice Appleton, may I be your guest until my apartment is ready?"

"Yes, Reese Bareden, you may." Head tipped back, silky hair falling behind her shoulders, she met his gaze. "And, thank you. I'm sure a few days will make all the difference. I only need a little time to—"

Reese bent down to kiss her.

He didn't plan it, hadn't even realized he would do it, but once he got there, with his mouth on hers, awareness reverberated throughout his system, making itself known…everywhere.

In his pants for sure, his head, as well, and maybe even in his heart.

That bothered him, so he made the decision to keep it brief, nothing more than a peck. Except that her mouth was insanely soft, and it all felt so damn *right,* he couldn't help but linger. He didn't kiss her the way he really wanted, and still it staggered him.

Her hands curled carefully against his chest, her fingertips pressing into his pecs, the telling gesture giving away so much.

She wasn't unaffected.

Great.

Finally managing to ease back, Reese studied her closed eyes and heated skin and knew he had to go now before he took things too far.

He ran the back of his knuckles over her downy cheek. All women were soft, damn it. But somehow, with Alice, the softness seemed amplified.

Reese said, "I won't be long."

She still didn't open her eyes. Instead, she swallowed, nodded and shooed him away.

That got him grinning and helped to subdue other, more disturbing reactions. Alice was the funniest and, yes, oddest woman he'd ever known. Everything about her was endearing. And a turn-on.

Somewhere in her past, she'd been taken by strangers. She'd been hurt, but he didn't know how badly. He only knew it was enough to get her armed to the teeth, to make her wary of one and all.

Enough to have her seek a life of isolation.

Eventually he'd find out everything. For today, he'd start with a few phone calls and go from there.

One thing was certain. Until he knew if she was still in danger, he wouldn't leave Alice Appleton unprotected. He had only planned to get clean clothes from his apartment, maybe his shaving kit, toothbrush...but, what the hell. He'd pack a bag, and until further notice, he'd be her roommate—and her shadow.

"Lock the door behind me." And with that reminder, he walked out before he changed his mind and didn't go at all.

CHAPTER FOUR

ALICE MISSED REESE the moment he left. Her apartment, that once felt peaceful with only her in it, now felt empty. Too quiet.

Even sort of lonely.

"Bleh." She turned to Cash. "It's ridiculous, isn't it?"

Cash gave her a sleepy yawn, wiggled a little on the couch and started thumping his tail when she walked over to rub his ears.

"I'm glad I still have you. But for how long?" She cupped his furry face and put her cheek to his head. "It breaks my heart, but you're not really my dog. Reese loves you, so someday, if he moves or gets involved with a woman, I might not be able to see you anymore."

Cash crawled into her lap and tried to lick her face. Dodging the majority of his sloppy affection, Alice gave a laugh that sounded far too close to a sob.

Damn it, she would not cry. God knew she had nothing to cry about. Not anymore. She controlled her life, and if things weren't exactly as she'd like them to be, well, she had no one to blame but herself.

Even with the pep talk, her throat went tight and her eyes burned.

A knock on her door had her sucking up the excess of emotion real quick.

Cash did a doggy feat of launching away while barking like a crazed beast.

"Cash, behave." Assuming Reese had forgotten something, Alice quickly wiped her cheeks and drew a cleansing breath. Going to the door, she put her eye to the peephole—and straightened with incredulity.

Taking his cue from her, Cash ramped up his barking to a berserk level.

"Shhh," she told the frantic dog. "It's okay." Maybe. But why in the world would—

"Open up, Alice," came a deep, compelling voice. "I know you're in there. I hear Cash."

As the dog recognized their visitor, his reaction transformed from outrage to utter elation. Giving a high-pitched whine, he turned circles and kept looking at her, waiting for her to open the door.

In a whisper, Alice reminded the dog, "You don't know him any better than I do."

"I can hear you, too, Alice." The amusement came through loud and clear. "Now open up."

She bit her lip to hold back the groan. Good grief, did he have supersonic hearing or something?

Heartbeat accelerated, Alice put a hand to her hair, but of course it was already tidy. She was *always* tidy. And boring. And too cautious…

Stop it.

She straightened her shirt, licked the lips that Reese had just kissed and unlocked the door.

Cash charged forward in excitement, but he didn't get far. "Hello, Rowdy," she said as he caught the dog's collar. Luckily, being around Reese had gotten her somewhat used to large men.

Because Rowdy Yates was that, and then some.

He was also drop-dead gorgeous in a devilish, careless, edgy way. Where Reese tempered his sex appeal,

Rowdy threw it out there without reserve, bludgeoning innocent bystanders with his raw magnetism.

"Hey, yourself." He went down to one knee to acknowledge the dog. "What a welcome! I missed you too, bud."

"Odd," Alice remarked at the dog's reaction. "He barely knows you."

"We're kindred souls."

She doubted that. The dog was sweet and mostly gentle. In more ways than one, Rowdy Yates represented walking, talking trouble.

Unlike Reese, he didn't speak in a falsetto voice to Cash. There were many, many other ways in which he differed from Reese, as well. Where Reese instilled trust and confidence, Rowdy brought out blushes and heart palpitations.

Standing there, one hand on her throat, the other crossed over her stomach, Alice wondered why in the world he'd come to visit.

His blond hair, darker than Reese's, was a little too long and a lot too messy, as if the wind—or a woman's hands—had recently played with it. He had beard shadow, not because he'd just awakened, but because he hadn't bothered to shave. He wore a snowy white undershirt with jeans so ancient the denim was threadbare in places.

All in all, he made a rugged, mouth-watering package. Alice gulped and asked with some hope, "Are you looking for Reese?"

"Nope." He scooped up the dog. "Instead of hanging out here while you analyze me, how about we take this little party inside?"

But they weren't having a party! And how had he known she was analyzing him? "I, ah…"

As if she had no say so at all, Rowdy strode in, and she could have sworn Cash smiled at her as they went past. Alice just managed to get out of Rowdy's way.

With the back view of him now presented to her, she couldn't help but notice his muscled tush—and the outline of a big folding knife in his back pocket. She'd barely met him, but it didn't surprise her that he'd armed himself. In fact, she'd bet he had another weapon or two hidden on his person.

Why was he here?

She had no reason to distrust Rowdy. But then, she had no real reason to trust him either.

Leaving the front door partially ajar, she followed him into her apartment.

They hadn't been properly introduced, but she knew Rowdy as one of the men involved in the violence yesterday. "You're Rowdy Yates, Pepper's brother."

"And you're Alice, Reese's neighbor." He gave her a killer grin guaranteed to make a woman's knees wobbly.

Alice didn't doubt its effectiveness—but he wasted it on her. So far, only Reese had the ability to overwhelm her with his presence.

"Alice Appleton." Given that Reese now knew her name, there didn't seem to be much reason for the continued subterfuge—at least, not in that. Concern furrowed her brow. "Is everything okay?"

"You tell me." Going to her couch as if he visited every day, as if they were somehow old friends instead of brand-new acquaintances, he dropped into a seat. Cash remained on his lap, a look of rapture on his dark face.

Given his exceptional good looks, it wasn't a hardship to study Rowdy. And in that study, she saw so many emotions. Self-assurance. Even arrogance.

But she also sensed his troubled thoughts. About what? Yesterday he'd been in the middle of extreme circumstances. Reese had told her that Rowdy's sister had been threatened. How powerless had that made him feel?

He appeared the overprotective sort. But now his sister was with Reese's good friend, Detective Logan Riske. Did that leave Rowdy somehow displaced? Did he have any other family to turn to?

She had family, and yet, she was still…alone.

"How long are you going to do that?"

Worry for him kept her from embarrassment, and obliterated her usual reserve. "Not much longer."

"Good." He got comfortable, one arm along the back of the couch. "I don't mind female attention—"

"I'm sure you're used to it."

"—but now it's getting a little disturbing. Almost like you're dissecting me or something."

"My apologies." After a moment of hesitation, Alice approached him, decided to sit close and even reached for his hand.

Wariness sharpened his casual posture.

She ignored his unease, and instead went with her instincts. "How are you, Rowdy?"

Taken aback, he scowled. "That's my question for you."

"I'm not the one who was threatened yesterday."

He tried to retrieve his hand, but Cash in his lap hampered him, and she held on. "That wasn't—"

"A big deal?" Very gently she patted his hand. "Of course it was. Guns were aimed at you, and that means you could have lost your life at any moment."

"I figured we'd get free."

Or had he resigned himself to death? Since he'd settled in, she knew she wouldn't easily get him to leave. Instead of even trying, she held his hand in both of hers and tried a different tack. "I met your sister yesterday. Only briefly and of course not under the best circumstances. She's very beautiful, and very brave."

"Yeah, that's Pepper for you."

"The two of you are close?"

He stopped straining away and instead scrutinized her. "Very."

"I understand that she was threatened, as well." She tipped her head and said without inflection, "Human trafficking, correct?"

His jaw locked as he leaned forward. "*Never* would have happened. I'd have taken those bastards apart with my bare hands before letting them—"

"I know." She squeezed his fingers to soothe him, to let him know the coarse language hadn't offended her. His hands were big and rough. Capable hands—not that it would have mattered. "Good men always feel that way, and yet, you know that women still get hurt."

Dark eyes narrowed in a scowl. "What do you know about that, Alice?"

Poor Rowdy. He hoped to turn the tables on her by deflecting her concern.

She wouldn't let him. "I can see your worry, Rowdy. Your vulnerability."

"What the fuck?" Indignation wasn't the only emotion coloring his laugh. "I am *not* vulnerable."

"The language doesn't shield you. In fact, it gives away your upset."

His teeth clenched. "I'm not upset either."

"Of course you are." His raised voice was as much an indicator as the guarded expression in his eyes. "About your future," she insisted, "about what to do next and how to proceed."

"Proceed with *what?* Sorry, sweetheart, but you're not making any sense."

And now endearments. It was a tactic meant to reduce her conclusions to insignificance. The little woman spouting nonsense. She shook her head in pity. Rowdy didn't know her fortitude, he didn't understand that it took a lot more than that to derail her.

"Your sister is in love with a police detective. Where does that leave you?"

"I don't know what you're talking about."

They both knew better. "For a man who treads a fine line of right and wrong, how difficult must it be to have a cop for a brother-in-law?"

He breathed hard, then muttered, "They're not married yet." Pulling his hand from hers, he set Cash aside and stood. After a moment, he shrugged. "But, yeah, I saw her today and it seems they're making plans at Mach speed."

Alice looked up at him. "You're opposed to the wedding?"

"No." He started to pace. "Logan's a good man. I like him."

"You trust him."

"Of course I do. What's with the psychobabble? Are you a shrink now?"

Her smile held understanding. "Can you pick a lock, Rowdy?"

A show of nonchalance couldn't hide his antagonism. "Yeah, sure."

"And yet, you're not a locksmith."

"I learned on the street." He took a single step toward

her. "Picking locks, along with a boatload of other talents, was a skill I acquired out of necessity."

Exactly how she'd learned to read people—out of necessity. Given the shift in his expression, now more concerned than combative, he must have come to the same conclusion.

To head off any intrusive questions, Alice tried to steer the conversation. "Does it reassure you to know that Pepper will be well protected?"

Rather than the idea sidetracking him, he jumped on it. "What makes you think she needs protection?"

How to answer? How to explain that she'd made many assumptions in a very short time? Stalling, Alice gave Cash a pat before she, too, stood. "You could call it a hunch if you want."

Rowdy planted his big feet apart and crossed his thick arms over his chest. "Here's the thing, honey. You're not the only one with hunches. And that's why I'm here." He chucked her under the chin. "I have a hunch you're running scared. It'll be easier on you if you just settle down and tell me why."

SHE DIDN'T SCARE EASY, he'd give her that. Even though he pressured her, he couldn't crack Alice's calm facade.

When she'd first started digging into his head, into his motives, Rowdy had told himself to take off. If Alice didn't want to share, then to hell with it. Let her be Reese's problem. God knew that one enjoyed doubting everyone and everything…but, yeah, that wasn't entirely fair. He'd given Reese, the astute bastard, good reason for doubt.

As if she'd read his mind, Alice asked, "Does Reese know you're here?"

He laughed. "No."

"You don't trust him?"

"Other way around, honey." It still burned his ass, but what the hell? Why not tell her? "What do you know about Reese?"

Without hesitation, right to the point, she said, "He's a good man."

"Yeah, I suppose he is. Not that I always believed it."

"You must not know him well."

Because if he did, he'd nominate him for sainthood? Rowdy bit back a snort. "Nope. Hardly at all, in fact." He grinned at her. "We had this little case of mistaken identity. Logan and Reese thought I'd witnessed a murder two years past, but it was actually my sister...." Sickness burned his stomach, sent acid into his throat.

Playing cavalier became more difficult.

Not that Miss Alice Appleton was easy to fool, anyway. He rubbed at an ache in his temple. "Scratch all that, okay? The bastard is dead now, and good riddance."

Voice soft, strangely comforting, she said, "So the murderer was the man who died in Reese's apartment."

A statement, not a question, but Rowdy confirmed it, anyway. "Yeah. Because of him, because of what he would've done if he'd known Pepper was a witness, we lived off the grid." He couldn't quite look at her, because damn it, she'd probably see too much, far more than she'd already surmised. "We managed to lay low for those two years, but after Logan and Reese exposed us, we became instant loose ends."

"So you would have been killed?"

He lifted one shoulder, hoping to shake off the tension that clung to every muscle. "Reese and Logan, and others, too."

"Everyone—except for your sister." In deep thought,

Alice whispered, "He would have kept her alive so he could sell her."

Rage ignited, so bright Rowdy couldn't speak, couldn't answer. He gave a barely perceptible nod.

Attuned to him in a way that he wasn't used to, Alice touched his arm. "It's a very good thing that he's dead."

And therein lay the crux of the matter: her easy approval of such things, a mind-set that death could be the answer to a problem.

He decided to focus on Alice and tune out everything else.

Glad that she'd helped him with that, he covered her hand with his own. "Hell of an outlook, honey." With alacrity he moved on to the purpose for his visit. "How does a buttoned-up gal like you get that indifferent about death?"

She tipped her head. "Buttoned-up?"

"Prim. Proper." At her look of confusion, he gave her a nudge. "Come on, Alice. You're a shrewd woman. I'm not telling you anything you don't know."

Distracted, maybe even a little insulted, she moved away from him to sit.

When Rowdy joined her, Cash crawled over to rest between them and gave a lusty sigh of contentment. She pushed her fingers into the dog's fur in a gentle stroke that could mesmerize.

"I'm worried for you, Alice."

Lost in thought, she said absently, "Don't be."

Not good enough. Yesterday, when she'd walked into the middle of the chaos, the death and the blood, he'd perceived something damaged in her persona, the same type of hopeless acceptance he'd seen in his sister—before she'd hooked up with Logan.

It bothered him because, almost instantly, he'd recognized Alice as a woman with dark secrets and a fair store of fear. How could any man turn a blind eye to that?

Measuring his words, hoping to reach her, Rowdy said with utmost seriousness, "The thing is, Alice, I know women, so I know—

She laughed. *At him.*

A little irate, he waited for her humor to subside. "That's funny?"

"Absolutely." Her smile was teasing—and made her look really pretty. "You're so incorrigible and untamed."

"Untamed, huh?" What the hell did that mean? She made him sound like a wild animal.

"Definitely." Leaning closer, looking into his eyes, she pretended to share a secret. "You're also incredibly big and undeniably handsome."

Ears burning a little, he tried to lean away from her without looking too obvious. It wasn't often he dodged a woman. Like maybe never. But this couldn't happen, so he tried to be gentle but up front. "You know I'm only here as a friend, right?"

Another of her silly laughs escaped, and damn, it sounded so sweet, it almost made him smile.

Her chastising look forewarned him. "We're hardly friends, Rowdy."

"We could be." *If she'd stop laughing at me.*

Now she sighed. "I'd like that, actually. Thank you."

The truth struck him. He was both relieved and a little embarrassed. "You weren't coming on to me, were you?"

"No, I wasn't. I'm sorry, but honestly, I wouldn't even know how."

He wouldn't tell her that she'd done a damn good job without trying.

She rubbed the dog's neck, then around and under his chin. "You and Reese share a similar look."

"Yeah?" Since Reese was polished, with a witty perspective on life, Rowdy didn't see it. Well, except that they were both blond and tall.

"You're big."

Since a statement like that had all kinds of connotations, he had to cough to keep from making a joke. With any other woman…but, yeah, this was Alice.

"And you really are handsome." This time it was his hair she tunneled her fingers into. "I'm sure women appreciate the 'bad boy' guise you've cultivated."

Bad boy? *Guise?* His neck stiffened. "I haven't cultivated—"

"But Reese is also big." Dropping her hand, she smiled off at nothing in particular. "And incredibly handsome. And he's…" Her voice faded. "He's *sooo*…"

Curiosity got the better of him. "What?"

She licked her lips and inhaled a deep breath, only to let it out in a long sigh.

Put off, Rowdy scowled at her. "If you start purring, I'm outta here."

A blush warmed her cheeks. She straightened her shoulders and refocused on him. "My point is that you and Reese might have similarities, but you also have differences. Like that giant chip on your shoulder and that cocky swagger—"

"I do *not* swagger." Did he?

"—that proclaims you a rebel." With a mere glance, she shared her sympathy. "You like butting heads with the law, walking that narrow path between saint and sinner, and we both know it. I think you enjoy it."

The sinner part he could attest to, but where the hell had she gotten the saint angle? "Sorry, doll, you don't really know me at all. What I do or don't enjoy. Who I enjoy it with." He warmed to his subject, ready to wrest the upper hand from her velvet grip. "In fact—"

Suddenly Alice stiffened, lifted her head as if she heard something.

"What is it?"

She put a finger to her lips as if in warning, then shook her head.

Cash watched her with the same confusion Rowdy felt.

As she rose silently from the couch, her gaze on the front door, she said, "So you saw your sister today? How is Detective Riske feeling?"

What the hell was she up to? She made not a single sound as she inched toward her door. "He's grouchy." Fascinated, Rowdy watched as she stopped to study the door a moment. "I don't think he likes being pampered any more than I would."

She gestured for him to continue. He obliged, but in case trouble intruded, he also stood. "Pepper isn't the typical mother hen. Far from it. Her efforts at coddling are as likely to drive Logan nuts as anything else."

As he spoke, Alice went on tiptoe to look out the door's peephole. Apprehension dropped her back to her heels.

With a huff, she jerked the door open. "You scared me."

There stood Reese, and it was obvious he'd been eavesdropping. It took him only a second to find his aplomb. "Sorry. I was about to knock."

She snorted.

That particular sound coming from that particular woman might have amused Rowdy. But under the circumstances, it didn't penetrate past his annoyance.

"Damn it." He hadn't heard a thing, hadn't even realized that Alice had left the door unsecured. "I'm slipping."

"No, you're fine." Alice waved off his disgruntlement. "It's just that I'm familiar with the sounds in my apartment."

"He wasn't in your apartment," Rowdy pointed out. "He was lurking around the hallway."

"Lurking?" Reese asked with a raised brow, but he couldn't very well deny it.

"I'm familiar with those sounds, as well."

Chagrined, Reese looked at Alice, gave her a half smile and then zeroed in on Rowdy.

Well, hell. He had hoped to be long gone before Reese realized he'd come to call, but too late for subterfuge now. Rowdy lifted his hands in surrender. "Busted."

Carrying a stuffed overnight bag and some clothes over his arm, Reese strode in, all the while letting Rowdy feel his discontent. "Care to tell me what you're doing here?"

"I'm just visiting." Rowdy nodded at Reese's load. "But it looks like you're moving in."

As if someone had goosed her, Alice jumped. "What? No."

Dismissing that reaction, Rowdy whistled low. "Fast work, Reese. I had no idea."

Alice started to speak again, but Reese cut her off. "So, now you know. Make note of it, okay?"

Alice subsided with a wide-eyed look of surprise.

So, it was like that, huh? Rowdy saluted him. Sure, there was no denying Alice's interest in Reese. Hell, she'd spelled it out, all the while going moony-eyed. Granted, he didn't know Reese that well. But he hadn't quite figured Alice as his type. Still, stranger things had happened.

Cash showered Reese with the same enthusiastic welcome Rowdy had received. Fickle mutt. "That dog loves everyone."

"No," Alice said, "he doesn't." Hands on her hips, she addressed Reese with accusation. "You were listening in."

"I'm a cop, Alice, remember? I'm trained to eavesdrop." Catching the back of her neck, Reese held her still as he lowered his mouth to hers. Alice froze, but she allowed it.

That *was* fast work.

The kiss lingered, and Rowdy lifted both brows. He meant what he'd said: he knew women, so he knew it wasn't in Alice's nature to get involved easily. Reese must've conjured some magic.

It wasn't any of his business, but damn it, he felt protective—maybe of both of them. And wasn't that a bunch of bullshit? Hell, Reese was a well-trained, astute, hulk of a cop.

Alice needed a gentle hand, but Reese…well, Alice hid something dark and dangerous. Rowdy saw it there in her eyes, the same shadows he faced every time he looked in a mirror. Would Alice's past cause problems for a reputable cop?

Tired of being a voyeur, Rowdy said, "You're going to make her faint."

With clear reluctance, Reese pulled back, and Alice struggled to get it together. It was amusing to watch, and her blush was as pretty as her smile, as uplifting as her laugh.

"Behave, Rowdy." She licked her lips, realized what she'd done and glared at both men.

Rowdy fought off a grin. The lady had grit—which meant she wouldn't easily give into fears or intimidation. Whatever she had in her past, it had to be something substantial.

It was nice that she had Reese's attention, but that wouldn't keep Rowdy from giving protection of his own. After all, Reese was limited by legalities.

Rowdy…not so much.

Judging by Reese's possessive posture—with both the dog and Alice—things were about to get real interesting.

That was just the way Rowdy liked it.

CHAPTER FIVE

THE DISGRUNTLED LOOK on Alice's face didn't deter Reese. He ignored it, just as he ignored Rowdy's smug amusement and rapt attention.

Because he wanted to, because for whatever reason, she was too damn tempting, he put his mouth to hers again. This time he kept it light, brief to the point of frustration, and when he lifted his head he smoothed her plump bottom lip with his thumb. "Where can I store my stuff?"

Somewhat dazed and definitely flustered, she looked around as if she didn't know her own apartment.

"I can hang my change of clothes in the hall closet, if that's okay."

She didn't look at Rowdy. She didn't really look at Reese either.

"Alice?"

"Mmm? Oh." After a deep shuddering breath, she pulled herself together. "Why don't I put your shaving kit in the bathroom? I, ah, have a shelf in there, so it'll be handy when you need it…tomorrow I guess. To shave." Pained, she did a verbal push to get beyond her stumbling speech. "Please do feel free to use the hall closet for your clothing. It's mostly empty, so there should be plenty of room."

"Right." Empty for now—but when she got her gun

back from Logan, she'd have yet another weapon stored there. "Thanks."

With a dismissive smile, she hurried off. Reese shot a suspicious frown at Rowdy—and saw him watching Alice's retreat.

No fucking way. Was that interest in Rowdy's gaze? It better not be. It damn well better be something else—what, Reese had no idea.

Turning to fully face him, Reese waited until he gained Rowdy's complete attention. To ensure Alice wouldn't hear, he kept his voice low. "What are you doing here? And don't give me that bullshit about visiting."

Rowdy followed his lead and spoke in a near whisper. "She's scary."

"Alice? Don't be stupid."

"A dog that doesn't bark is always the most dangerous."

"You're calling her a dog?" Reese knew that wasn't his point at all.

"I'm saying she's too quiet, and too proper." Rowdy took a seat again, and Cash abandoned Reese to join him. "She's also putting on a brave front, almost like she's been doing it so long she doesn't even realize it now."

No kidding. He'd figured that one out on his own. "What do you know of it?"

"Only that it bothers me."

So Alice hadn't confided in Rowdy either? Good. He wanted her to trust him first and foremost, not any other man. "Don't worry about it." Reese took his clothes to the closet. "I've got it covered."

"Somehow, Reese, I don't think you do."

Reese was ready to take him apart, but Alice reentered with forced cheer.

"Where are my manners? Rowdy, would you like something to drink?"

"No," Reese said, "he doesn't."

Confusion tripped her up. "You already asked him?"

"No."

Alice frowned at him.

Rowdy just smirked. "I'm good, Alice, thanks, anyway."

Before Alice could protest, Reese asked him, "So, you saw Logan? He's doing okay?"

"He's surly and complaining that Pepper keeps trying to shove a pain pill down his throat."

"He isn't taking his meds?"

"The antibiotics, sure. But the pain pills make him sleepy, so he'd rather suffer the discomfort. Thing is, if he so much as flickers an eyelid, Pepper can't bear it. She wants to 'comfort' him."

Imagining that, Reese grinned. Like him, Logan wasn't big on being coddled. It emasculated a man, especially a man who wanted to do the coddling. "I can see why that'd make him surly. At least he has a reason to stay in bed." Then, just to tweak Rowdy, he added, "With Pepper."

Rowdy slanted him a look. "If Alice weren't present, I'd tell you what to do with that sentiment."

That seemed to startle Alice out of some heavy-duty daydreaming. "What does it matter if I'm—"

He pushed to his feet. "I don't want to singe your ears, hon."

"Oh."

Hon? Reese collected her to his side again. "I was going to check in with Logan today, anyway. Maybe I can run some interference for him." And thinking that gave him an idea.

He looked down at Alice. "What do you have planned for the day?"

"Nothing much. I finished my work while you were—" she waved a hand at the couch "—sleeping. I thought I might give Cash a bath."

The dog flattened his ears, slunk off the couch and went behind a chair.

Bemused, Alice watched him. "Maybe instead I'll make a run to the grocery."

"Is there something you needed?"

She bit her lip. "I have a sweet tooth."

Somehow, the way she said that felt like an admission. Reese saw the same confusion he felt mirrored on Rowdy's face. "I do, too."

"Me, three," Rowdy said.

"Jelly beans are my favorite." She looked at both men.

"Chocolate ice cream," Rowdy said without hesitation.

Would he ever understand her? Reese wondered. "I'm up for anything, but I especially like caramels, and warm peach pie is always good."

"Mmm, sounds delicious," Alice agreed. "You're both in such great shape, you can probably eat anything you want without worrying about it."

"You're slim," Reese told her. "Surely you don't—"

"Diet?" She shook her head. "No. But I'm bad, I use food as…" Her voice trailed off.

"Comfort," Rowdy finished for her. "Pepper does the same thing. She says the worst for her was the evenings. But instead of a few jelly beans, she'd binge on an entire pizza."

Alice smiled over that. "I go through a bag of jelly beans a week. Sometimes two bags." She tipped her head at Rowdy. "Your sister is really beautiful."

"Yeah, she is," Reese agreed. "Logan is a lucky guy." Reese paid little attention to what he said. He was too busy trying to figure out Alice's thoughts. Was she making some sort of female-inspired comparison? He hoped not, because Pepper Yates was an extremely unique woman.

But then, so was Alice—only in a very different way.

"Maybe we can shop together on the way back from seeing Logan and Pepper." Holding her hand in his, he rubbed a thumb over her knuckles. "You'll come with me, won't you?"

She couldn't quite hide her pleasure. "You want me to?"

"I'm sure Pepper would like to see you again." He could keep Alice close by taking her along, and while there she could give Pepper someone else to focus on. Whether or not Logan would thank him for that, Reese couldn't say.

Touching her hair as if to straighten it, Alice asked, "When did you plan to leave?"

"I'm ready now if you are." He sent a pointed look Rowdy's way.

"And there's my cue to hit the road." As Rowdy walked to Alice, Reese saw the slight rise in her anxiety.

Rowdy, the dick, pretended that he didn't. "Thanks again for everything."

Everything? What the hell did that mean?

Alice stuck out a hand. "It was nice to see you again."

Ignoring her impersonal gesture, Rowdy hauled her in for a big hug, lifting her right off her feet.

Which meant her hand was now caught between their

bodies, against Rowdy's midsection, and that had Reese seeing red.

She all but groped him. Unwillingly, sure. By accident even. But still…

He stepped forward—and Alice disengaged herself.

She didn't go far. In a low, too-serious voice—as if Reese wasn't right there and more than able to hear every single word—she said, "If you ever want to talk, I'm here."

No, she was not. "What the hell does he have to talk about?"

"Not a thing," Rowdy said, his good humor obliterated by her offer. And then with exasperation: "You stole my line again, hon."

Reese stepped forward in warning. "You're pushing your luck, Rowdy."

Drolly, he said, "Yeah, wouldn't want to do that."

Reese started to fume, and Alice slipped forward to lead Rowdy to the door. "I'll see you out."

Cash launched into the fray, always excited by the idea of a trip outdoors.

As good an excuse as any, Reese decided. He took down the dog's leash. "No, I'll walk him out. I'll take Cash with me, so as soon as you're ready we can take off."

"Thank you," she said. "I only need a few minutes."

Rowdy didn't wait, so Reese had to hurry to get Cash hooked to the leash so he could follow.

He caught Rowdy in the parking lot. "Hold up, damn it."

Rowdy paused, then with a shrug, walked into the grassy area.

They stood there in silence a moment, watching as Cash chased a bee while also trying to piddle. He hobbled along on three legs—the fourth in the air—before running out of leash and landing back on his tail.

Rowdy shook his head. "I do like that dog."

"So does Alice. Good old Cash was my icebreaker." Dark clouds rolled over the sun, and a breeze carried the scent of rain. Reese surveyed the sky with interest. "It wasn't until she saw the dog that she stopped snubbing me."

"But she has stopped."

It gave Reese great satisfaction to confirm it. "I'll be staying with her a few days while they clean my apartment."

"Bragging? Hell, Reese, you may as well use a branding iron on her." Thunder rumbled, announcing a threat of storms to come. "Calm it down a little, why don't you."

Advice from another man, a man who'd just been in Alice's apartment, didn't go down smooth. "What's your interest?"

"Hell, I don't know." Rowdy leaned over to pluck a dandelion. "There's something about her. It's like she's guarded. Even hurt. Unlike most people, she's too alert, too intuitive, like maybe she's waiting for something to happen."

"Something bad."

"Yeah. And the way she rolled with that shit yesterday? A dead body doesn't shake her. And the stuff she says, how she says it…"

"I know." It unnerved Reese, as well, and made him determined to shield her.

"I want to find out what happened to cause her to be that way."

Reese wanted the same. "I'll handle it."

"So will I." Rowdy tossed aside the weed. "Don't

start huffing, Reese. It doesn't suit you. Sarcasm, sharp wit, that's more your speed."

Reese held silent, not a single bit of sharp wit coming to mind.

"You know I can find out things you can't. No, not by grilling Alice. I won't do that to her." When the stiffening breeze blew his hair, Rowdy shoved it back with both hands. "Hell, if I tried, she'd probably put me through the inquisition, all while showering me with concern."

Interesting. "That's what she did?"

"Totally threw me. Not even my sister tries that hard to get in my head." He narrowed his eyes at Reese. "She treated me like some damned abused mutt she wanted to heal."

As Reese knew, Rowdy had plenty of demons to deal with. He and Pepper had not had easy lives. Apparently, Alice saw it, too.

But was that her only interest in Rowdy?

"What did you tell her?"

"I denied everything." The baring of Rowdy's teeth didn't come close to resembling a smile. "Something's up with her, and we both know it. My guess is that you've already made plans to check into it, but your legal channels are limited."

"Duly noted." Sticking to legal channels had almost gotten him and his friends killed, in his own damned apartment.

Rowdy eyed him. "Give it a rest, Reese. That wasn't your fault. No one blames you." He stared toward the dog, now digging at a root. "I'm glad it's over."

But it wasn't, not yet. One scumbag might've died, but others remained. The tentacles of evil reached far and wide. "You know, I figured you'd be Lieutenant Peterson's problem right about now. Yesterday we rounded up parts of the human trafficking ring, but there are more connections, others to pull out of hiding."

"And you thought I'd be following leads?" He examined a few raindrops that landed on his forearm. "Now, Reese, would I ignore a direct order from your lieutenant to stay out of that?"

Yeah, he absolutely would. Where innocent women were concerned, few men could stand aside and do nothing. A man like Rowdy? No way would he stay uninvolved.

"If you trip up," Reese said, "Peterson will have your head."

"My head and my balls—at least that's what she told me."

They shared a quick smile before Rowdy sobered again.

"One advantage to living under the radar is that I made contacts on the street. And before you say it, yes, I know how to ask around without drawing too much attention. There won't be any blowback for Alice."

"If she's not from around here, you won't find jack shit." Rowdy had cultivated many friends in high and low places, but he didn't have unlimited boundaries.

"True enough. The thing is, I'm more concerned with any remaining threat against her. If she has legitimate reason to worry, I'll be able to find out."

Reese hated to have another man poking into Alice's business. Yet he knew it was true; Rowdy did have connections that might elude the law.

And if she was only skittish thanks to a traumatic past? Well, then, he'd deal with it. "Report to me."

"I don't report to anyone."

Temper spiking, Reese stood his ground. "Maybe now is a good time for you to start."

Static collected in the air as Rowdy continued to study Reese, until finally he flashed a genuine grin. "Yeah, all right. Don't implode. I just wanted to test the water."

"Keep out of the water."

Laughing again, Rowdy clapped him on the shoulder. Hard. "If I find out anything, I'll clue you in. You'll do the same?"

Damn it, he didn't want to. But maybe an alliance with Rowdy would be a good thing. He could think of him as a snitch, utilize his talents in different ways....

"We're on the same side in this, Reese. She's a hell of an actress, and she's putting up a brave front, but she's scared. I want to know why, you want to know why, and we both want to ensure that no matter what it is, it never touches her again."

Reese watched as Cash rolled to his back in a patch of clover. "All right. I'll tell you what I know so far. But understand this, Rowdy. She's off-limits."

"To me?"

God, he despised declaring himself. If this wasn't so important, he wouldn't. "It's nothing personal against you," Reese clarified. "Far as I'm concerned, she's off-limits to every guy other than me."

After Rowdy finished laughing, Reese told him about the kidnapping. They were both grim as death when they parted ways.

ALICE STARED OUT the passenger window, watching the wind bend trees, the rain flood the streets. The windshield wipers beat a frantic rhythm, and the defroster worked overtime.

She'd been halfway to Reese's car when the skies opened up and sent a deluge to soak her before she could even attempt to open an umbrella. Combing her hair now would be pointless. Already it started to curl.

Luckily she didn't wear makeup, or it'd be everywhere.

She'd changed into simple, plain ballet flats and a dark print summer dress that should have been modest and comfortable. But now wet, it kept trying to cling to her breasts, her belly, her thighs. Chills rose on her arms despite the warmth of the interior.

She loved it.

Often when out and about, she couldn't relax. She stayed too busy watching for threats, observing everyone and everything. She wondered how those people could be so different from her.

And she wondered if evil blended in with the mundane.

Right beneath the noses of the unsuspecting public, people were grabbed. Taken away. Mistreated. Abused.

Forced to do things they didn't want to do.

Never again would she be unaware of her surroundings. She stayed vigilant, for herself and for others.

Right now, though, on this stormy afternoon, few people could be seen. Even better, she was safe and sound in a car with the impressive Detective Reese Bareden.

Lightning seared the sky ahead of them, ramping up the downpour from a shower to a thunderstorm.

Feeling content, a little lazy and all too comfortable despite the weather and her drenched appearance, she sighed. "I love storms." She'd always found them sexy. Peaceful. A sign of fresh renewal.

Strung too tight, Reese muttered, "Me, too."

He slowed as a woman, holding a little boy's hand, dashed across the street. She almost lost her umbrella beneath a gust of wind. The kid laughed as he deliberately stomped in deep puddles. The poor woman was not amused.

Alice watched them hurry into a restaurant. She realized she was smiling.

"You like children?"

She redirected her smile at Reese. He, too, had gotten soaked to the skin. His dark polo shirt stuck to his broad, solid shoulders and chest. He'd pushed back his wet hair, leaving it in sexy disarray. His lashes clumped together over his bright green eyes.

"I love them." What would Reese's children look like? They'd be tall and no doubt blond. Surely confident and happy, like their dad.

"You don't have any?"

She shook off fanciful daydreams. "No, of course not." What did he think? That she'd abandoned a child somewhere? That she would live apart from her child? "I've never been married, or even in a serious relationship. I mean, not that serious." Not since the kidnapping had she even looked at a man with interest. "One day I'd like to have kids of my own, though."

"Boys or girls?"

"It wouldn't matter to me." The skies darkened with the storm so that it felt like early evening. Headlights danced over the rain-washed road and reflected off the wet surfaces of signs, buildings and other cars. "I thought men didn't like to talk about stuff like that."

"Stuff like what?"

He'd turned that back around on her, so she sought the right words. "You know what I mean. Things so personal. So…intimate."

"Intimate?" Reese kept his gaze on the road.

If he wanted to discuss it, fine. "Talking about children usually suggests a committed, caring relationship."

A muscle ticked in his jaw. "I like talking with you about anything."

Could that possibly be true? She couldn't miss the stiff set of his shoulders, how his hands gripped the wheel. Something wasn't right, but unlike with most people, she often had difficulty reading his moods and thoughts. "You're upset?"

"What? No." He shifted, trying to relax.

Alice studied him. "Would you fib to me, Reese?"

The seconds ticked by. It almost felt like he held his breath—and then he admitted, "If necessary, yeah, I would."

His honesty pleased her. She smiled at him to let him know.

Confused, he worked his jaw. "You want me to lie to you?"

"I don't think you would, not about anything important." She tipped her head. "You say you're not upset?"

"I'm not."

How wonderful would it be to totally trust another man? Did she dare? "Then what's wrong?"

His laugh was short and rough. "Nothing."

Something. Maybe she needed more information to figure him out. "Reese?"

"Hmm?"

"You've kissed me a few times now."

"Yeah." His voice went deep and dark. "And you liked it."

Such confidence, and such knowledge of women. Could a man be any sexier? "I did," she admitted. "I hope you'll want to kiss me again."

"Count on it." He glanced her way. "But next time, it'll be more."

He said that with so much heat, it stole her breath. "The thing is…I'm not sure I'm ready for more than that. Not yet, anyway."

He shook his head. "No, I meant… The way I kissed you was hardly a kiss at all." Again he glanced at her, then down over her body before giving his attention back to the slick road. "I want to really taste you, Alice. I want to feel your tongue…" He inhaled, shifted. "I want *more* of a kiss."

"Oh." The damp dress suddenly felt restrictive, especially over her breasts. She had the awful suspicion that Reese could see the outline of her stiffened nipples. "Yes, I'd like that." *A lot.*

"Good to know."

Thinking about it now, she wondered why steam didn't rise in the car. She plucked at the material of her dress, trying to rearrange it a little, but it was a futile effort, so she gave up. "I need you to understand, though. If you want to sleep with me—"

"No way can you have a doubt about that."

Her heart swelled. No, she didn't really have any doubts. "Thank you." Her eyes rounded after she uttered those absurd words. Had she really thanked him for wanting her? Oh, God, yes, she had.

Reese grinned. "You're welcome."

She had to clear her throat twice before speaking again. "The thing is, I'll need some time. I've already made it clear that I'm interested—"

"You are? Great. I thought so, but I appreciate the confirmation all the same."

Worse and worse. *Get to the point, Alice.* "I didn't want to confuse things, or lead you on."

"Okay."

His easy compliance only rattled her more. "I'd understand if you'd rather not wait for me. For me…to be ready, I mean." With every word, she sounded more ridiculous. "I don't know how long it'll take me, if it'll be tomorrow, or next week, or maybe even a month from now—"

All humor fled his expression. "Alice."

"—and I know you have other options. Pam and Nikki made that clear enough. You're obviously a very…sexual man."

"Like all men, sure. But that doesn't mean—"

Unwilling to hear him make excuses for her, she rushed on. "I don't mean to make things uncomfortable. I wish I was different, but I'm not."

"Alice." He reached for her hand, but she pulled away.

Lacing her fingers together in her lap, she stared out the windshield and tried to get it all said. "Even though you seem to have some interest in me now—"

"A lot of interest, actually."

"I'm not like most women." And she was glad other women were different, because she wouldn't wish her ordeals on anyone. "I can't just—"

"Be quiet, Alice."

The order got her back up, and pretty much guaranteed she couldn't go quiet. "I don't take orders from anyone!" Here she was, doing her best to be clear and up front with him, and he—

"Think of it as a request," he snarled.

He dared to sound angry! That annoyed her enough that she forgot her disjointed explanations on her possible hang-ups. "Maybe I would if you couched it that way."

"*Please* be still a moment, Alice. Let me think."

She pressed her lips together, but it wasn't easy to stay silent, especially when more than a full minute passed.

Finally he said, "If we're laying it all out there, then fine, I want you. You know that. Every damned time I'm near you I get hard, so it'd be impossible for you to miss."

She was just irked enough to say, "Braggart." The accusation came out before she could censor herself.

"I wasn't…" He scowled at her, but the scowl lifted into a crooked smile. "It *is* noticeable, and you know it."

More subdued—and on the verge of grinning herself—Alice nodded. "Yes." Most definitely, very noticeable.

"It's insane." This time when he reached for her hand, she accepted the gesture. His hand was big and warm, holding hers securely. "There's something unique, something very special about you."

She would have called it odd.

"But I'm not a kid who can't control himself. And now, knowing you were kidnapped…" His hand tightened. "The last thing I ever want to do is pressure you, or make you uneasy."

There went her grin. Ice expanded inside her, cramping her stomach. "Please don't pity me, Reese." She could take just about anything but that.

He made a rude sound. "Trust me, Alice, pity for a woman doesn't get me jacked." He released her to steer around a corner, onto a quieter, more suburban street. "I see you and I react. Can't help it. I also can't ignore what you told me."

"It doesn't matter."

"That you were kidnapped? The hell it doesn't. I need

to know what happened, if that's the reason you're reserved now. If it's something else—"

"I wasn't raped." She startled him with that blurted statement.

He swallowed hard, nodded. "I'm glad."

"But it was ugly, and awful and..." How much should she tell him? As a cop, he could find out some details on his own, so maybe she could just expand on that. She lifted a hand toward him and realized she was shaking. She tucked it back toward her lap. "It was a while before I managed to get away."

"Days?" He worked his jaw. "Weeks?"

She shook her head, unable to admit the truth. "The important thing is that I *did* get freed, and now...I don't know. If I'm hesitant, it's because I haven't felt like a woman for a very long time, and I haven't been that aware of men except to avoid them." She studied his strong profile and whispered, "Until you."

"And my dog."

Humor wormed its way in past her bleak memories. "Yes, and your dog."

"Thank God for Cash."

That sentiment nearly brought tears to her eyes. "I'm sure he feels the same way about you." After all, Reese had rescued Cash from sure death. But she didn't want him to rescue her from her self-imposed isolation and uncertainty.

She would rescue herself.

Putting her shoulders back, she faced him. "I might need a little time to adjust, but I want to give you whatever you want from me."

He accepted that with a nod. "I want everything."

Her mouth opened twice before she managed to squeak out, "Oh. Okay, then."

"While we get things back in order, I'm going to stay with you." He pulled up to a stop sign. "I want to have sex, Alice, that's a given, but I also want you to want it."

Never had she imagined this conversation. But then, never had she imagined wanting a man again. Not after everything else that had happened in her life. "Okay."

"While you're being so agreeable…" He pulled the car away again. "I don't want anything to do with Pam or Nikki or, currently, any other woman. So, get that out of your head." He gave her a hard glance. "And I don't want you involved with any other guys either."

That struck her as hilarious, and the laugh bubbled out before she could stop it. When he looked more murderous, she pursed her mouth to hold in the humor.

"Promise me."

"You have my word."

"Good." The car slowed again. "We can work on everything else, take it one step at a time. Starting with that deeper kiss. Sound good?"

Better than good. Her breathing hitched. "I… Yes."

He stopped the car, turned in the seat to face her. His gaze went all over her, narrowing on her breasts, her belly. Reaching out, he touched her cheek, smoothed back a hank of damp hair.

Breath bated, she waited for the promised kiss.

"Alice?"

"Hmm?"

"It sucks, believe me, but we're here."

"Here?" She looked up, and sure enough, he'd pulled into the drive of an impressive house, right up next to an expansive three-car garage. Only a few feet separated her from a nice overhang.

She'd forgotten where they were going!

"Buck up, sweetheart. We won't stay long." And

then, while the rain continued to pound down, Reese took the umbrella from the floor, opened it as he left the car and circled around to her side.

CHAPTER SIX

LEAVING THE UMBRELLA by the door, Reese allowed Pepper to usher them along the foyer to the living room, but drew up short at the sight of Logan sitting on the couch, his feet propped up on the coffee table, a pillow behind him and a throw over his lap. He knew Pepper had likely arranged his friend there, exactly like that, and he laughed.

Logan scowled. "I'd hate to see you have to turn around and leave again in this storm."

"Surely even Pepper wouldn't be that cruel."

Pepper said, "Ha-ha," at the same time Logan promised, "No, but I would."

"He doesn't like being sick," Pepper explained.

"I'm *not* sick, damn it."

"Wounded, then," Pepper snapped right back. "You heard what the doctor said. You have to take it easy."

"I'm seeing a whole new side to her personality." Logan pushed the throw away from his legs. "She didn't want to let me out of the bed even for company."

"And you're complaining?" Reese tsked. "From what I remember, that's where she always wanted to keep you."

Pepper cracked a smile. "He'll be more agreeable to that again after his arm is healed."

"No doubt."

"I'd be agreeable now," Logan grumbled, "if you'd only—"

Pepper smashed her fingers over his mouth. "Behave."

Stepping out from behind Reese, Alice said, "Thank you for allowing us to visit." She slipped off her shoes and placed them at the edge of the foyer rug. "I'm relieved to see you both in such good spirits."

Logan's attention shifted to her and locked there.

Even though Reese already knew what he'd see, he looked at Alice, too. The visual packed quite a punch.

Her usual persona was starched and standoffish, prim and proper.

But getting drenched had taken care of that.

With pink cheeks, tangled hair and dewy skin, her sweet summer dress outlining every understated curve on her willowy body, she resembled the woman from his dream.

No way around it, she was sexy as hell.

And damn it, Logan saw it, too.

"You might want to go dry off some," Reese told her. "Bathroom is all the way at the end of the hall, past the stairs and the entry to the kitchen, last door on your right."

"Of course." She put a hand to her hair. "There's a towel in there I can use?"

Logan continued to stare, so Alice shifted her attention to Pepper.

Belatedly Pepper shook off her surprise. "Sorry. I'm new here myself, so I'm not sure where everything is." She nudged Logan.

He still looked thunderstruck but managed a reply. "In the linen closet across from the bathroom." His gaze dipped over her once, then shot back to her face. "Help yourself to whatever you need."

Reese understood why both Pepper and Logan stared. Did Alice have any idea of the picture she presented?

Doubtful, since she smiled without a care. "Thank you."

As she walked off, they craned their necks to stare after her.

Annoyed, Reese toed off his own soaked shoes and strode over to Logan. "Knock it off already."

Logan blinked. "Damn, man, seeing her so wet—"

Every muscle on Reese's body clenched. He leaned toward Logan. "If you weren't already injured, I'd—"

In the middle of his threat, Pepper reached past Logan's bandaged arm to pop him in the other shoulder.

"Ow!" He jumped and then sucked in a breath at the pain it caused. "Damn it."

Devastated over what she'd done, Pepper petted him. "I'm sorry, but you were ogling her."

Logan gritted his teeth, then just as quickly tried to remove the discomfort from his expression.

Reese winced for him. Sure, Logan was manning up, trying not to make a big deal out of being shot, but any movement hurt, no two ways about that. He rubbed his own thigh in remembrance.

After a few metered breaths, Logan caught Pepper's hand and kissed her knuckles. "I wasn't ogling, honey, just making a surprised observation."

"An unnecessary one," Pepper insisted, unappeased. She tried to free herself.

Logan held on. "You were staring, too."

"I'm allowed."

Reese had to laugh. He saw a lot of fireworks in Logan's future.

Keeping Pepper contained, Logan slanted a look at Reese. "Seriously, Reese, you realize I was commenting on clothes and hair, right? I didn't mean wet as in—"

Reese cut off the half-baked, smirking explanation before Pepper killed him. He seated himself, saying, "Rowdy came to see her today."

Logan's eyebrows shot up. "You don't say." He was so surprised that he loosened his hold on Pepper. "Why?"

Bristling again, she pulled away to pace. "Not for the reason you're thinking."

"It might shock you, honey, but you don't always know what I'm thinking."

"Baloney." Pepper crossed her arms. "You're thinking Rowdy was there to hit on her, but you're wrong."

"I don't know about that." Reese didn't like having Pepper at his back. In the time he'd known her, he'd found her to be very unpredictable—as just evidenced by the way she'd set Logan up like a pampered sheik, then punched him in the shoulder. Her life had been unconventional, and her reactions were often the same.

She rounded on Reese. "Alice isn't his type."

Using his uninjured arm, Logan caught her elbow and pulled her back around and down beside him.

Appreciating that, Reese relaxed again. "You're that sure you know his type?"

"Bet on it." She thought about it a second. "I'm guessing he's worried about her and wants to protect her. Yesterday was...well, it wasn't something most people would take in stride. But she did."

"Yeah." Reese watched for Alice's return. "That's what Rowdy said."

Her eyes narrowed. “Then that’s what it is. My brother wouldn’t lie about it.”

Reese held up both hands. “Stand down, Pepper. I wasn’t maligning your brother.” Although in the recent past, he’d maligned both siblings more than enough to justify her current abrasive attitude.

“No, he was just exhibiting some possessiveness.” Logan grinned. “Isn’t that right, Reese?”

Reese shrugged, refusing to be baited into confessions, and instead concentrated on Pepper. “I thought you and I had come to a friendly cease-fire.”

“Poor Reese. Am I firing at you?”

“No, but you’re not currently armed either.” Thank God. “So what do you say?”

“You know you can blame all past transgressions on him being a cop.” Logan squeezed her shoulder. “A good cop is always suspicious of everyone.”

“Maybe,” Pepper conceded. Again leaving her seat, she approached Reese. “It’s mostly because you’re Logan’s friend that you can consider yourself on probationary forgiveness. But not if you start insulting my brother.”

“Glad to hear it—because I like you and Rowdy both.” He held up a hand to stall her from getting any closer. “It’s true. And I especially like that you make Logan happy.”

Logan, who looked anything but happy in that moment, again snagged Pepper to his side.

“But fondness aside, if Alice needs protection, I’ll protect her.”

“Who said anything about protection?” Logan shifted, struggled to hide a flinch from Pepper, and settled into his seat again. “Worrying about and protecting a woman are two different things.”

"But in Pepper's case, it required both."

After a long look, Pepper snorted. "Men are all the same."

"Obviously not," Reese denied, "but if you want to keep that narrow view, I won't debate it with you."

Logan groaned.

"So much for our truce." Pepper pushed once more to her feet. "I think I'll go check on Alice."

Damn it. Why was it he couldn't be around Pepper without sniping? Reese got to his feet, too. He even dared to catch Pepper's arm. "I like matching wits with you, Pepper, I really do."

"Is that what you were doing?"

"But if you're going to get pissed every time, it takes the fun out of it."

"Far as apologies go, that was totally lame."

"Maybe because I wasn't—"

She patted his face—a little more firmly than necessary. "Don't sweat it. I'll let you off the hook this time, but only because we're all still out of sorts today."

"I'm not out of sorts," Logan denied.

"Me either," Reese said.

Pepper rolled her eyes and said again, with more feeling, "Men!"

Reese waited until she'd left the room before he dropped into his seat tiredly. "Jesus, but she's right, Logan." He rubbed his face. "I'm on the ragged edge, here. Not enough sleep, a trashed apartment and…" He hesitated, but he trusted Logan enough that he had to bring him in. "Alice told me she was once kidnapped."

Logan sat forward, his injury forgotten. "When? Who?"

He shook his head. "She doesn't want to share the details, but she says she wasn't raped."

Silence filled the room for a moment until Logan asked quietly, "You believe her?"

"I don't know. I hope that's true. But whatever happened, it changed her life." He met Logan's concerned gaze. "One way or another, I need to find out everything."

Logan agreed. "She's still afraid."

Reese knew Logan was harking back to the moment Alice had walked into his apartment with the gun in her hand. *Sometimes it's better when they're dead.* Never would he forget how she'd said that, the expression on her face at that moment. Reese closed his eyes, sick with some anomalous need. "I don't have much to go on, but I think it's possible the threat is still around."

"That's why Rowdy visited her?"

No astute man would miss the aura of fear surrounding Alice like a fragile veil. "He suspected things, same as I did." Reese stared toward the hall. What was keeping Alice?

"She's safe with Rowdy, you know that, right?" Logan fidgeted, trying to get comfortable. "He's something of a lost soul, but he's not abusive, especially not to women."

"A lost soul?" What a lot of melodrama—but in Rowdy's case, apt. "He's been so used to looming over his sister, he probably needs a new target now just to keep himself occupied." He glanced at Logan. "Since you've usurped his position and all."

"He says he understands, and I know he's happy for Pepper." Logan eased back again with a sigh. "Once we're married we can all get settled into being related."

Reese moved away to look down the hall, but the bathroom door remained closed. Was Pepper in there with Alice now? What the hell were they talking about for so long? "At first I didn't like Rowdy sniffing around, but as you said, that was based off jealousy."

Logan stared at him in disbelief. "You admit it?"

"It is what it is." And he felt very possessive where Alice was concerned. "And since I can't always be there with her, it's nice to know Rowdy can keep an eye out, too." He'd spent the past few years doing just that for his sister. He and Pepper were as close as siblings could be.

They were steadfast people, unique but with a good moral compass. "She's been getting by on her own just fine, but now she won't have to." Whether or not Alice would appreciate the intrusion, Reese didn't know—and that was a good reason not to tell her just yet.

"God knows I'll have plenty of downtime, so I'll need a way to keep from going nuts." Logan cautiously flexed his injured arm. "Tell me how I can help."

WHILE ALICE WORKED a comb through her tangled hair, Pepper sat on the side of the tub, visiting. She wasn't a chatty woman, Alice noted. Not intrusive either. She was just…there. Friendly but quiet. Interested but not nosey.

"This is hopeless." Alice put the comb aside and smoothed her hair with her hands. It was neatly parted again, but continued to pull into wild waves. Making a face at herself in the mirror, she said, "It doesn't really matter, anyway. We're going to get soaked again when we leave."

Pepper studied her. "You want some warm tea or something?" Then she looked struck. "That is, if Logan has tea." She fingered a thick decorative towel over the towel bar. "I haven't even looked at the whole house yet."

"I'm sure you had other things on your mind by the time you got here from the hospital."

Pepper nodded, swallowed hard, then closed her eyes. "I could have lost him."

"But you didn't." Quickly, Alice sat beside Pepper. She'd done what she could to dry her dress, but it still stuck to her body in a very unattractive way. "I'm sorry he got injured, but I'm so thankful he showed up to help." Imagining what might have happened otherwise was too painful.

"Me, too." Pepper glanced at her, smiled and looked around. "You realize we're sitting in a bathroom talking."

Alice grinned. "I know. But I'm not in a big hurry to join the men." Not while she still resembled a drowned rat.

"Me either." Pepper tipped her head, watching Alice. "Thank God you keep weapons. Yesterday, Logan might not have been as successful otherwise."

"Do you?"

She snorted. "Damn right. Rowdy's always insisted. He even taught me how to shoot." She eyed Alice in speculation. "Are you a good shot?"

"Good enough." She could hit what she aimed at. "I go to target practice once a month."

That pleased Pepper. "Really? Maybe we could go together some time."

Just days ago, Alice would have avoided that much involvement with another person, but now…she liked the idea, and she liked Pepper Yates. "That'd be terrific."

Pepper beamed at her. "Not to jump all over you or anything, but do you think you'd like to attend our wedding, too? You saved us yesterday, so it'd be appropriate."

Saved them? "Oh, I didn't—"

"You *did,*" Pepper insisted, "so don't deny it. And besides, Reese will be there. He's Logan's best friend, you know."

It sounded wonderful, and she badly wanted to accept, but she didn't want to make assumptions about her new relationship with Reese.

Pepper misunderstood her long hesitation. "Am I being too grabby?" She wrinkled her nose. "I didn't mean to pressure you."

"It's not that. I'd love to be there." It surprised Alice to feel that way. "It's just that I wouldn't want Reese to misunderstand." Or feel smothered.

"It's not up to him. I can invite whoever I want."

But if she accepted, and things didn't work out with Reese, would he bring a different date? What if she had to stay through a ceremony, watching him with another woman?

Pepper bumped her with her shoulder. "I can almost read your thoughts." She grinned. "But trust me, Reese wouldn't dare. And besides, the only guests will be the ones Logan and I invite. And because I want to keep it small, we're not inviting any 'plus one' guests."

Alice bit her lip. Was she really that transparent? "In that case, thank you. I'd be honored."

"Terrific! I'll have to give you details when we get things figured out." She bobbed her eyebrows. "We'll wait for Logan to recoup so we can have a real wedding night."

Alice laughed with her. It was so nice having another woman to talk to, a woman unlike Nikki and Pam.

That thought gave her pause; Pepper might be different, but she still wasn't like Alice.

Again Pepper nudged her with her shoulder. "I can be really discreet, just so you know."

Alice didn't understand.

"If you want to talk about…stuff." Letting out a breath, Pepper said, "I see the mask, because I used to wear one, too."

Confused, Alice shook her head. "I don't wear a mask."

"Sure you do." Lifting a twisting lock of Alice's hair, Pepper smiled an apology. "The rain did you in."

Her shoulders deflated. She prided herself on a nice appearance, but she'd never figured on getting caught in a storm. "I know."

"No, I don't think you do. You look great, Alice. Not that you looked bad yesterday, but now, with your hair a little wild and that dress showing off your figure… It's a good look for you."

Eyes widening, Alice said, "I look like a used mop."

"Nope, not even." Studying her, Pepper shrugged. "Truthfully, you look sort of sexy."

Alice's face went hot. She was both flattered and horrified. "Of course I don't." Hand splayed over her chest, she looked down at her dress. Her sturdy bra kept her mostly concealed, but the dress did outline her meager bust. "Do I?"

"You didn't notice how the guys went all goofy when they saw you? They practically had their tongues hanging out. Reese was ready to beat his chest, he's such a possessive ape."

Still disbelieving, Alice shook her head. Sexy was not a word ever applied to her. Clean, neat, well-groomed, sure. Or as Rowdy had claimed, buttoned-up, and sadly, prim and proper.

But she was not—

"Anyway," Pepper said, interrupting her private angst. "You *are* disguising yourself. I figured it was on purpose. See, until recently, I did my own type of hiding. That cretin who died in Reese's apartment yesterday?"

Fascinated, Alice said, "Yes?"

"A few years ago, Rowdy and I worked for his club. Late one night, I saw him kill a city councilman. Cops were involved, so I couldn't go to them. I tried talking to a reporter, and he got murdered, too."

"Oh, my God." How horrific. Rowdy had left out a few details when he'd mentioned why he and Pepper had lived the life they had. Empathy welled inside her like a giant balloon, crowding out all other thoughts and emotions. Maybe she and Pepper had more in common than she'd realized. "That's why he was after you?"

"And my brother," Pepper confirmed. "Rowdy doesn't really run from anyone, but to protect me, he did."

That gave her great insight into Rowdy, too. What would it be like to have someone that dedicated to your well-being? Her parents cared, of course. Her sister, too.

But this was different. Alice touched her hand in understanding. "I've met your brother, and I'm pretty sure he'd do anything for you."

"True enough." Pepper didn't retreat from the touch. She looked down at her feet, but only for a moment. "We were in hiding for way too long. I had to look like a hag to ensure if anyone saw me, they wouldn't recognize me." Her mouth curled in distaste before she squeezed

Alice's hand and regained her grim humor. "It was such a drag, looking *bad* all the time."

Seeing her now, Alice couldn't imagine such a thing. "You're so attractive I don't know how you managed to *not* look good."

That made Pepper laugh. "You should have seen Logan when I threw off the dregs and reverted back to me. It was a hoot. Well, sort of. At the moment I didn't think so because I was worried about everything else." She leaned close to whisper, "Logan was undercover, so I had no idea he was a cop when I slept with him."

"Wow." No other words came to mind. "That must have been…interesting."

"Yeah, picture my shock when he arranged for Reese to show up and arrest my brother."

And that, of course, would explain some of the bad blood between Reese and Pepper. Her heart broke a little, imagining what Pepper had endured. "That must've been really awful."

"No kidding. I was so furious I wanted to take them both apart."

"Furious…and hurt?"

Pepper shrugged. "In the end, it worked out. And thanks to them, Rowdy and I are now free."

No more hiding. Alice envied her the freedom. "So you've forgiven the deception?"

"Yeah, sure. Don't tell Reese, though." She gave a devilish grin. "I like giving him a hard time."

Given her carefree expression, Alice believed it. Pepper looked truly happy—and well loved. "I'm glad you and Logan found each other, regardless of the path you took to get there."

"That's about it." Her fingertips tapped the edge of

the tub before Pepper said, "This is nice—talking with you, I mean. You're…comfortable."

Alice gave a short laugh over that dubious compliment. "Thank you. I've enjoyed it, as well."

"Maybe it's because we're both different."

Not exactly a subtle hint, but Alice just smiled. "Maybe." In such a short time they'd settled into an easy alliance. "Bullet wound aside, I'm glad to see that you and Detective Riske both fared so well after everything that happened yesterday."

"You worry a lot, don't you?"

About everyone and everything. "Sometimes." *Always.* "As you said, I'm…different."

"Different is good." Pepper sized her up. "You know what? I think we should do a makeover on you."

"On…me?"

"It's not an insult, I swear."

"I wasn't insulted." More like…intrigued. "I've never fussed much with the usual female stuff."

"You don't really need to, not with your dark lashes and brows. But it wouldn't hurt to loosen you up a bit."

"Loosen me up?"

"Is there an echo in here?" Pepper teased, but then suddenly stalled. "I'm rushing things, right?"

Alice waved that off. "No, of course not."

"You've probably got better things to do—"

"I think it's a wonderful idea." Would she enjoy being *loosened up?* Possibly. "I wouldn't mind looking more fashionable—that is, if it won't be too much work for you."

"Are you kidding? It'll be fun." Pepper paused to draw a breath. "God, it's been forever since I just had fun. Especially with another woman."

Alice got caught up in her excitement and her teasing mood. “You won’t expect me to go around in wet dresses, will you?”

“Reese has to be able to function, so, no.”

There was more laughter—until a tap sounded on the door.

CHAPTER SEVEN

REESE SPOKE THROUGH the closed door. "Are you ladies having your own private party in there?"

After winking at Alice, Pepper said, "Butt out, Reese."

"All right. But you should know that Logan is about to leave the couch to come look for you."

Pepper shot off the tub ledge and jerked open the door. Muttering, "He wouldn't dare," she rushed around Reese and down the hall.

Still sitting, hands in her lap, her ankles together, Alice wondered how Reese saw her.

Was Pepper right?

Could he actually consider her *sexy?* Not just available, but a woman he specifically wanted? It was such a foreign concept that her mind blanched over the idea—until she peeked up at Reese and saw the heat in his gaze.

Hello! He stared intently at her bare feet, her calves, up to her hands clenched together in her lap and then to her breasts, now rising with her deep breaths.

"Reese?"

Green eyes met hers. His voice sounded lower, rougher. "Why are you hiding in here?"

"I'm not." Knowing he might see her differently—and accepting that she wanted him to—changed everything. Alice felt shy and uncertain as she stood. "Pepper and I were talking."

"Oh?" Hands in his pockets, his gaze still moving over her, he leaned on the wall. His casual position blocked the doorway, keeping her in the bathroom with him. "Dare I ask the topic?"

"Their wedding," she blurted.

His mouth curved in an indulgent smile. "Girl talk, then."

"Well, sort of." What did he consider girl talk? "We discussed a lot of stuff. She's nice."

"She has her moments."

Her dress might be clingy, but then so was Reese's shirt, and Alice couldn't stop staring at his chest. No shirt would have been better, but a shirt outlining every muscle? Not bad. "We're making plans for some outings together."

"You don't say?" He maintained his casual stance but was now more focused. "What type of outings?"

"She wants to give me a makeover."

Abruptly Reese straightened. "Come again?"

Rather than go into detail—because, really, it made her feel too silly—Alice said, "And we might go to the shooting range to do some target practice together, too."

Blank surprise washed over his face. "Target practice? You…with Pepper?"

Rushing past that seemed wise, as well. "And I would love to attend the wedding after they finalize plans. That is, if you wouldn't mind too much."

Sidetracked, he stepped farther into the room. "Why would I mind?"

"Because you'll be there, and I didn't want you to feel…I don't know. Too crowded or anything."

He stepped closer until only a few inches separated them. "I don't know what that means, Alice."

He smelled good, all rain-damp and warm. She drew in a deep breath, filling her lungs with his scent. It was enough to leave her dizzy.

Reese tipped up her chin. "Alice?"

"I don't want you to tire of me."

Frowning, he lifted his hands to cradle her face. His thumb brushed her cheek. "That's not going to happen, so don't worry about it."

But of course it could. Maybe not today. And if Logan and Pepper married quickly, maybe not by the wedding. But Reese couldn't know what the future would bring. "How old are you, Reese?"

He cocked a brow at the odd question. "Thirty."

And yet he wasn't married, which had to mean he avoided commitment…didn't it?

"And you, Alice? Mid-twenties?"

"Good guess. I'm exactly in the middle." She felt far older, though. Somctimes she felt so emotionally tired, worn out.

Defeated.

"That makes you twenty-five?"

"Yes." Making the mistake of looking up at him, Alice said again, more softly this time, "Reese?"

Watching her with absorbed fascination, he brushed her bottom lip with his thumb. "That other kiss we discussed?"

The husky timbre in his voice sent her pulse racing. She went on tiptoe, lifting up to him, leaning in.

Ready. "Yes?"

"I don't want to do it here, in Logan's bathroom."

Disappointment dropped her heels back to the floor. "Oh."

Reese treated her to a knowing smile. "We need to get going, anyway."

So soon? She hadn't even made it out of the bathroom yet. "Is something wrong?"

"Other than me wanting to seduce you in a friend's bathroom? No." He kissed her forehead. "The weather isn't letting up, and I'm a little worried about Cash, that's all. I hope he's not one of those dogs that spooks over thunder and lightning."

The sweet sentiment warmed her even more than the anticipation of his kiss. Could Reese Bareden be more appealing?

She touched his bulging biceps. No, he couldn't.

Everything on him was supersize—his muscular physique, his attitude…and his caring. "I left my bedroom door open for him, with the radio on. He's probably under the bed right now. He goes there sometimes when I'm working."

"You're very good to him." Lightning flashed outside the small bathroom window, followed by a crack of thunder that reverberated in the floor beneath their feet. "To both of us."

He had that wrong, but she wouldn't correct him on it. "So our visit is about over?"

"Yes. Logan invited us to stay for dinner, but I said we had other plans."

That was news to her. "Do we?"

Again Reese kissed her, this time brushing his mouth over her cheek. "We're going to talk while we get your jelly beans." He trailed damp kisses along her jaw. "We'll pick up something for dinner, too…while we talk some more—" down to her chin "—and once we get home and check on Cash—"

"We'll do yet more talking?" Everywhere his mouth

touched, her skin tingled. Somehow he made *talk* sound very seductive.

Near her ear, he whispered, "I want to know you better."

Since she wanted to know everything about him, too, she liked that plan. Smoothing her hands over his solid chest, she nodded. "All right."

"Damn, Alice." His mouth opened on her neck, hot, damp. She felt the slightest of suctions, and her toes curled. "Agreeable women are such a turn-on."

Knotting her fingers in his damp shirt, Alice held on—until Logan said, "Get out of my bathroom, you perv."

Alice jumped away in guilt, and Logan quickly amended, "I meant him, not you."

"Pepper let you off the couch?" Reese asked. "You managed to convince her that a bullet to the arm hadn't handicapped your legs?"

"She's reasonable when necessary." Logan waited for them to leave the bathroom, but as he started forward, Pepper showed up and followed him into the john.

Biting back a laugh, Reese asked, "Going to lend him a hand, are you?"

Logan stood there, mouth open to say something, but Pepper shut the door in their faces before they could hear it.

Alice grinned. "They're funny together."

"Much more so than when they're apart." Taking her hand, Reese led her back toward the living room. His stride was so long, she had to trot to keep up.

"Why the rush?"

He immediately slowed, even pulled her up and into his side. "Apologies, but I need to sit down."

"Why?" Reminded of the dark bruises around his

wrists, Alice grew concerned. "What's wrong? Are you hurt?"

"I think I should call it the Alice Syndrome."

That made no sense to her.

Reese leaned down to her ear, even nipped her earlobe. "My attraction to you is difficult to contain, especially when you taste so good."

A flush warmed her skin. She tried to lean around him to see, but he didn't give her a chance.

"At the moment, there's nothing to see and I'd as soon keep it that way. So behave."

She always did, she thought with a sigh. "If you insist."

He gave her a quick look, shook his head and kept going.

Alice used the opportunity to admire Logan's home. They passed the modern and spacious kitchen, then the stairs leading toward a second floor and presumably the bedrooms.

The house was clean, open and uncluttered without being too masculine. "Detective Riske has a beautiful home."

"I like it, too." Reese drew Alice down onto the love seat with him. "You know, Logan did most of the decorating himself."

On their return, Pepper heard him and groaned. "He's almost too perfect, isn't he?"

Logan, who didn't act like a man recently shot, laughed. "I only need to be good enough to keep you."

"You're stuck with me and you know it." After a quick kiss, Pepper directed Logan to sit again but appeased him by perching in his lap. "Luckily," she said to Alice, "he's good at all the housekeeping stuff, because I don't really have the domestic gene."

Logan no sooner got settled than his cell rang, and he retrieved it from the table. Alice would have given him some privacy to take the call, but Pepper didn't move from his lap, and Reese seemed unwilling to stand again.

After a short greeting, she knew the identity of his caller: Lieutenant Peterson. She imagined working for that formidable woman could be a challenge for such alpha men, but neither one seemed to think a thing of it.

Logan said, "Reese is standing here now. I'll let him know. Yeah, shouldn't be a problem. Hang on." He lowered the phone, holding it to his chest. "Follow-up interview tomorrow. Is 8 a.m. okay by you?"

"Whatever," Reese said. "Not like either of us is working."

Pepper scowled. "Of course Logan isn't working. He needs time to heal." And then to Logan, "They interviewed both of you at the hospital. Why do they need to see you again?"

"That was cursory because Logan was in the hospital."

Logan agreed to that with a nod. "Tomorrow will be at the station, and more in-depth."

"You were *shot*."

Reese said, "Do you really think he's unaware of that?"

Logan caught Pepper before she could turn her anger on Reese. "That's the only reason they didn't call me in before this. All this shit usually takes place within twenty-four hours."

"If he doesn't answer questions," Reese told her, "he could lose his job."

Aghast, Pepper gathered steam.

"Shut up, Reese." Logan cupped Pepper's face to reassure her. "Trust me, it's not a big deal. I'm perfectly capable of doing interviews—and no, I don't need you there." He softened that by saying, "I love you, but some things a man has to do alone."

Reese laughed. "So says the man recently escorted to the john."

Pepper narrowed her eyes at Reese. "Our truce is becoming shakier by the moment."

Reese held up his hands in surrender. "If it helps, an association rep will be around." His smile twitched. "I promise no one will abuse him."

Logan glared at him. "Soon as my arm is healed..." He let the threat hang out there.

Knowing it was all bluster kept Alice from getting too anxious over their verbal sparring. It was sort of nice to see friends indulge in harmless baiting.

She saw that as a true measure of friendship.

After whispering something to Pepper, Logan put the phone back to his ear. "We'll be there. Yeah, Reese, too. Got it. Thanks." He disconnected the call.

Reese sat forward. "Who's doing follow-up on—" his gaze went first to Pepper, and then to Alice "—on the info we got yesterday?"

He didn't want to mention traffickers again. Given what Pepper had been through and how she was threatened, Alice appreciated the restraint. Pepper was clearly a strong woman, a true survivor, but that had to be an awful memory for her.

Alice knew all about awful memories.

For a few minutes, the men talked shop and occasionally Pepper chimed in. Alice did her best not to intrude.

When they finished, Pepper still wasn't happy. "You can't drive, not with your arm in that sling still."

"Reese'll pick me up." He glanced at Reese.

"Certainly, as long as Pepper understands that I'm an innocent bystander."

Appeased, Pepper asked, "How long will you be gone tomorrow?"

"Could be a few hours, could be all day." Logan hugged her with his good arm. "Depends on the questions they ask and the answers we have to give. Usually, the D.A. does the interview, and I.A. will watch on a live video feed. When the D.A. is done, I.A. might have additional questions."

"In that case…" Pepper glanced at Alice. "We could bump our shopping trip up to tomorrow. What do you say? Are you free?"

Since she set her own hours, it wouldn't be a problem. But was she ready for that yet?

Pepper swayed her by saying, "God knows I need some new clothes now that I'm not playing the wallflower anymore, and shopping will help keep my mind off things."

"All right, then."

Reese started to object, but Logan jumped in first. "Great idea."

Plans were made around Alice, and before she knew it, everything was arranged.

It struck her that she'd not only let Reese into her life, but Rowdy, Logan and Pepper, too. Reese and his friends swept her along with their camaraderie, their openness and caring.

She hadn't known any of them long, but they'd had such an impact on her, she already knew she didn't want to lose them. As usual, though, much was out of her hands. Everything would change once they learned of her past.

And with two detectives involved, how could she keep her secrets buried?

HALFWAY HOME, the rain slowed to a soft drizzle. In the seat beside Reese, Alice looked drowsy, almost languid. Hopefully relaxed.

It pleased him that she and Pepper had gotten along, but he worried about them being out and about alone together.

Logan, without knowing of their plans, had actually encouraged them.

With any luck, Rowdy would be available to keep an eye on things. He'd check with him later—when Alice wouldn't know.

"What are you thinking?" she asked. "You're so quiet."

"I was wondering about this shopping trip of yours."

She smiled toward him. "I haven't shopped with another woman in a long time." As if distracted, she fussed with the hem on her dress, now wrinkled from the rain. "My sister and I used to go out together a lot. The last time we shopped, it was for her prom dress."

With Alice, it was often what she didn't say that gave him pause. "Your mother didn't go?"

"Not that time. She and my dad were on a business trip. My sister had decided not to go to prom so Mom didn't think she'd be missing anything. Then Amy got asked by a special boy, and we had to scramble to get things together. It was pretty wonderful, and she looked so beautiful that night."

It was hard to imagine dark secrets in the soft, caring picture Alice presented. "You're older than her?"

"By six years."

"So you two weren't close?"

Hesitation hung in the air between them. "Despite the age difference, we used to be." She turned away to stare out the window at the sodden landscape. "I don't see her very often now."

He wanted to ask why but didn't. "Your parents?"

She held silent.

"You can tell me, you know."

More time passed. Reese heard the shushing of tires on wet pavement, the lazy, rhythmic slicking of the windshield wipers.

He heard his own heartbeat in his ears.

Shifting around to face him, Alice curled her legs up on the seat, rested her cheek against the back, folded her arms around her waist.

She let out a breath.

Reese felt her watching him, and he knew she was measuring her words.

"My family is pretty wonderful. Supportive and caring. Smart and friendly."

Like Alice.

"Mom is a teacher, Dad an architect. Amy is still in college. She's going to be a nurse."

To Reese that sounded nice enough, much like a typical middle-class family. "So why don't you see them more often?"

"Because I love them." Her voice thickened with emotion, breaking his heart. "A lot."

Though he couldn't imagine anyone not loving Alice, he had to ask. "They don't feel the same?"

"After I was kidnapped, things changed." She corrected that with a shake of her head. "That is, I changed. They were thrilled when I returned, but it had been so long...." Her voice trailed off. "I wasn't the same person anymore."

To a captive, a day could feel like a week, a week like a month. Reese prayed that Alice had been rescued sooner than that. "You were still a daughter, a sister. I'm sure they—"

"Loved me? Yes." Expression stark, she looked away. "But he kept me for over a year."

Shock rolled over Reese, cramping his guts, locking his jaw. "Jesus," he whispered, wishing he could somehow change the reality of what she'd suffered.

"I didn't think I'd ever get away." She hugged herself, chin down, her voice breaking. "I thought that was my life."

Knowing how the memory still hurt her left Reese hurting, too. She'd survived, and she said she hadn't been raped. What could a kidnapper possibly have wanted with her?

The silence grew heavier, almost suffocating. Reese tried to get into cop mode, to think logically instead of with emotion. "You said he. It was a man who took you?"

"A man that had me taken."

"Did you know him?"

She shook her head—and curled tighter. "No."

His heartbeat thundered. He wanted to pull over and hold her, console her. Make absurd promises that he wasn't sure he could keep.

But he didn't dare interrupt the moment of confession.

He needed to know.

Keeping his tone calm, no-nonsense, Reese asked, "Do you know why he took you?"

"Yes."

She didn't elaborate. As a man, he wanted to let it go, to see the wary shadows lift from her gaze. But as a cop, logic won out and he forced himself to push for more. "What did he make you do, Alice?"

"The one thing I'm good at." She swallowed hard. "I had to be his secretary."

That…didn't make a lot of sense. Reese spared her a quick glance and saw that she'd huddled into a small, vulnerable form—as far from him as she could get.

"Will you explain that to me?"

The sun peeked out from behind the clouds, reflecting off all the wet surfaces. Steam rose in suffocating waves. Birds came out to sing.

"You were probably already digging into my past."

"I was." Reese saw no reason to deny it. He was a detective, and she knew it.

"You'd have found out, anyway." Her shoulders lifted on a big breath. "But I don't like talking about it."

"That's why you avoid your family?"

She nodded. "I can't bear to trouble them with my… unpleasantness. They're so happy, burdening them with the real worries of life, the life I now know exists, doesn't seem fair."

"A life with kidnappers?"

A rainbow stretched across the sky. His tires hit a puddle in the road, causing a big splash.

Alice drew in a shaky breath, looked at him. "A life with human traffickers."

Reese's blood ran cold. His hands tightened on the steering wheel. "That's what he was?"

"He pretended to be a hotshot businessman. And I guess he was that, too. But he also bought and sold women." She paused, chewed her bottom lip a moment. "I haven't told many people about it."

"Because it's so ugly?"

She nodded. "You're a detective, so you already see stuff like this. You can deal with it."

"Yes." But she thought her family couldn't? "You

can tell me anything, remember?" Screw keeping an emotional distance. He reached for and found her hand. "You won't burden me."

Her fingers locked on his. "I told my family just a little of it, and they were so sick. My sister had nightmares, my mom cried. And my dad…" Big tears clung to her lashes, and her words thickened with heartache. "My sweet, gentle dad broke his hand punching the wall."

Reese could picture it in his mind; too many times he'd witnessed fathers trying to deal with the loss or injury of a child. "I can't imagine a dad reacting any other way." Her shuddering indrawn breath wrenched him. "That's not your fault, honey. That's human nature."

"That's loss of innocence. That's reality—a reality few ever have to face." Easing her hand away from him, she sat up straighter and pushed back her hair. "I don't want to talk about this anymore. Not right now."

He needed to know more. He needed the kidnapper's name, and he had to know if justice had been served.

Because if it hadn't, he'd be taking care of that himself.

He considered everything she'd shared, and he pieced together what he could.

For over a year, she'd been forced to act as a secretary to a scumbag trafficker. Inconceivable.

She hadn't been raped. She had escaped. How? Who had helped her?

They were almost to the grocery store, and Alice trembled all over. If he pushed her any further, she'd lose her fragile grip on control. As a detective, he knew that could get him answers; people spilled their guts in moments of weakness.

But he couldn't do that.

Not to Alice.

Mind made up, Reese reached for her hand again. He needed the brief contact, whether she did or not. "You can relax, honey. We'll put it on hold for now."

Her rigid shoulders drooped. She squeezed his hand like a lifeline. "Thank you."

Reese felt like an abusive ass, but he nodded to accept her…gratitude.

Shit. He wanted many things from Alice, but not that. Not even close. Definitely not over confessions he'd wrung from her.

As he parked in the grocery lot, she opened her seat belt, then hesitated until he'd turned off the car. Uncertainty filled her dark-eyed gaze. "You know, once you've heard it all, it'll probably change everything."

He realized he was learning to read her, to understand what she didn't say. "You mean how I feel about you?"

"Yes." And then, a little self-conscious, "Whatever it is you feel."

He felt plenty, all of it unfamiliar and disconcerting. "Somehow, I doubt it, but I guess we'll find out." He leaned forward, brushing his mouth over hers. "In the meantime, you might try trusting me, okay?"

Instead of agreeing, she touched her fingertips to her lips, let out a pent-up breath—and turned to get out of the car. Reese had to hurry to catch up with her.

He had a feeling Alice would always stay one step ahead.

CHAPTER EIGHT

IT WAS RIDICULOUS, but the closer it got to bedtime, the more antsy she became.

In part because of what she'd told Reese.

But mostly because of what she hadn't told him.

He behaved the same, a little outrageous, far too attentive, sexy and downright wonderful. About everything.

He helped cook dinner. He helped clean up afterward. He played with Cash while she checked her messages and emails.

At the speed of light, he already filled her life.

Alice knew she wanted more. More than a casual relationship. More than sex.

More than temporary.

But a man like Reese would always demand honesty, and her personal truths would likely drive him away.

Such a conundrum. A balancing act.

Hearing Reese return from taking Cash out, she closed her computer. Ears attuned, she heard him lock the door, heard him talking softly with the dog.

Heard his footsteps coming down the hall.

With little decided, she turned her chair in anticipation of seeing him—and there he was. Cash came in around him, but Reese held him back.

"It's muddy out there, so I had to wash his paws. I tried drying them, too, but easier said than done."

Alice smiled. "It's okay." With her emotions so jumbled, she could use some unconditional puppy love right about now. She patted her thigh, and Cash bounded forward.

Hands in his pockets, his mouth tilted in a crooked smile, Reese propped a shoulder in the door frame. "He acts as if he hasn't seen you for days instead of minutes."

Sinking her fingers into the dog's long, silky fur, Alice hugged him. "He's the sweetest dog ever."

"Or perhaps you're just a very accepting woman." He stepped in. "Are we interrupting your work?"

"No. I'd just finished up."

He lifted a crystal paperweight shaped like a rose. Engraved on the front were the words: Sisters are Forever. "Very nice."

Needlessly, she explained, "My sister got me that."

"Special occasion?"

Nervousness began uncoiling inside her. "When I… returned home." Her throat constricted. She hugged Cash closer. "After the kidnapping."

As if the dog understood, he whined and laid his head over her thighs.

"I see." Reese returned the paperweight to her desktop and looked around her room. "Tell me more about what you do."

"Being a virtual assistant?"

"Yes. I don't know much about it."

So, he didn't plan to pry right now? Tension receded, making it easier for her to breathe. Her work was a safe, comfortable topic. "I do a lot of stuff."

"Like?"

"Set up programming, marketing, advertisement. I do copywriting for presentations and manage social calendars. Filing, travel plans, sometimes I even help develop brands for small businesses." She watched Reese stop before an ornate clock on the wall. It neared ten-thirty.

Her bedtime.

Reese moved on to her file cabinet, read the names on the front of each drawer. "Sounds like you do it all."

What was he looking for? Surely a utilitarian, locked file cabinet held no fascination. "Whatever the client needs, I can usually handle it." She was a top-notch assistant—a curse she would live with forever.

"You communicate through email?"

"Mostly, yes." A throbbing started in her temples, thanks to the intrusion of a nasty memory. She rubbed it away. "Sometimes with conference calls." She avoided Skype and visual conferencing because she didn't want to be identifiable.

Reese pondered that. "You never receive physical items?" She could almost see him thinking, picking apart her methods and finding reasons for them. "Actual mail or anything? Maybe a business item that the client wants you to review?"

"It's rare, because I'm not part of product development. But when the client insists, I have a post office box that I check twice a week." She made the trip two towns over to avoid a trail. In every way possible, she kept her anonymity. Not easy, but doable, when you were careful enough.

And she was very, very careful.

"I see." He touched the top of her oversize flat-screen monitor. "How do you get paid?"

His continued questioning set her on edge again. Though she trusted Reese and enjoyed his company—even craved it—nervousness began ramping up. She closed her hands over the arms of her chair, her grip tight as she instinctively rejected the intrusion into her privacy. "I get paid through online accounts."

"Convenient."

Did that sound like an accusation? "Yes."

He didn't look right at her, instead choosing to circle her desk, his attention on folders, even paper clips. "Do you ever actually meet your clients?"

Too quickly, she said, "No."

As if he understood her reticence to meet others, her need for isolation, Reese nodded.

She braced herself for the more personal questions to come. Now he would insist on knowing it all. And she wasn't ready. Apprehension flooded her system, but she kept her expression composed.

She'd learned to do that during her captivity—to hide all emotion. Reactions gained attention, and sometimes retaliation. Better to fade into the woodwork, to get her job done as unobtrusively as possible.

Silent and efficient.

Blind to the cruelty.

Cowardly.

Having circled the small room, Reese now stood in front of her. "Alice?"

Distress got a stranglehold on her. She met his gaze, wishing she could will away the past, wishing she could convince him to stay, wishing she could put off this confrontation forever....

He studied her face, and concern pulled his brows. "It's getting late."

Bedtime. A time when her thoughts would relentlessly circle memories she badly wanted to bury. "Yes."

"Shhh. Don't panic."

He'd known she was?

Reese touched her cheek, ran two fingers along her jaw. “I don’t relish the idea of folding myself onto your couch again.”

Confirmed. He wanted to leave her. Her heart tripped as she stood, her mind searching for words to convince him to stay.

Cash sidled out from between them and headed out of the room, probably going to the aforementioned couch.

They stared at each other. Her voice quavered as much as her nerve. “I…I don’t want you to leave.”

Rock-steady, he held her gaze. “I’m not going anywhere.”

Just that fast, anxiety deflated. “You’re not?”

“The path your thoughts take…” He shook his head, that cocky, crooked little smile in place again. “I want to share your bed, honey.”

Share her…? As in sleep with her, under the covers with her, his big body *right there,* hot and solid, comforting and so tempting…

“Just sleep for now. Not sex. But I’d love to stay closer tonight.” He brought up her chin. “May I, Alice?”

Elation burst through her. “Okay.” More than okay. Already her toes curled, and a sweet ache unfurled. She breathed a little faster.

“Not for sex,” he chided again.

For tonight, for right now, she’d take what she could get. “Okay.”

His smile curled more. “Not just yet, anyway.”

She nodded. She wasn’t ready yet—but now she knew she would be…and soon.

He cupped the back of her neck, his mood shifting in some intense, indefinable way. “Now seems like a good time for that kiss we discussed.”

Before she could even absorb what he’d said, he

touched his mouth to hers, warm, barely there at first, then more firmly. He moved his mouth over hers, parting her lips, angling his head to fit her more surely.

On a sound of wonder, Alice sank against him.

Wrapping one arm around her, he gathered her closer still, drew her in until her breasts pressed into the solid muscles of his body. Her heart thundered.

So did his.

She felt his tongue, tentative at first, touching her bottom lip, the edge of her teeth.

She held on tighter.

His exploration grew more curious, deeper, bold as he dueled with her tongue, and finally seductive, consuming.

She tasted *him.* And that, combined with his touch, his scent, overwhelmed her. Heat pooled between her legs, her nipples drew tight and somehow the two were connected, throbbing together.

God, it felt good to be aroused again, to react normally, to want a man so much. Not just any man, but this man. Reese Bareden. Macho, sexy, caring.

The whole package.

And he was here, with her. Judging by the hardness of his body, he wanted her just as much.

Amazing.

A groan snuck out as she ran her hands over his broad, solid chest, up to his shoulders, down to his biceps. So hot. She held on to him, ensuring he couldn't leave her. Not just yet.

Reese sank a hand into her hair, palming her skull, keeping her right there with him. Dazed, incredibly excited, Alice relished the hungry way he took her mouth.

His arm around her loosened, but only so he could open his big hand over her back. She felt the gentle press of his palm between her shoulder blades, then down the length of her spine. Stopping short of her behind, he brought it up again. Down once more, slower this time, almost as if he fought himself until…

He opened his hand over one cheek, caressed, delved down…

The press of his fingers nearly stopped her heart.

With a low sound deep in his throat, Reese suddenly released her.

Mouth tingling, adrenaline pumping, Alice stared up at him. Never before had she seen his green eyes look so bright or so burning.

He sounded hoarse when he said, "Already I'm going to have one hell of a time sleeping. Any more of that and I'll have to take the couch so I don't rush you."

Reflex clenched her hands tight in his shirt. "But you already promised to sleep with me." And she already anticipated it with all her heart.

One way or another, she'd hold him to it.

His quick laugh turned into a groan. His hands covered hers, not to pull her away, but in reassurance. "Stop thinking I'm backing out on you, or anything with you. Okay?"

So he hadn't been? "Okay." Still a little breathless, Alice nodded. "Good." And she thought to add, "Thank you."

He thumbed the rioting pulse in her wrists. "You have an amazing ass."

No one had ever said anything so outrageous, so wonderful to her before. The compliment warmed her clear through to her soul. She grinned at him.

With a shake of his head, Reese said, "Go." He pried her hands loose, turned her and planted a light swat on her behind—the behind he claimed to admire. "Do whatever you have to do before bed. It's time we turned in—before I forget myself. Again."

Alice was counting on him doing just that. Soon. Very, very soon.

SHE WORE A long white nightgown that looked like something straight out of a Victorian fetish catalogue. Sleeveless. Flowing. Opaque enough that he saw only shadows…a tease to his tested control.

Already taut in places that didn't bear close scrutiny, Reese tried not to dwell on the image she'd made coming into the bedroom: face freshly washed, hair just brushed, her small feet bare and that long white gown swinging around her slim ankles as she marched to the bed with transparent eagerness.

It should have shredded his ego that a woman wanted to sleep chastely with him instead of indulging in raw, hot sex. But instead, with Alice…it broke his heart a little.

She'd be wrecked if she knew that. Pity was not a sentiment she'd welcome.

She wasn't all that keen on concern either.

And she despised prying.

Too bad for her that he couldn't let it go. If she were another woman, sure, he could take what he wanted and dismiss the rest. But with Alice…no. Not possible.

She'd beamed at him from the other side of the bed until, teeth locked, he'd shucked off his clothes and gotten under the covers, hopeful that she hadn't seen his erection beneath snug cotton boxers.

Ha. Alice made no bones about checking him out at every opportunity.

But she hadn't remarked on it. She'd just crawled into the bed beside him, still smiling, smelling like lotion and toothpaste and like Alice herself, warm and soft and so desirable his teeth ached.

Cash, tail thumping in excitement over having them together, had bounded up, circled the bed once to say, "hey," to each of them and then collapsed near their feet. Reese turned out the light, stretched out on his back, and a second later Alice cuddled close.

"Okay?" she asked.

Torturous. But he'd said only, "Perfect."

Now, half an hour later, Cash's doggy snores softly floated on the quiet air, mingling with the hum of the air conditioner.

Thank God she didn't leave the windows open at night, but then, he wasn't surprised that she'd locked up, checked everything twice and checked it again.

At some point, as naturally as if they'd slept together dozens of times, she'd turned, scooting back against him until he spooned her. That lush little ass—such a surprise—snugged up close to his groin, taunting his efforts at gentlemanly restraint.

His arm draped over the significant dip of her waist. He badly wanted to open his hand over her belly, so much so that his palm tingled. The thin barrier of that boner-inspiring gown wouldn't hinder his touch at all.

No.

Leaving his hand lax on the mattress in front of her, Reese squeezed his eyes shut and resisted temptation.

His roiling thoughts refused to calm. Visuals continued to slam into his brain. Without meaning to, he dipped his head so that his nose brushed Alice's baby-fine hair. He inhaled deeply.

Without saying a word, her hand covered his, fingers twining together.

At times, Alice could be so deceptively peaceful.

He knew her well enough now to know it was a ruse; at all times, she remained aware, alert. Of everything.

She surprised him every other second. With her hurt. Her courage.

Her sexual openness.

He could take her now. He knew it whether she did or not. She might have issues clouding her desire, but he could get her past that easily enough. A few kisses, a touch—and she'd be ready.

But this time, with Alice…damn it, he wanted more.

And so he would wait. He needed to know everything that she tried so hard to keep hidden. If he wasn't a detective, maybe, just maybe, he could let it go. Leave it in the past.

But he couldn't. It was in his nature to uncover mysteries. Especially when he feared there could be danger involved.

Danger to Alice.

Maybe he should tell her that. Maybe if she knew sex hinged on complete honesty, it'd be incentive enough for her to come clean. To bare her soul.

To him.

He'd work on that—

"Reese?"

Her soft voice, coming to him in the dark…even that turned him on. "Hmm?"

Untangling her hand from his, she squirmed around to face him, her breath on his chest, her knee so close to his dick that he twitched.

"You seem antsy. Are you okay?"

Suffering a raging hard-on seemed *antsy* to her? He counted to three to take the sting out of his voice. "Overwrought with lust, but otherwise well enough." As she turned her face up to him, he said, almost in desperation, "No, shhh. It's fine. I'm enjoying this, holding you." Torture, yes, but the sweetest kind.

"Me, too." She wiggled closer—and there it was, her leg against his boner.

Ah, God. He locked his teeth.

"I've never slept with a man before."

His eyes widened in the darkness.

"I've had sex," she said softly, her fingers now toying with his chest hair. "I didn't mean that."

Reese tried to relax. Impossible while she employed her unique brand of foreplay.

"Only a few times, and it wasn't all that memorable. That was before…"

"I know." If she started talking now, they'd never get any sleep. He wanted her well rested. Tomorrow was D-day, the day he'd get answers. But if she knew that, she'd never doze off.

Alice might think she hid it from him, but he saw her angst anytime she thought he might press for more information. She wanted to feed him details in dribs, maybe hoping that'd lessen the impact…of what?

How did she expect him to react?

He knew she was familiar with weapons, that she held her own in moments of crisis. He knew she jumped at every whisper of wind.

Such an enigma.

Yet the way she composed herself, her face a blank facade, told him more than an outpouring of emotion ever could.

It was in those contained moments that he most keenly felt her pain. It was that pain that had him holding back now. Whatever had happened, whatever she'd done, whatever shame she bore, it couldn't compare to her suffering.

"Even back then," she whispered, her fingers getting ever closer to his left nipple, "I never shared my bed overnight."

His heart beat so hard, it was a wonder it didn't rattle the bed. He flattened her hand to his chest to keep her still. "You need a larger bed." The full-size mattress wasn't nearly big enough for her, him and Cash, to boot. The proximity of her body was almost a necessity; there wasn't room for him to ease away.

He heard the smile in her voice when she said, "Until you, it wasn't an issue."

"I have a king-size bed."

"Much better suited to a man of your size."

Did she shift her leg against him on purpose, to punctuate that comment about his *size?* "We'll stick close, that's all." He locked her to him, his only defense. "It's fine."

She relaxed again. "If you're sure."

He throbbed all over, skin hot, muscles clenched, need escalating with each touch of her moist breath. But he wasn't a wimp, so he wouldn't budge—not when he knew Alice wanted him to stay.

"Go to sleep now." He hugged her, kissed her forehead and pretended to fall asleep. Tomorrow he'd take care of work obligations.

And after that…he'd take care of Alice.

THE STORMS LEFT behind air too muggy to breathe. Even inside the bar, the sluggish cooling system couldn't fight the humidity. Rowdy rubbed the back of his neck. Perspiration stuck his shirt to his back and curled the ends of his unkempt hair.

Not that he gave a damn.

Restless, he sipped his beer and thought far too much about too many women.

Even without a reason to worry, his sister stayed on his mind. He should relegate that duty to Logan now—but he knew he wouldn't. Pepper was the most important person in his world. To his dying day, he'd do what he could to keep her happy and safe.

That brought his thoughts to Alice. Too intuitive for her own good, Alice nettled him on many levels. Not with any intimate interest, regardless of Reese's concern. But she was alone, vulnerable, emotionally guarded. Sure, she would deny that, at least to him. Maybe not to Reese.

Either way, it didn't change the facts. Something or someone plagued her. Rowdy planned to figure it out.

It complicated his intent, the way she made him feel so defensive. And wary. How the hell had she so easily gotten to him? And why did she want to pick at his psyche, anyway? Women approached him all the time, but *not* because they wanted to understand him.

Never that—thank God.

Staring toward a tableful of women without really seeing them, Rowdy drank his beer. So far tonight, his questions had gone unanswered. He had a few leads, but nothing solid. A few sources checking into facts, but they could be unreliable.

He wouldn't give up.

As his gaze moved around the room, a woman smiled at him, but he didn't encourage her. Another lifted her drink to him in a suggestive toast. He glanced beyond her.

Everything came full circle as he realized he once again searched for Avery Mullins, the third woman on his mind.

He got why his sister had taken up permanent residence in his thoughts. It didn't take a shrink to know that he'd lost everyone—except her. Now that she'd found her happy-ever-after with a good guy, he felt at loose ends. Picking up on his protector role with Alice made sense.

He could roll with the punches when necessary, but he liked playing guard dog. Alice could use his special street savvy, and assisting her gave him a solid purpose. So he thought about her. Made sense.

No problem.

But Avery…what the hell was it about her? Rather than lie to himself, he admitted that he came to this particular dive, repeatedly, on the chance he'd run into her again.

That last time they'd crossed paths, he'd had goons after him intent on a beat-down. You couldn't live his life and not make enemies left and right. Elusive and cautious as he might be, every so often the disgruntled bastards caught up.

If it hadn't been for Avery assisting him out a back exit, he would have had to crawl from the bar, bloody and battered. Two men he could handle. Maybe even three. But five armed and muscled bullies lessened his odds of getting away upright, on his own steam.

Without too many questions asked and only a little condemnation, Avery had lent a hand to protect him. He'd repaid her by stealing a couple of kisses.

Lousy little pecks under shitty conditions and a definite time crunch. That's all they'd shared.

Added up, those kisses totaled less than five seconds, so they hardly counted.

Yet…they'd stuck with him. *She'd* stuck with him.

It wasn't because she amused him without even trying. Or that her forthright manner was adorably honest. It wasn't even the way she looked at him with heated awareness—all while denying an attraction.

With Avery, he was more likely to get insults than come-ons.

She'd stuck with him because he needed to have her.

That's all it was, all it could be. Once Avery gave in to the chemistry, he'd get her naked, over him or under him so he could sate himself until he got her out of his system.

And then he'd move on, as he always did.

As often as he came by hoping to see her, she had to be avoiding him. That last time, along with the kisses, he'd managed to wrangle her name from her.

While withholding his own.

Necessary then, but now…now Rowdy Yates was in the clear. He could offer a proper introduction.

If only she stopped dodging him.

While thinking of Avery, his gaze snagged on a petite blonde wearing a barely there mini dress. Great legs. Tiny waist. Come-and-get-me smile. He should take her up on it…except that he wasn't all that interested. Damn.

He transferred his attention to a tall, willowy brunette. She stared at him with blatant invitation. Fake boobs, but what did he care?

No. Still nothing.

He finished off his beer, sulking when he never sulked and wondering if he should just take a woman—any woman—to prove to himself…what?

On this particular night he didn't need the company. Sure, he had a lot on his mind, but it wasn't the disturbing stuff that sometimes plagued him in his dreams.

It wasn't the hell of a past reality, dark and gritty and sharp, clawed with disturbing images of what he'd—

"You know, if I was gay, we'd get along just fine and dandy."

CHAPTER NINE

STARTLED, PULLED from thoughts of his flawed psyche, Rowdy turned his head, and there stood none other than Avery Mullins. A headband held her incredible dark red hair off her face. Given the kiss of sun on her nose and cheeks, she'd spent a few hours outdoors earlier in the day.

At a few inches over five feet, probably weighing no more than a buck-ten, she presented an enticing little package—a package that had his muscles twitching to attention.

Though her opening salvo held plenty of attitude, her blue-eyed gaze avoided his as she finished tying a clean, crisp apron around her waist. Had she come directly to him at the start of her shift?

It appeared so.

Rife with satisfaction and anticipation, Rowdy relaxed back in his seat. "Knowing you're not gay is a relief."

"Shouldn't be. It's nothing to you."

Extra snippy tonight. He felt challenged. Hell, he felt alive. "I'm curious what you meant about us getting along."

"The women you eyeball." She finished with the apron and, with nothing else to do, picked up his empty beer glass. "Very bad taste, if you don't mind me saying so."

He didn't mind her saying anything as long as she stuck close. "'S that right?"

"If I courted women, we'd never be competing, that's for sure."

Using his foot, Rowdy pushed back the chair opposite him. "Take a seat and tell me about it."

"Can't." She tipped her head at the crowded floor. "I got called in on my day off because someone called in sick. With only one full-time waitress and two part-time, this place is always short staffed. So, as of five minutes ago, I'm on the clock."

"And I'm a customer." So this was her day off? And she only worked here part-time. Interesting.

"Yes, you are." She lifted the glass. "That's why I was going to get you another beer."

"Not just yet." Maybe not at all. He needed to stay sharp if he hoped to do some snooping into Alice's past.

"No?" She looked skeptical. "Since you usually drink two, I just assumed…"

"You know my habits?" Had she been around on his visits, and he hadn't known it? Before he left tonight, he'd find out her schedule. "In that case, I should introduce myself, right?"

"You're no longer incognito?"

He no longer had dire threats hanging over his head—but no reason to dump his sordid past on her. "Rowdy Yates."

"Like the old Clint Eastwood character?"

"Guess my folks were comedians, huh?" Or too drunk to make logical decisions. Whatever.

"More likely you're making it up."

Rowdy shook his head. "We'll eventually get together." And top of his list was giving her a screaming, unforgettable orgasm. "When we do, I damn well want you saying the right name."

"I..." As if she'd read his thoughts, she swallowed whatever she'd started to say and referred back to his offer to sit. "I should be working."

He let his gaze dip over her for one tantalizing peek. "You can take a minute, right?" He loved the way this particular woman dressed down in jeans and Ts. "I'll make it up to you with a big tip."

She waffled. "I am on a tight budget."

"So, do us both a favor. Take the tip—and tell me how it is we wouldn't be competing for the fairer sex."

Challenged, she said, "Sure, why not?" She dropped into the chair and propped her elbows on the table. "That blonde?" Using the beer glass, she pointed in the general direction of the crowded floor. "Horrible breath. She's a chain smoker. Probably been outside twice already to puff away. By this time of night she's so stale you pick it up from six feet away."

He wouldn't kick her out of bed for being a smoker, but he wasn't keen on it either. "And the brunette?"

"Very unpleasant..." She stopped, flattened her mouth and gave up with a shake of her head. "Actually, she's a big-time bitch."

Whoa. Rowdy's left eyebrow shot up. It was the first time he'd heard Avery curse. "To you?"

"To *everyone*. If she doesn't have a legitimate complaint, she makes up something. She's so annoying, I'm the only one who will willingly wait on her."

Probably insecure, then. Definitely not his thing.

He enjoyed strong women. Confident women.

Redheads.

Had he actually missed Avery that much?

To shake off his odd mood, Rowdy teased, "Aren't you the little critic today?"

"Just a few observations on my part."

"I'll scratch them both off the list, then," Rowdy promised.

She still looked disgruntled. "Hey, if you don't mind kissing an ashtray or listening to nonstop complaints, go for it. They both look agreeable."

Yeah, he'd go for it—but with Avery, not a substitute. "I appreciate the feedback. Anyone else I should avoid?"

She shrugged. "To each his own, but I'd steer clear of that one in the corner, too, the one with the short brown hair."

Rowdy looked and admired. Nice. Long legs, shapely bod, plenty of attitude. "What's wrong with her?"

"Nothing if you like a lot of ink."

"Tattoo?"

"Plural. And they're weird. I mean, not the usual stuff you'd see on a woman. They're not pretty, just extremely noticeable."

"I don't see them."

"Because she's facing you. One runs up the back of her calf, and another is across the top of her shoulder."

Rowdy nodded, but again, while he didn't get turned on by tats, they didn't really bother him either.

"Thanks. Thing is, though, I wasn't looking at any particular woman." Giving up his careless slouch in the seat, he sat forward, forearms on the tabletop, attentive, even enchanted.

Avery glanced at his shoulders, over his chest and… away.

He'd felt her attention like a stroke. Eventually, she'd stop denying him. "Actually, if you want the truth, I was thinking about a lady I saw earlier today."

Her back stiffened. "Only one? I'm shocked." She started to stand.

Rowdy caught her wrist.

Awareness arced between them, and they both froze, Avery staring at his hand, Rowdy appreciating her softness and warmth.

Smoothing his thumb back and forth over her wrist, Rowdy noted the new heat in her cheeks mixing with the slight sunburn. "Want me to tell you about her?" A pulse tripped in her pale throat. He wanted to put his mouth, his tongue, right there. He wanted to free her silky hair, taste her flushed skin, breathe in her heady scent—

She swallowed, lifted her chin. "I assume she's a woman you plan to sleep with."

"Wrong again." At the moment, Avery was the only woman he wanted. "I didn't visit her for that."

"So, she's a relative?"

Another assumption? He shook his head. "I only met her recently."

"Too old? Too young?"

Did she honestly think he slept with every woman he met? "No, smart-ass. She's probably mid-twenties."

"Hmm." Avery eased away from his hold to tuck her hand beneath the table. "I take it she's not sexy enough for you, then."

Rowdy gave it some thought. "You know, in a quiet, sort of naive way, she's really sensual." And intrusive, but he could forgive her that since she had good intentions.

"Wonderful." Avery's tone turned brisk. "Glad to hear it. Sounds like you're all set."

Shades of jealousy? Nice. "I already told you, it's

not like that. I think she might be in some trouble, and I hoped to help her. That's all."

"What kind of trouble?"

"I don't know yet. But I'm working on it."

"So this—" she gestured at the small table, at his empty beer glass "—your lack of company or interest in drinking, that was you…fretting over her?"

Did she have to make that sound so absurd? "I don't *fret.* I was strategizing." And sulking, but that was such an aberration, no way in hell would he admit it to someone else.

"I should assume she's not married? Doesn't have anyone else to assist her?"

"Not married, no, but from what I can tell, she's taken."

"Ah." More antagonistic by the second, Avery regained her feet. "I guess that makes her off-limits."

Rowdy stood, too. "Sometimes."

"Sometimes?" She looked ready to throw the empty beer glass at his head. "So if the woman you like has a significant other—"

"It's not about me liking her." Taking care not to move too quickly, Rowdy circled the table to close the space between them. He wanted to lessen his odds of getting hit with a projectile. "It's about me respecting the other guy."

Tipping her head back, Avery stared up at him. "And in this case you do?"

Rowdy couldn't help it. Recognition brought a slow grin. "Yeah, I do." He actually liked Reese, respected his ability and intuition, and even enjoyed his company. "Crazy, huh?"

"Why is it crazy?"

"For one thing, because he's a cop."

Sounding tart, Avery said, "And here I thought you avoided the police."

Yeah, he used to. For the most part, he still would. "Guess this cop is different."

"Or," Avery said with emphasis, studying him, picking him apart in profound ways, "it only seems that way because you're now different."

Son of a bitch. The truth stunned Rowdy. Yeah, since Logan and Reese had obliterated the biggest threat against his sister, he *was* different.

Funny that only Alice and Avery had ever dared enough, or cared enough, to analyze his motives. It bugged the hell out of him that Alice did it.

But with Avery… "Damn, woman." Appreciating her insight, Rowdy trailed the backs of his fingers over a long hank of silky hair. "I just realized that you missed your calling."

She put a theatrical hand to her chest. "You're saying I'm not meant to be a waitress in a sleazy, broke-dick bar about to go under?"

Broke-dick? He grinned. She really was feeling sassy tonight. He liked it. He liked her. Maybe too much.

"Nope." He wanted to swing her off her feet. He wanted to kiss her the way she needed kissing. But the new, different Rowdy restrained himself. "You're meant to be the bartender."

"I…" She eyed him. "The bartender?"

Ignoring her confusion, Rowdy again surveyed the crowd, this time bypassing the customers and instead taking note of the structure, the furniture, improvements that could be made.

A good cleaning and fresh paint would go a long way in making the place less seedy. More appropriate lighting. A little rearranging to better utilize space…

"You think I should be the bartender?" Avery waved that damned glass like a spotlight. *"Here?"*

"Absolutely." She might not advertise it, but Avery had a take-charge air stemming from independence instead of arrogance. She presented a great appearance without flaunting her body, and somehow drew more attention because of it. She listened, heard things and had a grasp on the customer base, as just proven with her observations.

"You're delirious." She patted his chest in dismissal. But once her hand connected with his body, the pat turned to a curious caress—until she caught herself and quickly withdrew.

Rowdy felt his interest expand. "We could continue that in private."

"Yeah, uh..." She cleared her throat. "Thanks, but no thanks. I'm working."

And that was her only reason for turning him down this time? Though he'd hopefully hidden it, her touch almost leveled him—and made him more determined to have his way. "I think you'll love being bartender—once the place changes from broke-dick to thriving."

"I hardly think that's possible."

"Should we make a bet?" Finally, he had another cause. And this one would be no less challenging than uncovering the threat to Alice Appleton. He felt a rush of adrenaline and couldn't wait to make plans.

Nose in the air, Avery said, "I'm not a gambler," and she started away.

Catching her by the apron strings, Rowdy hauled her back around. "Where can I find the proprietor?"

"Usually anywhere but here." She let out a strained breath, saw he was dead serious and nodded toward the back rooms. "Tonight you're in luck."

Luck, fate, whatever. He'd take it, especially when it came hand in hand with Avery. "Perfect, thanks." He started to turn away.

This time she drew him back by grabbing a handful of his T-shirt. "What are you going to do?"

He planned to do all sorts of things, most especially to this particular woman. Rowdy took the glass away from her and set it on the table.

"Rowdy..." she warned.

Grinning, honest-to-God happy, he caught her upper arms and lifted her to her tiptoes. Her soft lips parted on a gasp, then softened more when he pressed his mouth to hers. Keeping the kiss light wasn't easy, not when she tasted so good and felt so...right.

"That's number three," he breathed against her mouth. "Not all that satisfying, I know, but if my offer gets accepted, I promise to improve on that soon."

Her heavy eyes brightened. "Your offer?"

Almost by rote, she fought the chemistry. Once he saw her on a more regular basis, he'd find a way past her reservations. "Do me a favor and stick around tonight. I can't very well promote you if you keep dodging me."

She laughed. "And you figure to promote me...how?"

"I'm going to buy the place."

Her eyes rounded and her mouth opened, but she held silent. Yeah, he liked that reaction.

Rowdy chucked her under the chin. "Let me take care of business, and then we can discuss your new salary." He leaned closer to say, "You're going to like working for me, Avery. You have my word on that."

As he walked away, he heard the loud release of her pent-up breath, and then a low snarl of frustration.

He didn't look back—but he did grin in triumph.

Soon, Avery Mullins. Very, very soon.

DISGUISED BY THE shadows in the bar, the man stood back against the wall, watching as Karia moved toward the prey. Her hesitation pissed him off, but she'd learn. He'd see to it.

Finally, her mouth quivering with nervousness, she approached the bar. Sitting on a stool, she turned to face the room and leaned back on her elbows—just as he'd instructed.

Dougie, the bartender, glanced at her back—at the tattoo visible on her shoulder, and gave a small smile. He moved down the bar to speak quietly with a group of men.

With little fanfare, the men approached Karia, and seconds after that, with false smiles and scripted dialogue, they left the bar together.

Perfect.

Smug with satisfaction, he held back, remaining in the shadows, watching the door. He'd give them three minutes, no more. Then he'd go after Karia.

He didn't want her going off the rails, sneaking away from him, or spilling her guts about things meant to be kept secret—details that formed the support of his enterprise.

He didn't want her to lose her nerve, because he'd hate to have to kill her. But if she blew it, if she didn't follow the carefully laid out directions, he would snuff her like a spent candle, and then he'd find another woman.

He'd done it before, and he'd do it again.

Luckily, the women knew that. Fear, he'd learned, proved to be quite the motivator.

ALICE AWAKENED ON a gentle sigh, a slow stretch and stirring warmth from deep inside. Even through her closed eyelids she knew the sun had risen, which meant she'd slept late. Amazing.

She never slept past the sunrise. Actually, she never slept the whole night through. Sleep, like peace of mind, was a rare commodity, always warring with her conscience.

Usually losing.

But last night, she'd faded into a peaceful slumber, surrounded by warmth and security.

Surrounded by Reese.

So many things he'd given her—the care of Cash, affection and caring, sexual interest.

And now this.

That last kiss had been a revelation. She touched her mouth, remembering, savoring.

Anticipating more.

Turning her head, she looked at the other side of the bed—and found it empty.

Her heart sank like a stone. Sitting up, hands fisting in the sheets, she listened. But her senses told her what her heart feared.

Her apartment was empty.

Raging anxiety spiraled out, trying to take hold. Deliberately, Alice drew a breath, then another, slow and deep, reaching for control, for that elusive calm.

She'd been alone for a very long time, mostly by choice. Being alone now was no different. It was—

No. She couldn't, wouldn't accept that.

Throwing back the sheet, she climbed from the bed and made a frantic rush out of the room. The bathroom door and her office stood open, and empty. Her feet made a quiet patter on the hardwood hallway.

The sunny living room greeted her with a deafening silence.

How could Reese sleep with her and then just go? How could he kiss her and say he wanted more and then walk out of her life as if—

A key sounded in her lock, causing her stomach to drop. Eyes wide, heart stuttering, she froze.

The door swung open, and Reese, fully dressed, stepped in with Cash. He spoke softly to the dog as he hung the leash on the wall and closed the door with a quiet click.

She held herself so still that it took a second for Cash to spot her. With joy lighting up his face, he levered back on his haunches, shook his butt then leaped forward.

That drew Reese's attention. He turned, a smile in place—until he saw her.

Just that quick, warmth faded under concern.

The next thing she saw was sympathy.

Disgusted with herself, embarrassed and maybe even shamed, Alice knelt down and hugged Cash close. She loved the dog, and she needed an excuse to hide her hot face.

Unfortunately, Cash was too excited to be still. He kept jumping, and in her kneeling position, she didn't have great balance.

He knocked her on her can.

Laughing around her humiliation, Alice let Cash crawl up into her lap, then nuzzle against her face, her neck. His paws tangled in her gown, and his tail wagged so hard it jiggled his entire body.

Knowing Reese had seen her stricken expression, she waited for the inquisition, but when she looked up, she saw him striding into the kitchen without a word.

"Uh-oh," she whispered to Cash. "Did I make him uncomfortable?"

Cash's only answer was more joyous snuffling and wiggling.

Reese returned with a mug of coffee in one hand, a dog chew in the other. "Cash, c'mere boy."

Cash abandoned her quickly enough for Reese's bribe. He took the chew to the other side of the couch and began gnawing.

"He's been out twice," Reese told her. "Fed, walked and frisky as ever."

"Thank you." Still on the floor, legs sprawled, gown twisted, Alice regretted the exposure left by Cash's defection.

Reese came to stand by her feet. "Quite the picture you present. Somewhat like a collapsed confection."

She didn't understand him, so she didn't reply.

After a moment, he offered her a hand. "Either you come up off the floor, or I'll have to join you there. And if I get on the floor with you while you're like that, I might not be able to control myself."

What in the world did that mean?

Hand still extended, Reese said, "You're the only woman I know who could look so damned desirable while rumpled from sleep, dejected from God knows what and cowering."

"I don't cower!" But she knew she had been. Biting her bottom lip, she scowled and accepted his hand.

He hauled her upright—and into his body. As if nothing else had transpired, he said cheerfully, "Good morning, Alice."

How would she ever keep up with him? Alice mumbled, "Morning."

Keeping the coffee out of reach with one arm extended, the other arm looped around her waist, he kissed her forehead. "Everything okay?"

God, she felt like a needy child. She'd worked too hard for independence to backslide now. Forcing her chin up, she met his gaze and willed her voice to be steady and strong. "I thought you'd left."

"No, you thought I'd snuck out while you slept." He stepped back and handed her the coffee. "I like to think I'm a little more honorable than that."

"You're very honorable." She sipped the coffee. Perfection. Was there anything he didn't do well? As far as she could tell, no, there wasn't.

And of course, that meant he'd also be good at relationships, even dysfunctional relationships with damaged, needy neighbors.

"I'm sorry." Feeling like a wounded mouse, Alice wanted to limp off and hide. But that wouldn't do. "I should have known—"

"Yes, you should have." Reese gestured for her to join him in the kitchen.

Reluctantly, she went along, sitting in the chair he pulled out for her.

After getting his own cup of coffee, Reese sat across from her. Brows drawn, expression stern, he stared at her. "If I spend the night and you wake up alone, instead of assuming the worst, look for a note or wait for a phone call."

Now that she understood nothing had changed—Reese hadn't left, hadn't lost interest—she found her backbone again. "Don't leave without waking me, and I won't have to."

His left brow lifted. "So, I'm to give you notice of my comings and goings?"

She hesitated, but… "Yes." So much daring made her pulse race. It was exhilarating. "If you stay the night with me, you owe me that courtesy."

Seconds ticked by—and he smiled. "All right."

Wow, she'd just successfully debated with an ultra-appealing alpha male. Her entire mood lightened. "How long before you have to go?"

"Soon." He set his cup aside. "While you slept in—and I'm not complaining about that, just so you know—it occurred to me that you'd done all the sharing last night. Hardly fair, is it?"

She tucked her messy hair behind her ears and struggled to keep up with him. "It's okay. You had—" *have* "—questions."

"Yes, and with each answer you give, it seems I have more." He held up a hand. "No, don't draw wrong conclusions again. I'm not ready to launch into a cross-examination."

Yay.

He moved the cup a little, turning the handle. "I just wondered, don't you have a few questions of your own?"

None that she could voice first thing in the morning, after making a fool of herself, on only half a cup of coffee. But she could tell he wanted something from her. She licked her lips. "Yes?"

Proving she'd given the right answer, Reese smiled and held out his arms. "Let me have it."

She gave him a blank stare.

"Questions, Alice."

She wracked her brain and came up with a subject of interest. "Family."

"Everyone has one, don't they?" He took another drink of coffee, visibly sorting his thoughts. "Mine is large. Mother, father, brothers, sister, nephews and a niece, aunts and uncles, cousins…even my grandparents are still around."

"Wow."

"There are a lot of us, and despite the occasional conflict, we're a good group. Dad is hilarious. Overly educated but still a comedian. He makes my mom nuts, but she loves him."

Fascinated, Alice pictured them all together, and that made her wonder. "Did you get your size from your father?"

"And he from his father, and on down the line. The men are mostly all big, some bigger than me. A few of the women are tall, too, but obviously with more feminine features."

"Your mother?"

"She's average height. Around five-five. By the time I was twelve, I towered over her. When she wanted to lecture me, she made me sit in a chair in front of her. Said it hurt her neck otherwise."

Alice smiled. "You said brothers and sisters?"

"Two brothers, one sister. And yes, being the only girl, she's bossy but kind, so we tolerate her." He grinned to let her know he was teasing. "She has sons, and my oldest brother has a daughter."

Caught up in the picture he painted, Alice asked, "What were you like in high school?"

"Pride demanded I get good grades and do well in sports. I was cocky, I guess. Full of myself."

"Were you popular?"

"I didn't want for friends."

"Or girlfriends?"

Grinning, he said, "Not exactly, no." He reached for her hand, worked his thumb over her palm, examined each finger. "During my junior year, I got dubbed 'Bare it All Bareden,' a name that stuck after a bunch of cheerleaders caught me naked in the locker room."

She almost blushed for him. “That must have been so embarrassing!”

He rolled a shoulder. “You’d think so, right?” Before she could question that, he went on. “The girls, all fifteen of them, claimed to come in on me accidentally. I mean, who would think a football player would be in the locker room getting dressed after practice? Better still, none of the other guys were around. I hadn’t really noticed since I’d just stepped out of the shower, buck-ass.”

“Oh, my.” The visual crowded into her brain and stuck there. Reese young and naked and still damp… “They set you up?”

“Let’s just say the guys helped the girls work it out in exchange for favors.” Lifting her hand, he kissed her knuckles, turned her hand over to kiss her palm. “High school guys are notoriously horny, and there’s not much they wouldn’t do for sex.”

Curling her fingers, Alice tried to ignore how the sensation of his mouth there was felt all over her body. She wanted to hear the rest. “I take it you weren’t angry?”

“At the girls? No. They were just curious because of the rumors.”

Suspicious, she narrowed her eyes. “What rumors?”

His gaze met hers. “Size rumors.”

Drawing a blank, she shook her head in incomprehension.

“You know,” Reese said. “Am I big all over? That sort of thing.”

She recalled Nikki and Pam commenting on the same. Studiously keeping her gaze on his face, Alice said with confidence, “You are.”

The green of his eyes deepened. “Yes, I am.” This

time he kissed her wrist, lingering, provoking. "Back then, I enjoyed the bragging rights."

"And now?"

His smile came reluctantly. "As a grown, mature man, I'd like to say it doesn't matter." The damp heat of his tongue almost stole her breath. He closed his mouth over her wrist, lightly bit and murmured, "But I still enjoy showing off."

Even sitting in a chair, she felt herself swaying. She swallowed hard and rasped, "Showing off?"

Slowly, maintaining his hold on her wrist, Reese stood and came around the table. He tugged her up and against his big frame. Serious, heated, he searched her face, her eyes, finally her mouth. "I'll fill you up, Alice. And I swear you'll enjoy it."

He bent to kiss her—and she knew without a single doubt what type of kiss it'd be.

Before they made contact, she stumbled back, taking Reese by surprise. "Sorry, no."

His chest rose and fell, but he didn't insist. "All right."

So honorable of him.

So dumb of her. Desperate to explain, she said, "I only got up a few minutes ago."

He let his attention roam over her body. "Great nightgown."

"Thank you." Was Pepper correct? Could simple clothes affect him so much? Apparently. She smoothed the rumpled cotton of her gown. "The thing is, I've only had half a cup of coffee. And I haven't brushed my teeth yet." *And I'm an awful coward.* "Pepper will be here soon, and I won't be ready."

"I'm not rushing you."

Good Lord. Then what would rushing be like? She could barely wait to find out. “Okay.”

His smile quirked, spread until he laughed. “Alice.” He stepped up to her before she could dart away. “I can’t stop thinking about getting inside you—”

She groaned.

“—but I’m not saying it has to be right away. I want you to want me, too.”

Seriously, he *had* to know. “That’s not the problem.” But verbalizing the problem wouldn’t be easy, because the problem itself was complex, a mangled mix of her past, her present intent, demons and determination.

“Hey.” He tipped up her chin. “I can wait until we work it out.”

Because he felt confident that they would? She hoped so. She wanted that more than she’d wanted anything since…since she’d lain awake at night, praying for escape, silently begging for a way out of a living nightmare.

She rubbed her forehead, refusing to go down memory lane yet again. Looking at Reese always helped to lighten the darkness, so she smiled up at him. “Okay.”

“You are the most agreeable woman.” He bent and kissed her before she could dodge him. Mindful of her feelings, he kept it light, almost teasing. “I have to go. Have fun with Pepper, but be careful. You have my number if anything comes up.”

CHAPTER TEN

ALICE STEPPED OUT of the changing room in the cuffed jean capris, peasant top and wedge sandals. Pepper looked her over with a big smile, then proclaimed the outfit, "Perfect."

It would be her fifth, which was only a third of what Pepper had purchased.

Alice toyed with the loose ties at the neck of the shirt. "It's comfortable." So far, everything Pepper had helped her choose was easy to wear, affordable and complimentary.

"That outfit, with your new hairstyle..." Pepper whistled. "Reese will go nuts."

She touched her hair, now parted more to the side, trimmed just enough to make it fuller and deliberately tousled. She liked it, too. "It'll be easy to replicate."

"The makeup, too. Honestly, you have such great bones, you can't go wrong."

No one had ever noticed her bones before, so she had to wonder about that. When Pepper's phone rang, Alice darted again into the changing room to dress in her regular clothes.

They'd been shopping for hours now, before and after lunch. Alice admired the pale, iridescent pink on her nails and toes, thanks to a professional mani and pedi.

Pepper had encouraged her to be worked over, head to toes, and she'd had so much fun.

Except for the sensation of being watched.

Off and on throughout the day, Alice had felt the scrutiny but no alarm. Sometimes being so observant was a curse.

Most likely the attention had been men admiring Pepper. Her new friend had the kind of "stop traffic" looks that never failed to draw male appreciation.

When she stepped back out of the room, Pepper accompanied her to the cashier, saying, "That was Logan. They're done at the station finally, so I guess we should call it a day."

Alice smiled. "I know you're anxious to see him again."

"It's new to me," Pepper admitted. "I'm probably smothering him, but he'll just have to get over it."

"He adores you, so I'm sure he doesn't mind." She paid with a credit card, then retrieved her additional packages.

"He does." Pepper gave a happy sigh. "I've always loved my brother, but there haven't been many other people in my life that I could care about."

They started out to the parking lot where they'd met up. "Rowdy is a very interesting person." At loose ends now, but Alice trusted that he'd find his way. He struck her as a very resourceful man.

"He's the best of brothers and a terrific ally if you ever need one."

A hint? An offer? Alice grinned. "Reese told you he came to visit me?"

"Yeah." She stopped by Alice's car. "I won't pry, but if you ever need anything, I can be a pretty good ally, too."

"Thank you." No way would she unload her issues on Pepper, especially since her new friend had only recently found peace of her own. She deserved happiness, not drama.

"I don't want Logan to overdo it today, but what would you think about getting together for dinner after he's healed up a little? We could all four go out. Someplace not fancy, because I don't do fancy much."

"That sounds perfect, thank you. If Reese is willing, I'd enjoy it."

Pepper snorted. "Reese is all kinds of willing. All you have to do is get on board." She laughed. "Take advantage of the time he has off."

Good advice. Alice said, "I think I will."

Laden with her own packages, Pepper left her with a wave, going to the other end of the lot where she'd parked. Alice waited until she saw Pepper get in a car, then she checked the time.

With any luck, she'd return to the apartment before Cash lost patience and soiled the floor. This was his usual nap time, but when she wasn't around, his routine always differed.

She unlocked her car, stored her packages in the back and opened the windows to let out the steamy heat. While she waited for the air-conditioning to kick on, she did her usual survey of her surroundings.

The mall did plenty of business with cars coming and going, women walking along in small groups, couples with children. Alice appreciated the sight of normalcy—until the hairs on the back of her neck stirred.

Visually seeking the source of the alarm, she noticed a slow-moving van. Nice, new, silver…nothing to elicit suspicion—until it stopped beside a truck parked on the outskirts of the lot, away from the rest of the congestion.

Eyes narrowed, Alice put her car in gear and drove closer. Using care, she retrieved her dark sunglasses and slipped them on, then pulled up by the end of a line of other parked cars. Near enough now to watch, but hopefully not that obvious. Other drivers went past in front of her, then continued on, helping to disguise her scrutiny.

The side door of the van opened, and a young lady stepped out. The driver of the truck met her before she'd taken two steps. Her right arm sported a thick gauze bandage, loosely taped in place. Otherwise she looked fine, dressed nicely enough in jeans and a halter, her long brown hair tidy.

For reasons Alice couldn't understand, her heart lurched.

Holding on to the girl's elbow, the truck driver spoke through the passenger window. He smiled, and though Alice couldn't hear what he said, her mind conjured all sorts of awful dialogue.

Things she'd heard before. Arrangements. Deals.

Okay, so maybe to the casual observer, it'd only look like the man assisted the young woman into his truck.

Alice saw it differently.

Why was she being moved from a van to a truck? Why in a parking lot? What had happened to her arm?

Even as she told herself she could be overreacting, Alice gave over to her screaming instincts. Waiting until the van pulled away, she put her car in gear and followed the truck at a cautious distance, always keeping at least two vehicles between them. Through the rear window of the truck, she watched the driver and his passenger, attuned to nuances in body language.

Alert.

Her senses churned, her stomach burning, her mouth dry.

Possibilities, spurred by a remembrance of things

she'd seen, things she'd reluctantly taken part in, mixed with fresh resolve, pushing aside all other considerations. Cash was home safe. Pepper had already driven away. Logan and Reese were together, just leaving the station.

She had no one else to worry about—except the young woman in the truck.

Her hands squeezed the steering wheel, steadying her nerve and helping her to focus. The outside shaking abated, but inside, she remained a bundle of jitters.

The truck drove in the opposite direction of where she lived. Farther and farther from her personal sanctuary, from her self-imposed exile, her lonely haven.

In and out of side streets, nearer and nearer to the wrong side of town.

Twice, Alice almost lost the truck. She closed the distance a little, scared spitless on many levels. While she rationalized her actions and tried to plan for outcomes, troublesome doubt returned her thoughts to Reese.

She had absolutely no illusion about how he'd feel at the prospect of her trailing possible trouble. But their relationship was fresh, new, so testing the boundaries would be expected, right?

Neither of them had spelled out any stipulations yet.

Stay out of trouble. Did he really *need* to spell that out?

Never did she want to outright lie to him, but for sure he would ask. She'd been gone all day. It was time for dinner. And Pepper had already assured Logan she was on her way home, so Reese would expect her to be at the apartment when he got there.

That is, if he came straight home.

Home. She couldn't start thinking that way. Right now, their arrangement was far from concrete.

And she'd just come full circle in her thoughts.

Nervous sweat dampened her palms, the back of her neck. With each mile covered, the area got more disreputable. Not that location mattered all that much when the monsters crawled out. They lurked everywhere, in high society and poverty, in business and in everyday life.

Her courage waned as they passed the bus terminal. Few people were out beneath the heat of the midday sun. They left behind businesses and went into a residential neighborhood, except that everything seemed abandoned.

The driver steered around a corner, dark and ominous and empty except for the crumbling brick facade of an old motel with single-story units that formed an L. The truck drove around to the back.

Alice paused before falling into that trap; her car idled on the street, her doors locked, her senses alive to warning signs. She quickly surveyed the area and decided to take an adjacent street separated from the motel only by an overgrown empty lot. She coasted along the curb until she finally spied the truck pulled up to a more open area at the rear entrance.

Neglect fell like a dark stain over the abandoned motel. Jagged glass clung to the frame of a broken back window. Weeds grew up through crumbling blacktop in what used to be a parking lot. Graffiti covered some of the individual doors. An awning hung haphazardly, ready to drop.

No one had inhabited that wretched place for a very long time.

So, why would the man take the girl in there?

Wishing she'd been wrong, Alice put her car in Park. Quickly locking up, she glanced around but saw no one.

Farther down the street, a siren blared, and in the distance she could hear the traffic on the highway.

With trembling hands she confirmed the contents of her purse. Satisfied, she drew a calming breath and went in pursuit of the woman, her steps hurried up the broken sidewalk to the front of the motel.

Circling the building, she peeked around and saw the man holding on to the woman's wrist while he worked keys in the dead bolt of a locked door. The unit he chose was at the end, with windows on two walls—but the windows were boarded up from the outside.

What to do, what to do? Wait for him to get inside, so they were out of the way of prying eyes?

Or act now, in case others were inside?

It would be awful enough confronting one man. But if she had to face two, or even three…

She lost the opportunity for choices when the door opened and the man urged the woman inside, then started to follow her.

Damn, damn, damn.

If he locked that door… *"Hello!"* Hearing her voice break the silence nearly made her hysterical.

But it didn't change her mind.

Alice hastened her step, all but jogging down to the remote unit. "Excuse me, please," she called even louder.

Incredulous, the man stuck his head back out the door. He had reddish-brown hair, a tidy goatee and a pocked complexion. He glared at her, looked beyond her, around then back to her with fury. "What?"

Moving her lips in the semblance of a smile, Alice waved to him. "Could you help me, please? I think I'm lost, and I don't see anyone else—"

"Get lost, lady." He started to move away.

Oh, God. Alice slipped her hand into her purse. Closer and closer she got to the door. “My phone died. I only need to make a call.” Her heart thumped so hard it hurt. “Please.”

Anger darkened his eyes. His insulting gaze crawled all over her. A smile stretched his mouth. He muttered something to the woman inside the room before holding the door open for her. “Fine. Come on in, and we can get you sorted out.”

Bile tried to crawl up her throat. She did not want to get close to him. Vision closing in, she nodded. “Thank you. That would be very helpful.”

Her skin crawled as she walked past him, and when she saw the room, she thought she might faint. Dark, with peeling paint on the walls, exposed pipes from the defunct heater/air conditioner and stained carpet. It was bare except for an older wooden desk, no chair, and a mattress on the floor. The girl stood in a corner, her back to the wall, her expression watchful, horrified.

Alice turned in time to see him locking the door.

He leered at her, saying, “Stupid bitch.”

In answer, Alice pulled out her Taser.

ROWDY DROVE AS fast as he dared. What the hell was she doing? He’d tailed Alice from the shopping mall, curious, a little concerned when she headed away from her apartment.

Never in a million years had he thought she’d pull a prank like this.

It took him a bit to realize she was tailing someone herself. Why, he didn’t yet know, but he’d find out when he caught up to her.

Unfortunately, he got hung up at a light, stuck behind a couple of other cars. He saw Alice turn a corner.

He knew the area, and he knew there wasn't a damn thing there for her.

Nothing…except trouble.

TREMBLING ALL OVER, Alice held the Taser steady.

Nostrils flared, hands curling into fists, the man all but spit out, "What the fuck is this?"

Finding her voice wasn't easy. "I've already flipped the safety into the armed position. I know how to use it, and I know it will incapacitate you."

"You're *insane.*"

"Sometimes I wonder." Getting enough oxygen into her lungs proved impossible. She all but panted—and still felt light-headed. "Don't move. I will seriously fry you if you do." The Taser had a fifteen-foot range, but in the small confines of the motel room, she was far closer than that.

Too close.

Without looking away from the man, she asked, "What's your name?"

"Hickson."

Alice shook her head. "No, not you. I don't care about you." She tipped her head toward the girl. "I meant her."

Hickson snarled. "She's not your concern."

Alice wanted to shoot him. Bad. "I'm making her my concern."

The girl fought back tears. "Ch-Cheryl."

"What's wrong with your arm, Cheryl?"

"T-t-tattoo."

Disgusted, Hickson said, "Stop that goddamned stuttering!"

Alice scowled, and when the girl stammered again, saying, "S-sorry," she lost her fragile grasp on control.

Heartbeat thundering in her ears, she whispered, "I don't like you." And with that, Alice pulled the trigger.

Teeth clenched and muscles bunched, Hickson gave a guttural scream of agony. His body went rigid, bowing hard as an incapacitating pulse overrode his motor functions, robbing him of any threat. It went on and on—because Alice continued to squeeze the trigger. His knees gave out, and he collapsed to the floor. Alice glanced at Cheryl. The girl covered her ears and sank to her haunches, her eyes squeezed shut.

Seeing that put her on autopilot.

Using her left hand, Alice retrieved the restraints from her purse.

The second she let up on the Taser, she was on Hickson, using the nylon straps to bind his arms behind his back. She leaped away just as quickly.

Cheryl whimpered.

Sympathy for the girl tore at Alice. She wanted to bludgeon Hickson over the head, but if she did, she might accidentally kill him, and what would Reese think about that?

Having a man in her life was proving problematic already. But she couldn't think about that now.

Her Taser allowed her to shoot three times, thirty seconds each. She had to hurry or odds of them walking away would diminish.

She didn't know the circumstances here, but she recognized Cheryl as a victim, Hickson as a creep. He could have a cohort or a buyer due to show up any minute. She just didn't know.

On a slow breath, keeping that Taser steady on Hickson, she withdrew another nylon restraint from her purse. "Cheryl, calm down."

"Oh, God, oh, God!"

"I can't get you out of here if you don't help."

That got her attention. She sniffled, wiped her nose with a shaking hand. With wretched uncertainty, she asked, "Get me out? To go wh-where?"

"Away from here." After that…well, she'd have to figure it out.

Hickson groaned, so Alice zapped him again.

His body flopped, jerked.

She let up and watched him slump boneless to the floor. Cheryl wasn't helping much, so she'd have to rely on herself. She went back to Hickson, this time tightening the nylon around his ankles, under his pant legs. Luckily he didn't wear boots; she was able to get them really tight.

When she finished, she tossed a nylon tie to the poor girl still slumped on the floor, now wide-eyed with confusion. "Cheryl, I need you to attach his ankles to that pipe."

Cheryl tripped toward a protruding pipe.

"No, the other one." Alice watched her. "The wet, moldy, dripping pipe."

"Are you a…a cop?" Cheryl asked while looping the nylon through the ankle restraints and around the pipe. There was barely enough room.

"No, sorry."

Cheryl hesitated. "Are you working for someone else?"

"I'm self-employed." Her attention on Hickson, Alice watched, ready if he moved a single muscle…

All he did was moan.

Cheryl threw herself away from him, doing a crab crawl backward until she ended up in the middle of the disgusting mattress, her knees pulled up, her arms around her shins.

Hickson was completely immobilized, far enough away from the door that he wouldn't be able to reach it. And cuffed to the pipe that way, he'd have a hard time sitting up.

Alice decided she would leave him there until she formulated a plan. On the desk was a phone, some change, a slip of paper with a number. Alice gathered it all up. "Does he have a wallet?"

"I don't know."

Alice had no intention of getting close to him again. "All right. Come with me, please. Quickly."

Hickson groaned again as they sidled out of the room, being sure to stay out of his reach. At the door, Alice peeked out, replaced the Taser in her purse and motioned for Cheryl to follow.

As she hustled past the truck, she paused, then decided to take a risk. "Wait." She dug the small folding knife out of her purse, went to one knee on the gritty, rough blacktop and cut the air valve off a tire.

If Hickson did find a way to get loose, he wouldn't be driving anywhere.

Her knee hurt as she stood again, but she paid it no mind. "Come on."

Cheryl followed as she darted back to her car, this time crossing the field. Weeds caught on her clothes; disturbed insects swarmed upward.

Alice tried to be vigilant, looking around for prying eyes. She saw no one. "Does anyone else know about that place?"

Swiping at the mascara tracks staining her cheeks, Cheryl hurried behind her. "Yes."

She should have known. Creeps gravitated to each other, often running in packs like wild dogs. "Do you know when they'll go back there?"

Cheryl shook her head.

Alice said, "I'll figure it out." How, she had no idea. Eventually she'd have to tell Reese. Or better yet, she could call… No. She wouldn't do that.

Maybe she could trust Rowdy. Reese was the law, and he saw things as black-and-white. But Rowdy understood the fine balance between right and wrong. He would balk at venturing into illegal territory—as Alice herself had just done. For right now, Rowdy's propensity suited her just fine.

As long as he didn't tattle to Reese. Honorable men, she knew, had this weird loyalty to one another.

Decisions, decisions.

She unlocked her car with the clicker before they'd even reached it. "Get in."

Alice circled around to the driver's side while Cheryl crawled in, her fearful gaze going everywhere, waiting for more hurt to come her way.

Alice started the car and drove straight ahead, then took the first left, and another. No one followed.

They were safe. *For now.*

Beside her, Cheryl held herself so stiffly that Alice wondered if she planned to leap out at any moment.

"What would you like to do? I can either take you to the police—"

"No." Cheryl gripped the door handle.

"Or," Alice said, understanding, "I can rent you a hotel room, or even put you on a bus."

Cheryl fretted, unsure of her offer. "A b-bus?"

"No strings attached."

A sob tore from Cheryl's throat. *"Why would you do this?"*

"I want to help," she said gently. "That's all. I swear."

Close to hyperventilating, Cheryl watched her. "I believe you're not a cop. But h-how can I be sure you're not working for the competition?"

"What competition?"

"The other dealers? A supplier?" She pressed into the door, cowering. "How do I know you won't take me somewhere and d-d-do awful things?"

Drugs and dealers. *What awful things?* "So this… It's about drugs?" She hadn't figured it that way at all. Alice waved a hand. It didn't matter, not right now. "Whatever's going on, I just want to get you someplace safe. I swear."

For the longest time, the only sound was of Cheryl's erratic breathing. Alice pulled into more traffic, willing to give her time to think, to compose herself.

Suddenly Cheryl ripped at the bandage on her arm. Her sobs escalated as she exposed an odd tattoo, a design of overlapping numbers and lines. "He marked me so they'd know." She used the wadded up bandage to scrub at her still raw skin. "That's why I had to get the tattoo. Others will see it and kn-know I'm carrying the drugs. They'll know who I'm with, that deals are made—"

"Shhh." Keeping her eyes on the road, Alice reached out to touch her arm lightly. "Please, don't hurt yourself, Cheryl. Please."

Defeated, Cheryl curled in on herself. "I want to go home."

Relief took the strain out of Alice's backbone. "You have family?"

She nodded hard, eyes squeezed shut, lips trembling. "I ran off from college. Everyone told me he was no good, that he'd hurt me. But I didn't believe them, and I ran off with him and n-now my parents are probably—"

"Worried sick," Alice finished for her. "That was him I met? Hickson?"

"No." She shuddered in revulsion. "He's just the guy who gets us tattooed."

Us. More than one girl? "Do your parents live far away?"

"A few hours." Cheryl scrubbed at her eyes, wiped her nose.

Driving one-handed while she reached into her purse, Alice produced a pack of tissues. "Use the visor and try to clean yourself up."

Cheryl sobbed a rough laugh. "Do you have everything in that purse?"

Everything she might need. "I like to be prepared."

Alice knew what to do now, and that shored up her courage. She drove toward the bus terminal. "I'll get you on a bus, with enough money for a cab from the station, and you'll be home before nightfall. It'll be okay. I promise."

Thank God, this time she could make a difference.

Maybe a big difference. Alice glanced at her. "While I drive, tell me everything, please. Especially about that tattoo."

FURIOUS, ROWDY HUNG back in the churchyard, watching through binoculars as Alice went into the bus station with a bedraggled woman who looked to be young: nineteen, maybe twenty. Slim, pretty, but now with swollen red eyes and blotchy cheeks.

What was Alice up to?

After falling behind, it had taken him a few moments to locate her again. To expedite his search, he'd pulled into a quaint stone church sitting atop a rise that overlooked the rest of the area. Using binoculars, he'd spotted her car, then located her at the motel just as she'd hauled ass out of the place with the other woman. Thinking she ran from someone, Rowdy started to rush to her rescue—but his alarm had faded when Alice paused long enough to sabotage the truck tire.

No one in hot pursuit.

Settling back, he'd watched her high-step across an overgrown lot that probably hid snakes, rats and too many insects to count. He tracked her as she drove through the neighborhood, circled around and headed toward the highway. He thought she'd finally be heading home, plus one passenger, until she pulled into the bus station.

Confusing.

Twenty minutes later, Alice emerged alone. Sun glinted off her brown hair—had she done something with it? It looked different. Rowdy rubbed his chin, still on high alert.

She smiled as she slipped on sunglasses and—after checking the backseat of her car—unlocked it and got in.

Undecided for only a moment, Rowdy pulled out his cell phone and thumbed her number before she could leave the lot.

"Hello?"

She sounded breathy, probably on an adrenaline rush. He shook his head. "It's Rowdy."

"Rowdy?" And just like Alice, she asked, "Are you okay? Is anything wrong?"

All kinds of things were way wrong, but he'd save that for a face-to-face. "Go back into the bus station and wait for me there."

"Go…" She twisted around in her seat. "Where are you?"

"I'm where I can keep eyes on you. Now hustle your ass back inside and stay put. I'll be there in less than half an hour."

Silence. Alice got out of her car, shielded her eyes from the sun and searched the area. "Did you watch me as I shopped with your sister?"

"Why?"

"I felt someone."

Damn. For the second time in their short acquaintance, he wondered if he was slipping.

"Rowdy? Why are you following me?"

"Inside, hon. I'll explain when I get there."

Even from a distance, looking through field binoculars, Rowdy saw her frown. "I don't like taking orders from you."

"Would you rather take them from the police?" He saw her go still. "Maybe from Detective Reese Bareden?"

"That's blackmail!"

"Whatever it takes." He and Reese had a deal, so Rowdy would end up telling him, anyway. Whether Alice realized that yet or not, it was a moot point.

As he said, whatever it took.

Head down, she turned a stiff circle, probably scheming, trying to think up options.

"Make a decision, Alice."

"Fine!" She relocked her car. Stride stiff, she marched toward the station entrance. "I'll be inside."

"Fine," he repeated back to her, and damned if he didn't have to fight a smile. "See you soon." Rowdy disconnected the call, but watched until he saw Alice reenter. He waited a few seconds more to see if she'd come right back out.

She stayed put.

And good thing, because his gut told him to get back to that motel, to stake it out, so that's what he did. Just as he'd observed Alice, he watched the motel—from a safe distance away, this time inside a condemned house, up on the second story.

The floor trembled under his feet, almost as if it'd give out any minute. But he'd been in worse places.

Hell, he'd lived in worse places.

He'd give it a few minutes, not long because he didn't want to leave Alice unprotected. But if someone showed up, he didn't want to miss it.

Every so often, he checked the perimeter. No way did he want to get caught spying on…whatever the hell she'd gotten into. Best to keep his guard up.

He was about to call it quits when a black SUV approached the dilapidated building. Two average-looking lowlifes went inside.

They wore jeans and printed T-shirts and both were armed.

One came right back out, scoping the area, cell phone in hand while he made an urgent call. Rowdy couldn't hear from this distance, but he didn't need to be a lip reader to pick up on the fury.

Finally the other two joined him. The one he hadn't seen before rubbed at his wrists. He looked waxy from pain, walking unsteadily.

What did Alice do to him?

When the guy noticed the flat tire on his truck, he cursed a blue streak—until one of the other men grabbed his shirtfront, slammed him to the brick wall and apparently gave a credible threat.

Subdued, emanating menace, they all three climbed into the SUV. Rowdy read the plates, committed them to memory and lowered the binoculars.

Whatever had gone on here, it wasn't good.

Alice, Alice, Alice.

Little Ms. Goody Two-shoes had put herself at the center of danger.

Now what?

THE PHONE SHATTERED when it landed against the wall. Those around the man jumped, sickening him with their weakness. "Get out."

In a rush, they scattered, filing out the door like frightened mice. Idiots.

He strode across the floor to stare out a window. God, he hated it when his people fucked up. Wasting precious time on discipline—or retaliation—meant he wasn't utilizing that time to make money. If Hickson wasn't so competent in other ways, he'd have him beaten to death and dumped in the river.

Instead, he had to find a way to drive home the seriousness of his error, to ensure such incompetence never happened again.

And he'd have to find the do-gooder broad, because no way in hell would he let her interference go unpunished. He showed no weakness, ever. He exhibited power, only power, and that's what kept them all in line—and kept his profits rolling in.

Yes, the bitch would have to pay.

Maybe, just maybe, he could kill two birds with one stone.

CHAPTER ELEVEN

NECK MUSCLES TENSED, thankful that the questions were over—for now—Reese left the room. It was a follow-up interview, and he wouldn't be surprised if a third came about.

It wasn't every day that two detectives, their lieutenant, a supposed witness and deadly perps all ended up in a shoot-out at one of the detectives' residences.

A fuck-up of that magnitude could take months to sort out.

He got that any officer-involved shooting was a big deal. Add to it the recent corruption at the station with a few cops on the take, working for the very scum who had died in his apartment, and yeah, no wonder the D.A. and I.A. were being so thorough.

Reese knew without a shadow of a doubt that both Logan and Lieutenant Peterson were on the up-and-up. Okay, so he'd once suspected Peterson. He'd been way off base on that one.

In a low voice, Logan said to Reese, "I found out a few things."

"The kidnapping?"

"Yeah." He glanced toward the lieutenant, walking ahead of them. "It was big news when Alice reappeared after being gone for so long. Course the press got hold of it. The thing is, she claimed not to know much—not who had taken her, or where. According to her, some anonymous man rescued her, dropped her off with money to get home, and that was that."

"Bullshit," Reese said low.

"That's what I figured, too. Thing is, a lot of women were recovered right around that time. Separate from Alice showing up."

Damn.

Logan watched Peterson's back, ensuring she didn't overhear. "Someone killed the traffickers, set the women loose and then…vanished."

"They interviewed the other women?"

"Yes, and most had the same tale. That they were freed by some anonymous champion."

What exactly had Alice been involved in?

Lieutenant Peterson glanced back at them. "If you two hens are done whispering, how about we grab some coffee?"

Reese wanted to talk more with Logan. He needed dinner.

And he needed Alice.

But before he could find an excuse to decline, Logan checked his watch and said, "I can take time for a cup."

Great. Coffee. Hadn't they seen each other enough for one day? Of course, under normal circumstances, they would naturally gravitate to the coffeepot, so maybe it was better not to make Peterson suspicious by varying things.

"Is your arm bothering you?" she asked Logan without a lot of concern or sympathy. Peterson was not a woman to indulge coddling.

She was hard. And cold. And thankfully, honorable.

This time, Reese spoke ahead of Logan. "More likely, it's that he has Pepper Yates waiting to tuck him back into bed."

Peterson gave a small smile. "I'm surprised you didn't get grilled more on that whole situation."

Reese wasn't at all surprised. "Any man who saw Pepper understood Logan's predicament."

Logan just smiled.

At thirty, Peterson was the youngest lieutenant in the state. She was on the short side, deceptively slender, with short brown hair and big blue eyes. She'd be a looker if she didn't favor containing all femininity within structured business suits and a ball-buster attitude that put many a man in his place—which was whatever place Peterson deemed appropriate for him at the time.

Somehow, Reese doubted that place was ever in a bed, naked, going deep. He could be wrong, but he just couldn't see it.

"Pepper was never really a witness," Logan argued, but he kept his voice low, aware that I.A. and the D.A. were still around.

They'd first answered questions for the district attorney, and everyone knew Internal Affairs watched through the two-way mirror. They'd had their own store of questions afterward.

"What about you?" Peterson asked. "You and the neighbor connecting?"

Prying, or just conversation? Reese wasn't sure. Peterson's motives were always murky—which accounted in part for why he'd once doubted her integrity. Not a sterling moment for him.

Logan repaid him by answering. "He and Alice—that's her name, Alice—are an item now."

"Is that right?" Peterson arched a brow. "I take it you disarmed her before getting too cozy?"

God knew he'd be forever ribbed over the way Alice

had shown up on the scene, gun in hand, a haunted look in her eyes.

Sometimes it's better if they're dead. That stark statement coming from a woman like Alice—understated in appearance and manner—had left everyone speculating.

Reese shook his head.

"What's this?" Peterson teased. Disconcerting both detectives, she stepped ahead and opened the door to the break room for them to enter. "Reese Bareden is without a comeback? Now, you know all sorts of scenarios are coming to mind."

"She's very sweet," he said, and walked past the lieutenant into the room. He counted it a blessing that no one else sat at the long table.

"Just like a sweet Ma Barker, huh?" Peterson let the door fall shut behind Logan.

"Sit," he told Logan and Peterson as he went to the coffee machine and filled three cups. He tried not to let the lieutenant's ribbing get to him. That'd only make him fair game for everyone else at the station.

"Cream and sugar in mine," she said. "So, tell me about her."

"Who?" Reese stalled, looking for a way out.

Logan grunted a laugh—and tried to hide his discomfort.

"Alice…what's her last name?"

He didn't want to say. He didn't want Peterson to start digging. Damn it, Alice had too many secrets, and until he knew what they entailed, he didn't dare have her exposed.

An image of Alice in the bed that morning—baby-soft hair fanned out on the pillow, her face utterly relaxed, expression peaceful—contradicted any ideas of her being trouble.

But deep down, something continued to whittle at his peace of mind. He would protect her to the best of his ability, but against what? Who?

"He has a thing for her," Logan said, filling in the too-lengthy, telltale silence. "Give him time to get a grip. He's still reeling."

"What kind of thing?"

Juggling all three foam cups, Reese returned to the table. "A none-of-your-business thing." He set one cup in front of the lieutenant. "Do you want me snooping into your love life?"

He waited for her to deny that a love life existed. He waited for her sarcastic reply.

Instead, she blushed.

Oh, ho, what was that about? Lieutenant Margaret Peterson, red-faced? Reese glanced toward Logan and caught his friend's reciprocal expression of surprise.

"Margaret," Reese teased, dropping formality as he took a seat. "What have you been up to?"

She slapped a file folder down on the table. "Work." Avoiding eye contact, she sipped her coffee. "Detectives Rhodes and Garland took over on our follow-up after that mess in Reese's apartment. They got the buyers, some other traffickers, freed a truckload of new victims and, overall, they've wrapped things up nice and tight."

Reese let it go. For now. Finding out info on the human traffickers was more important to him than speculating on Peterson's uninspiring feminine side.

"Glad to hear it." He turned the file around and opened it to peruse names. "Anyone else hurt?"

"Nope. It was a clean bust. The bastards had only just set up house, so gathering everything was easy. The thing is…" She sipped at her coffee, her demeanor going somber, flat. "They closed off the neighborhood, searched the whole area and found a body in a dilapidated house a few doors down. A young female, bound and gagged."

"Damn." Logan ran a hand through his hair, wincing at the pain caused by the movement. "Got an ID?"

"Not yet. There's a good chance it's unrelated to the traffickers. Early estimate is that she died recently, within the past twenty-four hours."

Reese thought of Alice, of a dark history, and kept quiet. His thoughts churned. He wanted to see her, to hold her.

"Anything to go on?" Logan asked. "Any ideas?"

"It might not be anything, but then again, it could be." She reached for the file, pushed aside a few papers and withdrew a photo. "She had a very odd tattoo on her forearm."

Reese studied the photo but couldn't quite make out the design of the tattoo. "What is it?"

"Lines, numbers. So far, no idea what it means. But it's unique," Peterson said, "and it's the only clue we've got. We're hopeful that it'll tell us something."

ROWDY WATCHED ALICE pull into the apartment parking lot mere seconds before he drove in behind her. After retrieving her from the bus station, he requested—because *telling* her anything would probably get her back up—that she drive straight home. He informed her that he'd be following her more closely this time.

Thank the heavens, she'd done as asked.

He didn't like letting her drive, but didn't see a way around it. Even now, as he caught up to her on the walkway in, he could see her trembling.

Nerves. The adrenaline dump after her escapade.

Crazy Alice.

He narrowed his eyes against the sun, now streaking the sky in shades of crimson, pink, purple and neon yellow. He said nothing as they walked side by side into the apartment complex, but his concerns shuffled around again and again, making his head ache.

He knew she'd once been kidnapped, though Reese didn't have all the details yet. From the moment he'd met her, Rowdy had figured she was afraid of something.

From what he'd seen today, she mostly had herself to fear.

Near her apartment door, she asked, "Are you coming in?"

"Damn straight."

She gave him a sour look. "Cash will need some attention." She unlocked her door. "I'll have to take him to the yard—"

The second the door opened, Cash launched out. His body wriggled and squirmed in maniacal excitement.

Alice did a fair job of subduing the dog while hugging and stroking him, talking to him in a soft, sweet voice. She reached inside for the leash. "When he's excited," she said over Cash's loud whining and yapping, "I have only moments before he wets the floor."

"I'll go with you." Rowdy took the leash and attached it to Cash's collar. He would have offered to take the dog out on his own, but…well, he didn't trust Alice alone just yet. "C'mon. We have a lot of talking to do before Reese shows up."

Cash practically dragged him down the steps. Rowdy took Alice's hand and hauled her along.

Once outside, Cash continued in his effusive greeting…while peeing. Funny dog. Luckily they were already on the grass, and Cash missed his shoes.

At this time of early evening, no one else was about

outside. Likely most were at dinner, which was where he needed to be. Chasing after Alice had helped him work up an appetite.

Maybe once he finished up here, he'd head to the bar, grab a sandwich…and maybe a woman.

Maybe Avery.

Yeah, he liked that idea.

Alice stood back, her arms crossed, her annoyance palpable. "I want to know why you were following me."

He shrugged and gave Cash a little more leash. "Reese asked me to keep an eye out."

She did a double take. "You're serious?"

"Why not?" Shadows stretched across the parking lot and the small grassy area. "It's what I do."

And he was good. Thanks to querying the right people, he knew that Alice was from the area. He didn't know why she'd been kidnapped, but he knew someone—known mostly as a wraith—had rescued her. Reese wouldn't find out shit about the heroic bastard, because apparently the elusive phantom had the law under his control. For all intents and purposes, he moved with impunity and kept a tight lid on his involvement.

But there was no taming the street, and when monumental things happened, when powerful men ended up dead, word spread like wildfire.

"You're not Superman, you know." Alice tapped one foot. "You don't need to transfer your attention from Pepper to me."

"Actually, honey, I think I do." He shrugged. "Especially given what I saw today."

She stiffened up. "I'll never sleep with you."

Whoa. That was one hell of a mental leap she'd

taken. Rowdy grinned at her daring. "Sorry, doll, but I didn't ask."

She deflated. "Do you think I'm attractive?"

Damn it, he did not want to go down this road. When women asked these weird questions, there was never a right answer. "There's something about you, yeah." His gaze went over her slim body and delicate curves, then shot back to her face. "But Reese has already laid claim, in case you didn't notice."

Her frown eased away. "Not that you're asking."

"No."

"Because even if Reese wasn't interested—you are saying he's interested?"

"Without a doubt." How the hell had they gotten off track like this? Cash tugged, so Rowdy meandered farther across the yard.

Alice followed. "Even so, you wouldn't be. Not like that." She shaded her eyes. "May I ask you something, then? Since you're not interested that way?"

"Uh..." Feeling as if he'd lost control of the entire situation, Rowdy tried to distract her. "I think Cash is done. Maybe we should head in."

"Okay." She took the leash from him. "Come on, boy. Let's go get a treat."

Hopefully she was talking to the dog. Rowdy trudged along behind her, trying to figure out a way to get things back on track.

He started with: "About today—"

"I'm thirsty. Would you like a cola or something?" She opened the door and let Cash in. He made a beeline for the couch, so Rowdy followed. He liked the dog.

Hell, he liked Alice, too. But Alice confused the hell out of him. "Sure. Whatever you've got will be fine."

"Make yourself comfortable."

Cash must've thought she meant him, because he crawled up and over Rowdy's lap, his whole butt still wagging.

Grinning, he watched Alice go into the kitchen. Seconds later he heard ice clinking in a glass.

Figured Alice wouldn't just hand him a can.

She returned with two frosty colas…and sat close beside him on the couch.

Shit. She was by far the pushiest female—who didn't want sex—that he'd ever met. "Alice—"

She shoved a glass into his hand. "I'm not interested in you that way either."

No kidding. Anyone with eyes could see she was majorly hung up on Reese. "I know."

"But I do like you."

He toasted her with the cola and took a long drink.

"I want a man's perspective, and since we've already cleared the air, I should be able to talk to you without misunderstandings. You're not interested, I'm not interested and, hopefully, Reese is."

A man's perspective? On *what?* Dread crawled all over him. "Reese hasn't made it clear to you?"

She frowned in uncertainty. "He's kissed me a few times."

"There you go." And then, curious despite himself, Rowdy asked, "Only a few kisses, huh?"

She nodded. "Reese is a wonderful kisser."

"I'll take your word for it."

Cash army-crawled over to her and, with a smile, she gave him the promised treat, then stroked his back as he gnawed on it. "I'm concerned about…anything else."

Rowdy had a hard time following the conversation. "Anything else with Reese?"

"With him seeing me. I'm not sure… That is…" She

visibly screwed up her courage. “I’m afraid he’ll see me, all of me, and be disappointed.”

“Why would he be—”

“I’m not at all like your sister.”

Rowdy shook his head fast. “Let’s not go there.”

“Or the neighbors who hit on him.”

Now he lifted a brow. “Neighbors, plural?”

She didn’t seem to hear. “I’m just…me. Very average me.”

She was a galaxy away from average, but none of that had anything to do with body issues. Trying to relax, Rowdy set aside his glass and stretched out his legs. “Women always look at that the wrong way. When a guy’s attracted to a woman, he wants to see her naked. Period. Big boobs, small boobs—”

“Hey!”

“A little over or a little underweight, who cares? Naked is what we want.”

“We?”

“With women we’re interested in.” She continually tried to trip him up. “Not me with you, but Reese with you.”

She stared at him with rapt attention.

Rowdy shifted, cleared his throat. “He’s not looking for any imagined flaws, you know.”

“And if they’re not imagined?”

Jesus. What the hell was she hiding under there? He ran a hand over his head. “It’s not that he’s turned on in spite of a lack of curves, or too many curves, or… whatever.” He couldn’t begin to guess at her particular hang-up. “It’s that he doesn’t even see it. All he sees is a woman he wants, and the promise of getting busy.”

“In bed, you mean.”

“Or on the couch, the floor, in the shower or on the

table. Wherever." Hoping to tease her just a little, he said, "Guys aren't nearly as picky as women."

Alice took a second to chew on that. "It's not… Okay, let's say I'm fine with my body. I mean, it *is* average, like me, but I guess that's okay." Then she asked, "You're sure he won't mind that?"

Fighting off a smile wasn't easy. "Get naked, and I promise you Reese won't be complaining."

She thought some more, then went resolute. "Okay."

Just like that? Reese would owe him ten times over.

"The thing is," Alice continued, "I have…character flaws, too."

Compassion almost smothered him. Gently, Rowdy said, "No, you do not." Hell, reckless daring aside, she was about the sweetest woman he'd ever met.

"I do, but I hide them well."

Something else to discuss with Reese…maybe. Rowdy didn't like the idea of betraying Alice's trust. Maybe if she and Reese got together, Reese would be able to figure it out without his help.

"Look," Rowdy said, taking her hand. "It won't matter. Reese is an astute guy, and he's sensible. Whatever the problem is, try trusting him."

"Why do men always say that?"

"Because women are always distrustful?" And that, finally, brought him back to his reason for being here with her now. "What happened today?"

She shook her head. "It was nothing. Just a young lady that needed a helping hand."

"Bullshit."

"Rowdy Yates, do not curse at me."

"Then don't feed me a line." Sitting forward, forearms on his knees, he studied her. "Something went down. Something dirty. You stuck your little nose right into the middle of it. Was that planned or happenstance?"

"If I tell you, will you tell Reese?"

"Maybe." Not if he could convince her to tell Reese first. "Let me hear it, and then I'll decide."

Indecision held her for several heartbeats before she complied. "I see when other people are upset or scared. I don't know how, but I do."

"Like a sixth sense or a gut reaction." Rowdy had them, too—hell, that intuition had damn near bludgeoned him when he met Alice—so he didn't question her. "Go on."

"I saw her—her name is Cheryl—get passed from a van to a truck in the parking lot at the mall. It felt wrong to me, so I decided to follow her."

Rowdy listened as she relayed chilling details laced with foolhardy bravery. She could have been killed. If Hickson hadn't been alone in that room, if she hadn't gotten out before the other two men showed up, if she'd misfired the Taser—so many things could have gone wrong that it left him cold.

"I left Hickson in the room, trussed up with nylon restraints."

Rowdy could only stare at her.

"After I Tased him, while he was still stunned, I bound his wrists and ankles," she said defensively. "And then I had Cheryl fasten him to a pipe in the wall."

"He's not there anymore."

She paused. "No?"

"Two other goons showed up and freed him only minutes after you'd left." It hadn't been quite that close, but she deserved to worry. He watched her, waiting for her fear.

"Well," she said with a lack of concern that bordered

on relief, "I guess that takes care of one problem, then. I don't have to worry about sending someone to find him."

Like that would have been easy? Challenging her, Rowdy asked, "Who would you have sent?"

"I was thinking…you."

He sat back in surprise. *"Me?"*

She patted his hand. "Reese could handle it, of course, but he would have all kinds of questions, and he'd probably get annoyed, being that he's a detective and all that."

"What the hell was I supposed to do with him?"

As if sharing a confidence, she leaned closer, her expression sincere, guileless. "I was thinking you could question him. Maybe find out about any other people involved so we could get them all."

Get them all? She was a walking disaster waiting to happen. Rowdy tried to find words but came up blank. He pointed at her, couldn't form a rational sentence and stood to pace away.

"What?" she said, jumping up to follow him. "Should I have just ignored her?"

Finding his voice with a vengeance, Rowdy pivoted to face her. "You should have called someone! Reese or, sure, me. But *before* you did anything, not afterward."

Her voice rose with his. "By then it might've been too late."

"Hell, you could have called a cop, any cop!"

"You don't like cops!"

Temper ignited. *"I wasn't involved."*

They both stared at each other, equally stunned by the outburst.

Rowdy couldn't believe it when her mouth twitched.

As if to placate him, she patted his shoulder. "You're scaring Cash."

He glanced at the dog and saw Cash watching him… while still gnawing on his chew treat. The dog was attentive but not really worried.

He and Alice had that in common.

Fuck, fuck, *fuck*. Alice Appleton would make him insane in very little time.

He sucked in a breath, flexed his hands to loosen his fists and tried to get it together. In a much calmer voice, he asked, "Are you home for the rest of the night?"

Prim, composed, she folded her hands together. "Yes."

Good. He started around her. "Reese should be here any minute now. Tell him everything. He deserves to know."

Fleeing her insane effect on him, Rowdy started out. He didn't want to yell at Alice. He didn't want to dictate to her.

Damn it, how would anyone keep her safe when she had such disregard for her own hide?

Now she looked worried. "But…where are you going?"

"I have a late appointment with a real estate lawyer." And after that, he'd head to the bar and find some feminine company, preferably Avery. With any luck, she'd help him expend pent-up energy in the best way known to man—through grinding hot sex.

"What?" Alice trotted after him. "Real estate? Why?"

Anxious to be gone, Rowdy opened the door. "I'm buying a bar." He started out. "Lock this. And, so help me, Alice, you better stay put."

He pulled the door shut, waited until he heard it lock then took the steps two at a time.

He'd give her the rest of the evening to talk with Reese—and then he'd share his own report. Poor Reese.

He might not know it yet, but Alice was about to turn his world upside down.

WITH ROWDY GONE, Alice's courage faded, and she started shaking again. Talking with him had held off the aftereffects, giving her a different focus.

Now, it all came flooding back. That squalid little airless room, the soured breath of Hickson, how his body had flopped around while being Tasered…

Men had shown up right after she'd left.

What if she'd hesitated a little longer? What if Hickson had struggled or Cheryl had gotten more hysterical? She didn't have enough tools in her bag to handle those circumstances.

Her composure fractured, and she covered her face. Memories of another time slithered over her, a time when she hadn't helped anyone, not even herself.

She could never be that vulnerable again.

She needed to show more care, gain more skill. And maybe she should have called Reese. But he'd been far away, and she hadn't known Rowdy was following her.

So, really, this was partly his fault. If he'd told her, maybe…probably not, but *maybe* she would have asked for Rowdy's help.

She did trust Reese, both with issues of safety and with her heart. Not that she had a choice where her heart was concerned; he was far too appealing for her to keep any kind of distance.

Thinking of Reese took her along a natural course, imagining how he'd look when he returned, how he'd smell and feel and taste. She could really use a hug or two from him right now. Or a kiss.

Or…more.

Reese's unique brand of comfort was like an exciting drug, buoying her confidence, making her feel prettier, braver, less guilty. Thoughts of him beat back the panic and uncertainty.

If he would just come home and smile at her, she could stop stressing over "what-ifs" and all the possible scenarios that might have taken place if things had gone wrong. She could concentrate on how to proceed, how to use what she'd learned to assist others.

How long she paced and fretted, she couldn't say.

When Cash barked, she jumped a foot, then jumped again as a key sounded in the lock.

Reese.

Time for confessions. But first she had to somehow compose herself. She had to compartmentalize all the worries, sorting them to a corner of her brain as she'd learned to do to survive.

Should she bombard him with the day's events first thing? Should she start by telling him about her past so that he'd better understand? Should she—

He unbuttoned his shirt as he stepped in, and he looked so good, so solid and safe and amazingly sexy, Alice knew what she wanted first, what she needed right now.

She needed Reese.

CHAPTER TWELVE

EVEN WHILE BENDING to greet Cash, Reese noted Alice's scrutiny.

And her scraped knee.

He nodded at her leg. "What happened there?"

Eyes dark and warm, she looked down at her knee. "It's just a scratch." Slicking her little tongue over her upper lip, she ogled him. "You're taking off your shirt?"

"It's hot as hell out there, and getting grilled has a way of making it worse." But mostly it was hearing the details of Alice's abduction that left him sweating.

They'd talked briefly after finishing the coffee, when Peterson had gotten a phone call. Logan had only uncovered what was in the press—which meant what Alice herself had shared. Sketchy details. A few names. A time frame.

Logan had also confirmed that Alice did, indeed, have CCPs in order for her weapons. *Why does she need conceal and carry permits?* He had a million questions for her, but mostly he wanted to hold her.

She inched closer. "It went okay?"

It made Reese smile, how she stared fixedly at his chest, not his face. "It's fine. I'll be back to work Monday." How could she expect him to keep his hands to himself, to give her the time she'd requested, when she showed such naked hunger? "You've seen my chest before, honey."

She nodded and whispered, “You take my breath away.”

With a final pat for Cash, he stood again—and shrugged the shirt off. “Is that so?” He tossed it over the back of the couch.

“Yes.” Alice drifted her attention over him. “It’s the same as you seeing me without a shirt.”

“Not even close.” But damn, he couldn’t wait.

Her heated examination dipped down to his abs, and then snagged on his fly.

The way Alice looked at him was almost as good as a stroke. *Almost.*

“Alice,” he all but groaned. “Up here, please.”

She dragged her focus back to his face.

“I need to take Cash out. Change out of these clothes into something more comfortable.” And cooler. “And I could use something to eat. I haven’t had dinner yet and I’m—”

“I’m sorry.” Visibly trying to rein herself in, she nodded. “I didn’t mean to—”

“Don’t apologize.” Not for wanting him. “I like the way you welcome me home.” And damn it, with Alice there, he knew any place would feel like home.

Flustered, avoiding his gaze, she said, “Cash just came back in.” She sidestepped to the kitchen doorway. “I skipped dinner, too. But I can fix you a sandwich while you change—”

“Or you can tell me what you really want.” To hell with food or changing into shorts; he’d prefer to be naked with Alice.

She shot back around to face him, her expression… eager. “Could I?”

Heat rolled through him. “Absolutely. I have the evening free, so I’m all yours.” Slowly, remembering her in that white nightgown, how her small body curled into his through the night, Reese approached her. "I don't want to rush you. We can go slow." *Torture.* "But I know you enjoy kissing me."

"I really do," she said with feeling.

Lust deepened his voice. "You enjoyed sleeping beside me, too. I know you need more time, but how about we do those things again—together this time."

"Kiss…in bed?"

God, he hoped she was willing. "Sounds good to me." He touched the side of her face, slipped his fingers into her hair—and realized it was somehow different, the adjustment subtle but still evident. "You changed it?"

Big brown eyes dark with desire gazed at his mouth. "It?"

"Your hair."

"Yes." Her hands trailed over his shoulders, his pecs, back up again. "My hair," she murmured, as if she had no clue what they were talking about.

Half smiling, finding her so endearing in her sensual distraction, Reese cradled her head in his palm, stepped closer to breathe her in. "I like it."

"Reese?"

With a hand opened on the small of her back, he urged her body into fuller contact with his. No way would she miss his erection, but he didn't care. "Hmm?"

Cuddling her hips against him, she whispered, "I don't want to wait anymore."

Reese closed his eyes, fighting the urge to take her to the floor right now. That little catch in her voice almost did him in.

When had he ever suffered this level of lust? *Never.* Only with Alice.

He did not want to rush through this first time with her.

"Do you suppose Cash is distracted enough?" Once

he got her in bed, he wanted to give her all his considerable concentration—and he wanted to make it very good for her, so good that she'd want many repeat performances.

"I'll give him another treat." Alice rushed off before Reese could stop her, came back with two treats, and after a quick pat to Cash's head, presented him with the gifts.

The dog's ears went up, and his eyes gleamed with gluttony.

"There." Standing again, expression expectant, Alice faced him. She bit her bottom lip, shifted her stance. "Should we go to the bedroom?"

Reese didn't understand the sudden turnaround, but he wasn't about to question it. "If that's what you want."

"I do." She snagged his hand and hauled him down the hallway at a near trot. "I thought about you all day, in between shopping and manicures and talking with Pepper."

She rushed them into her bedroom.

Closing the door, Reese turned her to face him. "You enjoyed yourself?"

"What?"

"With Pepper." He assumed all women enjoyed shopping, but Alice was unlike any woman he'd ever known.

Her face went bright red. "How was your day?"

Interesting reaction. Had she posed her own question to keep from answering his? "Just fine."

"Good." She looked away.

Had Pepper said something to upset her? God knew the woman could be pushy—

Alice reached for his belt. "Let's chitchat later."

Talk about pushy. It wasn't like Alice to be so assertive. He couldn't help but wonder what had brought about the change.

Catching her hands, Reese said softly, "Slow down, honey. I've been waiting for this forever—"

"We haven't known each other that long."

"Feels like forever all the same." He tried a smile that hurt, he was so hard. "Kissing first, okay?" He took her mouth before she could say anything more. Kissing her was a unique pleasure. "Open up for me, Alice."

On a gasp, she did as asked and Reese sank in, tasting her, stroking with his tongue. He angled in for a deeper kiss, both of them already panting…and Alice's hands returned to his belt again.

He caught them, brought them up to his shoulders then went to work on the buttons to her blouse. Kissing her jaw, her throat, he murmured, "You need to catch up."

She went very still, her fingers clenching, digging into his shoulders.

He loved it.

When the shirt was open enough, Reese slipped his hand inside and…over her left breast.

Her hands fell away from him, her breath hitching as he touched her.

Ah, God, she felt nice. Small, firm, her nipple drawn tight. "Perfect."

Putting his other hand into her shirt, too, he cuddled both breasts, brushed his thumbs over her nipples. Watching her face, he lightly caught each one and tugged with the gentlest touch.

She moaned before shrugging the shirt off her shoulders.

It fell to the floor.

Cheeks flushed and her bright gaze locked on his face, Alice stood there.

Her bra was a surprise. Sheer beige edged by black lace. In a voice that sounded like gravel, Reese whispered, "You little tease." Never had he suspected Alice would wear such sensual underwear.

Breasts shimmying with her fast breaths, she bit her lip in nervousness. "I like nice underwear," she explained.

"Great. I like it, too." He especially liked it on her.

Would her panties match? He couldn't wait to find out.

"You've been walking around in front of me, wearing this sexy stuff without me knowing." Nothing about Alice was ever expected, so he should have realized. She hid so much behind her straitlaced facade.

Knowing she hid *this* really turned him on—maybe because he'd be the only man aware of it.

Dragging the back of his knuckles down the silky skin of her rib cage, over her narrow waist and flat belly, Reese touched the closure to her capris.

Senses heightened, lust pounding through him, he opened the snap.

"Rowdy said you'd like my body," she suddenly blurted.

Freezing, his brain going blank, Reese stared at her. His mouth opened, but nothing came out.

Alice just watched him, waiting for confirmation.

In a croak, Reese demanded, "Rowdy said *what?*"

Maybe because outraged disbelief filled his tone, Alice sucked in a breath and shook her head. "Never mind." She nodded at his hands on her waistband. "Go on."

Go on... She had to be kidding! "Not on your life."

A red haze filtered into his vision. He took a step back, thoughts of mangling Rowdy uppermost in his mind—

And Alice shoved down her zipper. "It's not what you think!" Hastily, she worked the capris down over her narrow hips.

Even in a rage, he noted that the panties did indeed match. Minuscule, more lace than anything else, barely covering her…

"I was worried about you wanting me, and Rowdy assured me you would. That's all I meant."

His brain throbbed at the dual assault of raging jealousy and red-hot lust.

She kicked the pants aside and stood tall, stoic—insecure. "So…do you?"

God Almighty. Could a woman be more appealing?

He didn't think so.

Unable to get his gaze off her body, Reese took in every delicate curve, each tempting swell. Her thighs were long, trim, her bone structure delicate. "You shouldn't be discussing things like that with Rowdy." He shook his head, amending that statement. "With *any* other man. If you have questions, come to me."

"I had questions *about* you." She shifted her feet, laced her fingers together. "Reese, I'm in an agony of suspense here. You're just staring at me. Do something, please."

"All right." Later, he'd talk to her about inappropriate conversations and timing disclosures. Hauling her up to him, he took her mouth with all the hunger clawing inside him. She wilted against him—for about three seconds. Then she became a very active participant, her hands all over him, her body squirming against his.

She sucked at his tongue, teased him with her own and, this time, when she went after his belt, he helped her.

The second she got his slacks open, she slipped a small warm hand inside.

"Alice." A weak protest at best.

Curling her fingers around him, she kissed his shoulder, his chest, lightly bit his right pectoral muscle. "I could just eat you up," she whispered.

Reese tried to tune out the visual her words provoked. If he went there, he'd be a goner for sure. It was enough, more than enough, feeling her small hand holding him, squeezing, stroking—

"Alice…baby, stop. I'm a hair away from detonation." Catching her wrists, Reese drew them behind her and held them captive with one hand. He searched her face for any signs of uneasiness. "Okay?"

Eyes heavy, lips moist, she nodded. "You really are big."

Swallowing became difficult. "Yeah, but we'll be a perfect fit." He leaned down and drew her nipple into his mouth, dampening the material of her bra.

Her back arched on a soft cry.

Eyeing his handiwork, seeing the now wet material cling to her nipple, Reese said, "So pretty." He moved to her other breast.

Voice going high, Alice said, "It's a front closure!"

Hint, hint?

He smiled around the lust and, using two fingers, opened her bra. Pale, smooth, high, her breasts were enough to waylay his good intentions. Releasing her wrists, Reese hurriedly stripped the bra off her, then went to one knee.

Her hand settled in his hair, stroking, curious, a little unsure. "What are you going to do?"

"The same thing I did to your nipples. But—" he

touched the tip of one finger to the silky triangle of her itty-bitty panties "—here."

"Oh."

Leaning into her, Reese used his tongue to stroke, opened his mouth over her.

"Oh."

With both hands he palmed her sweet little backside to keep her from moving away. Her scent was indescribable, and he nuzzled closer, made a hungry sound of need.

"I..." A moan, soft and deep, sounded seconds before she wove her hands into his hair, holding him closer. "I want a turn, too."

He'd never survive her special brand of sweet torture. "Not a problem." Unless he died of pleasure.

Knowing he had to hurry it along or it'd be over before he got started, Reese caught the tiny waistband of her panties and slowly dragged them down her slender legs to unveil her.

God, she was sexy, standing before him in a wealth of mingled nervousness and excitement. Her soft inner thighs drew him, so he kissed each one, moving higher and higher, sucking gently on the sleek skin, trailing with his tongue.

When he was just shy of tasting her without the barrier of her panties, Alice wailed, "Not fair!"

He cupped a hand over her. "How's that?"

"I want you naked, too. I want to do...*things* to you, too."

He didn't want to give up his exploration of her body, but he also didn't want her so tense. Standing, he asked, "You want me to strip off my slacks?"

She gave a sharp nod. "Yes, please."

It seemed impossible to find humor in the middle of

such lust, but there it was, tugging at his smile, making him want to hug her close and laugh.

Instead, he toed off his shoes, saying, “I’m not modest, you know.” He bent to remove his socks. “There’s no reason to frown.”

“I’m concentrating.”

On his dick, yeah, he knew that. Hell, he felt her hot gaze all but penetrating his slacks. Reese teased her, saying, “They didn’t dub me ‘Bare it all Bareden’ without reason.”

“So, get to the baring part.”

“Such impatience.” And damn it, he started to feel a little unnerved by her intense scrutiny. He’d never done a striptease. Before Alice, sex had been a natural progression, without all the fanfare and discussion. A kiss, a touch, clothes gone, penetration, completion.

Now, with her, it felt like so much more. Important. Special.

Somewhat uncomfortable with that thought, he removed his wallet and cell phone to put on the nightstand, then shucked off his slacks, taking his boxers off at the same time.

Nipples tight and knees locked, she parted her lips on a sharp breath. “Oh, my.”

Reese started to lift his arms, to make some silly comment about giving her what she wanted, but she turned suddenly and scampered up to the center of the bed. His heart nearly stopped over that particular view.

Going to her back, Alice held out her arms. “Enough foreplay. I need you.”

Foreplay hadn’t factored in. He wanted to explore every inch of her because every inch was so enticing. But Reese found himself taking the two big steps needed to reach her. In the back of his mind, he reminded himself to not forget the condom.

But everywhere else, with every other fiber of his being, he immersed himself in Alice's unique sensuality, her scent and taste and her beautiful, slender body.

Half covering her, locking his teeth at the feel of her breasts cushioning his chest, Reese stroked down to her hip. "No rushing, Alice. I need to know you're ready."

"I am." She clutched at his shoulders. "I promise."

"How about I see for myself?"

He kissed her lips, her cheek, moving his hand over to her lower belly. She kept her thighs tightly pressed together, her eyes wide on his face, watching him.

"Open your legs for me."

Her nails stung his shoulders—but after a few seconds, she eased her hold…and spread her legs.

Reese teased her ear with damp kisses. "Nice, Alice. Thank you."

She held her breath while he slowly trailed his fingertips down, over her pubic hair, lower.

"Breathe, honey."

"Can't." She tightened everywhere, waiting.

Slipping a single finger over her, Reese parted her, touched deeper until he found her wet and hot. Pushing in, he whispered against her jaw, "What about now?"

She gasped in a breath, then let it out on a moan.

"That's it." Small and tight, she clamped around him—and got wetter. His erection strained against her thigh; he hurt with wanting her. But more than his own pleasure, he wanted hers.

First. Complete. A done deal.

He withdrew, pressed in again, gauging his moves by the raggedness of her breathing. Nuzzling his way down to her breasts, he asked, "What about another finger?" and as he drew in her nipple, he pushed in a second finger, filling her, loving her reaction.

Groaning deep in her throat, she lifted her hips and let her knees fall apart. He sucked harder, nipped carefully with his teeth and brought his thumb up to touch her clitoris.

"Oh, God." She moved with him, her head back, eyes closed. "Reese. That's… I'm…"

It was a wonderful thing to render Alice Appleton speechless.

Keeping up the rhythm of his thumb, Reese moved to her other breast, drawing on her easily, gently, curling his tongue around her. Her scent intensified; the sweetness of her skin and hair, the hotter musk of her arousal.

"This," he told Alice, moving his tongue over her nipple, "would feel even better between your legs."

Taking him by surprise, she arched up, her mouth open on a silent cry, her eyes squeezed tight. Locking her hands in his hair, she held him there, her hips writhing, her wetness bathing his fingers as she came.

It was so hot, so unexpected that Reese knew he was a goner. The second she uncoiled and her tension seeped away, he sat up and grabbed for his wallet. Hands shaking, he opened a condom and rolled it on.

But when he looked back at Alice, he caught her dazed smile, and he had to kiss her again. Then once more. "You are incredible."

"I am limp."

He carried her hand down to his cock, wrapped her fingers around him. Heat washed over him. "Limp is okay," he promised in a low growl, "as long as you're still with me."

"I'm very much with you," she purred back, stroking

him once, twice. Her thumb brushed up and over him, and he shuddered clean down to his toes.

Pulling her hand away again, he moved over her. "Next time," he promised her roughly, "I'll be a little less voracious." He settled between her legs, using a knee to open her even more.

"I hope not." Holding his face, looking into his eyes, she wrapped her legs around him.

He saw so much emotion in her gaze, both wonder and excitement, that it should have made him uneasy.

It didn't, not with Alice.

"You like me a little lost, is that it?" He positioned himself, her creamy wetness bathing the head. Hot. Slippery. How the hell could he still form a coherent thought?

"I think," Alice whispered, going serious, "that I like you any way I can have you."

That did it. He kissed her hard—and thrust in.

It was a tight fit. Always. But with Alice being so small and delicate…he thought he might die from the exquisite pleasure of her squeezing around him.

She'd gone still beneath him, breath suspended, her nails again leaving half-moons in his shoulders.

He knew she needed a minute—a minute he didn't have. He braced on his forearms, jaw clenched, shoulders bunching as he fought for control. Tension squeezed around him like a vise, and he knew he'd break at any second.

"Reese?"

Her tiny voice pained him; he held himself as immobile as he could, but no way could he reply.

Her puffing breaths met his lips. She shifted a little, probably trying to accommodate him but only inciting him more.

It felt as if lust boiled inside him, churning, rising.

"Reese?" she whispered again, this time with a question. He heard her swallow, felt her deliberately ease. She let out a long, broken breath. *"Reese."*

Well, now, that sounded different.

He met her dark, smoldering gaze, saw her face flushed with need—and realized that she was with him after all.

He withdrew slowly, watching her, fascinated with her shuddering reaction. He knew he stretched her, that as he slowly sank back in she felt a measure of discomfort.

It was there in her halting breath. In the way she arched and tensed. How her lips parted and her thighs strained against him.

But he saw the rising pleasure, too.

God, she was amazing.

Keeping the rhythm slow but steady, he kissed her jaw, the corner of her mouth. With one hand, he reached beneath her hips, positioning her just enough that each penetration stroked along her clitoris—making her wetter, hotter.

Anticipation showed in her heavy-lidded gaze as she touched his shoulders, his chest—and finally locked eyes with him.

Wondering if he'd ever tire of having Alice watch him in just that way, he drove deeper, rocking them both, wringing a small cry from her.

He went still deep inside her. "Okay?"

She licked her lips and nodded. "Again…ah…"

Reese felt her pulsing around him.

"Again, please."

The break in her voice told him that she was close to another climax, and suddenly he wanted that more than he wanted his own release. Leaning into her, Reese moved harder, faster, heat pouring off him, her scent and her escalating cries filling his head.

Suddenly she clenched, her slim body bowing hard on a deep, throaty groan.

Reese could literally feel her tighten around his cock, feel the milking spasms of her climax. The sounds she made, raw and real and exciting, pushed him right over the edge.

He gathered her close, put his face in her neck and ground out his own release.

AN INDETERMINATE AMOUNT of time later, Reese awoke, aware of Cash snuffling against the bottom of the closed door. Still sluggish both in body and mind, he lifted his head and looked at Alice.

She rested on the bed beside him, not curled close as was usually the case with women, but sprawled out, exhausted, limp.

Naked head to toe.

The covers completely off the bed.

Tumbled around her face, resembling a halo, her soft brown hair reflected the muted light of sundown through the open window.

But sweet as she might be, Alice was far from angelic.

Thank God.

Now without that haze of blinding lust, Reese studied her body. Slim, pale. Intrinsically female.

Her nipples were the same soft pink as her lips.

And thinking of lips…he sat up carefully so as not to disturb her, soaking up the sight of her, her belly, her thighs—and between them.

So damn pretty.

Again he noted the scrape and bruise on her knee. Had she fallen? He didn't wonder about it long, not when she had that leg bent, showing him everything.

Using just his fingertips, Reese touched the soft triangle of hair. Much more of that and he'd be on her again.

Instead, he transferred the touch to her pale belly, teased over a sharp hip bone, along a rounded hip.

Alice stirred, mumbled an incoherent sound and turned to her side away from him.

Why, thank you, Alice.

She had a great ass. Later, when he didn't have Cash at the door, he would spend more time on that curvy little tush.

On *all* of her.

The more Reese studied her, the more he liked what he saw. The more special she seemed.

At thirty, he'd seen plenty of naked women, some with truly remarkable bodies, some beyond beautiful, all of them sexy.

None of them compared.

He couldn't pinpoint what it was about Alice that set her apart. It wasn't just her trim body or sincere face, her nurturing nature or cautious approach. It was…everything. Every inch of her, every facet of her character.

Cash whined, urging Reese from the bed. He didn't want Alice to wake just yet. In fact, it astounded him that she slept on. He knew her to be ultra-aware. The fact that he could sneak around the room without disturbing her must mean she trusted him, at least a little.

He wanted her to trust him a lot.

Grabbing up his wallet and cell phone from the nightstand, his boxers and slacks from the floor, he eased the door open, using his knee to keep Cash from bounding in.

"Shhh," he whispered to the dog. "You're okay. We didn't leave you."

Cash leaped and twisted and woofed a few times, as if he'd been days without a visitor instead of a few hours.

It remained a challenge, reassuring the dog after finding him abandoned in a sealed box in the middle of the road.

"Love your enthusiasm, boy. And the fact that I don't see any puddles. Give me a second, and I'll take you out."

Cash amped up the excitement over that idea, so much so that he made it nearly impossible for Reese to pull on his slacks.

Clearly, the dog enjoyed being outdoors. Perhaps it was time for him to consider a house instead of the apartment. He could afford it. The apartment was just easier, or at least it had been up until he'd rescued Cash.

The dog deserved room to run, maybe in a big backyard. He'd have to give it some thought.

In nothing more than his slacks, Reese snuck out the front door with Cash on a leash. Though it wasn't entirely nightfall yet, security lights flickered on over the parking lot. Reese strode out to the requisite tree, propped a bare shoulder against the bark and gave Cash enough leash to do his business. While he watched the dog sniff an imaginary trail, his thoughts wandered to Alice.

He'd meant to ask her about her day, to find out if she and Pepper had gone shooting or if—with any luck—they'd stuck to shopping. He'd planned on dinner, conversation, a little necking to ease her into things....

Alice had sidelined those plans easily enough.

The second he'd walked through the door, he'd known something was up. Amazing how she could remain so secretive about some things but didn't even try to hide her attraction to him.

She'd seemed almost frantic to have him.

And he'd loved it.

Once she awoke he'd fix her dinner, shower with her and then take her right back to bed for a slower, more thorough taste. It didn't matter that he'd buried himself inside her not that long ago. Already he burned with need, especially knowing she remained in the bed, so relaxed—and so naked.

Yeah, once she awoke, the last thing he'd want to do was talk about shopping.

With that decision made, Reese pulled out his cell phone. Better to get the deets from Rowdy so he could concentrate on more important things with Alice.

Namely, her sudden decision to move their relationship into scorching-hot intimacy. He didn't know why she'd suddenly lost inhibition and caution, but he was more than grateful.

CHAPTER THIRTEEN

THE FOOD SUCKED. Another thing he'd address once he got all the legalities out of the way. Not that he'd expected much from the bar, at least not in the way of food.

Leaving the dry crust of the meager sandwich on his plate, Rowdy finished off a pickle, the last chip and turned on the stool, elbows back on the bar, to peruse the room. Right now, it wasn't that busy. But he knew, despite the lack of ambience and finer amenities, they'd soon have a crowd that would stay 'til closing.

Hard-core drinkers liked a dive as much as, sometimes more than, an upscale joint.

Once he took over, he'd keep it casual, Rowdy thought. At fifteen-hundred square feet, the building had enough room to add a few things, like billiards and a jukebox, especially once he got rid of the pole dancing. He'd offer the ladies, all three of them part-time, full-time positions instead. Once fixed up, the parking area would be big enough for eighteen cars. The adjoining parking lot, with another twenty spots, had proposed a reasonable agreement for usage.

He planned to offer affordable drinks with a limited but fresh menu. A variety of sandwiches, maybe chili, a soup of the day, fries.

Few came for the food.

But if he opened earlier in the day, that could change.

And why not? He'd already looked into the liquor license. Might as well ensure he had a food permit, as well.

First he'd have to pass the background check that came with the liquor license. The idea of someone poking around in his private life, even in a cursory way, sent itchy alarms down his neck. He had nothing to hide—nothing, that is, that should prevent him from keeping the license.

Rather than continue stewing on things he couldn't change, Rowdy searched the room until he spotted Avery. Far as distractions went, she was perfect. He watched her and knew she made a point of not looking at him.

Too bad.

He didn't want to go home alone. Not tonight.

Some nights were just like that.

Restlessness gnawed on him, amplified by old memories. He needed to be busy, but right now he had nothing more to do. Unfortunately, doing nothing alone was not the same as doing nothing with someone.

Anyone.

But preferably Avery.

She strode past him on her way to the kitchen. Rowdy stopped her with a hand on her arm. And just that, such an impersonal touch, sparked a fire inside him. He stayed silent, enjoying the feel of her smooth warm skin.

The skin of her…arm. God, he needed to get laid.

Pausing, she looked at his hand, then up to his face. "How was your sandwich?"

"Stale bread."

"I'm not surprised. Our so-called cook doesn't know his butt from a biscuit." She leaned closer. "He's not all that conscientious about cleaning either." The whispered words sent her breath warm across his ear.

A shudder ran over him. He couldn't wait to feel her breath in other, more interesting places. "When I take over, that'll change."

She leaned away to scrutinize him. "So you're serious about that?"

"Already have it in the works." As long as he passed the background check. "I'm serious about you being the bartender, too."

She chewed the corner of her mouth, considering him, then surprised him by dragging him away from the bar and toward a corner table.

He went willingly, curious what she'd do, what she had to say.

With privacy assured, she turned to face him. "In most places, the bartender is the most coveted job. So why me?"

Suspicion? He supposed she had reason. "You're competent."

"You barely know me."

But I want you. Rowdy shook his head. "I'm a good judge of character." And she had character in spades. "Bartending isn't easy. Other than the financial management, it's the most important job, so don't think I'm doing you a huge favor."

"I'm aware." She held up a hand and ticked off points on her fingers. "You stand for hours on end. You get hit on in rapid succession, with the pushiest, most determined men also being the most inebriated. Drugs are rampant behind the bar. You have to have a great memory. You—"

He put a finger to her mouth—and somehow felt the touch in his dick.

Thinking of her mouth and his dick at the same time left him muddled. He had it bad.

Shaking his head, Rowdy tried to clear the lust. “Back up to the drugs.”

Somewhat dazed, her plump lips still pressed to his finger, she stared up at him.

Maybe now would be a good time to kiss her again. Keeping her gaze locked with his, he eased closer.

Suddenly she blinked hard, drew two breaths and took a step back so that his hand fell away. “You didn’t know?”

A lost opportunity. He never should have hesitated.

“About the drugs?” Sure, he suspected. Drugs were a problem everywhere, in every bar. But specifically here? He didn’t doubt it. “Enlighten me.”

Instead, she pursed her mouth. “I don’t think so. You aren’t the owner yet, and I don’t want to cause a firestorm and then get stuck in the middle of it.”

“See, this is why you’ll make a great bartender. You’re circumspect.”

“I’m not an idiot,” she corrected.

Rowdy eyed her sedate clothing and approved. “As to getting hit on, I doubt most bartenders have to worry about that.” Avery, with her petite figure and that sweet face, would have her hands full fending off the drunks. “It’s nice that you dress in a way to discourage the hopeful.”

“You included?”

He ignored that. Damn it, he was hopeful. “And I assume you can learn the job?”

“Already know it inside and out.”

Fascinating. “I take it you’ve worked as a bartender before?”

"Last job, yep. And I tried to get the job here, but instead I ended up the barback."

"Barback?"

"You know, the one who stocks the bar, keeps the ice bin filled, cuts up the fruit and garnishes, cleans the glasses…."

"I know what it is." But it surprised him that she'd been hired for the position.

"For this place," she added, "the barback also needed to supply protection for the bartender." She lifted her shoulders. "I fell short in that category, so within three days I was told I had to waitress, which for the others also includes dancing that stupid pole. I refused that part, but I'm more competent than the others, so it's allowed."

Disbelief slammed into Rowdy. Someone had expected her to play bodyguard? Asinine. "What happened?"

"Which part?"

He growled his frustration. "The part where you fell short as protection." He already knew Avery wouldn't be caught sliding around on a pole for the delectation of drunks.

She hesitated some more. "How do I know this won't go any farther?"

"You can have my word, if that counts for anything."

For what felt like a lifetime, she studied his face. Rowdy resisted the urge to narrow his eyes in irritation. He was many things, most of them shady as shit.

But he wasn't a liar.

Finally she nodded. "The drugs I mentioned? Well, some big guy—I think probably a supplier—came in on my third night, and he was really furious about something. Looked like he'd already gone up against a Mack truck, and he had his sights set on Dougie."

"That's the bartender here now, right?" Rowdy was familiar with the wiry, hyper guy usually serving up drinks. He had dark, thick hair held in a stubby ponytail, and sported a stud in one ear. Despite the foulness of the bar and the sketchy clientele, he smiled a lot.

"None other."

"Someone came after him?"

"With a switchblade." Avery shuddered. "And I was supposed to look out for him."

The constriction of rage and concern had Rowdy straightening to his full height. "Some dumb fuck actually expected *you* to go up against a blade?"

The language filled her blue eyes with censure. "Obviously I'm not physically equipped for a conflict like that."

"You're not equipped for a conflict with a pillow!" She was small and soft and—

Cutting off his observation, she said, "So I called 911." Her mouth flattened. "*Big* mistake."

The concern continued to throb inside him. "You didn't get hurt?"

"I almost got fired!"

From this dive? Big frickin' deal. Might've been doing her a favor. Except then he wouldn't have met her, and now, having met her, he *needed* to have her. "I take it cops are unwelcome."

"Very much so—because of the drugs as much as anything else." She rubbed at her temples. "Dougie didn't get hurt too much. A cut on his arm that required some stitches. Once I yelled that the cops were coming, the guy took off."

"Thank God." If the dude had turned his rage on

Avery instead, they might not be here talking now. "Does he still come around?"

"The knife wielder? No. Disappeared." She gave him another look. "You should really find out more about the inner workings here before you tie yourself to this place. I have a feeling that once you stop the drugs…" She fumbled midsentence, staring at him with those big blue eyes the color of the sky. "That is…you would put a halt to that, wouldn't you?"

A tendril of her silky red hair drew his fingers. He toyed with it.

He wanted to toy with her. In bed.

"Count on it." He would run a legit business even if it killed him. He didn't particularly want to give the cops a reason to hang around either.

Avery slumped in relief. "Then I'm glad you plan to take over. And if you want me to bartend, count me in. I'd be more than happy to quit my second job."

"Second job?"

"You didn't think I supported myself working here, did you?"

There was a lot he didn't know about Avery Mullins—but he wanted to find out.

"I'm better than Dougie, and more honest, so I'll expect a raise over what he makes. But I don't need a barback, so you'd still be ahead."

He'd be protecting her, so he shrugged an agreement.

"You're going to cause a ruckus, you know. There are a lot of regulars who get their supply from Dougie. They won't like being cut off."

Rowdy wondered if the drugs covered more than the recreational variety but didn't want to entangle Avery further. "I'll take care of it."

She smiled, and her happiness stroked over him.

Still fingering that loose curl, Rowdy stepped closer, lowered his voice intimately. "Why don't you come back to my place after work?" Wasn't much of a place, but it had a bed, so…

Her eyes widened. As if she only then realized that he had her hair wrapped around his finger, she frantically freed herself. "Sorry, no."

Rowdy fought back the expanding discontent. "Tomorrow?" Knowing what she'd say, he asked, "Day after?"

"I can't, Rowdy. I'm sorry."

Okay, time for straight talk. It was that kind of night, the kind where heading home alone wasn't an option.

The kind where lousy memories crawled in and refused to quiet—unless he found a way to block them. So far, sex worked the best.

He stepped around Avery, cutting off her escape, and then casually—without threat—corralled her into the corner. "I'm taking someone home with me tonight."

She made a face at his confidence. "So cocky."

"I like it when you talk dirty."

Swatting at him, she said, "You assume it'll be that easy for you, huh?"

"With you? No. With another woman?" He shrugged. "But I'd prefer it be you."

Something flashed over her features, something like indignation, disbelief. Maybe sorrow.

She lifted her chin. "And if it's not me?"

He wouldn't lie to her. "Then it *will* be someone else."

Anger tinged with hurt narrowed her eyes. "Go on, then."

When she hurriedly ducked away, Rowdy let her leave. He felt the loss even as he tried to deny it.

Screw it.

Eventually he'd win her over. He'd uncover her reasons for refusing, and he'd figure out a way around her objections.

In the meantime, he eyed his other options. A slinky brunette caught his attention. Her slow smile and approving once-over issued a sensual invitation.

Yeah, it was a hell of a thing, but he was male through and through. He wanted Avery, would have been happiest with her company—but he wasn't immune to a raunchy sexual offer. Not if it'd get him through the night.

He started to move toward the woman when his cell phone rang. He pulled it from his pocket and glanced at the number.

Reese.

Blowing out a breath, Rowdy put his needs on hold and accepted the call. "Hey, Reese."

"Rowdy. How'd it go today?"

Shit, shit, shit. Obviously Alice hadn't come clean yet. If she had, Reese wouldn't sound so congenial. Had Reese been delayed, or had Alice balked at sharing? "You're with Alice now?"

"At the apartment, yes."

Feeling his way, Rowdy asked, "What did she tell you?"

Reese let a beat of silence pass. "We didn't do much talking before she…fell asleep."

Asleep, huh? He checked his watch and saw that it wasn't that late yet. Interesting. So the duty of a recap would fall to Rowdy.

Rubbing the back of his neck, he turned away from the brunette and moved to a quiet booth where no one could overhear him. "It'd be good if you were sitting down."

Grim resolve sounded in Reese's tone. "I'm outside with Cash."

Away from Alice. Maybe that would be better. Reese would have a minute to collect himself before he confronted her. Alice personified frustration, but she had tender feelings. Rowdy wouldn't want to see her hurt by angry words. "I suggest you brace yourself. It's not good."

A low curse, and then: "Tell me."

Doing exactly that, Rowdy related all the details of Alice's caper, leaving nothing out. With each word, Reese grew increasingly grave.

Rowdy understood. Ms. Alice Appleton had a knack for driving protective men insane.

When he finished the tale, Rowdy asked, "Are you going to wake her up for a chat?"

"As soon as Cash finds a spot suitable for his preferences."

Picturing that helped Rowdy find a smile. "Your dog does like to smell every blade of grass."

"Yes."

The impatience he heard was *almost* funny. "Good luck, Reese. I have a feeling you're going to need it."

"Go fuck yourself." But then, being the fair sort, Reese added, "I appreciate this, Rowdy. All of it. If she'd been on her own today and something had happened—"

"She escaped unscathed." How, Rowdy still didn't know. Dumb luck, or…skill? "By the way, Alice is from the area. She was living here when she got kidnapped and moved back after she got away. I didn't find out much, but apparently she was rescued by some mysterious vigilante with inconceivable connections."

"It just gets better and better," Reese growled.

"That's all I have for now, but if I find out anything

else, you'll be the first to know." After hanging up, Rowdy turned and found the brunette still waiting. She wouldn't be a challenge.

She wasn't Avery.

But she was better than sleeping alone on this disturbing night, with only his disquiet for company.

REESE STEWED IN turbulent silence. An early evening breeze blew over his face and bare chest, but it did little to cool his escalating temper.

What the hell had she been thinking?

Did he even know Alice? Did he know what she was capable of? How far she'd go?

What if she'd shot someone? Rowdy had said she'd been carrying her gun, but supposedly only Tasered the thug.

A fucking thug. Supposedly a man capable of coercing a woman. A woman Alice had "rescued."

His eyes burned, and his heart punched against his ribs.

What if the guy had overpowered her? She could be locked in a room right now, at the mercy of a brutal goon, and how would Reese have found her?

He'd stupidly thought she was shopping! His biggest concern had been Pepper's influence.

Cash finally came loping back, his tongue hanging out, his tail wagging. Anxious to talk to Alice, to say God-knew-what, Reese decided to head in. Somehow he'd get to the truth, all of it, every second of her past and whatever she had planned for the future.

He turned with a long stride—and almost collided with Nikki.

"Hey there, Reese." Dressed in heels, a tight mini-skirt and a halter, Nikki looked dressed to kill. Smiling at him, she flipped back her long blond hair.

"Evening." He tried to keep walking.

She blocked his way. "I haven't seen you jog lately." She stared at his slacks. Or more specifically, the fly of his slacks.

"I've been busy." He was busy *now.*

Moving closer, she touched his right biceps. Voice throaty, breath tinged with alcohol, she whispered, "It's a nice night, isn't it?"

With his current mood? No, it was a piss-poor night. "Pleasant enough." Locking his jaw, Reese tried to step around her.

Cash came up alongside him, sniffed at the hem of Nikki's skirt, and she reacted as if a skunk climbed her leg. "Oh, my God, shoo! Get away." She swatted at the dog's face. Yelping, Cash cowered away in fear.

Furious, Reese knelt down to the dog. "It's okay, buddy. She won't hurt you." Tail tucked, his body curled tight and his brown eyes sad and watchful, Cash huddled as close as he could get to Reese's side.

Reese stroked his back, kissed the top of his head. "Shhh. It's okay now."

Nikki realized what she'd done. "I wasn't trying to hurt him," she explained. "It's just…I don't want dog hair on my clothes."

Reese barely managed a nod.

"What's wrong with him, anyway?" Nikki gave a nervous laugh. "The way he's carrying on, you'd think I beat him or something."

Regaining his feet, keeping one hand on Cash's head, Reese stared down at Nikki. "He's a rescue." Repressed fury had him talking through his teeth. "Someone had left him for dead, so no telling what he suffered before that. Probably abuse."

Again she chuckled nervously. "I'm sorry. Really."

"If being near the dog is that big of a problem for you, avoid me when I have him out." Preferably she could avoid him *always*. But he wasn't quite rude enough to say that. "Now, if you'll excuse me."

"Reese, wait." She put one hand on his bare chest, the other at his side right above the waistband of his slacks. "Really, I am sorry. I've never been around animals much, and I can't say I'm a fan. But I would never deliberately hurt an animal. I'm not a monster."

Reese believed her. Taking his bad mood out on Nikki wouldn't accomplish anything. "Thanks."

"Maybe I could..." She looked at Cash with loathing as her fingers stroked through Reese's chest hair. "I could probably try to get used to him."

"There's no point." Beyond common courtesy and social civility, he had no interest in Nikki.

"But Reese..." Her thumb touched his right nipple. "Let me make it up to you."

"Yeah," he said, catching her wrist with his free hand. "Let's not do that."

"Please." She licked her bottom lip—and went after his nipple again.

How she thought that was going to help matters, he couldn't guess. He looked down at Cash and found the dog watching with a wealth of expression. "I should get Cash inside."

"But I want us to get along. You know I do."

She wanted more than that, but it wouldn't happen. "You're on your way out, and you've been drinking."

"Only a little." She leaned into him, her breasts to his chest, his hand holding her wrist caught between them. "And I was just heading to the club. I'm happy to stay in if you're…free."

"I'm not," he said as gently as he could. He suspected she operated under liquid courage. Sometimes two drinks could take away a lot of inhibitions or demolish good judgment. "And you shouldn't be driving."

"See." Now she pressed her pelvis against him, too. "I should stay home with you instead."

"Reese, there you are."

Alice's high voice startled him and Nikki both. They turned as one, and there she stood…barely dressed, her hair a little wild, her face pinched with antagonism.

Cash leaped toward her—and despite her obvious irritation, Alice knelt to receive him with a generous amount of petting.

Knowing how she felt about the dog, Reese was thankful she hadn't been out during Nikki's mishap.

Nikki looked at Alice, looked at Reese and turned back to Alice. "Well, well, Alice. You're all out of sorts tonight."

Standing with Cash at her side, Alice pushed her hair back. She'd pulled on a T-shirt, no bra, shorts and no shoes. "I'm fine." She zeroed in on Reese, her gaze telling. "Are you coming in?"

If he went in now, he just might shout. Alice wasn't a woman he wanted to shout at. At the moment, he wasn't sure what he wanted to do with her.

Walking away wasn't an option.

Reporting her antics to the authorities didn't sit right either.

Making love to her until she moaned again… But, no. He had to deal with her recklessness first. He had to find a way to rein her in, to get to the truth, to uncover her every secret.

To keep her from getting into more trouble.

Nikki still clung to him—peeling her away wouldn't be easy. Hopefully Alice would understand the circumstances.

He wanted everything from Alice, except jealousy or doubt.

"Why don't you take Cash in with you?" He held out the leash. "I'll be right there."

She stood her ground with her narrow bare feet planted, the breeze ruffling her tangled hair.

She didn't look at Nikki, and she didn't take the proffered leash. In a chilly voice laced with steel, she stated, "I'll wait with you."

Great. Jealous regardless, and apparently ready for battle. Just what the situation didn't need.

Nikki bounced her gaze back and forth from Reese's frustration to Alice's bold antagonism. Antagonism won.

Alice smiled, but it was not a friendly sight.

"Ooookay." Twittering a laugh, Nikki eased away. "I think I'll just excuse myself from this volatile domestic dispute." She patted Reese on the chest—and Alice's jaw ticked.

It fascinated him, this new aspect of Alice's personality. Possessive. Forceful.

But then, sounding like her usual reasonable, kind self, she said, "Why don't I call you a cab, Nikki? You probably shouldn't be driving."

"No need." A car swung into the parking lot, and a horn beeped. "My ride is here."

Reese turned to see a young man put the car in Park. He opened his door and poked his head out. "Sorry I'm late," he called to Nikki. "Traffic."

Tilting in against Reese, Nikki whispered, "Second

best, but tonight, I'll take it." And with that, she strutted to the car, much to the delighted anticipation of her date.

"I think she's drunk," Alice said on a sigh, "so I suppose I shouldn't take umbrage."

Given the stunt she'd pulled today, what she'd gotten involved in, umbrage over a pushy neighbor should have been the last thing on her mind. "I can see your nipples."

Alice looked down at herself with a distinct lack of concern. "I dressed in a hurry."

Taking her arm in a gentle but firm hold, Reese started them toward the apartment. Cash trotted along behind, his trauma with Nikki temporarily forgotten.

He'd gotten them halfway up the stairs when Alice said, "I grabbed the first T-shirt and shorts I saw. No time for underwear."

He tripped over his own feet.

"Besides," Alice said, peeking up at him. "I was hoping I could talk you back to bed. No reason to get dressed for that."

"Oh, no, you don't." Reese took the key from her and unlocked the door. "You will not distract me again. We have some serious talking to do."

"About Nikki?"

Anger started boiling to the surface again. "No, not about Nikki." After relocking the door, he went into the kitchen and fetched a treat for Cash. If this kept up, Cash would end up overweight. He'd have to get back to running—and maybe take Cash with him.

With the dog settled, Reese squared off with Alice.

She scowled up at him. "If I disappointed you, just say so."

"Disappointed?"

"In how I did—" she gestured "—you know, in bed."

Reese stared at her, distracted after all.

"You don't have to drag it out," she said. "Just tell me what I should do differently."

Reese shook his head to clear it. Oh, he was definitely disappointed. At her lack of trust, at her irresponsible disregard for safety.

At whatever illegal caper she'd blundered into.

"That was one hell of a turnaround, Alice. One minute we need to wait because you aren't ready, and then suddenly you're insisting we go straight to bed."

Confusion showed in her big dark eyes. "My boldness displeased you?"

"Hell, no. I loved it." He'd fallen for it hook, line and sinker, not a single suspicion aroused. "The sex was amazing. *You* are amazing."

Pleasure flushed her face, and she beamed at him. "Thank you."

"But you shouldn't have used it against me."

Going blank, she asked, "Used it…?"

Reese crossed his arms over his chest. "I talked with Rowdy." The words fell like a sledgehammer between them.

A silent gasp parted Alice's lips.

A sick churning of regret and maybe hurt brought Reese within an inch of her, towering above her, crowding her with his size. "And now I know why you suddenly had to have me."

CHAPTER FOURTEEN

"YOU'RE DERANGED." How in the world could Reese think anything had motivated her other than his awesome appeal?

His eyes widened a little at her insult.

Using both hands, she shoved him back a little. Or at least, she tried to. But since he was six and a half feet tall, every inch of him carved with strength, she only managed to surprise him.

"Look at you!" She cupped a hand at his jaw, rasped her thumb over his bristly beard stubble. Even that small touch set butterflies rioting inside her. Softer now, her voice an awed whisper, she said again, "Look at you."

"Alice."

Disregarding the warning tone in his voice, she ran both hands over his broad chest, those sculpted biceps, down to his incredible abs—which tightened more beneath her gentle touch. "You want the truth, Reese? You want to know why I was suddenly so—" she couldn't force the word *horny* out of her mouth, so she settled on "—ready?"

Green eyes narrowed again, showing his disagreeable mood. "The truth would be nice."

No way could she miss that insinuation. She gasped so hard she nearly choked herself. "I have not lied to you!"

"Lies of omission count, Alice." He settled both

hands atop her shoulders, close to her throat. "And I have a feeling you've omitted a lot."

She should probably feel threatened. She'd had some pretty awful experiences with big, powerful angry men. Reese was bigger and more powerful than most, and right now he was all but incandescent with anger.

But she didn't feel fear.

Not ever with Reese.

That did scare her a little because it felt so incredibly right to lean on him, to rely on him. She'd worked long and hard to find her independence again, to regain her self-worth.

And now, all she could think about was Reese…and how she wanted to share it all with him.

Knowing she had to confess, she let out a breath—and wrapped her arms around him. "You're right."

Surprised again, Reese held still…for three beats of time. Then he gathered her close. "Convince me I haven't been used."

"I can't." She tilted her head back to see him and gave him the truth he claimed to want. "I did use you. After what happened today, I was so shaken I didn't know what to do. I felt like crying, or shouting, or just curling up tight and hiding somewhere. I haven't felt like that for a while now. But then I realized you'd be home soon, and instead of falling apart, I wanted to get closer to you. I…" She pressed her cheek to his chest. "I wanted you to make me feel better."

Broad, warm hands coasted up and down her back. She felt the beat of his heart against her cheek, the expansion of his hard chest as he drew in slow, deep breaths. "And did I?"

Alice nodded. "I was going to tell you everything. Rowdy insisted. I knew if I didn't, he would."

Reese stiffened. "And if Rowdy hadn't been involved?"

"I'm sorry, but I honestly don't know. You're a cop," she said quickly, hoping he'd understand. "You naturally feel an obligation to do things the legal way."

"That's not a bad thing, honey. The legal way works when you let it."

"No, it doesn't, not always." Time to stop stalling. Alice gave up the comfort of his big solid body, but as she stepped away, Reese caught her hand.

She saw the questions in his eyes, the doubt he still felt about her motives. She couldn't blame him.

"Let's sit down." She gave him a gentle tug toward the couch. "It's a long story."

"Rowdy told me much of it."

Rowdy knew only the tiniest bit. Alice waited until they were both seated. As usual, Cash rushed over to sit with them. She patted her thighs, and he climbed into her lap, rolling to his back so he could stretch his head out to Reese's thigh.

Smiling, Alice scratched his belly—and avoided looking at Reese. "Today, I saved a woman."

Reese said nothing.

"Even if it upsets you, I feel good about it." A quick glance showed the seriousness of his expression, both somber and acutely focused. "There were so many times I prayed for someone to save me."

"Someone did." Reese rubbed under Cash's chin. "Rowdy says the guy is a wraith, but that he has incredible influence with the law."

In doggy heaven, Cash dozed off.

Alice loved the dog with all her heart.

She realized now that she loved Reese, too, and that

was a whole lot trickier. It meant she couldn't hide anymore. He'd have to know the truth.

And she'd have to accept the consequences.

"It surprises me, the things Rowdy can uncover." She licked dry lips. "He didn't get a name? Any details?"

"No." Scooping up the dog, Reese moved him to his opposite side so that he could sit nearer to Alice. With two pats, he resettled Cash, who was just as content to doze nearby.

Reese turned to her with all his considerable concentration. "I'm hoping you'll share those with me."

She would tell him what she could and hope it was enough, but not too much.

Stretching out one arm along the back of the couch, Reese more or less caged her in. "Logan also did some checking for me."

Wow, he'd been busy. Surveillance of her shopping trip, background checks on her past. Did all that curiosity mean that Reese cared—or that he suspected her of something?

Trying to sound curious instead of wary, Alice asked, "Did Logan uncover anything?"

"A little."

Her heart beat faster. She wished he hadn't moved Cash; being near the dog helped relax her. "For instance…?"

"I know what you told the cops when you were recovered, what you told the papers when you showed up again. And I know you have permits for your guns." He stared at her a moment. "Now I want to know the rest. Who took you, how you got away, why you're still so afraid—"

"I'm cautious, not afraid." *Liar.* So many times, fear overtook her. "Not as much, anyway."

He dismissed her protests. "And I want to know what happened today, and why."

The why was easy. "That young lady needed my help."

"No, Alice. There's more to it than that. I think maybe you're trying to make amends for something. I think you're still hiding a lot. But it's time to stop hiding."

Alice closed her eyes. Reese had no idea—and she'd really wanted to keep it that way.

Touching her chin, he brought her face up, waiting until she opened her eyes. "It's time to let me in, Alice."

She nodded, but she couldn't decide how to start. Fear. So much awful fear. "I don't want things to change," she finally admitted.

"Between us?"

"Yes." Once he knew it all, how could he possibly still be interested?

"You have to tell me sooner or later."

"I know." Dread smothered her, tightened her chest and made her stomach churn. "I think I've known that since the day I met you."

"Then let's get it all out in the open and deal with the consequences. The longer you wait, the harder it's going to be."

Knowing he was right, Alice fell back on an old tactic, forcing herself to relax her muscles, to compose her expression.

Hide emotion.

Hide fear.

Hide everything, so that she didn't really exist. That made it easier to get through—

"No." Reese turned her, his gaze bright with furious

determination. He kissed her hard, pressing her head back. "Don't do that, damn it. Not with me."

She blinked in surprise, shaken and thrown off.

Appearing pained, Reese put his forehead to hers. Voice guttural, his hands tight on her shoulders, he said again, "Not with me, Alice."

REESE FELT THE pounding of her heartbeat, but he couldn't make himself pull back.

He wouldn't let her hide, not anymore, not from him.

How many times had she had to do that during the year of her captivity? How many times had she faded to a quiet little mouse, hoping not to be noticed? Hoping to survive?

How many times had she been singled out, anyway?

God, it killed him to think about it, and Alice had lived it.

He kissed her again, more gently this time, moving his lips over hers, taking relief from the fact that she was here now, with him. "I need to know, Alice."

She nodded—and surprised him by offering comfort. It was there in the way *she* kissed *him,* so tenderly, on his chin, his jaw.

She rested her head on his shoulder. "He had me taken right after work."

The emptiness in her voice sent chills down Reese's spine. He smoothed back her tangled hair. "Can you tell me who?"

"His name was Murray Coburn. He's dead now."

Sometimes it's better when they're dead. Reese had to agree.

"I was locked away at night." One breath, two. "I'm not sure where he kept most of the women—the women he sold. But I stayed in his home. Wherever he went, I went. Always."

For a year. For an entire fucking year. Rage burned Reese's eyes, made his muscles twitchy with the need to find and kill a man beyond his thirst for vengeance.

"At first, for the longest time, I assumed he was going to murder me," Alice whispered. "But after a while, when that didn't happen, I didn't know what to think. Then he told me I needed to be his secretary. He said he had studied my background, my history of employment, and that I was just the conscientious, attentive assistant he needed for his business dealings. He said he couldn't just hire someone because he needed someone he could trust. He said—" she swallowed hard "—he said knowing I'd die if I didn't do a good job would be all the incentive I'd get."

Reese found it near impossible to fathom such a thing. But he believed her. "You did what you had to do."

"I'm sorry, Reese, but you don't understand how it was. *What* I had to do…"

Reese stroked her, encouraging, wanting for her to get it out there so they could deal with it.

"I told you he was a human trafficker?"

"Yes, you told me." And Reese feared where this would go.

"I was complicit in it all."

"No." Never would he believe that.

She nodded sadly. "In so many ways, I'm as guilty as he is."

"No." After he got all the facts, he'd find a way to convince her.

"I set up his meetings, arranged for pickups. For… sales."

The words choked her, and when Reese brushed a thumb over her cheek, he found it damp with tears that continued to fall.

His heart felt trampled. "You were forced, Alice."

"But I knew what he was doing. He made sure of that. Everyone knew. Everyone in the office, that is. So many immoral people, all of them as ugly and evil as him."

"The police?"

"Couldn't touch him," she said simply, stating it as a fact. "He always covered his tracks, and he had corrupt friends in high places. Whenever necessary, he had an alibi. He taunted me with it. And he told me if I ever tried to leave he'd steal my little sister and sell her, too, and then he'd rape me. He said he didn't want to." Her hands knotted against his chest. She pressed closer, her voice raw, broken. "Even when he made me be naked around him, he said that I repulsed him, but that he'd rape me anyway if I gave him trouble."

Dear God. Reese hauled her into his lap, trying to wrap himself around her, wanting to somehow protect her from a past already buried deep in her soul.

"I still waited and prayed, but I never had a chance to get away, not once. I couldn't stop things, couldn't risk my sister. If it had only been my life…"

"Your life is very important, Alice."

She swallowed hard. "The things he threatened, what I knew he did to others, that would have been worse than death."

Needing her to understand, he tunneled his fingers through her hair, cupped his hand around her skull, pressed a warm kiss to her forehead. "I'm very, very glad that you survived."

Tucking her face under his chin, she said against his throat, "I feel so guilty."

"I wish you wouldn't." But knowing Alice, he accepted that she'd take that guilt to her grave.

"When Murray hired a new bodyguard, I knew right away that he was different."

Ah, the wraith. Thank God. "Who was he?"

"I can't tell you that. No, please, Reese." She struggled back to see him, those big brown eyes liquid with tears, her nose pink. "He saved me. He saved *everyone*."

There was that. *But who was he?* "You said he hired on as a bodyguard?"

"Only undercover as one." She chewed her bottom lip, and more tears tracked down her cheeks. Impatiently, she used the back of her hand to swipe them away. "I'd been such a coward, worse than useless to all the injustice. But he gave me hope. And then he gave me freedom."

Leaning in close to her, his voice barely above a whisper, Reese said, "I'd like to thank him."

"I'm sorry, but you can't."

Unacceptable, yet how could he push it right now with her shaking uncontrollably, waiting, he knew, for criticism and censure?

More than his insistence on legality, she needed reassurance. Reese was more than happy to give it to her. "I think you're the bravest woman I know, Alice. Not many would be able to survive what you did and come out of it so caring and sweet."

She choked on disbelief. "I'm not sweet."

Using two fingers, Reese lifted her chin and kissed the tears from her cheeks. "Yes, you are. Sweet and wonderful, and I don't ever want you to forget it."

She searched his face and must have seen the sincerity there. On a small sob, she launched herself against him, squeezing him as tight as a slight, sad woman could.

Alerted by her cry, Cash lifted his head. Reese reached back with one hand and soothed the dog. "It's okay, boy. *She's* okay." He pressed his mouth to her temple. "Aren't you, Alice?"

"Yes." She nodded hard, gave him another squeeze then sat up to speak to Cash. "I'm fine, baby. Go back to sleep."

After watching her a second more, Cash gave Reese a quick glance and dropped back to the couch with a loud doggy sigh. At least Cash trusted him.

Now to work on Alice. "How did it all end, honey? Can you tell me that?"

"Yes." This time she used both hands to wipe her cheeks. A little more composed, she explained, "It was during an arranged meeting. Murray made me go along. I think he'd caught on to…the new bodyguard."

Which would have put everyone at risk. "He'd been nice to you?"

"Yes. Maybe that's why Murray decided to kill everyone. Instead…" She hesitated, exhaled out a shaky breath. "All the bad guys died."

All the bad guys? "What happened to the wraith?"

"He had backup."

Someone in the police force? Could it have been a sting? "How do you know that?"

"We were at the loading docks in an old crumbling warehouse. A truckload of women had arrived early, but when Murray ordered the driver to come open the trailer, he didn't answer. He was…dead. Belfort, the buyer, panicked, and everything seemed to happen at once. He thought Murray had double-crossed him, and

Murray thought the same of Belfort. Shots were fired from a distance, and Dugo, who'd come along with the buyer to protect him, got hit in the chest. He died. Belfort was badly wounded—I don't know if he lived or not, but I know he didn't get away. The women were all rescued. And Murray…"

Reese waited.

Voice fading, she focused her gaze somewhere in the past. "Murray died, and good riddance."

For a time, Reese just held her, keeping her close, reassuring himself that she had survived and that nothing that awful would ever happen to her again.

He kissed her forehead, her ear and cheek, hoping she'd understand that nothing had changed with her truths.

After some time had passed, Alice eased back to see him. She searched his gaze. "Are you disgusted with me?"

"I'm proud of you." And heartbroken, and enraged on her behalf.

Disbelief had her leaning away.

Reese touched her precious face, the corner of her mouth. "Anything else?"

It took her a minute to speak. "The police came, but we were already headed out of there. He gave me cab fare and a number to call if I had any trouble." She knew what Reese would ask before he finished formulating the question. "The number was for a limited time. It doesn't work anymore."

Disappointing, but that would have been a long shot, anyway. "Where did you go?"

"Home to my family. That's where he said I should go."

"He told you not to tell anyone about him?"

"No." Looking at his collarbone, Alice drew her small, cool hand along his chest. "He wouldn't do that."

Even at the worst of times, Alice seemed preoccupied with his body. Reese liked that. He more than liked her. Teasing her, he touched her chin and whispered, "Up here, honey."

On a sigh, she lifted her gaze to his. "It was my decision to censor the story. There wasn't much I could tell, anyway. I knew him only undercover with an alias. And he was long gone. Telling any of that to the police would only have confounded them, and it would have kept me with an open file. Instead, I told them the deal had gone bad, and everyone started shooting."

"Close to the truth."

"Yes. Close enough that they had what they needed from me."

Reese considered the plausibility of that. Any good cop would be able to tell the difference between shots fired at close range and shots from a sniper. But maybe they wrote that off as a cohort, either of the buyer or the seller, who got away.

"What was his alias?"

"Why does it matter?"

Because she still wasn't telling him everything. Did she hope to protect her savior because she thought Reese would go after him—which he might, if for no other reason than to get more answers—or because she still, to this day, had contact with the guy?

Watching her face for any sign of deception, Reese said, "Tell me."

She gave in with a lot of tension. "The name he used was Trace Miller."

The truth, as far as he could tell. "Thank you." He'd do a search, but if the guy was half as good as he seemed, there wouldn't be much, if anything, to uncover. "Now, about today…?" Reese prompted.

Alice drew a breath. "Today," she said, "I saw that girl, and I knew something wasn't right. I *felt* it."

Because cops survived off gut instinct, Reese accepted that. "You should have called the police."

"By then it might've been too late. I'm trying to make a difference, Reese. I want to believe that I'm stronger now than I was back then."

She meant morally—and that frustrated Reese. "Do you honestly believe there was anything you could have done to change things?"

"Maybe not, but I still should have tried."

"And died in the process? And then what?"

She shook her head.

Reese didn't let her turn away. "He would have grabbed another woman, Alice. He would have replaced you."

Shaken at that idea, she stared at him, her eyes haunted, her skin going pale. "Oh, my God, you're probably right."

"By enduring, you surely spared someone else."

Her bottom lip trembled, shredding his heart. "I never thought of that."

"You were too busy being guilty to see what I see. To see what others will see." He brushed his thumb over her delicate but stubborn jaw. "Your family included."

"That's a really wonderful way to look at it." A small, shaky smile appeared. "Thank you."

On that high note, Reese decided it was time to jump up to the present. Hoping to keep her in a better mood, he picked her up and started across the floor.

"Are we going back to bed?"

Reese looked at her, saw the flush on her skin, the heat in her eyes, and he almost lost his resolve. Alice and her one-track mind.

Damn, he was a lucky man.

"We're going to the kitchen."

As he entered the room, she eyed the table with interest, her thoughts clear on her face.

Shoring up his resistance, Reese shook his head. "No, I won't take you over the kitchen table." The idea had merit, but this was too important to put off for any reason. "But I will feed you. I don't know about you, but I'm starved."

"Oh." She looked disappointed for only a second. "We didn't have dinner, did we?"

"And you haven't yet told me about your newest exploit." Remembering how close she'd come to danger worked to temper the lust. Flattening his hands on the table in front of her, Reese leaned in, nose to nose, wanting her to understand the seriousness of the current situation. "No fudging, and no omissions. I need to know everything, Alice, even the smallest detail. And I need to know it tonight."

CHAPTER FIFTEEN

ALICE BIT INTO the peanut butter and jelly sandwich and thought it tasted better than anything she'd eaten in years. Her world felt…brighter, an enormous weight lifted off her shoulders.

She'd shared her biggest shame, and yet Reese hadn't turned away. He was such a good man, a detective even, and yet he didn't blame her.

It meant so much, more than she'd realized was possible. "Before I go to bed, I think I'll email my mom and dad."

"I'm sure they'd love that." He set a glass of milk in front of her. "But why not a phone call?"

"It's late and I don't want to wake them." They'd been apart so long now, she'd prefer to ease into things. An email, a request to visit…

Maybe even a reunion, this time without all the barriers of her shame and their regret.

Reese filled his own glass with milk, took his seat next to her and gave her such a severe, serious look that she almost squirmed.

He lifted his sandwich. "You're okay now?"

"I won't sob on you anymore." How humiliating that she'd left his chest wet with her tears. "I'm sorry about falling apart."

"Don't be." He ate half the sandwich in a single bite. "I'm glad you told me."

She was glad, too. It felt better not to carry the burden alone. “Thank you for letting me.”

Because he’d more or less insisted, he shook his head.

“I’m not really much of a crier.” She pulled at the crust on her bread. “There never seemed to be much point.”

“Everyone gets emotional now and then, and you certainly had reason.”

“I bet you don’t cry when you get emotional.”

His smile went crooked. “No, but I hit up the gym and lift weights until my entire body aches.”

Eyeing that awesome body, Alice could believe it. “That helps you to get things back in balance?”

Shrugging one boulder shoulder, Reese said, “It expends energy. Sometimes I run, too, but usually I do that just because I enjoy it. It’s a good time to think about things, to put them in perspective.”

“Things with your job?” she asked, and then digging a bit more, added, “Or with personal relationships?”

“Usually the job.” He turned his milk glass just a little, his thoughts hidden from her. “Rapes, missing teens… Those cases get to me more than murder sometimes.” His gaze met hers. “Many of the murders we see are between creeps. Bad deals that got out of hand. That sort of thing.”

Alice’s heart pounded. “So…you’re saying when a really bad guys dies, it’s hard to mourn him.”

“Impossible, actually. I do my job. I follow all the leads. I uphold justice. But I’m not going to lose sleep over it.”

Would he feel that way if he ever knew the extent of what she’d done?

Reese’s eyes narrowed as he studied her. “But a kid

alone on the streets, or a woman who's been brutalized, yeah, that plagues me."

"Does that happen often?"

"Once is too often, you know? We get domestic abuse calls all the time. Usually it's drinking that got out of hand, and the one who called us regrets it later. Once we're involved, we're involved."

"I think that's a very good rule, actually."

"Yeah, me, too. Because you just never know." He blew out a disgusted breath. "Last year there was a case of a man who'd used his wife as a punching bag too damn many times. Our first call there was due to a neighbor. The wife denied being hurt." Reese tightened all over. "But she had bruises, and there was something in her eyes…."

Swallowing became difficult; Alice had seen that look too many times, on too many women.

She'd even seen it…while looking in the mirror.

His hand on the tabletop curled into a fist. "Once we got involved, we found a macabre history of broken bones and concussions." Deliberately, he shook himself out of those memories. "She'd married him when she was sixteen. For twelve years she put up with that abuse."

"I hope he got a very tough punishment."

"If death is tough enough."

Oh, God. "You didn't…?"

Reese shook his head. "The bastard went after the neighbor who'd called the cops. He broke in, drunk and raging." With satisfaction, he said, "The neighbor shot him dead. Self-defense. He had a permit for the weapon. No charges were brought against him."

Alice bit her lip. "The woman?"

"Last I heard, she went home to her family, and they were attending counseling together."

Alice sincerely hoped the woman was happier now. She had not a single doubt that Reese would have done everything in his power to ensure that outcome. "You're very good at your job."

He gave a short laugh. "I hope so. At the very least, I'm as honorable as I can be."

"Of course you are." She couldn't imagine a more honorable man.

"I appreciate your faith." He sent her a smile. "You know we had some corruption at the department. Having crooked cops around complicates everything. Peterson has a handle on that now, but cleaning house is going to leave us shorthanded for a while. I've got a stack of shit on my desk, open cases that I need to get to."

"I understand." She had her own workload piling up. "I suppose on Monday, we'll get back to business."

He eyed her. "I have a feeling that you, Alice, will be my business."

"You mean personally?" It still amazed her that Reese wanted her. Not as much as she always wanted him, but enough.

He shrugged. "With what Rowdy told me, probably professionally, too." He finished off the other half of his sandwich, watching her as he chewed. "Speaking of that…since you're feeling better now, let's get on with the rest." He nudged her plate toward her. "You can talk while you eat."

So he'd only fed her to help her regain control? Considerate and practical. "What happened today, you mean?"

"Yeah, that." Crossing his arms on the table, he scowled at her. "What the hell, Alice?"

The sudden shift in his tone left her feeling defensive. How could he forgive her for what she'd taken part in—forced or otherwise—so long ago, but take issue with her for getting involved now? "She needed help."

"Apparently so. But what you did was reckless, and it's as likely you could have been caught and hurt instead of helping her."

What he said…she'd realized that all on her own. "I know. That's why I was thinking I need to be better equipped, and I need to get a better plan."

Reese choked. Coughing and wheezing, he held up a hand to fend off her assistance. After finishing off more milk, he took a moment, his shoulders bunched, his expression dire.

When he caught his breath, Alice didn't give him a chance to start lecturing. "She had a bandage loosely wrapped around her arm. I thought she'd been hurt, Reese, maybe wounded."

Incredulous, he stared at her. "And so you decided to jump into the middle of it?"

Okay, so that sounded bad. Alice tried to reassure him. "Turned out she wasn't injured at all. She'd just gotten a new tattoo."

That got Reese's attention, not that he hadn't already been focused on her with the force of a laser beam. "A tattoo?"

"Still red and swollen." Alice chewed her bottom lip, remembering. "I found her at the mall parking lot, and it seemed to me she'd just gotten it, probably someplace close. Like maybe only a few hours before. The tattoo was part of why she was so upset."

Reese stared at her. "What did it look like?"

She tried to picture it in her mind. "An odd design made up of numbers and lines twining together." Knowing it was important, she said, "Cheryl told me that the tattoo is used as identification for people carrying drugs—mules, I think she said they're called. The lines and numbers indicate what drugs are being carried, where they're from and how much they'll cost."

His eyes flared. "No fucking way."

Alice frowned at him for the language. "I know, unbelievable, right?" For the next twenty minutes she relayed everything that had happened. She didn't skip a single detail since, clearly, Rowdy had already spilled the beans.

With every word out of her mouth, Reese looked more livid.

Somehow, Alice had to make him understand. "Cheryl was not transporting drugs by choice. She'd moved to the area to be near a guy—I don't know his name because she didn't say. But the relationship, at least on his part, was just a ruse, a way to lure her in. He told her that if she loved him, she'd move the drugs for him."

Though his gaze darkened, Reese stayed eerily silent.

"There are more, Reese. Cheryl said that Hickson—the creep I left bound in that disgusting motel—gets the girls tattooed. I don't know who he works for, though. Cheryl did a lot of crying, and she kept worrying that I might be with some competing drug dealer or something, but I believe the girls are coerced, maybe even *forced* to transport drugs." As Alice spoke, her temper rose again. "I'm certain they're tattooing them against their will."

Reese looked stunned by her deductions. Did he

think she was too naive to piece it together? It didn't take a genius—or a detective—to see the truth.

Thinking of how Cheryl had tried to scrub away the tattoo, Alice leaned in closer to Reese, anxious to help. "I remember the van that brought her to the mall parking lot. And the truck I followed, too. I didn't think to memorize a license plate, darn it, but it occurs to me that they probably met at the mall because the tattoo parlor is nearby."

Alarm had Reese's shoulders going rigid. "Stop right there."

Driven by new urgency, Alice tuned him out. "I could visit the area, maybe look around a little. I might see the van or truck again."

"Alice—"

"Nothing dangerous this time," she said with a flap of her hand. "I could just check out the locations of the local tattoo parlors."

His hands locked onto the edge of the table. "No."

"Maybe I could even stroll inside to see if anyone had a design like that and—"

He shoved back his chair. "No."

"—because I might be able to match up the tattoo artist with the design."

Eyes red and nostrils flared, Reese jerked to his feet and loomed over her.

His mood finally sank in, and Alice stared up at him, bemused. "You're upset with me?"

He opened his mouth, closed it again. His jaw clenched. His big hard hands curled into fists.

"Reese?"

After running a hand over his head, he pointed at her and snarled—actually *snarled,* "I think you're fucking wonderful, remember that."

"Oh. Okay." *Fucking wonderful?* What did that mean?

"But," he said, his tone hard edged, "what you did today—not a year ago, Alice, but *today*—was as foolhardy as it gets."

Fascinated, Alice watched him.

He dismissed her awful connection to a wretched human trafficker, but was outraged over her saving a single girl?

Knowing he didn't blame her gave her new confidence. He was right that Murray would have replaced her. Without Reese, she never would have considered that.

But now, *with Reese,* she felt like she could actually deal with the past, possibly bury it once and for all, and make a difference in the future.

She smiled at him.

He didn't smile back. The seconds passed in silence.

Pivoting away from her, Reese pulled out his cell phone.

A little deflated by that reaction, Alice waited as he punched in a single speed-dial number. She was somewhat curious who he'd call right now, but more wary than anything else.

"Logan?" Reese stared at her while he spoke into the phone. "I've got a problem." His jaw ticked when he nodded. "Yes, Alice."

Frowning, Alice straightened in her seat. So, now she was a problem? *She had rescued a woman.* Why couldn't he see past everything else to what good had been done?

Reese held her gaze. "We need to bring her in for questioning." He nodded. "I know."

For questioning? *To a police station?* Oh, but…

"Peterson should be there." He rubbed the back of his

neck. "Rowdy, too. Yeah, he stepped in it while chasing after her. I can explain everything in more detail tomorrow. No, I won't." His attention all but pinned her in place. "She won't be out of my sight."

So…did that mean he'd be spending the night with her again? Given his current mood, he might want to sleep on the couch. She hoped not. She wanted him back in her bed.

She wanted him again—period.

"ONE LAST THING." Reese walked over to her, put two fingers under her chin and lifted her face. "We have a vigilante running around."

Uh-oh. Alice tried to shake her head, to caution him against sharing that, but Reese held her chin.

"He carries a lot of clout, had cooperation from the law and apparently he's good enough to kill Alice's kidnapper without anyone knowing who he is."

Oh, no. Alice's heart sank. She couldn't let this happen, couldn't let someone else take the blame for what had occurred that day.

Her rescuer hadn't killed her kidnapper.

Alice had taken care of that herself.

THE ROCK-SOLID FIST struck him in the gut, knocking him back into the wall where his head smacked hard. Stars danced behind his eyes, and his guts ached. He thought he might puke.

But Hickson took the punishing blow without fighting back. What other choice did he have?

"One girl dead, and now another on the loose." The icy gaze drilled into him, driven by disgust and rage. "I should fucking kill you."

Shaking his head, as much to clear it as to offer a denial, Hickson said, "That wasn't my fault."

"Not your fault? You let a woman best you? You let her shackle you to a wall?"

When Woody Simpson, the boss, got in these moods, there was no reasoning with him. But he had to try, anyway. "I didn't mean for Marcia to die. She flipped out after getting the tat, screaming bloody murder. I only hit her once to shut her up."

"You hit her hard enough for her to fall and crack her skull on the concrete."

"Well…yeah." It'd been plain dumb luck that she'd crumpled like that. In hindsight, he knew he should have just muffled her and waited until he had her in the motel, on the mattress, to smack her around.

Woody backhanded him this time, but with the brass knuckles in place, it hurt the same as a punch. He tasted blood.

Phelps and Lowry snickered, the bastards. They'd been riding his ass ever since they found him bound in the room. "That other bitch had a Taser, and she damn near killed me with it."

Woody laughed without humor. "Why didn't you disarm her first thing?"

"I didn't know she was like that! She looked like a mouse. Like a schoolteacher or a librarian. Said she was lost and just needed to use my phone."

"You're a fucking idiot, Hickson. You know that, right?"

He rubbed his goatee and swallowed his pride. "Yeah, I know."

"I want you to find her."

"Cheryl, or…the bitch that jolted me?"

"Yes."

Hickson shook his head again, this time bewildered. "How am I supposed to do that? I don't know her name. She could be anyone."

"You said she helped Cheryl? That was all about doing a good deed for the twit?"

"Yeah." Hickson brightened as he remembered. "Yeah, she got riled up when Cheryl cried."

"So, go to Cheryl."

Hickson went blank.

Rolling his eyes, Woody strode to his desk. "Cheryl probably went running home to Mommy and Daddy. I have her address. Get her alone, and get her to talk. She probably knows the woman, or at least knows a way to get in touch with her again."

"If she doesn't?"

"Find out what you can." Woody handed over a slip of paper with an address on it. "Cheryl should at least know the make of her car, if nothing else. You better hope it's enough for me to extinguish this problem, and fast. Because if it's not, if that woman causes me any more trouble, you'll be the one to pay."

Straightening away from the wall, Hickson accepted the address. He had a reprieve, and he wouldn't blow it. "When I find her, what do you want me to do with her?"

Woody sat back in his desk chair and smiled. "Bring her to me."

REESE REMAINED IN an odd, antagonistic mood. Alice thought it might be from worry, but she didn't know what to do about it.

She wasn't a woman who could ignore the pain of others. Never again.

While Reese spent an inordinate amount of time outside with Cash, she'd emailed her family, sending them her love and apologizing for being so distant. She told them she now realized her mistake withdrawing, and promised to visit very soon.

Every so often, she'd peeked out at Reese, but no one bothered him. He sat in the grass, tossing sticks for Cash, playing with the dog, even wrestling with him a little.

Seeing him like that put a lump in her throat and a smile on her face. He was such an amazing man, so caring, so decent—the antithesis of the monsters who had used Cheryl.

When he finally came in, she was ready for bed.

He went into the bathroom to wash up and brush his teeth, then into the bedroom. Uncertain, Alice trailed after him, watched him take off a shirt, strip off his slacks. Wearing only those dark sexy boxers, he turned to her.

With iron will, she forced her attention to stay on his face. "Will you stay here with me tonight?"

His brow went up. "I'm not going anywhere."

"I mean here." She gestured awkwardly at the bed. "In the bedroom, in bed with me, instead of the couch."

"Is that what you want?"

"Yes." She nodded hard. "Very much."

On his way to the bed, he said, "I appreciate that you're always honest with me, Alice."

A gibe? Because, seriously, he knew she wasn't always, entirely honest.

Now, as midnight came and went, Alice knew she couldn't sleep. Not like this.

Not with Reese still irate.

His body remained tensed, his arms behind his head instead of around her.

Her awareness of him was so keen that she felt the lack of his affection like a douse of ice water.

So unfair.

At the foot of the bed, Cash snored, every so often running in his sleep. The dog jerked again, and Reese moved his foot against him, saying, "Shhh…"

Cash settled.

Alice glanced toward Reese, but in the darkness she couldn't see much more than his outline. It was torture, being with him like this, but with invisible barriers keeping them apart.

An accusation escaped her before she could think better of it. "If you didn't want to get busy, you shouldn't have stripped down."

A moment of stillness nearly smothered her, then slowly, oh, so slowly, Reese turned his head toward her. She prepared herself for his annoyance, more of his anger.

He said, "Get busy?"

"That's what Rowdy calls it."

She heard a sound—maybe of his teeth sawing together.

"Rowdy is very informative," she told him.

The bed dipped as Reese came up to an elbow. "I wish you'd stop talking about Rowdy."

But Rowdy had given her so much hope. He'd said all it would take was Reese seeing her naked, and he'd be ready and willing.

Instead, she saw him in nothing more than boxers, and she was the one who wanted to die of lust.

"He's been helpful." So helpful, in fact, maybe she should try out one of his suggestions.

Reese dropped flat in the bed again.

Enough already. Determination got Alice's feet to

the floor in seconds. She found the lamp on the nightstand and turned it on.

Momentarily blinded, she shielded her eyes.

Reese did the same. "What are you doing?"

"I'm testing Rowdy's theory."

Up on one elbow again, he frowned. "What theory?"

Cash gave them both a sleepy look and bounded down off the bed. He went over to the closet, dropped down with a huff and curled up to sleep with his nose close to his rump.

Working up her courage, Alice looked back at Reese. "This theory." She reached beneath her gown and took off her panties, then made a show of tossing them aside.

Going utterly still, Reese said nothing. His gaze burned over her, hot, expectant, before settling on her face.

He waited.

Alice drew a fortifying breath, thought of the rewards of brazenness and peeled the nightgown up and over her head. The cool wash of the air-conditioning tightened her nipples.

Reese wasn't shading his eyes anymore, and he no longer looked angry.

Buoyed by his rapt attention, she straightened in front of him, naked head to toe.

Reese's chest expanded. His biceps bunched.

Alice chewed her bottom lip. Interest definitely sharpened his demeanor, but Rowdy had led her to believe he'd react differently. More…physically.

Had she expected him to jump her?

Yes, she'd been hopeful.

Shaking her hair back over her shoulders and lifting her chin, she tried staring him down. "Say something."

Reese lifted an eyebrow over the order. He did a slow

visual examination, pausing to scrutinize her breasts, her belly.

Between her thighs.

"How did you scrape your knee?"

Disappointed that he hadn't made a move yet, she shrugged and said, "I think it happened when I knelt down to cut the air valves off Hickson's tires."

His gaze hardened. "I hope like hell no one will be able to track you down from that stunt."

His concern made her feel guilty. "No one is after me, Reese. I promise, I'm *fine*."

He looked over the length of her legs. "Yes, you are."

Just when she thought she couldn't take it anymore, he tossed back the sheet and got out of bed.

A very noticeable erection strained his snug boxers. Alice braced herself, excitement unfurling…but instead of coming to her, he went to the door.

Watching Reese leave the room, Alice felt wretched, dejected, exposed… Until he returned with something in his hand. "Cash, you want a treat?"

The dog had been ignoring them, but at Reese's offer, he rolled to his feet with a lurch.

When Reese led Cash out of the room, Alice hurriedly got in the bed and pulled the covers up to her chin. Insane, but now she felt shy. Who knew seducing a man was so nerve-racking?

Reese walked back in, stalled when he saw her bundled in the middle of the mattress, but then continued on to the bed. He sat down beside her. "Have a change of heart?"

"No." Definitely not that.

"Then, what's this?" He gave a gentle tug to the blankets.

"I don't know." And then with annoyance, "You just stared at me."

"That's bound to happen every time I see you naked, so you may as well get used to it."

Clutching the blankets tighter, she wondered if that meant he'd be around for the long haul, that he'd want to see her naked a lot. "I wasn't all that sure you were interested."

Reese considered her, stood—and pushed out of his boxers.

CHAPTER SIXTEEN

ALICE'S EYES WENT wide. God love the man, she would never tire of seeing his body.

When he snatched the blankets away from her, tossing them to the floor, she gave a startled yelp but then just froze. What else could she do?

She pressed her thighs together and folded her arms over her chest. "I'm cold."

Wearing a half smile and nothing else, Reese stretched out next to her. He took his time pulling her hands away, arranging them over her head so that she was stretched out on the bed. After looking her over with appreciation, he cupped a hand to her breast, used his thumb to tease her nipple and said, "Don't be nervous about tomorrow."

Tomorrow? What was he talking about?

"I'll be there with you." He lightly caressed the other breast, too, then moved his hand down to her belly.

Alice sucked in a breath. His hand was warm, a little rough.

"Logan doesn't bite, and Peterson doesn't bite too hard."

He slipped his fingers lower, pressing them between her thighs, and her breath rushed out. "I don't want to talk about that." She wanted him to kiss her, but when she tried that, he gave her only a warm peck.

Against her lips, he asked, "Do you still have contact with him?"

With his fingers playing against her, she couldn't think. "Who?"

"Your savior." He kissed her again, this time deeper, hotter. "Trace Miller."

Her brain stalled. "Reese…"

He nuzzled her neck, his beard shadow prickly, his breath warm and soft. "Do you?"

"I…" She felt his tongue and started breathing harder. "Sometimes."

He barely moved his fingers, pressing them there, his palm over her mound. It made her nuts. It made her want to move her hips, but she held still. Barely.

Opening his mouth over the sensitive spot where her shoulder met her neck, he treated her to a damp, tantalizing love bite. "How often?"

Unable to think beyond her growing need, Alice tilted her head more, giving him better access, encouraging him to do more of *that,* and hopefully less talking.

And damn it, her hips moved after all.

"How often, Alice?"

"He…" Reese opened his mouth on her again, sucked at her skin, and she knew he was marking her. It was so erotic, so sexy. And it felt *so* good. "Occasionally he…checks on me."

Reese looked at her, his gaze sharpened. "Have you seen him?"

"No." She shook her head. She didn't need to see him. She knew Trace would be there if she ever needed him. "I…I haven't seen him since he got me the weapons."

"The CCPs?"

She had no idea what that meant.

"The conceal and carry permits. He got those for you?"

"I guess. Yes. He gave me papers." She tipped her head back, moaning softly as his fingers both excited and teased. "But I haven't seen him since."

Relaxing against her again, Reese nipped her earlobe, dipped his tongue inside. "Are you sure?"

Who knew her ears were so erogenous? "It's been forever." She moved against his hand to get him back on track.

Taking the hint, he whispered against her skin, "Spread your legs."

Even that, the coarse timbre of his voice, sent sweet lust coiling tighter. Knowing what he would do, anxious for him to do it, Alice opened her thighs.

Teasing over her moist flesh, he parted her, barely entered her, stroking and exploring until his fingertips were slippery wet—then going high in the briefest touch to her clitoris.

Her hips lifted in reaction; her gasp faded out to a vibrating groan.

Green eyes heated, voice lower still, Reese whispered, "Right there, huh?"

How in the world could he continue talking? Why did he want to, anyway? Barely able to breathe, Alice nodded.

"Like this?" He drew his fingers up and over her again, and her body clenched in delicious ways.

"Yes." Exactly like that.

"What about this?" Slowly, he worked two fingers deep inside her. Against her cheek, he murmured, "So snug, Alice. Nice and wet. Hot."

That felt wonderful, too, and again her hips moved despite her best efforts to keep still.

"And this?" He used his thumb with amazing impact.

Holding her breath, her body taut with need, Alice nodded hard.

In a soft, raw growl, he asked, "And this?" before closing his hot mouth over her right nipple. He tugged with a gentle, insistent suction that sent new sensations flooding her body.

Oh, God, it was incredible. Almost too much. Alice lowered her arms so she could hold him close. A climax built inside her, throbbing, receding, coming back stronger, closer.

His fingers filled her, his mouth pulled at her and he kept up that slick, rhythmic friction with his thumb, working her until she knew she couldn't hang on any longer.

Head back, heels pressing into the mattress, her fingers tangled in his hair, her body arched hard. He stayed with her, letting her ride out the release until only little reverberations of pleasure remained. She collapsed flat to the bed again, struggling to get enough oxygen into her lungs.

Reese released her nipple with a soft lick that made her moan. Slowly, he withdrew his hand, and even that, the rasping of his fingers leaving the tight clasp of her body, sent off more aftershocks.

In seconds he was off the bed. Alice got her eyes focused in time to see him open a condom packet. Lethargic, still tingling in select places, she soaked up the sight of his awesome physique. Renewed interest started a pulse beat of need between her legs as she watched him roll the rubber on his engorged shaft.

Large, capable hands. Tensed shoulders and thighs. Six and a half feet of undeniable strength and raw masculinity. Disheveled blond hair and darkening beard shadow only made him sexier.

Alice could barely believe he was here, with her, and that he wanted her. Again. "You are so beautiful."

Reese glanced at her with burning eyes. "You're seeing through a haze of satisfaction." He strode over to her, settled atop her and wedged her legs apart.

Alice loved the press of his weight, the blanket of his heat surrounding her. His broad, sculpted shoulders made her feel smaller and more female, but in such a wonderful way.

Cupping her face, he kissed her and said, "Let's see if I can get you there again."

She inhaled deeply of his wonderful scent and ran her hands over the crisp hair of his chest, already halfway there.

Balanced on a forearm, Reese adjusted, using one hand to guide himself—all the while holding her gaze in his. Alice felt him there, ready to thrust in, and her body trembled in anticipation.

He waited, breathing deeper, his expression strained as he teased the head of his erection against her. "So damn wet," he murmured.

"Do it," Alice whispered. She curled her fingers against his pectoral muscles, lifted her hips on a wave of expanding need. *"Do it."*

His green eyes darkened, narrowed—and he thrust in, burying himself deep. They both groaned, and seconds later he took her mouth in a consuming kiss.

They moved together, harder and faster and within minutes the pressure began to build. She freed her mouth to gasp for air.

Reese rose up on straightened arms. "I want to see you come again."

The idea of him watching her might have been embarrassing, except that release rolled over her too soon for her to give it much thought. She grabbed for his biceps, thrilled at his rock-solid strength. Crying out over and over, she let the pleasure take her.

Watching her, Reese muttered a low curse, and she felt him pumping into her as he gained his own release.

Carefully, he lowered his body down to hers, his heartbeat pounding fast and strong against her breast.

Her brain buzzed; her body went limp. Even getting her eyes to open was a chore too difficult. All she could manage was deep breathing that tried to lure her to sleep.

After a few minutes, she felt Reese lift away from her, leaving her skin exposed to the cooler air. She couldn't react, could do no more than lay there in a state of contentment.

Reese left the bed, but not for long. He returned, spread the sheet and blanket over her, called Cash up into the bed and stretched out beside her. He pulled her close, his arm around her waist, his leg over hers.

Cash walked the perimeter of the mattress, came up to snuffle her neck and ear then crashed at the foot of the bed.

"Sleep, both of you," Reese muttered around a yawn.

Something, some strange sense of unease, tried to worm its way into Alice's exhaustion. It didn't succeed.

Tucked warm and secure against Reese's body, she faded into sound slumber.

THE NEXT MORNING, Reese watched Alice sleep—his brain buzzing with questions. Sex with Alice was something special. Real special. Every time he thought he had her figured out, she surprised him again.

Wrapped around her, replete from a mind-blowing release, he'd slept like the dead—and awakened with a damned smile.

Seconds after getting his eyes open, the problems all came swarming back.

How did Alice contact the wraith? Did she use her computer? Had she lied about the phone number?

It had been dirty pool, using her lust against her. Unfair but effective. He felt bad about it…a little.

But as a detective, as a man physically and emotionally involved with her, he *needed* to know.

If it weren't for her sexual interest in him, if he hadn't snuck the questions in while she was in need, would she ever have told him?

It seemed doubtful.

Were there more secrets that she kept from him?

Hoping not, he kissed her bare shoulder, and wanted to go on kissing her. All over.

He'd been pissed when they went to bed last night, rightfully so. But knowing what she'd been through, how she'd rehashed it all for him, he couldn't make himself walk away. She didn't want to sleep alone.

He didn't want to sleep away from her.

Last night had been…amazing. It was such a contrast for Alice to be so contained in most aspects, only to let it all loose in bed.

With him.

It made Reese smile again, thinking of how she'd stripped off that gown, how she'd stood there buck-ass, challenging him to ignore her.

Not likely.

Since the day he'd met her, he stayed so aware of her that she plagued his thoughts. He wanted her always, but when she showed her daring, her vulnerability, he had no resistance at all.

A unique blend of curious innocence and hot carnality, Alice tempted him on every level.

There were many ways he wanted to take her, many positions he wanted to explore with her.

Hoping both she and Cash would sleep a little longer, Reese eased the coverings off her narrow shoulder, down the dip of her tiny waist, past her rounded hip. He dragged the blankets all the way to her adorable knees.

Such a great ass.

There were many things he had to figure out, but damn, it'd be easy to obsess over having her again and again. He'd love to get her on her knees, take her from behind, burying himself deep while holding her breasts in his hands…

On a deep stretch and wide yawn, Alice turned to her back. She settled again with a sigh—then popped her eyes open. Immediately her gaze clashed with his.

Finding him so close, realizing he'd uncovered her, left her eyes nearly crossed.

"Morning." Reese cupped her breast, enjoying the way her soft nipple immediately beaded tight. "Sleep well?"

She bolted upright, and it so startled Cash that he nearly fell out of the bed. His long ears perked up in interest. He looked from Alice to Reese and back again.

Alice grabbed for the blankets and pulled them to her chin.

Amused, Reese said, "Cash doesn't mind seeing you naked. And I enjoy it." He gave a playful tug to the blanket, but she held on.

"How long have you been awake?"

That sounded like an accusation, making him

grin. “Only a few minutes.” Lacking her modesty, he stretched and got out of bed. “I’ll take Cash out, then how about we shower?”

Still a little foggy, she dropped her gaze over his bare body and swallowed. “Together?”

“Yes.”

Another look, longer this time.

Much more of that, and he’d be sporting a boner. “Alice…”

Her grip on the blanket loosened. “Okay.”

It was a nice thing, to be wanted so much by Alice. “Be right back.” He pulled on slacks, grabbed up his wallet and cell phone, and by the time he hit the door, Cash was with him. “Good boy. You’re learning, aren’t you?”

Cash waited like a gentleman while Reese attached the leash, and on the way down the steps, he only pulled Reese off balance twice.

The progress the dog made pleased him. In such a short time, Cash had learned to hold it until he got outside, and he hadn’t chewed up anything in, oh, a day or two. Definitely getting better.

Alice had a lot to do with that. Her gentle, calm nature went a long way toward reassuring Cash and helping him recover from any past abuse. The fact that Alice worked from home, so therefore spent more time with the dog, helped, too.

She was a good influence—on Cash, on Reese.

But she still had those damned secrets.

Reese took out his phone and dialed Rowdy.

On the fifth ring, Rowdy answered with a grouchy, “What the fuck, Reese? Do you know what time it is?”

“Sleeping in?”

“I had good reason.”

Ah. "Company, huh? Sorry about that."

"Don't be. Was time for her to go, anyway. Hang on a sec."

Reese heard Rowdy talking low, heard a grumbled female protest, insistence from Rowdy, then the louder sounds of a woman scorned.

Had Rowdy wakened her just to tell her to leave? Brutal. But that was Rowdy, hard-edged, coarse and apparently inconsiderate to women.

Not his sister, who he cherished.

And being truthful, Rowdy had never been inconsiderate to Alice either.

Reese winced, remembering how he'd gotten answers from Alice last night. But damn it, he'd had good reason.

What possible excuse could Rowdy have for kicking a woman out of bed?

Feeling like a hypocrite, Reese considered calling back when Rowdy might be less occupied. He was about to disconnect when he heard the woman's complaints soften to pleas.

Low conversation, followed by a gruff, suggestive laugh, filtered through the phone lines.

A door closed, bed springs squeaked and Rowdy said, "So what's up?"

Unbelievable. "You're alone now?"

"Yeah. And given I was occupied for most of the night, I'd like to get a little more sleep. So unless you have a good reason for this call…?"

"I do. I wanted to talk while I'm outside with Cash."

"Meaning away from Alice?"

Exactly, but Reese didn't want to say that. "The girl that Alice helped yesterday—do you know anything more about her?"

"Not a thing. She'd already taken off on a bus by the time I caught up. I asked, but Alice said she'd only given the girl money, not bought the ticket, so she didn't know where she was headed."

Reese didn't buy it. Alice wasn't one to leave things to chance. "You believe her?"

"Hell, no. Alice is a little too sharp for blind trust."

That Rowdy knew her well enough to understand that rubbed Reese the wrong way. "She told me the girl had a unique tattoo."

"Told me that, too. So?"

Damn it, he did not want Alice confiding in Rowdy. Jealousy was a son-of-a-bitch, so Reese did his best to deny it.

He heard a toilet flush, heard water run. "You still there, Reese?"

"Yeah." Pinching the bridge of his nose, he said, "It could be unrelated."

"I need coffee, so if there's a point to this, let's get to it."

"All right." Going to the requisite tree—the spot Reese now thought of as his "taking out Cash tree"—he leaned against the trunk and gave Cash enough leash to explore. "Peterson found a similar tattoo on another girl."

"No shit? Maybe a new fad, huh?"

"The girl was dead."

Rowdy fell silent. "You said it was like the tattoo Alice described?"

"From what I could tell, yes."

"One girl running, another dead, both with the same tat. That's one hell of a coincidence."

"I know." Since Alice often surprised him by joining him outside, Reese kept watch on the apartment doors while telling Rowdy what he knew about the tattoo. "You think you can keep an eye out?"

"Sure thing. I've already noticed a couple of tattoo parlors not that far from the mall. I'll check them out."

"Thinking of getting inked?"

Rowdy snorted. "Not my thing. But I'm buying a bar, so I scoped out the area."

Buying a bar? That was news to Reese. "You're serious?"

"Yeah. Alice didn't tell you?"

Damn it. There was a lot Alice didn't tell him. "She hadn't mentioned it, no."

"It's not a big deal. I figured since Pepper was settling down here with Logan, I may as well do a little settling of my own."

A bar counted as being settled? To Rowdy, probably. "Is it nice?"

"Hell, no. It's a total dump. But I have plans for it."

Interesting. "I owe you, so if there's anything I can do, let me know."

"Maybe. We'll see." Rowdy paused. "So…I guess I'm up now after all. Might as well go check on those tattoo parlors. I think I get the gist of the design, but if you can text me over a photo, it'd help."

"I'm not officially back on the clock yet, so it'll probably be a couple of days before I can do that. But soon as I can, I'll take care of it."

"We're meeting at the station today?"

"Early afternoon." Which would give him time to prepare Alice first. If what she'd said was true—and with Alice, he wouldn't swear to anything—she hadn't been in a police station since the days immediately after her knight in shining armor rescued her.

Thinking that soured Reese's mood real fast. How often did she touch base with the elusive bastard?

"Don't worry about it then," Rowdy said, adding with thick sexual innuendo, "I'll see if Peterson will give me a peek."

Innuendo was wasted on Peterson, but he still chuckled. "She'll neuter you if you're not careful."

He heard the grin in Rowdy's tone when he said, "Later, Reese."

After disconnecting, Reese called over Cash, and together they went in to find Alice. Anticipating a shower with her, thinking of how he'd help brace her for the interview at the station, he walked in…and found Alice sitting in the kitchen.

Eating jelly beans.

"For breakfast?" he asked.

The look she gave him didn't bode well. Body slumped in the chair and her head propped on a fist, she tossed back two more jelly beans while glaring at him. She looked pissed, but when Cash came over and leaned on her leg, she made him feel as welcome as ever.

While getting the dog fresh water and food, she said, "I forgot last night, and then again this morning." She ate more jelly beans.

Hmm. Alice hit her candy the way some people hit alcohol. Reese crossed his arms and leaned against the counter. "Forgot what?"

She cast him a dirty look and set the dog's dishes back on the floor. Snatching up the bag of jelly beans, she marched into the other room.

Hands on his hips, Reese took in her stiff spine and squared shoulders as she left. She expected him to chase after her, to ask her what had her upset.

As if he didn't already know.

But damn it, he was the one with a bone to pick. Let her stew, he decided, and went about making coffee. He was filling the carafe when she stormed right back in. She ate three more jelly beans while staring a hole in his back.

"Something on your mind, Alice?" He added the water to the machine and turned it on.

"I'm mad at you."

And so she went on a jelly bean binge? "Care to tell me why?"

"I thought we'd be more comfortable on the couch, away from Cash. I don't want to upset him."

Instead, Reese pulled out a chair. "Soon as I get my coffee."

Her eyes narrowed. "You want to do this here, in front of him?"

"Plan to shout, do you?"

"Maybe." She hunted through the bag for a red candy. "It'll be better if I just go take my shower while you get your caffeine fix."

Before she got too far away, he spoke softly, calmly. "I thought we were going to shower together."

"Why?" She kept her back to him. "Did you want to *interrogate* me more?"

A sneer from Alice? Great. He must've really hurt her feelings, and suddenly he felt guilty. "Until I get all the answers, yes, I'll keep asking questions. But that's not why I wanted to shower with you."

She pivoted to face him. "Why, then? Did you hope to get busy in the shower, too?"

Forget guilt. It annoyed him that she kept using Rowdy's term for sex. "Actually, yes."

Her chin lifted. "I was hoping so, too. I've never had sex in the shower." Taking two steps closer, the bag of jelly beans clutched in her hand, she lowered her tone from annoyed to more curious. "How's that work exactly?"

Leave it to Alice to turn him on in the middle of an argument. There was nothing conventional about her, and he liked that. A lot.

Slowly pushing back his chair, coffee forgotten, Reese approached her. She didn't storm away.

Nice. Definitely not the typical female response.

He took her shoulders and turned her around so that she faced the fridge. Staying close to her back, he aligned their bodies. "First I'd wash you all over," he whispered near her ear. "My hands would be soapy and slick and they'd slide over your wet skin."

She held still and nodded.

So quick, so easy to turn her on. Even in the middle of anger and hurt feelings, she didn't deny either of them.

That was a very special thing—because their relationship was special. He wondered if Alice realized it.

"Here," he said, caressing her breasts, moving his palms over her nipples. "And here." He lowered a hand over her stomach, pressed it between her legs.

Her head fell back to his shoulder. "Would I wash you, too?"

He was already half hard, and with her provoking question, he went fully erect. He could practically feel her small hands working over him, and he said hoarsely, "If you wanted."

"I would."

Yes, she would. Alice never held back during sex. If only she was that honest the rest of the time.

Unwilling to have that thought intrude, Reese

blocked it and instead concentrated on the here and now with Alice. "After we're both nice and clean—"

"And excited."

Taking the bag of candy from her, Reese tossed it onto the counter. "I'd position you in a way to make it easier. Like this." He took her wrists, helping her to plant her hands flat on the front of the appliance. "Leave them there, but step back a little. Widen your stance, but keep your legs straight."

Her ass cuddled into his groin.

Biting off a groan, Reese held her hips. "That's it. Now arch your back."

She did, and he thought he'd lose it. He trailed his hands up her taut body, over her waist to her breasts. "I could take you like this, with the water running over us." He matched action to words, pressing the hard ridge of his erection to her sweet bottom. "It's a favored position of mine. I can easily hold your breasts and play with your nipples while going deep."

She groaned.

Giving up, Reese said, "I'm sorry if I upset you."

Her nipples were tight, her breath broken and fast. "Okay."

Damn it, he'd just had her last night, not that many hours ago. But with Alice, it didn't matter. Each time he had her just made him want her more. "I *had* to know, Alice." God, he hated to admit the truth, even to himself, but she left him strung so tight… "I was jealous." Of a fucking phantom—her white knight.

Another man, one who'd been there—thank God—when she needed him most.

Alice turned so suddenly that they both stumbled. Since he'd been leaning into her, lost in lustful visions, she ended up flattened against the refrigerator, his body crowding into hers. "You were jealous? Seriously?"

Trying to reorder his thoughts, Reese cupped her face. "And worried. I can't protect you if I don't know everything."

"Okay, I get the protection part. You're a detective."

Did she think he went around getting intimately involved with every woman who faced danger?

"But…jealous?" she said with a puzzled frown. "Of Trace? With *me?*"

That annoyed him. "Why not you? You're the most fascinating woman I know."

"Trace saw me only as a victim."

"Then heroic as he might've been, he was also a blind idiot."

Alice considered that, her thoughts almost transparent. She touched his chest, brushed her hand over his left nipple—which had a very different effect than when Nikki had done it—and she made up her mind.

Smiling, she grabbed his hand. "Come on."

"To the shower?" *Please let it be to the shower.*

"Yes." She hauled him into the bathroom and went to work on his slacks. "But Reese?"

His pants loosened, and she put her small hand inside, wrapping her delicate fingers around him. He caught his breath. "Hmm?"

"I *really* enjoy sex with you."

Damn it, why did that offend him? Because with Alice, he wanted it to be more than just sex.

How much more, he didn't yet know. But definitely… more. A lot. Maybe…everything.

Thoughts like that were way too heavy for the moment. Reese managed a nod. "Ditto."

"Please, don't mess things up by playing games, okay?"

"Maybe not that game," he conceded. He took her hand and removed it from his person, then bent to lift her nightgown up and over her head. "But there are other games, Alice, games that you'll absolutely enjoy."

Naked, excited, she stared up at him. "You'll show me?"

Hiding his smile, he turned on the shower, took her hand and helped her step inside.

"Give me two minutes to brush my teeth and shave." He trailed the backs of his fingers over her belly, then lower. Meeting her gaze, he said, "I don't want to leave you with whisker burns."

She released a trembling moan and nodded. "Please, hurry."

So incredibly sweet. So fucking hot. And so trusting—at least with this.

Somehow, some way, he'd earn her trust in all things. But for now, he considered this a great start.

CHAPTER SEVENTEEN

DESPITE THE FACT that they were headed to a police station, where she was sure she'd be questioned endlessly, Alice felt pretty good. After amazing sex in the shower, she'd fallen back into bed for a nap.

An hour later, she'd awakened in a cocoon of warmth, Reese holding her close to his chest, Cash curled behind her knees. Any movement at all would have disturbed them, so for a while she'd stayed still, relishing the comfort, the nearness.

The sense of being loved.

In a relatively short time, Reese and Cash had both become a part of her world. It seemed impossible to imagine an entire day without either of them. She enjoyed caring for Cash, and even arguing with Reese had its obvious rewards.

Sex in the shower and a nap—who knew that would be the result of a disagreement? For her, it was energizing and fun.

But how did Reese feel about their situation?

He'd be returning to his duties soon. She had her own stack of projects to catch up on. Would they be able to work out a compatible routine?

She glanced at Reese now, driving down the busy streets. Dressed in his work clothes, wearing dark sunglasses, apparently lost in thought, he still made her warm and melty all over.

It probably didn't matter, Alice decided, what he wore or—preferably—didn't wear. Freshly showered and shaved, hot and sweaty from a long day or, as was the case this morning, slumberous and affectionate.

She loved him. Period. She wanted every moment she could have with him, as many moments as he would give to her. But if she told him that, would he pull back? Would he consider her too clingy, too smothering?

While she'd been dressing for the day, she and Reese in the bedroom together, her parents had called. Both of them on the line, both excited to talk with her.

Reese had smiled at her, ready to give her privacy.

She didn't need it. Not with this, not with him. But instead of finishing with his clothes, he'd sat on the side of the bed and pulled her down to his lap. She'd leaned on him, his arms around her, his chin on the top of her head, while talking.

Her mother claimed that she'd read between the lines, that even in an email, she'd recognized that Alice was moving forward now—that she was ready to let them back in.

Around the joy and laughter, Alice had heard the tears in her mother's voice, the gruff emotion in her dad's. Over and over, her parents said that they loved her, that they couldn't wait to see her again.

Why she'd kept them at such a distance, she could no longer say. What had once felt important, even insurmountable, now felt…insubstantial. Even absurd.

She loved her family and they loved her.

Regardless of her past, of what she'd done, their feelings for her hadn't changed—Reese was right about that. She never should have let so much time pass away from them.

She would never let that happen again.

Unfortunately, her folks were on a vacation for two more weeks. They offered to return immediately, but Alice rejected that idea. They would all get together for dinner after they returned, preferably when her sister, Amy, had time away from her heavy class load. God, she'd missed Amy.

A lot of uncertainty remained in her future, but she had her family back, and for now at least, she had Reese and Cash. That was all pretty darned wonderful.

"I'd like to meet your parents."

Had he read her mind? "I was just thinking of them."

"Happy thoughts, I take it, given your smile?"

"Very happy." She let out a sigh. "You'll love my folks and my sister." Imagining what they'd think of Reese had her biting back a grin of pure pleasure. "They'll love you, too."

Alice watched him, but the *L* word had no noticeable effect on him.

"I promise to be as charming as possible." As Reese pulled into the police station parking lot, he reached for her knee. "You're not worrying about the interview, are you?"

"No." She trusted Reese. He kept telling her everything would be okay, so she would believe him.

"If not your folks, and not the interview, then what? And don't bother denying it, honey. I can tell you're fretting over something."

Honey. She liked that. "You think you know me that well?"

"Getting there."

Maybe it was time to stop stalling. Before they met up with his lieutenant, she had a giant truth to share. "You're right. I do have something on my mind."

He parked the car and removed his sunglasses. Pity

that, because seeing his eyes always made things more difficult for her. He had that type of penetrating gaze that made her want to squirm one way or another, even when she didn't have mammoth revelations to share.

He rested his left wrist over the steering wheel, stretched his right arm along the back of the seat.

In his crisp white button-up and necktie, he looked as comfortable as he did shirtless with his slacks undone. Wearing a slight smile, he moved his gaze over her face. "I'll be with you the whole time today." Using his right hand, he smoothed back a lock of her hair, briefly brushed a thumb over her cheek. "I promise."

"I'm glad. Thank you."

"All you have to do," he said, his tone grave, compelling her to follow his will, "is tell the truth."

"I know. That's not a problem." Not anymore. She'd given it a lot of thought, and she knew he was right. She wanted everything from him, so she needed to give him everything in return. She only prayed it'd all work out.

"Then what's wrong?"

She'd put it off long enough. Too long, really, given that they were due inside in minutes. "There's something I need to tell you before we go in."

Dread took the smile off his mouth. "I'm listening."

A deep breath didn't help, so she blurted out the truth. "Trace didn't kill Murray."

His expression fixed, voice carefully modulated, Reese said, "No?"

Alice reached up, laced her fingers in his. "He wanted to. Very much."

Slowly, Reese's gaze hardened. "You're telling me the bastard is still alive?"

What a conclusion he'd drawn! "Oh, no, he's definitely dead."

Taking that in, Reese frowned and studied her.

Her heavy heartbeat tried to shake her, but Alice tamped down the uncertainty and shared with him something she'd never told another human being. "I killed him."

That admission caused Reese's face to first go blank, then hot with some unidentifiable emotion. By small degrees, his neck stiffened, his hand tightened on hers. "What did you say?"

"I shot him in the chest, and he…died."

Reese tried to pull back, but Alice held on. She wasn't ashamed of killing Murray. She had no regrets in that regard.

But regrets with Reese…yes, she had plenty of those. "I'm sorry," she said in a rush, wanting him to understand. "It wasn't my secret to share. I wouldn't have shared it now except that I don't want you telling an inaccurate story."

The turbulence gathering in his eyes made her uneasy.

"Reese…"

Logan tapped on the driver's side window, making Alice jump.

With a low curse, Reese squeezed his eyes shut and put his head down.

Not looking at her.

He opened his fingers, releasing her hand, so she withdrew it. The chill of rejection sank in, but she would not second-guess her decision to be honest. Not anymore.

Not with Reese.

Rather than sit there waiting for him to make up his mind about…whatever decision he needed to make, Alice opened her door and got out.

Logan and Pepper looked at her with curiosity. "Everything okay?" Logan asked.

She wasn't sure. Reese might need time to come to grips with her disclosure, so she started around the hood, saying, "It might be best if we just wait inside."

Logan frowned. "Wait for *what?*"

She reached out a hand, hoping Pepper would join her. She didn't want to go in that police station alone. "For Reese to—"

Shoving open his car door, Reese emerged like a turbulent storm. His gaze pierced her, stopping her in midstep. "Don't even think it, Alice."

She thrust up her chin. "Or what? You'll arrest me?"

Scowling fiercely, he opened his mouth, then shut it again.

When Rowdy pulled up, Alice felt incredible relief. Maybe she'd get a second to talk alone with him, to ask his advice on how to—

"*No,* goddamn it." Reese slammed the car door so hard, it drew attention from other people in the lot.

Pepper murmured, "Uh-oh," at the same time that Logan whispered, "Shush."

Shoulders bunched, Reese strode over to her, clasped her chin and lifted her face. "No, Alice."

Refusing to be cowed, especially with his friends standing right there, Alice stood her ground. "No, you won't arrest me?"

Grim humor brightened his green eyes. "Actually, that part's still up in the air."

Pepper snorted.

Logan said in reproach, "Reese, for God's sake."

"What I meant," Reese said, ignoring the others, "is that you will not continue to look at Rowdy as a damned confidante."

How dare he try to order her around that way? Her friendship with Rowdy was not an illegal activity. "I will if I want to," Alice said as she pulled away.

Pepper interjected, saying, "Rowdy? Seriously?" She applauded. "Perfect choice, Alice. I've always found my brother to be completely reliable."

Now Logan scowled. "*I'm* reliable."

"Yes, you are." Pepper patted his chest. "But I don't want Alice coming to you for private talks."

Logan blustered. "I didn't mean *her*." And in an aside: "No offense, Alice."

"None taken."

"I meant *you,*" Logan told Pepper.

"Of course." She cuddled up against his uninjured side. "We are getting married, after all. Oh, and that reminds me, Alice. We've set a date. Can I still count on you to attend the wedding?"

Alice made a point of not looking at Reese. She could *feel* his pulsing anger as he stood there beside her. "Absolutely, thank you."

Logan looked at her, looked at Reese and laughed.

Reese didn't find it funny. "Shut up, Logan."

Alice bit her lip. She should have told him sooner, of course. He needed time to order his thoughts, to adjust to the new information. Not that she thought he'd actually arrest her. And she wasn't even sure he could. After all, Murray had needed killing, and she'd led a mostly quiet life since then, at least until Cheryl…

Reese shook his head. "The path your thoughts take."

Did he know her thoughts?

"You're like an open book, Alice." Then, under his breath he added, "At least most of the time."

Wide-eyed over his observation, she wondered what

to do next—and Reese took her hand. It reassured her, and she started to smile up at him.

Just then, Rowdy joined the ranks. Alice looked him over from his dark T-shirt, well-worn jeans and scuffed brown work boots, up to the eyes he had squinted against the bright sunshine.

Keys jangled in his hand as his long legs brought him closer. He took in the various expressions and asked, "Fireworks?"

"A little, yeah," Logan told him.

Grinning, Rowdy hauled Pepper right out of Logan's hold and hugged her off her feet. "Kiddo, what did you do now?"

"Not me," Pepper said, and she pointed at Alice. "Her."

Maybe going into the station alone wouldn't be so bad after all. Alice took a step toward Rowdy, but Reese wasn't letting go. "No, you don't." He brought his arm up to her shoulders and locked her in close to his side.

Then he just stood there.

Looking a little mean.

Logan lifted a brow. "What are we doing?"

"Looks to me like he's going quietly insane," Rowdy said. He tipped his chin at Alice. "Is this your doing?"

Alice slumped a little. "Yes."

"What'd you do now?"

"Well—"

Reese startled everyone when he snarled, "Even with me *standing* here, you two are doing it!"

Rowdy slowly straightened, at the same time releasing his sister. "Doing *what?*"

"Confiding," Pepper said with a grin. "Reese doesn't like how close the two of you are getting."

Alice tipped her head back to see Reese. He had his eyes narrowed in a way that made her uneasy.

Didn't seem to bother Rowdy, though.

Still, to be on the safe side, she hurried to explain. "We're just friends."

"Men and women are never *just* friends," Reese said, his hostility coming through loud and clear.

"Usually, I'd agree with you." Rowdy folded his arms over his chest. "But not this time."

"You see?" Alice stopped leaning out of Reese's hold and instead cuddled in closer. "Rowdy and I already cleared up any issue of sexual attraction. That was one of the first things we discussed."

Reese dropped his incredulous gaze down to her.

"Shit," Rowdy said. "It's not like that, Reese, and you know it."

With silky menace, Reese asked, "Do I?"

His provoking tone finally started to get to Rowdy. "You damn well should."

Logan choked. "Jesus, Reese. Get your shit together, man. I'm almost embarrassed for you."

Reese seemed uncaring what anyone else thought.

But Alice cared, darn it. "This is absurd. Rowdy isn't interested in me, and I'm not interested in him. Not that way. It's just…well, he's like a girlfriend."

Rowdy shot around to stare at her. "I am *not* your girlfriend, Alice."

Pepper barked a laugh; Logan rubbed his mouth.

Worse and worse. Alice drew a breath, let it out slowly. "I didn't mean that in an insulting way, Rowdy. Anyone can see you're all man."

Falling into her brother's shoulder, hanging on to his arm, Pepper laughed harder.

"Damn it, Pepper, you're not helping." Rowdy handed her off to Logan. "Can't you control her?"

"Not even when I have two good arms."

Alice spoke over Pepper's hilarity. "I only meant that I'm comfortable talking with you. Period. Only talk."

"Glad you cleared that up." Rowdy nodded toward his sister. "Seriously, though, if Reese is going to go red-eyed over it, Pepper can help you with…that stuff, instead."

Pepper looked shocked. "*What* stuff?"

"C'mon, kid. You know you'd be better at this than I am."

"Me? What do I know about any of that? You're the only one I ever confided in."

"And now me," Logan insisted again.

"I'm *sorry.*" Starting to feel like a complete imposition, Alice rubbed her forehead. "This has gotten out of hand. I didn't mean to bother—"

Reese spoke up, saying, "You're not a bother, Alice. Ever." He frowned at Pepper and Rowdy both.

"True," Rowdy said.

"And actually," Pepper chimed in, "I did enjoy shopping and hanging out and stuff. I haven't really had anyone to do that with either. Not for a really long time."

Reacting to Pepper's somewhat sad admission, Rowdy and Logan both reached for her, each one grabbing an arm to pull her into his side. While the men sorted out that one, over Pepper's grumbled complaints, Reese tipped up Alice's chin.

Speaking in a low whisper, he said, "You won't mention that to anyone."

"What?"

Disbelieving, he said succinctly, "What you told me in the car."

"Oh. No, I won't." And then, a little worried: "Will you?"

"Not today, no. I need time to think about things before I decide how to proceed."

Of course he did. "I'm sorry I didn't tell you sooner."

His hand left her chin, cupped around her jaw. "I'm sorry I got angry. But no more lies, Alice, not even lies of omission."

Oh, so he hadn't been upset with Rowdy? It was the whole killing Murray thing that had him so hostile?

She didn't realize that the others had gotten quiet and were listening in until Reese said, "Seeing how the two of you seem to relate so well, I'm fine with Rowdy being your girlfriend—if you still want him."

Her face went hot. She glanced back and saw everyone watching in various stages of amusement. Rowdy had his hands on his hips, his head dropped forward as he shook it.

"I didn't mean it like *that*." Alice pushed at Reese, but he didn't budge. "Don't get everyone riled up again."

Wearing the slightest of smiles, Reese held her closer. "Stop shoving away from me, okay?"

He sounded so sincere, she nodded. "Okay. Sorry."

"And stop apologizing," Rowdy added. "It isn't necessary."

Reese gave him a look, and Rowdy lifted his hands in mock apology.

Pepper spoke up. "I'm not sure how great I am at being a girlfriend, but I'm happy to try. And now that I've started on wedding plans…Reese will be the best man, Rowdy will give me away, so…would you want to stand up with me?" She rushed on, saying, "It won't be fancy at all. Just Logan's family and our group here.

But…I sort of want the whole white dress and veil and flowers."

Like a very satisfied man, Logan kept her tucked close, and he kissed her temple.

It surprised Alice to see Pepper in a sheepish, uncertain mood. It also made her heart flutter to think of attending a wedding with Reese. "You will be such a beautiful bride." She tried not to grin too much. "And, yes, I'd be honored."

"Perfect! One detail down, a hundred more to go."

Rowdy checked his watch. "We're going to be late if we don't head in now."

Logan agreed. "The lieutenant is not someone you want to keep waiting."

Looking around as Reese led the way through the station, Alice tried not to remember the last time she'd been brought in by police.

Many aspects of this station were different, but the basics were the same. Reese wanted to stop by his desk, but as they neared it, he drew up short.

"Dash?"

Sitting on a bench along the wall, Logan's younger brother looked up. Clearly surprised at seeing the group, he did a double take and then came to his feet. "Hey, Logan, Reese." His gaze moved past them to Pepper, Rowdy and Alice. "Having a party, huh?"

The joke, probably meant to deflect the attention, fell flat.

Alice noted that he'd spent some time in the sun recently, and though tanned, he now had added color in his cheekbones and along his straight nose.

Pepper noticed, too. "You went back to the lake?"

"No chance right now. We've been busy." With

Dash's sun-streaked light brown hair and the same dark brown eyes, Alice could see the resemblance to Logan.

Dash rubbed a hand over his shoulder. "Worked alongside the crew today. We had a big foundation to pour, and the sun was brutal."

Ah, so he was in construction. That made sense. Dash wasn't as muscled as Reese—few were—but he had a lean, fit body, honed from physical activity.

He stood on a par with Rowdy, a little taller than Logan's six feet, but not as tall as Reese.

My, Alice thought, seeing them all standing there together. They were an impressive lot, and more than a few female officers were giving them the eye.

Logan moved forward. "So, what are you doing here, Dash? Is something wrong?"

"Everything's…fine." There was a strangely awkward moment before Dash said, "I came to see you."

"Then you should have gone by his house," Reese told him. "He's not back to work yet."

"That's right. Damn." Dash ran a hand over his neck. "Like I said, it's been crazy at work."

Logan gave him a funny look.

"So…" Dash waffled. "If you're not working, what are you doing here?"

"Something's come up with Alice." Logan gestured at her. "You remember Alice, right?"

"Sure." He held out a hand. "Nice to see you again."

Alice smiled at him, took his hand in a brief greeting, but anyone with eyes could see he had *not* come to call on Logan.

Especially when Logan asked, "So, what's up?"

"What?"

Logan shifted, rearranging the sling on his arm. "You came to see me?"

"Oh, yeah." Putting his hands in his back pockets, Dash said, "I, ah…"

Alice heard her heels on the floor before the lieutenant came around the corner with a purposeful stride. She stalled when she saw them all together, did her own waffling, but then shot into professional mode.

She didn't even look at Dash.

Well, well. Alice picked up the signs, but when she looked at Reese and Logan, it was as if neither of them had even noticed the tension in the air.

Rowdy seemed too antsy at being in a police station to pay attention to much beyond all the armed officers. She glanced at Pepper, but like Rowdy, Pepper spent her time gazing around uneasily.

The big wall clock showed they were only tardy by five minutes, but still Reese said, "Sorry we're late."

Her tone clipped, irritation clear, Lieutenant Peterson said, "It's just as well since I had to attend a special meeting."

"What special meeting?" Logan wanted to know.

The lieutenant's speculative gaze landed on Alice. "I've been informed that we can talk about the possible connection of the tattooed girls, but the rest is off-limits."

Oh, shoot. Alice knew only too well what that meant: Trace had put the kibosh on any further snooping that might lead to him.

Reese didn't take the edict well. "What do you mean, *off-limits?*"

Alice almost winced.

Stepping closer so that no one else would overhear, the lieutenant said, "I mean that orders came down the chain of command. I was told in no uncertain terms to back off. Any and all discussions of her time as a kidnap victim are forbidden. Most especially any discussion concerning third-party vigilantes."

CHAPTER EIGHTEEN

LOGAN LOOKED STUNNED. "The hell you say."

Reese started to speak, and Peterson said, "End of story, Detective."

Reese knotted his hands. "How did anyone even know?"

"I have no idea." Again Peterson looked at Alice. "Perhaps you should ask her?"

Both Logan and Reese turned to her with accusation. Shaking her head, Alice fought the urge to physically retreat. "I haven't spoken to anyone."

Pepper, Rowdy and Dash held silent. To Alice, it felt as if they'd all tried her and found her guilty.

Slowly, eyes flinty and untrusting, Reese turned away from Alice to address Peterson. "A word, please?"

"Certainly," she agreed, gesturing for Logan and Reese to follow her into her office. Her own annoyance overflowed as she quipped, "As long as it's the right word, not the forbidden word, I'm all ears."

Not liking it but unable to change things, Reese agreed.

That's how it worked.

He said to Alice, "Wait here." Slanting a sharp look at Rowdy, he added, "She doesn't go anywhere alone."

"Got it covered."

"Thanks."

The commands didn't bother Alice near as much

as watching him go. Blast the man, he had demanded trust from her and so she'd shared her biggest secret.

But did he give trust in return? No. How could he think that she'd instigated a gag order? Why would she confess to him and then do that? It didn't even make sense. And if he'd just asked her—privately—she probably could have explained. But, no, instead he—

"Alice?" Looking very put upon, Rowdy pointed out the bench that Dash had vacated. "Why don't you and Pepper park it over there and…I don't know. Chat or something."

Encouraging her again to make Pepper her confidante?

Rowdy sighed. "If you need to talk to me…?"

"No, I don't." It was bad enough that she'd told Reese about Trace. No way would she tell Pepper and Rowdy, too. "What are you going to do, though?"

"I'm going to stay out of the way as much as I can."

Dash said, "I'll keep you company." The men moved to stand against the wall a few feet away—out of sight of the officers.

Poor Rowdy. He really didn't like anyone in law enforcement, and yet his sister would soon marry a cop. Not that she thought Rowdy would let that get to him for long. Rowdy was a survivor because he knew how to adapt to changing situations.

He would adjust to this, as well.

Putting Rowdy from her mind, Alice sank down to sit on the bench. She was both hurt that Reese had given her such an accusing look and nettled that he hadn't taken her at her word. In the car she'd shared her biggest secret, so he should trust her now.

Settling down beside her, Pepper nudged her with her elbow. "What's going on with you two?"

"What do you mean?" Alice hedged.

Pepper gave her a long, droll look. "You guys shoot sparks one minute, and antagonism the next. Are things not going well?"

"It's complicated." There were so many things on her mind, Alice couldn't even sort it out to herself. She had mostly forgiven Reese's sexual interrogation, and she'd confessed about killing Murray. But now, in the face of his continued distrust, she had to wonder if she'd made a monumental mistake.

"You know," Pepper said, "I've always found that things seem less complicated once I share them. Of course, Rowdy is the one I always shared with, and he has a great way of breaking stuff down so it's not so overwhelming."

"He does," Alice agreed. "He's such a…plain speaker." Rowdy never hesitated to tell her things, regardless of how intimate they might seem to her. But she couldn't tell him about Reese playing games in bed.

Given that Rowdy was a dominating personality, she could only imagine how he'd smile over Reese's methods of getting info.

Pepper looked down at her feet, offering in an offhand way, "If you'd rather talk to him, I understand."

"It's not that." Maybe she shouldn't have told Reese about Trace. Surely he wouldn't say anything to the lieutenant, not after being warned away.

What would Trace do if Reese didn't let it go?

Because somehow, she just *knew* Reese wouldn't.

Her head throbbed with possibilities.

"Alice?"

She squeezed her eyes shut. "I might have really screwed up."

"How so?" And then, with suspicion, "What did Reese do?"

"Nothing." Yet. But if he pressed the matter…

"I'm not buying it." Pepper studied her. "Reese did something, and now you're upset. God, he can be such a jerk."

"No," Alice denied. "He's not a jerk, but he is occasionally autocratic. And stubborn. And maybe a little *too* protective."

"Yeah?" Grinning with interest, Pepper asked, "What else?"

"Actually, he's pretty wonderful." When he wasn't being distrustful or asking her too many questions. Her face flushed at the reminder of how he'd gotten his answers. "Most of the time, anyway."

"Not perfect—same as everyone else, I guess, huh?"

Not perfect, but close. "I guess."

Alice nudged her again, playfully this time. "I won't pry, but remember what I told you. You can trust me if you ever want to talk."

Maybe a different perspective would help. She eyed Pepper's encouraging smile and figured, what the heck. "Reese used sex against me."

Pepper's smile slipped. "Come again?"

"He wanted to know things…about my past. Things that, I take it from the lieutenant's dictate, won't be discussed here after all."

"Wow." Fascinated, Pepper sat back. "I wondered what that was all about."

"I'm sorry I can't tell you details."

"Obviously not, since it's forbidden." Worried now, Pepper asked, "You aren't in any trouble, are you?"

"No, it's nothing like that."

"Good. I'm glad." She searched Alice's face, then prompted her with, "So Reese wanted these answers...?"

She nodded. "I didn't want to tell him. I mean, we truly haven't known each other that long."

"Pfft. I loved Logan right from the start."

Love. Wide-eyed, Alice said, "You did?"

"Sure. I didn't realize it at the time, not until he double-crossed me in a really rotten way. Then it was so crushing, I knew I more than liked him. If I only liked him, it wouldn't have hurt so much, and I wouldn't have been so obsessed with it all. With him."

Wow. "Logan double-crossed you?"

"Big-time. But that's another story, and right now we're talking about you."

"But...since you loved Logan, did you trust him?"

Laughing, Pepper said, "Shoot, no. I had secrets about my secrets." She sobered. "But looking back, I know that if I had trusted him sooner, we'd have saved a lot of time, and maybe he wouldn't have gotten shot."

Alice took her hand. "I'm sure that wasn't your fault."

"Maybe." Pepper let out a breath. "Let's get on to the juicy part of how Reese used sex against you."

Alice felt a gaze on her, and she glanced at Rowdy and got caught. Dash talked to him, and Rowdy nodded as if he listened and heard. But his attention stayed on Alice.

She blushed as if he could actually hear her, and Rowdy smiled.

Alice gulped and turned away. She should probably get through the story before Reese returned.

God, how did she even put it into words? "He got me...worked up."

"In bed?" Pepper asked in the same low voice Alice had used.

Alice nodded. "Then he asked me the stuff he knew I didn't want to talk about."

"Because he figured you were distracted with lust, huh?"

"Yes."

"That kinky bastard."

Kinky? Pepper didn't think it was…mean? Or underhanded.

"Let me guess." Full of sympathy, Pepper squeezed both her hands. "You're hurt? Embarrassed?"

"Well…yes." Who wouldn't be?

"It was pretty diabolical, I'll give you that. But tell me this—knowing Reese is a detective, and knowing he cares about you, did he ask about stuff that he needed to know? Or at least thought he needed to know?"

Alice dropped her shoulders. "Yes." In for a penny… "I came to that conclusion on my own. I knew I had to come clean about everything, but I had to figure out a way."

"So you *did* tell him?"

"Yes." She bit her lip. "After we were in the parking lot."

"Ah." Pepper nodded. "So that's why he was so hot under the collar? Well, that and he's jealous of my brother."

Alice didn't want there to be any bad feelings between Pepper and Reese. After all, Reese and Logan were best friends. She'd hate herself if she inadvertently caused an issue. "Reese trusts Rowdy. He's just…well, we don't have a clear understanding yet."

"Meaning you're falling for him, but he hasn't yet told you how he feels?"

Alice's shoulders slumped. "Pretty much."

"So, get even." Warming to that idea, Pepper said,

"You can make yourself feel better about how Reese used you if you use him back, and you can turn the tables on him and get answers of your own."

A little scandalized, Alice said, "I couldn't!"

"Of course you can. Payback doesn't have to be hell." Pepper bobbed her eyebrows. "It can be loads of fun."

Alice whispered, "Did you…?"

"With Logan? You betcha." Pepper leaned closer. "We'd had great sex, so even though I was pissed at him, I figured why should I suffer?"

Sex with anyone other than Reese would be suffering.

"We had to hide out in his brother's lake house. Shhh, the property's top secret, so don't tell anyone about it. Dash wants to keep it private, so only Reese, Logan and I know about it. Well, and now you. But anyway, each night when it was time for bed, I went to Logan. We'd have mind-blowing sex—and then…" Pepper got quiet.

Oh, no. She couldn't leave her hanging like that. "And then what?"

"I left him to go sleep by myself."

How…sad. "What did Logan say about that?"

"He didn't like it, but men do not turn down sex. Especially not sex with women they care about. And trust me, Reese cares about you."

God, she hoped Pepper was right. Still, she had grave reservations about the plan. "I don't know. Logan and Reese are very different men."

"True. But they're still men."

Both women jumped when Rowdy said, "Pepper is right. We're easy."

Heat rushed into Alice's face.

Rowdy chucked her under the chin. "I didn't mean to eavesdrop, but you two can't whisper worth a damn."

Pepper glared at her brother. "You had to be straining your ears!"

"Just be glad I took Dash up on his offer to get us drinks, or he'd have heard it all, too."

Looking mean, Pepper stood to face Rowdy. "Doesn't matter. He was there at the cottage when I got my *revenge* on Logan."

"Trust me, kiddo, no way did Dash feel sorry for him. For you, that was a lousy idea." He turned to Alice. "But for you—I say, go for it. Reese will spill his guts with a smile on his face."

There was that plain speaking Alice had admired. Now, though, in the middle of a police station with Pepper listening in, it wasn't quite so appreciated.

Luckily, Dash came back with four frosty cans of Coke, so nothing more was said on the subject. That didn't stop her from thinking about it, though, and forming some solid plans.

"HOW?" REESE DEMANDED. "How could anyone have known if Alice didn't say anything?"

Peterson took a chair at the long table. "You're sure she didn't?"

"Yeah." He rubbed the back of his neck. "She said she didn't, so she didn't. She wouldn't lie about that." But damn it, she'd killed a man and hadn't seen fit to tell him.

"Then I'd say someone has eyes everywhere."

"Which means," Logan said, pointing out the obvious, "he's someone with power."

"Yeah."

"Not that we're talking about this," Peterson pointed out. She tapped her nails on the conference table, then added, "Supposedly a certain senator ordered the gag."

A senator.

"My orders came from the captain." More tapping. "And he was quite clear on it all."

Logan sank into his own seat. "Maybe we're looking at this the wrong way. Could be the vigilante is more like a secret op or something."

"Maybe," Reese conceded. But damn it, he needed to know, whether Alice felt like sharing or not. "I trust her."

Logan lifted his brows. "Come again?"

"Alice." He paced the small confines of the conference room. "I trust her. She wouldn't be protecting the guy if he was hurting anyone other than the creeps who need it."

"Who needs it," Peterson pointed out, "is up to the judicial system."

"Maybe," Reese said again.

When Peterson and Logan both stared at him, he pulled up a chair of his own and leaned over the table toward them. "How many times has a ruthless murderer slipped through the cracks? How many times has evidence gotten botched and some asshole gets loose, only to kill again?"

Peterson rolled her eyes. "Not that we're discussing this."

"No, we're not." Reese made up his mind. He'd find out what he needed to know, but he'd trust Alice enough to keep others out of it. In his heart—damn, when had his heart gotten tangled up in this?—he knew she was one of the most moral, honest, caring women he'd ever met.

How could he betray her? He couldn't.

"Let's get this over with." He left the room to fetch

Alice and Rowdy. He found them with Dash and Pepper, drinking Cokes and joking around. "Alice?"

Her gaze met his, and she turned bright red.

What the hell was that about? Rowdy grinned, saluted him with his Coke and asked, "Can we common folk join the discussion now? I gotta tell you, being surrounded by the boys in blue makes me itchy."

Several cops glanced at Rowdy, but overall they ignored him.

Reese ignored him, too. "Dash, can you stay with Pepper? We won't be long."

"Sure. No problem."

Pepper started to object, and Reese said, "Alice?" He held out his hand. "Come on, honey. We're ready for you."

He hoped Alice understood his acceptance, but in case she didn't, as soon as she got close, he said low, "I'm sorry."

Blinking big brown eyes up at him, she asked, "For what?"

"For thinking, even for a second, that you'd somehow alerted Trace."

"You believe me that I didn't?"

Pausing outside the door to the conference room, Reese gave one sharp nod. "No more secrets between us. Right?"

"Um…" Like a deer caught in the headlights, she froze. "Okay?"

Reese smiled. It was an agreement, albeit uncertain, maybe even unwilling. "Good." He held her shoulders. "You ready to do this?"

"Of course."

So stubbornly independent. "It doesn't bother you,

does it?" He caressed her, fought the urge to kiss her. "Being here?"

Maybe having the same thought, Alice leaned into him, her face tipped back, her eyes warm on his mouth. "I thought it would." She put a hand on his chest, stroked up and over his shoulder. "But I got so involved chatting with Pepper that I forgot all about it."

Every time she *chatted* with Pepper, he worried. Not that he didn't like Pepper, because he did. But at all times, she was like a small, sexy explosion waiting to happen. The last thing he wanted was for her to influence Alice.

"The meeting is in here, Detective."

At Peterson's forceful tone, Reese gave Alice an encouraging smile and steered her into the room.

For the next forty-five minutes he sat back and let Logan and Peterson ask questions of Rowdy and Alice. It worked better to let someone fresh, someone uninvolved, get the info from them.

Alice handled it like a pro. It amazed him the amount of details she remembered, and how accurately she relayed them again. So often, witnesses got confused or mixed up about the order of things. Excitement and adrenaline caused a lot of people to miss specifics of the surrounding area, time frame, location, sometimes even the appearance of an attacker.

Not Alice. At all times, she remained alert, soaking up details the same way a detective might. Now, in relating those details, she didn't come across as phony or like she was making up anything. She shared what she could, and occasionally enhanced what Rowdy had seen while attempting to trail her.

The different perspectives from their accounts matched up.

When Peterson pulled out a folder, Reese realized that the lieutenant planned to show a photo of the murdered girl. He moved closer, sitting beside Alice, his hand on the back of her chair.

Alice must have realized what she'd see, because she braced herself. The subtle shifting of her shoulders, the tightness in her expression, might not have been obvious to the others, but Reese knew her. He saw the dread and the iron will that kept her in the seat.

"Is this the same tattoo?" Peterson laid the photo on the table, turned it and moved it forward.

On the other side of Alice, Rowdy's expression hardened. He cursed low.

With sadness filling her features, Alice took her time studying the photograph. "When did she die?"

"Recently," Reese said, not wanting to involve her with all the nitty-gritty. She'd already dealt with enough ugliness in her lifetime.

Alice lifted the photo to see the tattoo better. She drew in a shaky breath, blinked back tears.

Peterson said gently, "Take your time."

"It's similar." Alice dug in her purse and found a tissue, then drew a steadying breath. She didn't make a big deal of her tears, either to apologize for them or to seek sympathy. "Not exactly like Cheryl's, but pretty close."

"Same size?" Logan asked.

"Yes." Alice touched her own forearm. "From here to here," she said, indicating just above her wrist to just below her elbow. "About five or six inches long and less than three inches wide. It didn't circle her arm. It was sort of contained in a narrow rectangle but without a frame." She looked up at Peterson. "Cheryl's was still red. I think she'd just had it done."

Taking the photo back, Peterson returned it to the folder.

Logan said, "You're sure you didn't get a last name? Didn't see where Cheryl was headed?"

"I didn't want to pry." Peeking over at Reese, Alice shrugged. "But I did give her a phone number that she could call in case of an emergency."

Reese wanted to groan. "The police?" he asked hopefully. Or maybe the elusive Trace.

Alice shook her head. "She wanted nothing to do with the police."

Indignant, Peterson dropped the folder on the tabletop and sat back in her chair.

"You could've given her my number," Rowdy told Alice.

"Cheryl didn't know you. And right then, she wasn't feeling real comfortable with men."

Already knowing the answer, Reese took Alice's hand. "So, whose number did you give her?"

Wincing her apology, Alice whispered, "Mine."

REESE FELT THE way she held on to him, almost like a lifeline. The entire situation left her far more stressed than others would know. "Your cell?"

She shook her head. "A cell phone, yes, but not my regular phone." She skimmed the faces of Peterson and Logan before focusing on Reese. "I'm not an idiot, and I don't take chances."

"I know that." Not dumb by any stretch, but too daring? Too bold? Absolutely.

"I keep extra cell phones for…emergencies." Rushing beyond that, probably hoping it wouldn't draw notice—ha!—she added, "I've been carrying the phone since then, but Cheryl hasn't called, so I'm assuming she made it home okay."

A cautious move, to give Cheryl a different number. But that didn't excuse things. "Why didn't you tell me before now?"

Looking him in the eye, not really making any excuses, Alice said, "If Cheryl had called, I would have told you." She turned to face the others. "No one else has that particular number, so any call will be from Cheryl, or someone who got the number from her."

Keeping the annoyance from his tone wasn't easy, but Reese didn't want Peterson or Logan to get the wrong idea. Or maybe the right idea: that he didn't have control of the situation at all. "Anything else you haven't mentioned?"

She nodded.

Great. "Now would be a good time then, don't you think?"

"I told Cheryl we'd need a code of sorts in case anyone found her, or tried to coerce her in any way. The plan is that if someone is listening to her, she's to tell me that everything is peachy."

"Peachy?"

Alice shrugged. "It's not an everyday phrase, but it's not so obvious that others might understand. I told her if she said that, I'd know something was wrong, and I'd do everything in my power to help her."

So, she had planned to stay involved? Frustration rushed through Reese. He scraped back his chair and stood. "Everything being *what?*" She was one small woman, untrained, too soft—

Alice rose to stand before him. "Everything being… you."

"Me?" Damn it, he hadn't seen that one coming. Chagrined, especially with the others watching, Reese said, "So you think I'm in your power, do you?"

Alice nodded. "It's within my power to tell you. And, of course, if you know those creeps have found her again, you'll help her."

Irrefutable logic. What could he do but concede the point? "Of course."

The beatific smile Alice gave him made him feel like Superman. *Not* kissing her was difficult, he was so… Damn, he was proud. Of how she'd held it together under the difficult situation, and her faith in him.

Peterson cleared her throat. Logan frowned and Rowdy smiled.

Time to take charge. Again. Why was it that every time he got around Alice, he had to regroup? If he didn't take care, he'd end up with a boner for all to see.

Taking her wrist, he removed her hand from his chest and sought some needed distance from her influence. "I think that's all we need from you."

Unfazed by the dismissal, she resisted his efforts to guide her to the door. "You'll let me know your plans?"

Pushy. But so sweet, too. "Probably not." Before Alice could get too worked up over that, Reese got her to the door. "I need a few more minutes. Why don't you and Rowdy wait with Dash and Pepper?"

Confusion blunted her composure. "Reese?"

Definitely pushy. "I won't be long."

"But—"

Rowdy gently caught her arm and, with a nod at Reese, took her along with him as he exited the room.

The second the door closed, Peterson said, "Well. That was interesting."

Wasn't it, though? Reese sought words to explain

Alice's unique gift of deception and details, but Peterson gave her attention to Logan.

"Why exactly is your brother here?"

CHAPTER NINETEEN

GLAD FOR THE reprieve, Reese waited for Logan to answer.

"He probably came to catch lunch with me or something. He said he forgot I was off for a few days."

Incredulous, Peterson rose to collect her papers into a folder. "You're saying that he forgot you were shot?"

Logan shifted uneasily. "Dash knows a measly wound wouldn't keep me from working."

Reese snorted. The bullet that had torn through Logan's arm was far from measly. Helping Peterson along in her conclusions, Reese said, "Being Dash is in construction, he probably didn't understand that any officer-involved shooting takes you out of the action whether you like it or not."

"For one more day," Peterson agreed.

Forget that! No way in hell would Reese let her assign Logan as the lead again.

Not in this.

Not with Alice involved.

Of course, it was Alice's involvement that might get him excluded. Anyone could see they had a relationship. It was department policy to keep detectives out of cases that hit too close to home. An impartial detective was better than someone with an emotional vendetta.

Course, that hadn't kept Logan from going after the threat to Pepper.

Maybe he should just take charge before Peterson had too much time to mull it over. Given an opportunity, she might let her personal dislike of Reese make up her mind for her.

Crossing his arms over his chest, Reese leaned on the door—blocking the way. "So, we're dealing with drugs, possibly kidnapping and murder."

"How are we going to handle it?" Logan asked.

Peterson shook her head. "We're short-staffed, as you both know."

As if feeling guilty, Logan said, "I'm ready for full-go."

Reese nipped that idea real fast. "Pepper will tie you to the bed if you even try it."

Rounding on him—and then wincing with pain—Logan cursed. "Stop making it sound like she's my mother, will you?"

With the lustful way Pepper looked at Logan, no one would ever make that mistake. "Fine." Reese lifted a brow. "Tell her and let's see what she does."

A feral growl brought Logan to his feet. "She does not dictate to me."

"From what I've witnessed—"

Peterson laughed.

It so startled Reese that he did a double take. He and Logan shared a look of confusion.

"The power of women," she murmured, and then gave them both a quelling stare. "Starting Monday, Reese, you take lead."

Now that he had his way, he moved from the door. "If that's what you want." One way or another, he'd have worked it out, but it was nice that Peterson just handed it to him.

With her hand on the doorknob, Peterson paused. "Pick a team, then let me know."

"Of course."

Rather than depart, she emphasized, "Let. Me. Know."

"Right." It wasn't that long ago that Reese hadn't trusted her and had kept quite a bit from her. "Even injured, Logan will be useful, I'm sure."

"Gee, thanks," Logan said, completely deadpan. "Glad to hear I'm not totally useless."

"Pepper would deny such a thing with her dying breath."

Interrupting them with a huff, Peterson jerked the door open. And still she lingered, her gaze sizing up Reese once more. "Of course, you also have your little network of other trustworthy cops, now, don't you?"

"Guilty." He'd made it his business to know who was above reproach and who might be on the take. Peterson had ferreted out a lot of the problems, but these days, Reese left nothing to chance. He'd amassed his own group of loyals. They had come in handy more than once.

With a furtive look, Peterson ensured no one listened in. "If, until Monday, you choose to do some checking on your own time, keep it to yourself and make sure no one else finds out." And with that, she marched away.

Now that Peterson was out of the room, Logan asked, "What the hell, Reese? Care to tell me what that was all about?"

Ah, of course Logan had known he had a motive for his gibes. "You got lead last time." Unrepentant, he shrugged. "I needed her to give this one to me."

"But you made me sound whipped."

"If the whip fits..."

"Go screw yourself."

Reese couldn't keep a straight face. He grinned as he held the door open for Logan. "Actually, I'm happy for you. You two make a great couple."

"Jealous, huh? I figured."

Reese knew Logan was kidding, but still he nodded. "Yeah, sure. I'd like what you have."

Logan paused. "With Alice?"

"Now, there's the million dollar question, yes?" Did he want something that powerful, that permanent, with Alice? Despite her eccentric way of keeping secrets? Her off-limits background? Her lack of trust?

Probably.

"I'm thinking of buying a house."

Logan whistled. "For you and Alice?"

"Cash was the motivation, really. He needs room to run, more room than afforded by an apartment on the second floor."

"Cash, huh?" Logan idly rubbed the shoulder of his injured arm. "That's the only reason?"

"Are you taking your pain pills?"

"At night." Realizing what he was doing, Logan dropped his hand and affected a look of boredom. "The meds muddle me too much during the day."

Logan should about be done with his antibiotics, and he'd only need the sling a week or so longer. Thank God the bullet hadn't done more damage.

They'd been friends for a very long time. Reese trusted Logan with his life, so why not trust him with this, as well?

"The thing is," Reese said, wanting to say it out loud, "I can't imagine Cash playing in the yard without imagining Alice nearby, as well."

Staring off at nothing in particular, Logan shifted his stance. "That was awfully fast."

"Look who's talking."

Head down, he nodded. "Yeah, I know." Finally he looked at Reese. "It wasn't easy. Still isn't, really."

"But all the same, it feels right."

Logan lifted one shoulder. "That's about it."

Both solemn and introspective, they stared toward the women, again ensconced on the bench, their heads together in conversation.

Nearby, Rowdy stood with his arms crossed, his gaze watchful as he contemplated everyone and everything in the station with palpable suspicion. No, for Logan, it wouldn't be easy. Not until, if ever, Rowdy got settled.

When Alice blushed, Reese felt a stirring deep inside. Lust, but something else, too. Something...*more.* As Logan said, it wasn't easy. Hell, sometimes it was damned uncomfortable. "Wonder what they're talking about."

"I don't know about Alice," Logan murmured, "but Pepper doesn't do the usual girl talk."

"Shopping, cooking, makeup?" No, that wasn't Pepper. "More often than not, I think she's conspiring something."

"Probably." Logan studied her some more, then grinned and sent his good elbow into Reese's ribs. "Given the look on Pepper's face, I'd say they're talking sex."

Great. Just what he didn't need to know. Was Pepper sharing advice, or encouragement?

Veering off topic, Reese said, "You think Pepper will give you enough privacy to do some work over the weekend?" He eyed Logan's arm in the sling. "Off the clock, that is."

"She understands my job." Like a man satisfied, Logan had to pull his attention off his fiancée. "What'd you have in mind?"

"Rowdy is going to scope out the area tattoo parlors. If he reports back to you, could you do some background checks on the owners, managers and employees?" Alice noticed them and, with a secretive smile, started toward him. Watching her every step, wondering what she had planned, Reese said low, "See if anything jumps out."

"Not a problem." Before she got too close, Logan said, "Since it looks like you'll be busy, I'll get hold of Rowdy myself. I'll call you when I know something."

"Thanks."

Color still high in her face, her dark eyes mysterious, Alice stopped before him. "All done?"

"Yes." She sounded breathless. How soon could he get her alone?

With a mocking salute, Logan went to talk with Rowdy and Pepper.

Reese looked, but he didn't see Dash anywhere. "Where did Logan's brother go?"

Leaning into him, Alice whispered, "I think he followed your lieutenant."

"Why?"

"He's interested in her."

Reese snorted in disbelief, but when Alice didn't smile, didn't show any sign of jesting, he sobered real quick. "Not possible."

She chided him with a roll of her eyes. "Did you buy that nonsense about him coming here to see Logan? I don't know him well, but Dash doesn't strike me as a dummy. He wouldn't have forgotten that his brother was shot."

Reese had wondered about that, but with so many other things on his mind…

Well. Given that Logan and Dash were close, and Dash had been there with Logan when he'd gotten shot, had stayed with him at the hospital, too, it didn't seem feasible for him to just forget.

Dash and the lieutenant, huh? No, Reese couldn't bend his brain around anything that bizarre. He'd known them both a long time, Peterson as his superior, Dash as an extension of his close friendship with Logan.

Dash successfully played the field, with *play* being the operative word. He dedicated himself fully to his job and his family. But when it came to women, he gravitated toward beautiful, stacked…fluff.

Peterson was not fluff. Far from it. From what Reese could see through her "all-business" attire, she wasn't stacked either.

As to being beautiful…Reese supposed if he could look at her in an unbiased way—which challenged his imagination a lot—he could see a certain appeal. Maybe if a guy ever got her blue eyes softened with lust, or mussed her always tidy, short brown hair… No.

He shook his head, denying the possibility.

Petite, toned and bristling with intent. That was Lieutenant Margaret Peterson. Dash, who was far less serious than Logan, worked hard at his construction company and even harder at having fun.

He did not work hard for women.

Surely Alice had to be mistaken. Yet…she was awfully astute.

Did Logan realize? Of course not. If he did, he'd be on Dash's ass already. Reese groaned. "I hope you're wrong, honey."

She tipped her head. "Why?"

"Because no way in hell will the lieutenant appreciate Dash's interest. It's more likely than not that she'll only get more difficult, and I'll still have to work with her. That's why."

"Oh, I don't know," Alice said. She took his hand as they headed out to the parking lot. "I think Lieutenant Peterson just might surprise you."

For Reese, that idea was even more repugnant. He knew how to deal with *this* Peterson. The last thing he wanted was a new dimension to that ball-busting personality.

Pushing away impossible thoughts of Peterson in a sexual relationship, Reese slipped his arm around Alice. "You and Pepper seemed to find plenty to talk about."

Alice ducked her face. "She's very nice."

"To you." Reese opened the car door for her, then went around to the driver's side.

"She likes you, too," Alice said.

"Too?"

Smiling, Alice said, "You both bluster, but the mutual fondness is easy to see."

For Alice, it might be easy. "You think so, do you?"

She took his teasing comment to heart. "In some ways, you're very easy to read."

Reese wasn't sure he wanted Alice "reading" him. He wasn't used to it. But he supposed if he wanted to keep her around, and he definitely did, he should accustom himself.

He started the car and got on the road. After a minute, he cupped his hand over her knee. "Do you know what I'm thinking about now?"

"Yes." She covered his hand with her own. "You're concerned about the people involved in tattooing and drugs, and you're worried about me, even though I keep telling you not to be, and you're thinking about how much juggling you're going to have to do."

Damn. She'd nailed it. "Actually, I assume I won't have to juggle." He gave her knee a gentle squeeze. "Because you're not going to keep any more secrets."

"No, I won't."

"Good." He'd never get a better opening than this. Even though it was forbidden—maybe especially because it was forbidden—he needed to know how she contacted Trace. He put both hands back on the wheel. "So, how about you tell me how I can reach your buddy?"

CHAPTER TWENTY

ALICE BARELY HELD back her groan. Like a dog with a bone, Reese didn't want to let it go. "It would be…better if you didn't bother him."

Displeasure caused a muscle to tic in his jaw. "Better for you?"

"Better for everyone." Now that he'd removed his touch, she felt bereft. Physical contact with Reese always made her feel more settled. Putting a hand on his forearm, Alice gave him the truths he wanted. "If it's that important, I'll tell you. I swear. But it'd be nice if you trusted me even half as much as you want me to trust you."

"Shit."

She smiled. "I know. You don't like it when I turn things back on you. But it's the same principle, Reese."

"Not even close. He's a loose end—an unknown variable."

Alice shook her head. "He's not a threat. Not to you and not to me."

"Maybe. But that's something I'd like to conclude on my own."

After a lot of needless prying. "Why?" She didn't want to change Reese, so she had better learn to understand him. "Because you're a detective?"

"There's that, and the fact that I want to protect you."

"I'm not in any danger." Nothing immediate, anyway.

"Jesus, Alice. You don't *know* that." Frustration carved a scowl in his features, delineated every muscle in his arms and shoulders. "A woman is dead. Another woman is on the run. And you—" he scalded her with a burning glance "—put yourself into the thick of it."

"None of that has anything to do with Trace." Yet. But if Trace thought there was any danger to her…

Shoot.

Probably another truth she ought to share with Reese. She sighed, and even that made Reese more alert.

"All right," he said. "Let's hear it."

It was kind of a nice thing, having all that single-minded concentration from a man like Detective Reese Bareden. "There's no reason for you to reach out to Trace. If he doesn't want to connect with you, he won't."

Stopping for a light, Reese locked his jaw, waited.

And Alice added, "But if he does…you'll be hearing from him."

Going rigid, Reese slowly turned his head to stare at her in disbelief. "Just like that?"

"I told you he had great contacts. Now you've seen how great." The light changed, and Reese turned back to the road, maneuvering through the traffic.

Hands flexing on the steering wheel, Reese gave one nod of grudging acceptance. "He didn't want to be investigated, so he officially closed that option."

"Yes." Unofficially, though, Alice knew Reese would continue to pry.

"He must have some high officials in his back pocket."

Reese continued to look at this all wrong, staying suspicious of Trace. Or…maybe as he said, he was jealous. Hoping to pacify him, she said, "I'm sure I won't, but if I hear from him, I'll tell you immediately."

"Even if he tells you not to?"

She ran her fingers over his thick forearm. The hair there was soft, his skin warm, his muscles so well defined. "He wouldn't," she said simply.

Reese groaned. "God, you've got him on a pedestal."

Of course she did. Trace was that kind of man.

But then, so was Reese, and he was the man she wanted. Now, tomorrow.

Forever.

Her mouth went dry—with acceptance and with uncertainty. She needed to know if Reese's heart was involved. Falling in love alone would be…well, tragic. And she'd had enough tragedy in her life.

"Could you maybe take a day or two to think about it? To *try* to trust my judgment on this?" She cut him off before he could complain over her request. "And then, if you still want to know—"

"*Need* to know."

"—I'll tell you."

Quiet, thoughtful, Reese took the road toward their apartment complex. "One condition, Alice."

Her pulse sped up. "What is it?"

"I stay with you."

That sweet, familiar ache pulsed between her legs. "In my bed?"

Satisfaction kicked up a wicked smile. "That'd be my preference, but it's always up to you." He shifted, stretching out one leg. "I meant in your apartment."

"Oh." How would that work? Them living like… roommates? No, thank you.

As if to convince her, Reese said, "I don't want you alone until I'm sure that there isn't any danger."

Had they come full circle? She sighed. "Danger from Trace?"

"Actually, I was talking about the bastards using

women as drug mules." He shook his head, correcting himself. "But, yeah, your mysterious wraith, too. Hell, anyone from your past. Or…basically, anyone or anything."

Alice licked her lips. "How long do you think that'll take?"

"Days. Weeks." He checked the rearview mirror, switched lanes. "No telling, really. In cases like this, we could get a break tomorrow or still be floundering months from now."

Months! If it weren't for women being in danger, she'd hope for the latter. "I see."

Reese shifted his shoulders. "If that's a problem, remember that I still have my own place and a job that sometimes keeps me away for the better part of the day. I won't be underfoot."

Why did he look so uncomfortable? He kept adjusting his big body as if trying to settle in. "I wasn't worried about that." But if he only wanted to be with her as protection, should she tell him that she loved having him around for any reason?

"I like that Cash will be with you during the day." He glanced at her, then away. "But at night, I want to be right there with you."

"Okay." Hopefully, he'd solve the case quickly, but in the meantime she'd have an opportunity to make him fall in love with her. "I have a condition of my own."

He gave a nod of acceptance. "I'm all ears."

"No sleeping on the couch." And to make certain he understood, she added, "If you're there, even if it's just in the capacity of a detective, I want you to…sleep with me."

"Sleep, huh?" The quirky smile lifted into a full-fledged grin. "I can handle that."

"I mean it, Reese." She wanted no misunderstandings. "Even if I do something that annoys you. Or if we argue. You don't get to shut me out."

He surprised her by laughing. "I don't move in on women just to play cop, Alice. I'm worried, true, but I wouldn't get hard every time we talked if I only had protection on my mind."

Her gaze shot to his lap, to the impressive bulge there, and she let out a breath. "Oh." She reached for him, intent on touching. Stroking. "Good."

He caught her hand, kissed her fingers. Fondness softened his humor. "If we start that, I'm liable to wreck. Just give me five more minutes, and we'll be home."

"Okay, but hurry."

He answered by accelerating. "You're one of a kind, honey. Do you know that?"

Probably. Not many women had spent a year in captivity, forced to work for a monster. That experience had forever changed her, giving her a unique perspective on life. She knew what she wanted, and she'd go after it.

Reese might not realize it, but she wanted him.

For however long she had, she'd do what she could to win his heart.

And she'd start with Pepper's plan…as soon as she worked up her nerve.

WOODY SIMPSON LEANED back on the brick wall of the college bookstore, eyeing the merchandise as it passed. Sophomore girls with explosive sexual appetites, a few young teachers flattered by his attention, a volleyball coach with strong legs.

He admired them all, but it was the timid freshman,

her load of books hugged to her chest, her expression flustered, that drew him.

With Cheryl soon to be out of the picture, he needed a replacement to keep up with demand. The little babe with her insecurity and anxious hope would be easier to handle than the others. He watched her as she peered around the campus, a little lost, a lot vulnerable.

Perfect.

Pulling his hands from his pockets, Woody started toward her.

Sometimes it was too damn easy.

But in the back of his mind, he thought about a woman who might be more of a challenge. She'd certainly gotten the best of that dumbass Hickson.

His heart started tap-dancing in his chest. He wanted her. To tie up loose ends. To punish her.

To experience her—in every way he could think of.

To prove that no bitch would best him, ever.

Cheryl would lead Hickson to her.

And Hickson would deliver her to him.

Smile predatory, body hungry, Woody stepped aside—and "bumped" into the freshman. Her stack of heavy books went scattering.

"Oh, damn." Catching her shoulders, Woody stared into her startled eyes. "I'm sorry. Are you okay?"

She stared up at him, stunned, breathless, her lips slowly parting.

And just like that, another one bit the dust.

OVER THE NEXT eight days, Alice and Reese fell into a wonderful routine.

A routine broken only by spontaneous lovemaking. Many mornings Reese woke aroused, which meant he woke her with kisses…everywhere. Twice he'd come home for lunch…which Alice now knew meant a sandwich that he practically swallowed whole and fast, hot sex that he deemed "a quickie."

Every single night, regardless of how late he got in, he wanted her. In the shower. The kitchen. Her office. The bed.

They'd even ended up on the floor once.

Alice never objected.

She felt immersed in pleasure, her body in a constant state of tingling awareness. Fast or slow, in the bedroom or spread-eagle on her desk, the man knew how to send her over the edge. His stamina amazed her, but then, given his size and fitness, she should have realized he wouldn't tire easily.

Most mornings before Reese left for work, he took Cash for a jog. It gave Alice an hour to herself, but even then, Reese kept a cell phone on him, and he never left without first gaining Alice's promise that she'd lock the door behind him.

Cash loved it. As soon as he'd see Reese in his running shorts, he'd head over to the door and wait by his leash. Alice had coffee ready for Reese when he returned. After showering and getting dressed, he'd join her for breakfast at the table. Before heading off to the station, he always patted Cash, and he never forgot to kiss her goodbye.

It all seemed so domestic and so…enduring.

Cash felt it, too. In such a short time the dog had flourished. He no longer felt the need to stay right on top of them. They could actually leave the room without him following.

While Cash didn't exactly pine for Reese when he left for work, he still went berserk when Reese got home again.

In no time, Alice not only caught up with her work, but she also took on a new client who designed and built children's playground equipment. Of course, that made her think of kids, but she always snuffed the thought. Her relationship with Reese was still too new to start daydreaming about a family together.

Usually he got in by six. On those nights, they took turns cooking dinner and cleaning up afterward. But when circumstances dictated it, Reese could be out 'til well past dinner. A few nights ago, after a robbery at a local diner that left three people injured, he'd followed leads that kept him gone through half the night. In the end, he'd managed to catch the two men, and got beat up a little in the process. Nothing serious, but the bruising of a black eye lingered still.

As yet, they hadn't found out anything about the murdered girl or Cheryl's abductors. Reese and Logan shared a lot of private calls, and occasionally Rowdy stopped in for a hushed conversation.

Knowing Reese wanted to insulate her from his police work didn't make it any easier to be excluded. Just as she tried not to worry, Alice also tried not to smother him with too many demands. Reese hadn't asked anything more about Trace, so in return, she tried not to ask too many questions about the case.

It would all be easier if she knew Reese was falling in love with her. He was kind, caring, attentive and beyond sexual.

But did any of that equate to an emotional commitment?

Or did it just reiterate that he was a great guy?

So many times, she'd thought to implement Pepper's plan. The idea of taking charge in bed, *taking charge of Reese,* was incredibly tempting. She would love to have him so sexually excited that he shared his innermost thoughts.

About her. About their future—if they had one.

So far, Reese hadn't given her a chance. He left her so exhausted each night that he woke up before her every morning. If she smiled at him, he was on her. If she looked at him over-long, just admiring him, he took it as an invitation—which, she supposed, it was.

The chemistry between them hadn't waned and, in fact, seemed hotter than ever. Could that turn to love? God, she hoped so.

She paced the floor, wondering how to implement the plan, when she heard Reese's footsteps in the hallway.

An hour early!

Cash got to the door before she did; Alice stood there, probably looking guilty. After all, she'd been plotting his seduction and working herself up in the bargain.

As he came in, Reese knelt to say hello to Cash. Alice saw only the top of his head, the set of his brawny shoulders in his dress shirt, but she sensed a problem.

"Reese?"

"Should I take this beast out?" He rubbed Cash's neck. "What'dya say, boy? Wanna go out?"

Since Cash had been out twice already, he only sat there wagging his tail without encouraging Reese.

Alice strode forward. "What's wrong?"

"Who says anything is?" He reached for the dog's leash.

His avoidance alarmed her farther. "Reese Bareden. Don't you dare use that sweet animal as a way to dodge me!"

Giving up, Reese straightened to his full, impressive height.

He had another, freshly swollen black eye! And a split on the bridge of his nose. A cut on his lip…

Alice froze in place. "What in the world happened to you?"

One hand on his hip, the other holding Cash's leash, Reese dropped his head forward as if disgusted.

Alice waited while he grumbled to himself.

Finally he met her gaze. "A couple of yahoos got into a fight inside the station."

"And you used your face to try to stop them?"

"No, smart-ass." He moved closer, his expression fierce.

And tired.

Huh. So Reese was human after all.

"I got sucker punched when I told them to knock it off." His jaw firmed. "That was the shot to the eye. I got the rest when I *subdued* them."

"Oh." The discoloration beneath one eye had only just started to fade. Now the other eye was swollen and purple. She realized his tic was gone, his shirt torn and dirty.

Poor Reese. He'd apparently had a terrible day. She found one of Cash's chew toys and tossed it toward the center of the room. Cash went after it, then took it to a ray of sunshine to work it over.

Alice turned back to Reese. "You didn't kill anyone, did you?"

With a long-suffering sigh, he shook his head. "No."

"Good."

"But I wanted to."

She could see that. Though Reese tried to hide it, he still looked ready to chew nails.

Brushing at a spot of dirt on the front of his shirt, right over his chest, she felt the radiating tension in his muscles. Going brisk, automatically knowing he wouldn't want to be coddled, Alice asked, "How badly did you hurt them?"

His green eyes glittered with new intent. "Enough to get them cuffed and handed over to a uni."

"Remarkable restraint. I'm sure they deserved more." She opened a button on his shirt. Then another.

"Alice?"

"Hmm?" She continued until she had the shirt open, then pulled it from his slacks. Right where she'd seen the dirt, he had a bruise.

"What are you doing?"

"Undressing you." Leaning forward, she put her lips to his hot skin and filled her head with his intoxicating scent.

He dropped the leash to tangle a hand in her hair. "I'm a sweaty mess, babe."

"I know." While kissing her way across his chest, she opened his belt buckle. "You can soak in a cool tub while I fix you something to eat."

Using the hand he had tangled in her hair, he tugged her head back. "I don't need to be babied."

Alice slipped her hand inside his slacks and fondled him. "I wasn't trying to baby you." She felt her nipples go tight as his erection grew. "I just want you ready for me, sooner instead of later."

They stared at each other, and she watched his eyes go a smoky green. "God, that feels good."

Finally, she had some control. Excited but determined to do this right, she took away her hand and turned toward the bathroom. "My mouth will probably feel even better."

When Reese didn't follow her, she glanced at him

over her shoulder and smiled at the scorching way he traced her every step. "Come on, Reese. Let's get the show on the road."

SENSES HEIGHTENED, Reese watched Alice finish with the dishes. After she'd insisted he soak while she grilled chops and potatoes, he felt like a slug—a very horny slug who'd had too much free time to think about what she might do. He understood that Alice wanted to pamper him since he had a few new bruises. But a couple of lucky shots to his face weren't enough to slow him down. Piss him off, yeah. He'd been plenty pissed.

Until he saw Alice.

Even now, while loading plates into the dishwasher, she wore that small, sexy smile that made him nuts with need.

"You know I could've helped with that."

"I know." She bent to add in another plate, putting her rump on display. "But I want to do it."

Just as she'd wanted to undress him and prepare his bath? All right, so now what?

"I'm bathed," he told her. When was the last time he'd soaked in a tub? "Well fed, too." The dinner had been fast but filling. "I'm even wearing clean clothes." Clothes that she'd laid out for him. He would've definitely protested that, except that he had a feeling she'd deliberately chosen the draw-string athletic pants and soft cotton undershirt because they'd be easy to remove.

She dried her hands. "You could take Cash out one last time."

He glanced at the clock. Hell, it wasn't late. What did "one last time" mean? Unless…did she plan to keep him in bed the rest of the night?

Despite his best efforts at control, his Johnson jumped at the possibility.

Damned unruly body part.

“Sure,” he said, hoping she didn’t hear the lust sharpening his tone. “I can do that.” He left his chair.

“But Reese?” She came up to him, smoothed a small hand over his abs—abs now clenched tight with anticipation. A pretty blush warmed her cheekbones. “Make it fast, okay?”

“Not a problem.”

She got out Cash’s treat jar—a sure sign that she wanted uninterrupted time with him. “When you’re done, give him one and then come into the bedroom.”

Fascinating how her blush deepened, but her eyes didn’t waver. Bold. Sexy. Sweet.

He liked it. A lot.

Wondering how far she’d go, Reese dipped his head and took her mouth in a hot, possessive kiss. “Give me ten minutes, tops.” Sometimes Cash liked to explore every possibility before choosing the perfect spot.

Luckily, Reese didn’t run into anyone else in the lot, and Cash didn’t find any birds or squirrels to provoke him. With the promise of a treat, he urged Cash to hurry, and in record time he had him back in the apartment.

Reese hadn’t even been out long enough to work up a sweat in the thick humidity.

The second he closed and locked the apartment door, he heard Alice in the shower. Picturing her wet, naked, he started to join her—but he hesitated.

He didn’t want to steal her thunder.

Instead, he took a minute to play with Cash before giving him the chew treat. When he heard the water shut off, he went into the bedroom and sat on the side of the bed to wait.

Fully erect.

Every nerve ending sizzling.

Anticipation honed.

Wrapped in a towel, skin still damp and one hand lifted to remove a tie from her hair, Alice rushed in.

She halted at the sight of him. Those luscious eyes showed surprise, a hint of embarrassment, even a little disappointment.

Until determination overrode everything else. He saw the shift in her expression, in the way she moved.

Looking her over, Reese badly wanted to strip away the towel that kept her slender body hidden from his view.

Instead, he made himself sit there, the epitome of patience.

Movements measured for effect, Alice finished freeing her hair so that it tumbled down around her shoulders. "That was fast."

"You thought I'd linger?"

In a small, telltale sign, the hand holding the towel clenched, and her breathing deepened. "I'm glad you didn't."

She stood there a moment longer, maybe working up her courage—or figuring out how to proceed. As sexual as they'd been, as open and honest as she was in bed, this was new for her.

She dropped the towel.

Just like that, with no warning. Reese sucked in a breath, soaking up the sight of her. It didn't matter how many times he'd already seen her, this was a new attitude for her, and it fired his blood.

His gaze moved to her tight nipples, the damp curls between her legs, her soft, pale skin now rosy all over.

He did his own heavy breathing.

Beautifully bare, she turned and closed the bedroom door. He heard the quiet click like a blast of thunder.

"Damn, you have me tightly strung." Her ass was a special source of lust for him, and she knew it. "Come here."

Facing him, she murmured, "I'd like to get your clothes off, okay?"

"Great. Clothes off." He reached for her, but she shook her head.

"Raise up your arms so I can take off your shirt."

Reese started to strip it off himself, but she stepped between his thighs, and the sweet scent of her body filled his head.

Catching his shirt, she tugged it from his hands. "Arms up, please."

Jesus. Unable to recall the last time he'd been this frantic for sex, he lifted his arms.

Alice worked the shirt up, slowly, over his chest and arms until it cleared his head. After tossing it toward her discarded towel, she stepped closer still. Her plump pink nipples were right *there,* close enough to kiss. The spicy scent of her arousal mixed with the scent of her soap, the scent of his need.

She touched his shoulders with both hands, gliding her delicate fingertips over his skin, around to his nape, up and into his hair—which brought her closer, so close he couldn't resist.

He ducked his head to move his tongue over her left nipple.

Her fingers knotted in his hair. "Lay back."

Tension coiled tight.

"This time," she told him, "I want to touch your big, gorgeous body."

He met her gaze.

And she whispered, "Without you taking over."

CHAPTER TWENTY-ONE

REESE FELT RIGID enough to break as he tried to recline. Now he knew what she had planned, and it ratcheted up his temperature and his need until he couldn't get enough oxygen into his lungs.

"Relax."

With every second that passed, Alice gained new confidence. He wanted her to have that confidence. With him.

Only him.

Letting out a long breath and concentrating on unkinking his muscles, Reese put his hands behind his head.

Until she stroked him through the athletic pants.

Every muscle knotted again in expectation of more to come.

She cupped his balls, cuddling until he clenched his teeth. "I love how you feel."

"I love when you feel me." Speaking wasn't easy, but Reese hoped some errant humor might lighten the mood before he totally lost his grip.

She obliterated that plan when she stroked up along his erection, squeezing him through the material, then kept on stroking up his body until she sprawled out over him.

She kissed the bruised skin under his eye, then again

near the cut on the bridge of his nose. "Even battered, you are the most gorgeous man I've ever seen."

The way she rested on him, her breasts to his chest, one slender leg between his, the other outside his thigh, drove him nuts. "You said something about getting me naked?" *And using that pretty mouth on me...*

Her eyes looked darker, deeper. Full of secrets.

Secrets that, this time, he might enjoy.

Sitting up beside him, Alice touched his chest again, used her thumb to explore his nipple—almost making him leap off the bed—then moving down to his abs. "You stay in such incredible shape. I can't imagine any woman not wanting you."

Looking for reassurance? "Right now I only care about you wanting me."

"Of course I do." She bent to kiss his other nipple, and Reese bit off a groan.

Down to his sternum. *Such a hot little tongue...*

Over his abs. He locked his hands together behind his head.

She lightly bit his shaft through the material of the loose pants and his snug boxers, and before he could catch his breath again, she moved off the end of the bed and grabbed the waistbands of both. "Lift your hips for me."

No problem. Anxious to be rid of clothes, Reese lifted up so she could strip them down his thighs. She got everything as far as his knees—and zoned in on his dick.

He tried to finish kicking off the pants, but Alice lay down crosswise in the bed, giving him a good profile view of her body, and he stilled.

He could feel her breath.

Taking him in both hands, her hold firm, she shattered all thought. The way she watched him so intently kept him on a precipice of suspense.

She nuzzled against him, breathing deep, making a small purring sound of pleasure. “I love how you smell.”

Ah…fuck. Reese squeezed his eyes shut and concentrated on keeping it together.

There was no prelude, no teasing kiss or tentative lick. One second Alice held him—and in the next she slid her soft, moist mouth down around him.

A groan ripped from his chest. Without even realizing it, he pulled his hands out from behind his head and tangled his fingers in her hair. He’d had blowjobs before. Always enjoyable, absolutely.

But this was Alice. And that meant it went beyond the sexuality of the act. It was Alice’s scent, the way she looked while doing it, the soft sounds she made—how she meant so much more to him than any woman he’d ever known.

The emotional connection made everything different, more severe, sweeter and…*hotter.*

He couldn’t keep from growling, from urging her to take more of him.

Keeping her lips firm around him, she moved her tongue, teasing around the head.

She pulled back with a long, leisurely lick. “Good?” she asked with innocent curiosity.

His heart pounded. “Fucking great.”

“Mmm.” Pleased by that, she went back to work on him.

Not wanting to miss a thing, Reese rose to his elbows. He was draped across the bed. Alice rested on her belly perpendicular to him, legs bent at the knees, her pretty feet in the air, crossed at the ankles.

She could have been a posed centerfold model, she looked so enticing.

The fact that she had his dick in her mouth only enhanced the image.

Cupping his fingers around her nape, his thumb in the hollow of her cheek, he guided her, watching as her lips moved over him, as her fawn-colored hair fell onto the paler skin of his pelvis.

So fucking erotic.

Her narrow shoulders flexed each time she drew back, and her toes curled each time she took him deep again.

Two more strokes and he'd be in oblivion. And much as he liked the idea of her finishing him off with her mouth, he wanted her to come with him.

He tightened his hand in her hair. "You have to stop now, Alice, or I'm a goner."

She did, pulling away with another hot lick that damn near did him in.

Sitting up in a rush, she said, "Don't move." She finished yanking his pants and boxers off. "I'm going to grab a condom."

Gaze molten, Reese watched as she left the bed and rummaged in the nightstand. Seconds later, she crawled back atop him.

What a sight. Alice naked on her knees, her hair loose, her breasts free, her expression lustful…

She settled on him with her legs open around his thighs. "Lie back."

"Let me touch you first." *All over, with my hands and my mouth.* "You need to catch up."

She caught his wrist before he could reach her breast. "On your back, Reese."

Damn. Their gazes clashed.

Putting both hands to his chest, Alice whispered, “Please?”

As if in slow motion, fascinated with this new take-charge mood of hers, Reese stretched out again.

“Tell me if I do this wrong.”

Not possible, because anything she did at this point would only add to the growing sexual tension. But he nodded.

She worked the rubber onto him—and, yes, that tormented him in wonderful ways. As soon as she had that done, she straddled his hips. “Reese?”

God, she looked amazing poised over him like that. Urgent breaths lifted her breasts and left her nipples darkly flushed and puckered tight. Excitement pulled her belly taut. She bit her bottom lip as she searched his face.

“What is it, sweetheart? Tell me what you want.”

Instead, she took his hand and carried it to her body—right between her legs. Her head tipped back the second his fingers brushed over her damp curls, then lower, where he found her hot and slippery.

Ready—but not quite enough.

He pressed his middle finger barely into her, testing her, teasing the slick, swollen lips, then used her own wetness to glide that fingertip over her clitoris.

Whimpering, she clenched her legs around his.

With his other hand, Reese stroked her breasts. “You are so damn beautiful, Alice.”

Even now, lost in the carnality of the moment, she shook her head, denying that. “I’m just…me.”

I love who you are. Reese kept the words to himself and instead censored that thought to make it more acceptable to the moment. “You’re rare. And genuine. And, yes, Alice, beautiful.” He caught one nipple, rolling it gently, tugging carefully, insistently, until she groaned. "Especially now, like this."

That seemed to bring her around. Eyes heavy, she moved his hands away and instead scooted up over him. "I want you inside me." She flexed her legs, lifting up to arrange him for entry. "Now." And with that, she eased down over him.

Tight. Slick. He throbbed as she worked the head in, stretching around him. Lips parted, she paused.

Putting his hands on her taut thighs, Reese whispered, "It's deep this way, Alice. Tell me if I hurt you."

She nodded—and took more of him, her breath catching with every inch that went deeper.

Apprehension trembled through her as she tried to adjust to his size.

Reese didn't mean to, but his hands contracted on her soft flesh, keeping her from retreating again. "How does that feel, honey?"

She sucked in two fast breaths, pressed down more, and said on a moan, *"Wonderful."*

Nothing could be more of a turn-on, Reese thought, than watching Alice as she took him, seeing how she enjoyed the snug fit despite any discomfort she felt.

Still on her knees, she stopped short from taking all of him, her head down, her hands braced on his chest.

God, he needed her to move. He could feel her body clasping him, squeezing in little spasms; he felt her wetness and her heat.

"Reese?"

Sliding his hands down to her knees, he opened her legs wider so he could better see where they joined. Voice rough and deep, he ordered, "More, Alice."

Almost as if she couldn't help herself, she rocked once, then stopped. "Not…just yet."

Reese groaned.

And she asked in the softest of whispers, "How do you feel about me?"

He swallowed hard, doing everything he could to resist the urge to thrust up into her. She was so slight in comparison to his height and weight and bone structure that he could easily hurt her without meaning to, and he'd die before doing that.

This was her turn, and he'd give that to her no matter how difficult it might be on him.

She did another single slide of her hips before pressing down enough that they both gasped.

His cock swelled more, and he felt on the verge of exploding.

Breathy, strained, she asked again, "How do you feel about me?"

"You're killing me here, Alice."

"You want me?"

"Yes." More than that, he *needed* her. Not just now. Not just for the physical release. But for…everything. A scary thought, one he tried to abolish by saying, "Ride me, honey."

"Yes." She lifted, sank down again, taking a little more of him.

Almost there, almost buried inside her.

"As soon as you tell me how you feel."

It stunned Reese, but he finally caught on to her game. She was turning things around on him, using sex to get the answers she wanted.

Answers about his emotional commitment.

Admiration hit him first, followed by sultry acceptance. His heart thundered in his chest, and with every fiber of his being, he was aware of their connection, of the clasp of her body holding him so tightly and her hungry gaze watching for his reaction.

And still he wanted to see how far she'd take it. "I think you're incredible." He cupped a breast, plied her stiffened nipple with his thumb. "Now, ride me."

As he said that, he lifted up a little, and she gasped. He rocked up again, slowly, giving her his entire length by degrees.

Eyes closed, body accepting, she whispered, "Are you interested in more than…sex?"

While continuing those easy, shallow thrusts, he used both hands to play with her nipples. "With you, yes."

She groaned, gasped. "More than…ah! More than just…now?"

Now, tomorrow, next week and next month. "Yes." He lifted harder, sank deeper. Release beckoned, boiling closer to the surface.

"Maybe…" She gasped, cried out, closed her hands over his, pressing his hands into her breasts. "Maybe commitment?"

Commitment? Well, hell, that startling question almost blew it for Reese—until Alice took over, riding him hard and fast as she sought an orgasm. She lifted so that he almost left her, then dropped down to grind on him with breathy moans.

Jesus, talk about torture.

"Reese," she cried. "Tell me."

He caught her hips, holding her closer, trying to slow her down. "Let's talk about it after."

Closing her eyes on a shuddering groan, Alice held still. "Let's talk about it now."

With him buried deep inside her, her breath coming in pants, she waited for his reply.

Why not tell her? Caressing her hips, Reese said, “I’m insanely attracted to you.”

“To this?” She clarified by lifting up and sliding down again, slowly this time, so slowly that they both had to struggle.

“Yes, that.” Reese strained under her. “But also *you,* Alice. Talking to you. Holding you while you sleep.” He held her hips and kept her flush against his body, knowing he filled her, loving the way her breath caught, how her muscles contracted. “I even like arguing with you. And, honey, I *love* the way you do payback.”

But for right now, he couldn’t take a second more. He brought her down to his chest, rolled to put her under him and took over. “Okay?”

For an answer, Alice opened her mouth on his chest, and he felt her sharp little teeth, not hard enough to break his skin, but definitely enough to send a rush of pleasure through him.

Luckily, he brought her with him.

Four strokes, five—and they were both coming hard. Alice held him tight until the last waves of her climax receded. Lying fully atop her, their heartbeats in sync, Reese felt her ease—her body, her thoughts. It took him another minute to recover enough, and then he pushed up to his elbows.

She wasn’t asleep. Her eyes were drowsy.

Sated.

She touched the bruise under his eye with gentle fingertips. And then the mark she’d left with her teeth. “I’m sorry.”

“I’m not.” He smoothed back her hair. “I like it when you lose control.” He kissed her mouth and wanted to go on kissing her.

Her small laugh stalled him. "You're insatiable," she teased.

He put his forehead to hers. *Only with you.* But again, he held back. They still had so much up in the air, with killers on the loose and her safety in danger—far too much for deep declarations.

Cash whined at the door, giving Reese the perfect distraction. "He has impeccable timing."

"He's wonderful," Alice whispered. "Like you."

"Speaking of wonderful..." After levering off her, Reese sat on the side of the bed and rested a hand on her thigh. "That was...straight out of a fantasy." He brushed his thumb over her silky skin. "Thank you."

Her smile looked a little sad, but she stretched and then sat up. "It's still early. Want to go watch a movie with Cash?"

He'd had a shit day that had put him in a shittier mood—until he'd gotten home to Alice. And now, after being with her, he felt...content.

Very soon, he needed to tell her how he felt, maybe get her input on a house for Cash.

He also needed to expose drug dealers who were heinous enough to tattoo women the same way ranchers branded their cattle. He had to protect Alice from men corrupt enough to kill a woman rather than let her escape.

But for right now, tonight, Alice and Cash would fill a void he hadn't known existed until only recently.

"That sounds perfect." He smiled at her. "As long as I get to pick the movie."

FOR OVER A week he'd waited, spending many sleepless nights drenched in the sweat of his own worry. Hour upon hour, he'd sat in his car, afraid to leave, eating cold fast food and pissing in a cup so that he wouldn't miss it, if or when Cheryl finally left the safety of her parents' small home.

Luckily they lived in a congested area with a lot of side streets. Each day he parked in a different spot, sunup to sundown, cursing her and that goddamned busybody who'd interfered.

For a while there, he'd thought maybe Cheryl hadn't gone home after all. Or that she was so spineless, she'd never leave the house again.

Unacceptable. He had to get her.

Woody Simpson was not a man you wanted to disappoint. His wrath was so volatile, he could kill as easy as laugh.

But now, finally, in the wee hours of the morning, Hickson saw Cheryl as she slipped out the front door.

"Cheryl, you stupid bitch," he muttered to himself. It was because of her that the other one had been able to get the drop on him; because of Cheryl that he'd been made to look like an incompetent fool.

Using Cheryl, he'd find the nosy broad who'd dared to turn the Taser on him, and then he'd deliver her to Woody. That'd ensure she got what she deserved.

But Hickson wanted to dole out the punishment to Cheryl. And he would. Soon, very soon.

He started his car, staring as Cheryl walked out toward the street. She looked jumpy, watchful.

Probably still scared after running from Woody. Hickson snorted. Women were so fucking easy to intimidate, even easier to control.

Looking up and down the street, car keys in hand, Cheryl headed for a little yellow Civic. Hickson didn't see anyone else around, so he put his windows down, pulled away from the curb and rolled right up to her.

The second he approached, she went wild-eyed and started to run.

"Do it," he told her, "and I'll go talk to your family instead."

Big tears filled her eyes. She looked around, probably hoping for help.

Hickson didn't have time for her dramatics. "Call the police, scream, make a single wrong move…" He shrugged. "And they're dead. Every fucking one of them. Don't doubt it."

The tears spilled over. "Wh-what do you want?"

"Get in the car and we'll talk about it."

She didn't want to— but she also didn't want her family murdered. He'd been mostly bluffing about that. He didn't mind doing what had to be done, but he wasn't dumb enough or reckless enough to slaughter a whole family.

But Cheryl was too chickenshit to realize that.

Patience running thin, he leaned across the seat and shoved open the passenger door. "Get in. *Now.*"

Shaking all over, she joined him in the car.

The second her ass hit the seat, Hickson drove off. "Shut the goddamned door. And stop that sniveling!"

She obeyed the first but not the second.

Hickson rode to a quiet park, not stopping until he found a secluded area. He turned to face Cheryl, looked her over. She wore jeans and a long-sleeve T-shirt. For only a moment, that amused him. "Hiding your tat?"

She rubbed her forearm as if it still hurt. "I…I…"

"Where were you going?"

Confusion mixed with the stark terror.

"Today," he said, impatient with her hesitation. "Just now. You were slinking off somewhere, right? A new boyfriend?"

She shook her head hard. "No, I..." Swallowing, she swiped away her tears and met his gaze. "I had an appointment to see a doctor."

"Yeah?" He looked her over again, but she didn't look sick or hurt. "What's wrong with you?"

That trembling chin went higher. "I was going to have the tattoo removed."

Anger expanded. "That'd be a big fucking mistake." Before she could move, Hickson grabbed her wrist, then hauled her half over the console. He shoved up the sleeve of her shirt. "You see this? It *stays,* bitch. Do you understand me?"

Snuffling and sobbing, she fought to get away from him. Hickson tangled a hand in her hair and held her still. Now, with her truly hysterical, he said, "The one that helped you get away. What's her name?"

Cheryl bawled and fought—until he tightened his hand in her hair. "Who is she?" he demanded.

"I—I don't know."

He snatched up her arm—the arm covered by a long sleeve even on what promised to be a blistering day. "Wanna do it the hard way, huh?"

"I said *I don't know!* Alice something. She—she never told me her last name."

Hickson read the truth of that in her wide eyes. "All right." He rubbed his thumb over her wrist. "Tell me what you do know. And, Cheryl, honey, I hope it's enough. Otherwise you and I are going to take a nice long drive to the river."

Her slender throat worked before she finally got the words out. "She—she gave me a number to call." Frantically, Cheryl dug in her purse until she found the scrap of paper. Hand trembling, she offered it to him.

"A number? What the hell for?"

"She said…in case I—I needed her."

Hmm. Interesting. So the busybody had thoughts of playing in the big league? "That just might work." He pulled out his cell phone and offered it to her. "Call it."

Cheryl treated the phone as she would a two-headed snake. Hands pulled back to her chest, her expression horrified. "What—what would I say?"

Hickson grinned. "That you need her, of course."

"Oh." Tentatively, Cheryl accepted the phone.

"Ask her to meet you at the bus stop across from the tattoo parlor. And Cheryl? Pray that she agrees."

CHAPTER TWENTY-TWO

ALICE WOKE THE next morning in the usual way—or at least the way that had become usual now that she had Reese and Cash in her life. Reese spooned her from behind, one brawny arm over her waist, and even in sleep, his hand curled around her breast.

She loved his hands so much. Big and strong and so incredibly capable, whether he cooked, brushed Cash, or drove her insane with sensual need.

Cash rested at the foot of the bed, his head over her ankles.

She could hear both man and dog breathing heavily in their sleep, and a softball-sized lump of emotion lodged in her throat.

She loved them both *so* much. But last night she'd blown it. She'd gotten so caught up in the incredible pleasure of sex with Reese that she hadn't uncovered his feelings about her. She hadn't discovered if he was in it for the long haul, if his heart had gotten as involved as hers.

Sure, some of the things he'd said were nice. Better than nice. But they didn't give her a clue about a future together.

Swallowing down her worry, Alice put her hand over his, marveling at the size of his wrist, his fingers. She touched him gently, tracing along the seam of his middle and index finger—and suddenly felt the rise of his interest against her rear end.

She turned her head toward him. "You're awake?"

"Mmm." His hand contracted carefully, caressing her. "Awake and wondering what you're thinking."

Cash grumbled, snuffled away from her feet and stretched out again with a lazy sigh.

Alice turned to face Reese. He adjusted, moving his hand around her to her backside, pulling her half up onto his chest as he went to his back and stretched out his free arm.

Toying with his chest hair—another thing she loved about him—Alice said, "I was thinking how nice your hands are."

"Mmm." He traced the shape of one cheek, teasing her. "How nice my hands are when they're on you?"

"I do love that." Levering up to his chest, Alice gave him a long, serious look. "And I love waking up with you in the morning."

He brought her down for a kiss. "I'm fond of that myself."

"Before you, before this, I couldn't imagine myself being this comfortable. I haven't brushed my teeth, and I have to pee, and I know my hair is a mess."

Reese grinned like a rascal. "Ditto on all the above."

She smoothed down his short blond hair, now sticking up at odd angles. Her hand automatically went to his jaw, to the beard shadow that rasped against her fingers. "You are so natural about everything that when I'm with you, it feels…okay."

He put both hands on her butt. "It?"

Life, love, the entire world. Alice sighed. "Everything, I guess."

"You feel safe with me."

Very safe. Even if he didn't love her, she knew Reese would never purposely hurt her, and that he'd do everything in his power to protect her. "Yes."

"I'm glad, but Alice, I don't want you to get too comfortable."

Her heart stuttered. "With you?"

Scowling, Reese did a sudden turn, and Alice found herself under him.

He put his mouth to hers for a quick, whiskery kiss. "With me, I always want you comfortable. *Always*. Do you understand?"

She didn't, not really, but she said, "I think so."

Still looking far too grim, he searched her gaze. "You need to continue being cautious, Alice. There are dangerous people out there—"

"There always are."

"—who want to do you harm," he stressed, overriding her objection. "You have to understand the reality of what you did. By interfering with—"

"Rescuing."

"—Cheryl, you drew their attention. They could be looking for you right now. Until they're caught and their operation is shut down, you're in danger."

Today, she would not get distracted. Today, she would find the answers she needed.

Alice cupped his face. "Please, tell me, Reese. Does all this concern mean that you—"

A cell phone rang.

With a look of confusion, Reese turned his head toward the sound. "What is that?"

Like a dash of ice water, the sound of that particular ring froze Alice for a few seconds. Then she pushed at Reese's shoulders. "Move. It's my phone."

"Your phone?" He gave her enough space to wriggle out from under him. "It doesn't sound like—"

"My *other* phone." Worried that she'd miss the call, Alice stretched from the bed until she got the nightstand drawer open. On the fourth ring she finally snatched up the cell. She was very aware of Reese going quiet beside her. "Hello?"

"Alice? It's Cheryl. Y-you said I could call."

Dread made her light-headed. Alice scrambled to sit up against the headboard, her breath stuck in her throat, her stomach cramping.

Beside her, Reese came alert. "What is it?"

She put a finger to her lips, cautioning him to be quiet. "Cheryl," she said aloud, so Reese would know. "Is everything okay?"

Cheryl started to cry—and stammer. "Y-yes. Everything is…"

With her free hand to her mouth, Alice held her breath.

"…just p-peachy."

Oh, God. Alice could hear her own heartbeat in her ears. "I see." She didn't dare look at Reese. If she did, she'd lose her concentration—and her nerve. "Then I'm glad you called."

Cheryl gasped for air. "I'd love to—to see you."

Think, Alice. *Don't waste precious time. Just react.* She nodded to herself. "Are you back in the area?"

"I can b-be. Tonight?"

Alice chewed her bottom lip. "Does it have to be tonight?"

"I don't know."

Cheryl would surely prefer it be sooner rather than later, but rushing into this wouldn't save her.

It would only put others at risk.

Reese sat up beside her, not touching her, but close enough to let her feel his concern.

"If it could wait until tomorrow evening, that would work for me." And it would give Reese time to come up with a plan. *Please, God, let him have a plan.*

Reese stayed silent beside her, listening, waiting.

Trusting her.

"What do you say, Cheryl? Tomorrow evening?"

"I don't… Let me check my…my schedule." Cheryl breathed heavily, then it sounded as if she muffled the phone. Finally, when Alice feared she wouldn't come back, Cheryl said on a sob, "I'll call you back."

"No! Cheryl wait—" The call ended, and the silence seemed louder than a scream. Alice started shaking. "Oh, no. Oh, no, *no*."

Reese took the phone from her hand, put it to his ear then closed it. "It was Cheryl?"

Numb, afraid that she'd just left Cheryl to a god-awful fate, she nodded.

"What did she say?"

Alice bit her lip. Obviously Hickson, or whoever had Cheryl, wanted to get to her, too. Why else would they have Cheryl call?

Maybe they'd only promised to have her call back to give them time to think through a plan. Perhaps to avoid having the call traced.

Could you trace a cell phone call? She didn't know.

Please, please, she thought, let her bluff for more time be enough to keep Cheryl safe.

Reese caught her shoulders, turning her toward him. He'd shifted into cop mode. She saw it in his eyes, in the way he held himself even while naked in bed. "Alice? I need you to tell me everything. Right now."

Dreading his reaction, she nodded. "About that tattoo business…I hate to say you were right…."

"Tell me."

"I could be in trouble after all."

Rowdy stood outside a tattoo parlor, waiting as the morning fog dissipated. Oppressive heat already wafted from the blacktop. By noon the humidity would feel like a sauna.

Last night, he'd signed the final papers on the bar. It was his. He'd take ownership in a few more days. The current owner only needed a little time to clear out.

Owning property wasn't new to him. He'd bought the apartment building his sister had used while hiding from murderers.

But that was for cover.

This would be his livelihood. A legit occupation. Roots. Stability. An honest living.

A fresh start.

Exhilarating and terrifying—he couldn't wait to get started. He hadn't yet told Dougie, the bartender, that he'd be replaced. He didn't want anyone sabotaging things before he was settled in and supervising. And he didn't want anyone giving Avery a hard time.

Avery. Every damn time he thought of her, he breathed harder. How fucked up was that? He wanted her, sure. She was hot in a "play it cool" way. But he didn't breathe hard over the thought of a woman. Ever.

At least, he hadn't until Avery Mullins.

Now that he officially owned the place, would it be unethical to sleep with her? Not that she'd agreed, anyway.

Yet.

And not that he got all that hyped up over ethics. But

he also didn't want to do anything to cause problems at his own establishment.

Hands in his pockets, his head down but his eyes up, Rowdy strolled to a lamppost and took in the surrounding area. A light shone inside the tattoo parlor even though it wouldn't open for hours. Interesting.

The other nearby establishments—cigarette shop, cash advance, alterations and a novelty store—remained locked up, dark inside and out.

He didn't see a car near the tattoo place, but then maybe, like him, whoever was inside had parked down the street, out of sight.

Another light came on, this one in a back room. Rowdy badly wanted to go in, to check out things on his own. It'd be a piece of a cake. Locked doors rarely slowed him down. He could be in and out with no one the wiser.

But Reese had been clear about shit like that, and on the off chance he had the right place, he didn't want to dick up any of the legalities.

There weren't many cops he trusted, even fewer he'd assist. But Reese and Logan were different.

Good thing, since Logan would soon be his brother-in-law. He was starting to get used to that idea. Now, when he thought about it, it didn't make his stomach roil or send ice down his spine.

He even enjoyed working with them. Having been a street rat most of his life, Rowdy blended in more easily than cops did. Using stealth for a reason other than mere survival made it somehow less caustic and more meaningful.

A few minutes later, a drunk staggered out of an alley and went to the liquor store. When he tried the door and it didn't open, he dropped to sit on the front stoop. Half a minute later, he appeared to pass out, slumped against the door.

Shortly after that, two women parked in an alley near the alteration shop. They left the car but stood outside talking a moment. One smoked while the other laughed about a story.

Loitering, smiling at the women when they looked him over, Rowdy again surveyed the tattoo parlor. So far he'd checked on five in the area.

For reasons he couldn't pinpoint, this one felt right.

And then…bingo. A man came out, and damned if he didn't look like one of the men who'd shown up in that shitty little hotel shortly after Alice had vacated it.

Rowdy waited to see where the man would go—and he sensed someone approaching from his left.

He turned—and instead of a direct threat, he found a woman standing there, probably in her mid-twenties, light brown, shoulder-length hair, big blue eyes.

Doing what came naturally, Rowdy checked her out.

She looked killer in super-short shorts and high-heeled strappy sandals, with a skimpy halter that barely contained her breasts. No tattoo, but a lot of earrings in one ear, and just enough makeup to look hot.

She smiled at him.

Rowdy looked her in the eye and smiled back.

"Now, don't you look lonesome," she purred as she touched one finger to his shoulder, trailing it down to his chest.

"Just waiting."

"For what?"

He stared at her, saying nothing—which was exactly how he would have reacted regardless of what he was doing or why. He didn't allow people to pry, ever, under any circumstances.

Undaunted, she gave a cute pout. "Maybe I could keep you company."

Bold. He liked that, but in this neighborhood, he had to be careful. "You a hooker, honey?"

Playful, she swatted at him. "No, I'm not. Is that what you're waiting for?"

"No."

"Good. Because I work at the cigarette store." After nodding toward the building, she again teased his chest. "But for you, I'm willing to skip a day."

Pretending a reserve he didn't possess, Rowdy glanced away—and damn it all, he didn't see the man anymore. He scanned the street, the alleys…nothing.

"My goodness, you're a big one, aren't you?" She came closer until her body pressed to his, crowding him, making his senses go on the alert. "Wha'dya say, handsome?"

It'd be all too easy for a babe to hide a weapon. He wasn't a fool, ever, not even for a sexy body and beautiful face.

"Sorry, honey, not today." Hands on her upper arms, he eased her back a foot. "I'm waiting on someone." To shore up that story, he checked his watch. "Hopefully, I haven't been stood up."

"A woman?"

"You are one nosy little lady, aren't you?"

"I was just thinking that you could wait with me in the store." Smiling, she leaned around to see his face and cajoled in a singsong voice. "It's air-conditioned."

"Hold up." He used the excuse of retrieving his cell from his pocket to put even more space between them. On speed dial, he rang up Reese with the push of one button.

Reese answered on the first ring. "Rowdy."

"Hey, dude, you coming or not?"

Not being an idiot, Reese caught on real quick. "Do you actually need me?"

"Yeah, sure. But, hell, it's a hundred degrees here, with no shade to be found." Rowdy smiled at the girl. "I've got a little sweetheart here offering to let me cool off in the…" Rowdy tipped his head at her. "Where'd you say you work, sweetheart?"

She smiled brightly. "The cigarette store."

"Right." Then back to Reese: "The cigarette store. You know the one, right by the…" He looked around as if he didn't already know the name of the tattoo parlor by heart. "Killer Designz. Yeah, with a *z*."

"Shit," Reese said, understanding the silent message Rowdy conveyed. "I'm on my way."

"All right, but make it quick. I have better stuff to do than wait around on you." He smiled at the girl. "And she's standing right in front of me."

Reese didn't find the humor in that. "Damn it, Rowdy, are you in any danger?"

"Nope." To make sure that was true, he checked out the surrounding area again, but saw no one suspicious. "I'll give you fifteen, and then I'm heading in with the lady. After that, you can damn well wait on me."

Soon as he closed his phone, the little lady took his hand and started back-stepping toward the street, trying to haul him along with her.

"Not so fast, sweetheart." Rowdy Yates did not get dragged away by women—at least, not women fully clothed and on a street corner. "Before I let you distract me too much, I need to give my buddy a few minutes to get here."

She gave another pretty pout. "But he's already kept you waiting, and it *is* hot out here."

"True enough." When he didn't budge, she had to stop, too. "You should go on in. I'll join you if I can."

Undecided, she toyed with the end of her hair, shifted her feet, and finally opened her purse. "At least let me leave you my name and number."

The way she said that seemed genuine enough. She looked and sounded the same as every other girl who wanted to get him horizontal. Maybe he was making a big deal out of nothing.

Then again, she was in this place, at this time, and it seemed awfully coincidental that she'd come on to him right when he wanted to follow the other guy.

She scrawled some info on the back of a receipt, but instead of handing it to him, she clutched it to her chest. "How do I know you'll call?"

"Look at you." He let his gaze linger on her impressive rack as he murmured, "I'll call."

That compliment had her beaming. "Better still, let's set up something right now." She traced a pink tongue along pinker lips. "How about…tonight?"

Fast work, but he'd play along. "All right. Sure." No reason to make her suspicious. Not when she might have info he needed. "Where do I pick you up?"

"I'll meet you. Is midnight too late?"

Figured it wouldn't be that easy. "Tell me where, and I'll be there."

"The Drunken Dawg. You know it?"

Well, hell. Of course he knew it.

He'd just bought it.

His smile this time felt mean, but maybe she wouldn't notice that she'd hit a nerve. "Yeah, that works." He took the paper from her, glanced at it and shoved it in his back pocket. "Midnight, DeeDee. I'll be there."

Now that she'd gotten what she wanted, she turned to sashay away.

Rowdy focused first on how her shorts hugged a really nice ass, then dropped his gaze down the long length of those shapely legs.

And there it was, the fucking tattoo, not on her arm as expected, but down the back of her left calf.

Huh. So, sexy DeeDee wasn't so enamored with him after all. At least he knew he'd found the right place.

REESE HATED LEAVING Alice on the heels of her getting that damned phone call. It left him antsy and angry, but Rowdy wouldn't have pulled him away for anything unimportant.

On his way out the door, still shrugging into his shirt, he dialed Logan and brought him up to speed.

Once in the car, he called up Peterson. She needed to know about Cheryl, but he also mentioned that Rowdy needed him.

"You will update me immediately after you find out what's going on."

"Soon as I can. Sure." Rather than continue driving one-handed, he disconnected the call and put all his concentration on reaching Rowdy. He wore dark sunglasses and an absurd ball cap that, hopefully, would keep him from being too recognizable should he have to return to the area later.

Reese found Rowdy slumped comfortably on the curb, his back against a lamppost. Unsure how they should play it, Reese pulled up, let the car idle and waited.

Rowdy came over and got in on the passenger side. "Go right around the corner there, and then park it. Let anyone watching think that we're doing a deal."

"A drug deal?"

Shrugging, Rowdy said, "Why not? But we have to make it quick. Dealers and junkies don't sit around in the dealer's car shooting the breeze."

Keeping the details short and sweet, Rowdy told Reese about the lights on inside Killer Designz, and the guy he recognized who'd disappeared after the woman had come on hot and heavy.

"Could be a coincidence." But Reese didn't like it. He eyed Rowdy and, feeling edgy for many reasons, quipped, "Maybe she just liked your smile."

Rowdy took him seriously. "I wondered, since I do get hit on a lot."

Looking at him over the dark sunglasses, Reese said, "Braggart."

"Just stating a fact. Women have never…" He hesitated, shook his head. "Almost never been a problem for me."

Rowdy's love life was the least of his concerns at the moment. "If you don't think it has anything to do with the case, why mention it?"

"Because she had the same type of tat as that dead girl, same as the one Alice described seeing on Cheryl."

Reese cursed low.

"I didn't see it until she was walking away. Instead of being on her arm, it was on her calf."

Great. Now the sick fucks were mixing it up, putting the tats in different locations. "Wonder if there's any significance in that. If maybe a leg tattoo has a different meaning than on the arm."

"I was thinking the same thing. Could be for different buyers, or as a sign of what she's carrying."

"They could be anywhere," Reese mused aloud. "Back of the neck, shoulder, midsection…"

“Even a tramp-stamp.”

“Small of the back, right?”

“Yeah.” Rowdy gave it some thought. “You can ink just about anything on your body.”

“But we should assume it’d be a location easily seen. It’s not like these ladies can go around naked without drawing attention.” Reese glanced toward Killer Designz. “I need to get inside there.”

Hedging, Rowdy looked out the passenger window, then turned toward Reese in a rush. “It’d be easier for me.”

Reese didn’t even bother looking at him. “Forget it.” He put the car back in gear. “Where are you parked?”

Defiance held Rowdy silent until Reese started driving forward. Hands curled into loose fists, gaze unflinching, Rowdy directed him. “Turn right, circle the block. I’m up at the other end, by the park.”

Smart, not to be too close. Without showing it, Reese waited for the arguments to start.

“You’re a cop.”

“Seriously?” Reese pretended surprise. “I’ll be damned, I think you’re right.”

“One look,” Rowdy said, not amused by the sarcasm. “That’s all it takes. Everything about you screams *officer of the law.*”

“I’ll manage.” Somehow. But Rowdy might have a point. Unlike Logan, who had successfully pulled the wool over Pepper’s lustful eyes, Reese wasn’t quite as anxious to try the undercover routine.

But given that they were so short-staffed right now, he might not have a choice.

“That’s me,” Rowdy said, nodding at a beat-up truck.

Reese pulled up alongside Rowdy’s ride. No one paid any attention, not with the park filled with kids and young moms, people with their pets, joggers and walkers. "How is it you have a damned different vehicle every other day?"

"I rotate when I don't want anyone to tag me." He didn't exit Reese's car. "So, what are you going to do?"

It might not be routine, but he decided Rowdy had a right to know. "Cheryl called Alice."

Other than the pinching of his brows, Rowdy showed no discernible reaction. "She's okay?"

"Alice or Cheryl?"

He slashed a hand through the air. "I'm assuming you have Alice well in hand."

Reese stared at him.

"Keeping her safe, I mean." Rowdy rubbed his face with both hands. "Jesus, don't tell Alice I phrased it like that."

In many ways, Rowdy's rapport with Alice resembled the relationship he had with his sister—full of platonic concern, caring, protectiveness.

And good thing, since Reese's heretofore unknown jealous streak shone bright around Alice. "For now at least, Cheryl is alive. She wanted to meet Alice."

"No fucking way."

Not that Rowdy had a vote in the decisions, but… "You took the words right out of my mouth." Reese pulled down his sunglasses. "Cheryl called the extra cell Alice had, and she used the code Alice set up, claiming her life was *peachy*."

"You can't let her—"

"Absolutely not." Pushing the sunglasses to the top of his head, Reese rubbed his unshaven jaw. "Alice asked if she could make it tomorrow instead of tonight, and Cheryl said she'd call back."

"That's it?"

“Yes.” Reese saw a small group of women eyeing them. Two of the women had kids with them. The other three were whispering and laughing about…something.

“They’re just flirting,” Rowdy said. “Ignore them.”

So, even though he hadn’t looked, Rowdy knew they were there? Talk about situational awareness….

“Alice is probably going nuts worrying about Cheryl right now. Damn, man, I’m sorry I pulled you away.”

Alice had promised to let him know immediately if she got another call, and other than taking Cash out, she wouldn’t budge from the apartment. “You did the right thing.”

“I don’t know about that. Holding back was not my first choice.”

Reese turned to him with a frown.

Holding up a hand, Rowdy stalled his objections. “You said you wanted it by the book, so I’m trying.” Bracing that hand on the dash, Rowdy turned to fully face him. Tensed muscles showed along his arm, his shoulder. “But now you have to do the right thing, too.”

Reese narrowed his eyes.

“You have to let me check out Killer Designz.”

CHAPTER TWENTY-THREE

NEEDING SOME AIR, Reese got out of the car and walked toward Rowdy's beat-up truck. Was it stolen? No, he didn't think so. Put to the test, Rowdy was certainly capable of boosting a ride, but he'd only do so if necessary to keep his sister—or probably any innocent—safe.

This wasn't one of those times.

When Rowdy joined him, Reese said, "How many vehicles do you have?"

"Five. I told Pepper to pick one to drive." Hands in his back pockets, he gave a small grin. "Logan looked ready to blow a gasket."

"You weren't offended?"

"That he loves my sister enough to feel territorial? No."

Good attitude. "He doesn't want to change the dynamics of your relationship. He just wants Pepper to have a better life."

Rowdy laughed. "Save the pep talk, Reese. Logan doesn't need your help, and I don't need you to explain things to me."

Two women walked by, cutting close to them, full of sly looks, their hips rolling in an attention-grabbing sway.

Rowdy smiled at them, said, "Ladies," and then dismissed them. "So, tell me, Reese. You going to make the smart move here?"

Before he could answer, a dark-haired woman lifted her cell phone and took a pic of them. Rowdy looked her way, and she blew him a kiss. Her girlfriend giggled behind her.

Rowdy just winked.

"Un-fucking-believable."

With a lift of his shoulder, Rowdy discounted the attention. "Focus, Reese. You need to let me hit up that tattoo place. The assholes inside have already seen me in the area, so they won't think I made a special trip to check them out. And even if they're suspicious, they won't be after I meet with the chick tonight—"

"Not happening."

"—at my own damn bar."

After soaking that in, Reese strolled over to stand in the shade. Cash would probably like this place. He saw other people with dogs, some of them chasing Frisbees. "So you bought it?"

"Yup." Rowdy sat on the front bumper of the truck and continued to check out the flirting women. "There are drugs at the bar already."

"Most bars." Did he dare let Rowdy walk into danger?

"Yeah," Rowdy agreed, "but Avery says it's a big problem there."

"Avery?" That got Reese's attention.

Rowdy turned away. "She'll be the new bartender."

Since when did Rowdy Yates avoid eye contact? "A woman as bartender?"

"Your sexism is showing."

That was so ludicrous that Reese laughed. "Who is she?"

"I told you. She's a waitress who will replace the

bartender." Suddenly Rowdy looked struck. "Son of a bitch."

That whispered curse alarmed Reese. "What is it?"

"I just realized..." He turned to face Reese. "Avery was telling me the women she wouldn't date."

"What?"

He waved that off. "Inside joke. She's not gay, thank God."

"Okay." Where was Rowdy going with this?

"The thing is, she pointed out the smokers and the complainers—and a woman with unusual tats. I didn't see the tats because, at the time, it didn't matter to me. But Avery described them as 'not pretty.' She said the woman had her calf and her shoulder inked."

This was getting too close for comfort. "At the bar you just bought?"

"Yeah, and Avery said the drug use there was an issue." He shook his head, saying in an aside, "I promised her I'd clean that up, but I never imagined...."

"Your bar could be an exchange point."

Quick to change the subject, Rowdy pushed off from the truck. "The thing is, I'm to meet DeeDee there tonight, and I officially own the place. So this is on me, whether you like it or not."

Damn it, he hated feeling like things were out of his control. "You know, DeeDee is setting you up."

"Yeah, probably. But I can handle myself. And maybe the plan is just for her to feel me out a little, to see if I'm onto them. The way I figure it, I can lead her on, admire her tattoo and tell her that I've been thinking of getting one, too. Maybe she'll tell me what it means, but probably not. Either way, it'll explain why I was at the parlor, looking around, maybe throw the hounds off the scent a little, you know?"

Though it had merit, Reese hated that plan. Unfortunately, he didn't have a better one. "Normally I'd want you to sit on meeting with her, at least for a day or two. Give me time to look into it, maybe set up something so we could throw out a net and get everyone involved. Not just the muscle, but the main people, too."

"Yeah, I know. And if everything wasn't coming together this way, I'd agree. But with Cheryl calling, we need to gain some ground before Alice gets compromised."

"That won't happen." Even thinking about it set Reese's muscles in spasms and made his chest feel too tight. "I won't let it."

"I know." Hands low on his hips, Rowdy said, "But I'll be helping to keep an eye on her all the same."

He surprised Rowdy by saying, "Appreciate it." Hell, the way he felt right now, he wouldn't mind having the National Guard standing at her door.

After everything Alice had been through, he knew he'd gladly give his own life to ensure she never got hurt again.

"I'll hit up the tattoo parlor in a bit," Rowdy said, unaware of his dark musings. "Then I'll meet with DeeDee tonight and, hopefully, we'll find out something useful before Cheryl calls Alice back."

It was a horrible conflict for Reese. Never in his life had he turned a blind eye to injustice. But the idea of Cheryl reaching out to Alice made him sick with an urgent need to shield Alice from any and all possible danger—especially the danger posed in assisting a desperate young woman.

He couldn't take the phone from Alice; not only wouldn't she allow that, but it could be the only lifeline left to Cheryl. Neither could he insist on answering the call himself, because they all knew Cheryl was a tool being used to get to Alice.

His head throbbed, and his vision tried to narrow to Alice, *only* Alice. He was a damned cop, a detective, and he had a duty to serve and protect.

But in every second, Alice dicked with his concentration.

When two of the flirting women walked past again, eyeing him without reserve, Reese gave them an absent nod of greeting.

They reacted as much over that as they had Rowdy's attention, and he frowned. He preferred that they keep their sights on Rowdy and off him.

In an effort to focus, he said to Rowdy, "You know I should be paying you."

Rowdy barked a disbelieving laugh. "Fuck that."

But Reese couldn't let it go. "Police work with civilians all the time. And we pay."

"I said no."

So damn proud. Off to the side, Reese saw the women plotting. Shit. Rowdy wasn't the only one familiar with flirting females. Before Alice, he might have relished the fun distraction.

But now…it was a mere annoyance.

Before they interrupted, he said to Rowdy, his tone surly, "You think it's any easier for me? You think I like asking for your help? That I like owing you? Well, I don't."

Taken aback by the quiet attack, Rowdy scowled. "Didn't say that."

"Then let me even it up a little."

"Given the drug deals Avery told me about, it looks like you and Logan will already be lending me a hand. I can only do so much to keep out the criminal element." He grinned, because not that long ago, he'd been considered part of that element. "The rest is up to the boys in blue."

"That's my job. It's a given that I'll be there for that." He gave Rowdy a direct stare. "You know, with your background what it was, you might not realize this, but people—good people—like to lend a helping hand to those in their inner circle. And now, with Pepper marrying Logan, who happens to be my best friend, that circle includes you."

"Inner circle, huh?"

"Whether you like it or not."

With a half grin, Rowdy gave it considerable thought before making a quiet admission. "I have plans to renovate the bar. Right now, it's pretty shitty. Buying it didn't completely strap me, but it's going to be tight for a while." He gazed off at the playground area where kids kept the swings going high. "When I was solely responsible for Pepper, I couldn't…"

"Cut it too close?" Reese offered. He knew that Rowdy had looked out for his sister in every way imaginable, including keeping a store of cash on hand in case they needed to make a fast getaway.

"Yeah." The grin widened. "I never wanted to be caught without an escape plan."

Because Pepper had depended on him.

But who could Rowdy depend on? Back then, no one.

At such a young age, a ton of worry had been dropped on his shoulders. He'd had to grow up fast, and overall, he'd done an inspiring job—with everything. "I'm impressed you had enough for a cash deal. Few could swing it. As to manual labor, count me in."

"You like to sweat, do you?"

"Do I look like I avoid a workout?" Reese was big

enough and muscled enough that not even Rowdy—who wasn't a physical slouch himself—could downplay his strength.

Rowdy laughed. "You're a fucking hulk and you know it." He nodded toward the women. "Seems to me they're noticing, too."

Reese ignored that reference to their female audience. He plain and simple didn't care. "Once Logan knows your plans, he'll want to help, as well, and since Dash owns a construction company, he'll probably have all kinds of useful input."

"Jesus, round up a posse, why don't you?"

"They're your family now. You'll get used to it." Or at least, Reese hoped he would.

Slowly, Rowdy nodded. "All right, then. It's a deal. I'll keep you posted on what's happening and when."

The women chose that auspicious moment to intrude. The dark-haired one led the pack, coming up to Rowdy first. "Hi."

"Hi, yourself." Rowdy included the rest of the ladies with a smile.

The woman turned to Reese with a dreamy look. "Are we interrupting?"

God, he knew that smile, knew that look in her eyes and what it meant. He needed to get home to Alice, not play games with…well, beautiful and sexy women who weren't Alice.

Disgusted, he rubbed his face, knowing he was whipped, without much effort on Alice's part. All she'd done was accept him, and he'd fallen headlong into monogamy.

Last night she'd wanted confessions from him, but damn it, this was all so new. He wasn't even sure what he felt. He only knew that he felt it in spades.

When Reese just stood there, probably looking dumbfounded, Rowdy brought the woman's attention back to him with a touch on her chin. "Sorry, darlin', but he's newly taken and still fighting it. And, yeah, we are sort of busy at the moment. But if you like, I can give you my number, and maybe we can hook up some time."

She sighed. "It was a little unrealistic to think you'd both be available."

Rowdy laughed. "Should I be insulted that I was second pick?"

A blonde pushed her way around the brunette. "I'll take your number, no problem at all."

Grinning, Rowdy dug out a card.

Reese eyed him. He wasn't yet a businessman, so was the card strictly for hooking up with women? Probably.

"I'll be busy tonight," Rowdy told her, "but ring me tomorrow and we'll see what we can cook up."

Another woman asked, "All of us?"

"Works for me."

More than a little put out, Reese crossed his arms over his chest. Even before Alice, he wasn't in the habit of setting up orgies, yet Rowdy appeared to take it in stride.

It drove home just how different their lives had been.

The brunette gave him another sultry look, then daringly reached out to stroke his shoulder. "It's a shame you're unavailable. I'd have shown you a real good time."

"It's my loss," Reese told her.

"If things don't work out, let me know. We're at the park here nearly every day."

Doing…*what,* he wondered. Picking up strangers? "I'll keep that in mind."

Rowdy gave her a swat on the ass. "Move it along now, honey. We've got business to complete."

Laughing, she rubbed at her backside and led the others away.

"That one's going to be a handful," Rowdy murmured. "I like that. Doesn't even bother me that I was second pick."

Reese watched them go, until Rowdy gave him a nudge. "You having regrets, or looking for tattoos?"

"Tattoos." His only regret was that he was away from Alice right now. She'd be worried about Cheryl, anxious, and he didn't want her alone. "Other than a butterfly on one ankle and a rose on a shoulder, I didn't see any ink."

"Me either." Rowdy lifted one brow. "And I was looking *real* close."

Understandable, given the women were all hot. So, why didn't Reese care, damn it?

Rowdy laughed. "You're in love, dude, just go with it."

"Fuck off, Rowdy. We—or at least I—have work to do."

Unfazed, Rowdy watched him. "Why is it a problem? Alice is a sweetheart."

Why was it a problem? He had to keep a clear head, be unbiased, analytical…and he couldn't, not with Alice involved.

Rather than spill his guts to Rowdy, Reese came to a decision. "All right. You can go check out Killer Designz."

Brows up, Rowdy said, "Was that still in question?"

"But you're not going alone, and not without backup." To get things arranged, Reese pulled out his cell and put in a call to the lieutenant. After he explained what he wanted to do, he expected her to argue.

He expected her to refuse.

Lieutenant Peterson surprised him by enthusiastically agreeing.

Seemed everyone enjoyed going undercover except him.

SLUMPED IN THE corner of the small motel room, Cheryl suffered in miserable silence.

Her wary stare annoyed him. "Relax, will you? I'm not going to drown you." Yet. But after that debacle of a phone call, he was in a killing mood.

Unfortunately, in order to keep that pain-in-his-ass Alice from slipping through his fingers, he needed Cheryl alive. "I thought she would care about you."

"She—she does. She will. Let m-me call her back. I'll convince her, I sw-swear."

Studying her, Hickson rubbed his chin. "You're sure you don't know her last name?"

Cheryl shook her head hard.

Hmm… "Maybe she needs to hear you suffering to make her realize the enormity of the situation." He strode to her, kneeling down and grabbing her hair when she tried to scamper away. "Maybe she needs you doing a little wailing to know that your life is on the line here."

Cheryl did indeed wail, so loud and pathetic that he wanted to strike her. Instead, he tightened his hand in her hair, pulled her head back. "Just like that, Cheryl. You need to be that authentic when you call tomorrow. Do you understand me?"

"Y-yes!"

He looked into her eyes, saw the stark terror there, and knew she would do as told. Releasing her with a shove, Hickson gained his feet again. He needed a foolproof plan, one that would ensure Alice showed up alone, without the law, without enforcements.

Vulnerable.

Easy prey.

"Here's what we'll do." Pacing in front of Cheryl, he detailed every step, and he felt confident that in the end, he'd get what he needed.

He'd get Alice. His life depended on it.

REESE GOT HOME sooner than Alice expected. She'd just stepped out of the shower when she heard Cash bark.

Not that long ago, alarm would have overtaken her if someone had entered her apartment. Even if someone had knocked on her door.

But she'd learned to recognize Cash's different barks. She knew when he was afraid, protective, suspicious, and—like now—welcoming. She made the easy and comfortable assumption that Reese was back.

Wrapping a towel around herself, Alice came out of the bathroom. She smiled to see Reese on one knee, holding Cash by the face and talking softly to him while Cash's tail thumped hard in joy.

When Reese kissed the dog on top of his head, her heart expanded, getting so full that it threatened to break. To fight off the excess of sentiment, she strode closer to man and dog.

Her man and dog—whether they quite realized it yet or not.

"Rowdy is okay?"

"Up to his ears in female adoration, but otherwise fine." Reese stood, looked her over, and a familiar heat burned in his beautiful green eyes. "How are you?"

"I'm all right." She unpinned her hair and let it drop

down to her shoulders. "Worried, of course. I mean, I keep thinking about what Cheryl is probably going through right now. How scared she must be."

Instead of coming to her, Reese shoved his hands into his pockets and continued his perusal of her person. "Until she calls back, there's really nothing we can do."

"But I assume you have a plan." Blind faith had never been her forte—not until Reese. She needed to know that he had things in hand, that somehow he'd make it all okay. "You do, don't you?"

"Working on it." He tilted his head and studied her body. "How is it that every time I look at you, you get hotter?"

Alice felt a blush rising. "You're..." Well, she couldn't say smitten. In lust? Maybe. She settled on, "A charmer."

Cash looked between them, then trotted to the kitchen, hopeful for a treat.

Reese's slow smile made her toes curl. "Cash assumes we'll be having sex."

Because usually they were. But...maybe not this time.

Despite the warm way Reese looked at her, Alice could tell that he had more than sex on his mind.

"You're going back out, aren't you?"

His gaze cut to her face, and a cynical smile twisted his mouth. "So astute."

That sounded almost like an insult.

Or a complaint.

Alice held the towel a little tighter. "Obviously you have other plans or..." *You'd have already been on me.*

No, that was another thing she couldn't quite say.

She lifted her chin. "Or you wouldn't be waffling around, acting out of character."

"Waffling?" Taking his hands from his pockets,

Reese closed the space between them, lifted her chin with the edge of his fist, searched her face. "It's almost scary how you do that. How you so easily read me."

Ironic, because if she could read him better, she'd already know if he loved her. "You're in cop mode," she explained. "Anyone can see that."

If anything, that made him look more forbidding.

"I understand," Alice rushed to reassure him. "With Cheryl's call and then Rowdy needing you… What was that about, by the way?"

Instead of answering, his thumb caressed her chin, and he bent to take her mouth, startling her since he hadn't looked in a kissing mood.

Despite everything going on, all the threats and her worry, she couldn't remain immune to his mouth on hers. She groaned a little, reached for him…

But he ended the contact as abruptly as he'd introduced it.

Alice whispered, "Reese?"

He headed to the kitchen to give Cash a treat.

"Only half," he told the dog. "I don't want you getting spoiled."

Cash took the treat and went to his favorite spot in front of the balcony doors. Reese stayed in the kitchen, just looking out the window, silent and somehow distant.

Alice didn't know what to do. "How much time do you have before you have to go back out?"

Bracing his hands on the kitchen sink counter, he dropped his head forward. Alice took two deep breaths—and removed her towel.

Though he had his back to her, he seemed to sense the moment she was naked because his head slewed around and his interest burned all over her.

On the pretense of drying her shoulders, Alice avoided his gaze. "It's okay to tell me, you know. I won't kick up a fuss. I can tell it'll be something dangerous, and of course I'll be anxious. But I'm not the type to—"

She squeaked when Reese suddenly scooped her over his shoulder.

"Reese!" The towel slipped from her grip to land on the hardwood floor.

His hand covered her backside, holding her still as he strode toward the bedroom. He told Cash, "Stay," as he passed him.

So Cash was right? They *would* have sex?

Smart dog.

In her ignominious position, Alice could do no more than hang on and wonder what had gotten into Reese. One minute he'd been distant, then austere, then all over her.

She felt his hand moving, sliding down to her inner thigh, tucking in between for a fleeting touch.

"Reese!" she said again, but she didn't really struggle. What would be the point?

"Hush." He stepped into her room and kicked the door shut behind him.

"But…what are you doing?"

His hold was rougher than usual, and she could feel him shaking when he said, "I need you."

"Oh." Well, of course that was okay. Hanging over his shoulder, Alice said, "I need you, too."

He gave a dark laugh. "Always so agreeable, Alice." He dumped her sideways onto the bed and stood back to look at her.

She came up on one elbow but didn't bother to close her legs.

Peeling his shirt off over his head, Reese stared at her breasts, then down to her sex.

Alice licked dry lips. "Are we doing something different?"

"I'm going to get my fill of you."

Her heart skipped a beat and she went still. She didn't like the sound of that. *Oh, God, please don't let him mean that the way it sounds.*

But she had to know. So, she drew in a breath, shored up her courage and whispered, "Do you mean…for forever?"

CHAPTER TWENTY-FOUR

ALICE FELT ONLY nominal relief when Reese gave another humorless laugh, accompanied by a shake of his head. "I doubt that's even possible."

Well…good.

"No, I meant for the night."

The reprieve left her limp until his words sank in—then her heart started tap-dancing again. "Oh."

He opened his slacks and pulled down the zipper. "I'll have to be gone for a while, and I'm going to need to focus." His gaze clashed with hers. "By the way, Logan and Pepper will be here with you."

"I don't need babysitters."

"*I* need you to have company." He shucked off his pants. "I don't want to worry about you while I'm gone, but I will if you're here alone."

Mmm. The sight of his body always inspired her, and her fingers curled into the bedcovers. "I've been by myself for a long time now, Reese. You know I'm capable of taking care of—"

"Me." Naked, he stepped up to the bed and caught her knees, then opened her legs more. "You can take care of me."

The way he displayed her made her voice die in her throat.

His fingers kneaded her knees while he studied every

inch of her. "I feel almost savage. *You* make me feel savage."

Meaning *what?* Alice didn't understand this new mood of his. She'd seen many facets to his personality, but none this urgent, this dark. "I don't mean to."

"Doesn't seem to matter if you do it on purpose or not." He pushed her knees up—and wider apart.

Bracing herself, Alice did her best not to shy away. "Reese, tell me, did something happen?"

"You happened." He slid his hands down to her hips, then drew her to the edge of the mattress.

Her legs dangled over the side, and she floundered, grabbing on to the covers. "Reese…"

"You keep saying my name." He went down to his knees.

Between her legs.

"I like it." Lifting her legs over his shoulders and cupping her bottom in his big hands, he said, "You are so fucking beautiful."

Good grief, he was staring at her *there.* It was intimidating but also exciting. Alice dropped her head back and studied the ceiling. "Is this because of what I did to you yesterday?"

"It's because I want you. All the time, it seems." He brushed his lips along her inner thigh, his cool hair tickling her skin, his hot breath making her shiver. "Other women hit on me, and I don't care because you're always in my head."

Whoa, wait. "What?" She tried to lever up. "Other women hit on you? When?"

Nuzzling against her, Reese gave a soft growl that almost stopped her heart. "You smell incredible."

A thundering heartbeat made her weak, so she lay

back again—and felt his mouth and his tongue on her thighs, along the delicate skin of her groin, her belly.

"Oh, God."

"Be still, honey." Using just his fingertips, he teased over her lips, opening her, dipping in the tiniest bit, back out, in again. "You're already wet."

Alice squeezed her eyes shut.

He slicked two fingers into her, turning them a little, withdrawing. "Nice and wet."

That low, rasping voice washed over her, assuring her that he enjoyed this, enjoyed holding her this way. It was both embarrassing and exciting.

She waited, her breath held, her body tense in anticipation—and his soft, hot tongue licked over her.

In her.

Sank deep.

Sensation washed over her, arching her back and lifting her off the mattress.

With a hand on her stomach Reese brought her flat again, all without breaking the deep, intimate kiss. He locked his arms around hips, keeping her still, keeping her close. After another long, soft lick, he moved up to circle her clitoris with the tip of his tongue.

Alice moaned sharply, the pressure already building. He circled once more, teased and tasted, and then closed his mouth around her, sucking gently.

The exclamation of *"Oh, God, oh, God"* dwindled to indecipherable groans as the climax uncoiled inside her. Even against Reese's powerful hold, her body bowed again. She couldn't keep from rolling up to the pleasure, moving against his mouth in a rhythm that enhanced everything he did.

He was voracious, unrelenting, and oh, so incredibly patient, almost as if he didn't want to stop, as if he could have done this for hours.

She was almost there, reaching for the release, when Reese readjusted and put his fingers inside her again, filling her up, stretching her a little.

That did it.

Crying out, she gave over to release and slowly sank back to the bed.

She hadn't yet gotten enough breath into her lungs when Reese straightened, her ankles still up on his shoulders, and thrust into her.

It was so unexpected that she gasped…but her climax had left her wet and soft, and with a low, vibrating groan he filled her up.

Locking his gaze with hers, Reese brought her legs to the crook of his elbows and slowly lowered himself over her. Her legs ached from the position, but she felt him so deeply, loved the raw pleasure on his face, and already her sensitized nerve endings sparked again.

Opening his palms over her breasts, Reese rasped her nipples while driving into her, and Alice exploded with another orgasm.

Reese waited until the last shuddering spasm had faded, then he stilled. Eyes squeezed shut, he said, "I'm not wearing anything."

All but insensate, Alice lifted a limp hand to his sweaty shoulder. "I know." Still tingling all over, she tried to shift beneath him.

He sucked in a breath. "Don't."

"I love your body, Reese." She loved every single inch of him.

"I don't mean clothes." His teeth locked and he panted. "I skipped the rubber."

Eyes widening, Alice stared up at him. That admission brought her around some, although every muscle remained mostly unresponsive. Beyond curious but not really alarmed, she put both hands on his face.

After Rowdy's call, he hadn't taken the time to shave, and she loved the rough texture of his beard shadow, how aroused color slashed his high cheekbones, the way he held himself in check—just barely. "Why?"

"Didn't want to." He kissed her, then kissed her some more, slanting his head for the perfect fit before finally coming up for air. His big body strained against hers. "I still don't."

That damned emotion gathered in her throat again, choking her, making her eyes burn. She tried a smile that quivered too much, giving away her heart. "Then, don't."

As if he'd just been waiting for permission, Reese stopped holding back. Again he took her mouth, his kiss consuming as he pounded into her, keeping her legs pressed back so that each and every stroke entered her so deeply, she felt him against her womb.

When he suddenly threw back his head on a harsh groan, his big body drawn taut, Alice watched him, enjoying every nuance on his face, glad that she was the one here with him.

He dropped against her, his heartbeat shaking them both, heat pouring off him in waves.

Usually she relished the closeness, but this time she protested his weight with a small wiggle. "My legs are dead."

With what seemed like a great effort, Reese struggled up and helped to untangle her legs from his thick, muscular arms. He lowered them carefully, massaging her left thigh for a moment. "Okay?"

"It was worth it," she whispered.

Smiling, he separated from her and dropped down beside her again, but he kept a hand on her belly, his fingers spread out to encompass her from hip bone to hip bone. The seconds ticked by while they both held silent, each concentrating on breathing.

Reese moved his fingers in a gentle stroke. "You are incredibly delicious, Alice."

She had no idea what to say about that.

Turning toward her, he rose up on one elbow. "I haven't had sex without a condom since I was an ignorant schoolboy."

So that meant…something, right?

Far too serious, he smoothed her hair back, brushed her temple with his thumb. His brows came together, and his voice went deeper. "Even now, after just having you, I want you all over again."

Oh, no way. "I'm not sure I could—"

He kissed her hard and quick. "It's insane and unsettling, and I'm not sure I like it. Other women flirt with me and it makes me want you. Rowdy fills my ear with important info about the tattoo murders, and I want you. Lieutenant Peterson agrees to go undercover, and even that, something I never expected in a million years, gets overridden by thoughts of *you*."

It finally occurred to Alice: Reese was telling her how he felt.

Joy filled her, along with contentment and excitement, and she smiled at him. "I'm glad you don't want other women."

This laugh sounded honest, more lighthearted and sincere. He dropped flat again. "God Almighty, woman, you kill me." He took her hand. "And, no, I don't want other women."

"I don't want any other men either." *Ever,* she could

have added, but didn't want to push him when he was already struggling to share with her.

"Great. Glad we got that settled."

Alice wondered what exactly they had settled, but she only smiled and let out a breath. "So, we're exclusive." For now. "That's nice."

He, too, seemed to relax more when she didn't start digging for more details about this new exclusivity. "I'm sorry, but I have to leave soon." He lifted her hand to his mouth, brushed her knuckles over his lips. "I'll be out late."

Alice turned her head toward him. "Should I worry?"

"No, because it's my job, and I'm good at my job." Using her hand, he tugged her atop him. "Even when a certain sexy lady keeps shattering my thoughts and giving me mental fits."

"Hmm." Alice kissed his bottom lip, then his whiskery chin. "So, did you get me out of your system?"

He shook his head. "No." He brought her close for a deeper taste, lingering, somehow almost…desperate. "But you did give me plenty of incentive to get back home safely. In the meantime, let's go get some breakfast, and I'll tell you what's going on."

REESE RAN A hand over his whiskered jaw. He still hadn't shaved; being scruffy helped him to fit in. Parked across from the cigarette store, he waited in one of Rowdy's cars. The Ford sedan ran well but looked like shit.

Probably because that's how Rowdy wanted it.

With sunglasses in place, a ball cap on backward, a worn T-shirt and his most comfortable jeans, Reese drank a Coke and tried to look negligent. The hot afternoon sun baked the car. He was alert and ready but, thanks to Alice, not so tense.

And hell, even now, while on surveillance, he thought of her.

In his peripheral vision he saw Rowdy approach the tattoo parlor on the pretext of perusing a few designs in the front window. Unlike Reese, Rowdy looked the same as always—which meant he didn't stand out the same way a cop would.

It was an attitude thing, Reese decided. Rowdy was just as watchful, but on him it looked street-smart, not authoritative. Huh. He could probably learn a few things just by observing him.

Now, where was Peterson? He glanced at his watch. Rowdy could only window shop so long before someone got suspicious.

Reese glanced in the rearview mirror and saw a woman stride down the street. The color of that short hair looked right. The height and weight, too, but…no way could that be Lieutenant Peterson in high heels, a miniscule black shirt and a barely there white blouse unbuttoned so low he thought he might see her navel if he looked close enough.

The Coke can nearly slipped out of his hand. He resisted the urge to jerk around and stare, but heaven help her, Lieutenant Margaret Peterson looked like walking, breathing, smiling sex.

Her dark sunglasses kept him from seeing her eyes, but who'd notice her eyes anyway with her cleavage on display like that? Before this moment, he hadn't even thought about the fact that Peterson had breasts, much less that she could make them look so round and full and…

He shuddered, unsure how he felt about noticing her now.

Rowdy gave her the attention expected for any attractive woman, even going so far as to leer a little—real or fake? Hell, Reese didn't know. But when Peterson strolled inside Killer Designz, Rowdy followed hot on her heels, his gaze zeroed in her rump in the tight skirt.

Reese broke out in a sweat, and he didn't know if it was the heat of the sweltering sun, the high stakes of the situation or seeing Lieutenant Peterson as a sex kitten.

Oh, God. He shuddered again as he sank into his seat and tried to obliterate the image from his mind.

The sun continued to beat down. Sweat gathered on the back of his neck, between his shoulder blades, and at the small of his back where the concealed harness held his Glock.

The other gun, strapped to his ankle, wasn't as uncomfortable in the heat.

Minutes felt like hours, and still nothing happened.

Until Reese saw two men pull up in a black SUV. A chill went up his spine, and damn it, he didn't like it. The men glanced around as if looking for witnesses, but this wasn't an area where concerned citizens kept watch. It was more a "see no evil" type of habitat.

Reese used his sunglasses to hide his direct gaze, turning his head down as if playing with his radio.

The two men had a similar look, one in expensive jeans, the other in khaki slacks, both in black polo shirts with Bluetooth earpieces and mirrored sunglasses. They looked like professional thugs, and unlike him, they hadn't even attempted to blend in.

They spoke quietly to each other. One guy put in a quick cell phone call, nodded, and together they went inside.

In a nanosecond, Reese made the decision to follow. He felt it all going to hell, sensed an implosion about to occur. No way would he wait in the car when Peterson and Rowdy were likely sitting ducks.

Thank God, Logan is with Alice. If anything went wrong here, he knew she'd be okay. Logan would see to it. And with that knowledge, he managed to shove her from his mind so he could handle the situation as needed.

With professionalism, a cool head and deadly accuracy—in a freakin' ball cap and printed T-shirt.

As he left the car, Reese tugged at his loose T-shirt, peeling it away from his damp back to ensure it kept his Glock covered. He repositioned his cap, taking it off to let air reach his head, then settling it on again. Anxiety ramping up with every beat of his heart, he strode toward the tattoo parlor.

Killer Designz had a massive front window, so even while still a dozen feet away, he spotted Peterson—he would never get used to seeing her dressed like that—talking to presumably a tattoo artist. She stood with her hip cocked out, an "I'm up for grabs" smile on her painted mouth, and her hands on a counter so she could lean forward, which effectively kept the artist's attention glued to her rack.

Rowdy stood a few feet behind her, glancing through a book of designs. The two hoods were off to the side, pretending to peruse the body jewelry in a glass-enclosed case.

Like either of those goons had piercings.

A little bell jangled when Reese walked in. Cool air-conditioning washed over his heated skin. Rowdy glanced up and away, doing a good job of dismissing him. Peterson stalled a second but not for long. Her gaze moved to the two thugs and then away again.

Was that to let Reese know she was already aware of them? Maybe.

"Well," she said, her voice somehow throaty, "you're getting busy, and I don't want to hold you up."

The thugs, it seemed, were more concerned with Rowdy than Peterson, which made sense. Rowdy stood six-four, only a few inches shorter than Reese, with a fit physique that promised capability. In comparison, the Lieutenant was a diminutive little lady, and in that getup, she looked more like fluff than a ball-busting, high-ranking cop who'd damn near single-handedly cleaned up a very corrupt department with cold-blooded determination.

Shit. "Hey," Reese said. "You the only one working?"

The artist nodded at him. "I'll be right with you."

"Great." Hooking his sunglasses to the front of his T-shirt, Reese did his own perusing. That gave him an opportunity to surreptitiously scope out the interior in case they had to make a hasty getaway.

The lieutenant put a finger to her lips. "I like all of these," she said of the designs shown in a free-standing swing panel display. "But I saw a really unique pattern the other day, and I think I want something like that."

The artist watched her finger on her mouth as she dragged it back and forth over her bottom lip. "Can you describe it to me?"

"Sure. It was sort of long and narrow, with lines and numbers."

"Numbers?"

"Mmm-hmm." She rested her arm on the counter—which dipped her forward even farther until Reese feared she'd fall right out of the dubious constraint of that sheer blouse.

He stopped staring only long enough to realize that

Rowdy and the two goons were also paying very close attention to the straining buttons on her blouse.

"Like this," she said, and she used her damp fingertip to draw the size of the tattoo on her arm. She looked up with a slow smile. "Got anything like that?"

The guy concentrated on breathing for a few seconds. "Yeah, I think I might." Something glittered in his eyes. Lust, yes, but more than that? "Hang on a sec while I go get a different pattern book."

Was he onto her?

Staying loose, his ankles crossed, Reese leaned back on the counter as he flipped through a catalogue.

The artist turned and went through a curtain to a backroom.

Rowdy looked up at her. "Where you getting your tat, honey?" He used the excuse of a conversation to move closer to her—something Peterson didn't appreciate, given how she took a step away.

Heat flushed her cheeks, and damn if that didn't look genuine.

"I haven't decided," Peterson said. "Probably on my arm, but I'm thinking it might look great climbing the back of my leg, too." She turned, presenting that snug little ass to Rowdy and the two hired hands. She tipped her hip out again and looked over her shoulder with a smile. "What do you think?"

"I think you shouldn't mess with perfection."

Peterson did a slow bat of her eyelashes, and that was so disturbing, Reese almost missed hearing the lock on the front door click into place. He turned fast and saw that one of the men now barred the door. The other man, mouth twisted in a sick smile of anticipation, pulled out a Desert Eagle .50 cal with a long black suppressor attached.

Reese didn't wait for questions, for a better opportunity, or to see what Rowdy and Peterson would do. He thought only of controlling that deadly weapon.

Full force, he launched his considerable size and weight at the armed man. The complete lack of hesitation took the goon by surprise. Reese topped him by several inches and probably forty pounds, so the impact of his assault crashed them to the ground hard. As they fell, Reese heard a near-silent *pop, pop* and the shattering of glass.

He trusted Rowdy and Peterson to handle the other one, not that he had much of a choice.

While holding on to his wrist so that the bastard couldn't lift the gun, Reese deliberately thunked the man's head to the floor, then landed an elbow to his face. That slackened the guy's grip, and Reese wrested the gun from his hand.

"You're a dead man," the idiot snarled, renewing his effort to get the upper hand.

Reese used the gun to slug him hard in the jaw.

The man went limp at the same time something crashed behind him.

Twisting, Reese looked over his shoulder—and Peterson was all but naked!

Somehow, while he'd had his back turned, her blouse had gotten ripped, and yes, those were pale, full breasts spilling out all right. Jacking up her skirt, she produced her own weapon—a small handgun she'd strapped to her thigh—and pointed it at the man Rowdy had in a chokehold.

Belatedly, Reese found the wherewithal to follow her gaze, but Rowdy tightened his hold and the second man went to sleep, making Peterson's effort unnecessary.

They'd taken charge of the deadly situation with little fuss.

Neat, tidy, easy…

Until rapid-fire gunshots shattered the front window and pelted the walls and counter.

"Shit!" With alacrity, Rowdy released his man and dove for the front counter. His boots crunched over the sharp broken glass of a display case and the scattered, more gravelly glass of the big picture window.

Hunkered down in her high heels, her skirt still up and her blouse still open, Peterson scuttled ahead of him.

They both made it behind the dubious safety of the counter.

More shots zipped into the room, each one a dull ping that sent that debris scattering.

The shop was destroyed. It appeared the shooters wanted them all dead. Talk about overkill….

Utilizing professional detachment, Reese stayed plastered to a wall. As his man started to revive, he busted him again and let him slump supine to the floor. He glanced across the room, but Rowdy had choked the other one enough that he was breathing, but unresponsive even to the clamor surrounding him.

"Get over here," Peterson snapped when several more bullets littered the interior, exploding yet another case.

"Move back." As soon as Peterson got out of his way, Reese snatched up the Desert Eagle, ducked low and, on his haunches, joined them for cover. The damned counter wasn't big enough to properly shield three people.

"Sit tight." Rowdy slipped into the backroom.

Reese could just see him moving in a crouch, checking the small john, a supply closet and another backroom. He was unarmed, damn it, so he had no business playing hero.

"Rowdy." Reese kept his voice calm and in control. "Damn it, don't do anything stupid."

Rowdy returned, his expression grim. "We have to get out of here. The artist is long gone, run off out a back door."

If the owner could leave, that meant others could come in. Great, this whole fuck-up just kept getting better and better.

CHAPTER TWENTY-FIVE

"GONE WHERE?" Peterson asked, as she tried—unsuccessfully—to pull her torn blouse together.

"Hell if I know. But only an idiot would've stuck around once the shooting started."

To punctuate that, more shots were fired.

Where the hell was backup? Surely someone—anyone—had called in the gunfire by now. Even with suppressors, the denizens of the area had to know an attempted murder was going down.

Rowdy had been keeping watch out back, but for a second there, he stared at Peterson's chest.

The lieutenant said low, "If you don't want me to shoot you, use those eyes to keep watch out the back."

"I'm watching." He lifted his gaze but didn't smile. "And while it's clear, I'd suggest you hightail that sweet ass on out of here, *now,* while we can still go."

Ignoring the sexist remark on her body, Peterson checked her weapon and cursed. "That might be exactly what they want us to do." She narrowed her eyes on Reese. "What do you think? Not to give away an inside secret, but how do you feel about calling your little entourage?"

Few on the force knew that Reese had personally vetted some of the uniformed cops, forming a solid crew that was loyal to him. But calling them a "little entourage" didn't do them justice.

The men were smart, honorable and, above all, trustworthy. "Not this time." Calling in his own team on such short notice, bypassing on-duty officers, would draw too much attention and defeat the entire purpose of keeping an under-the-radar alliance.

Reese handed the gun with the suppressor to Rowdy, then pulled off his T-shirt and offered it to Peterson.

Rowdy lifted a brow and said to Reese, "Spoilsport."

"You're pushing it, Rowdy Yates." She took the shirt.

But damned if she didn't stare at Reese's chest as intently as Rowdy had stared at hers.

It was like a comedy of errors, bizarre in the extreme. If they weren't in such incredible danger, he might have laughed. "Lieutenant?"

"Right. Thank you." Showing off strong legs, Peterson struggled into the shirt without standing up in sight of the gunmen or sitting on the broken glass. The awkward position strained her thighs, especially in those heels, but she didn't seem to notice or care.

Reese pulled out his cell—and realized he'd busted it when he'd tackled the gunman to the floor. "Damn it." He sent a questioning look to Peterson.

Her head cleared the shirt. "Dropped my purse on the other side of the counter—with my phone in it."

They both turned to Rowdy.

He withdrew his cell and tossed it to Reese. "Knock yourself out." Then, with a hand at the small of Peterson's back, he helped to steady her, so she could get her arms free.

Before Reese could make the call, they heard groans coming from one of the downed men only yards away. He said as politely as he could manage under the circumstances, "I suggest we move before we get cornered."

"Damn it." Maneuvering in the limited space, she finished tugging the T-shirt down over her trim body. It fit like a damned tent, billowing down below her knees, more than adequate to keep her covered.

Taking the lead, she said, "If you have to shoot, make damn sure it isn't a bystander." And with that, gun held in front of her, she ducked through the back of the store.

Still holding the Desert Eagle, Rowdy followed right behind her.

Reese peeked around the counter to ensure no one followed. So far, both men were still out, and he hadn't heard a shot in the last few sec—

A bullet hit the floor in front of his face, sending him ducking for cover again. Not more than two or three minutes had passed, but under these circumstances, a minute could feel like an hour.

He joined the others in back.

As Rowdy had said, the store was empty. The second they cleared the doorway, Reese closed the door. There was a dead bolt on it, which to his beleaguered senses seemed fairly suspect. What happened in this narrow room that required such a sturdy lock?

He saw only shelves of supplies, a file cabinet and a single chair…in the middle of the floor.

His brain buzzed with possibilities, but for now, the dead bolt worked in their favor. He secured the lock and turned to assess the situation.

Peterson stood beside the back door, her spine flattened against the wall. At any other time, Reese might have paid more attention to how mismatched she appeared in those mile-high heels and a printed T-shirt so large it hung off one shoulder and fell below her knees.

Today was not that day.

He put in the call for backup, then pocketed Rowdy's phone. They had a squad car about five minutes out—which might not be soon enough if they got into a shoot-out in such close confines. "Is it clear?"

She shrugged the bared shoulder. "Looks like. We open into an alley that leads to the street. But since none of this was expected, are we willing to trust that it's not a trap?"

Reese weighed the options. "The angles are wrong unless they have a sniper." What to do? "If we stay here, we're sitting ducks."

"I have my car close by," Rowdy said. "That alley leads to a back street. I'm one block down in an empty lot."

"Don't even think it," Peterson warned. She chewed the pink gloss off her bottom lip. "Jesus, I never expected things to go so hot so fast."

"It's insane," Reese agreed as he tried to figure out what to do.

The jarring sound of the front door crashing open drew his attention. They wouldn't have five seconds, much less five minutes. Whoever came after them didn't worry about witnesses or the destruction of Killer Designz.

That could only mean they planned to kill all three of them and be long gone before the police arrived.

Reese removed the Glock from his back holster and traded it for the Desert Eagle.

Rowdy lifted a brow. "You want the bigger, badder gun?"

"I trust my weapon," Reese explained. And he wanted to ensure Rowdy could defend himself. "I know I've taken care of it."

"Thanks." Rowdy hefted it in his hand once, then launched out the back door before Reese could stop him.

"Idiot," Peterson muttered in a hiss.

Cursing softly, Reese divided his time between watching the locked door, as the sounds of assailants drew closer, and watching Rowdy as he darted to the end of the alley.

"What the hell is he doing?" Peterson asked.

Seeing Rowdy run without apparent fear of personal injury, Reese muttered, "I assume he's playing hero."

Luckily, Rowdy made it without a single shot being fired. At the end of the alley, near the street, he signaled that it was clear.

The lieutenant sucked in a breath and said, "Let's go."

Great. They'd either be killed or not, but sitting there waiting to be murdered didn't much appeal to him either. Reese followed her out, impressed that she could run so fluidly in those deadly heels.

Rowdy covered them, his gaze going everywhere as he waited for them to join him. Not a single shot was fired, and no more noise came from the tattoo parlor.

Together, they hustled toward the lot holding Rowdy's car. Soon as they reached it, they could let the officers know they were clear.

And with any luck, they'd be able to round up the shooters.

But Reese wouldn't be holding his breath; so far, luck hadn't been on their side.

Two questions pounded through his brain as they reached safety.

Just how big was this operation—and how far would they go to find Alice?

THE PHONE CALLS had come in rapid order.

First the warning call from Killer Designz, letting

him know that people were snooping around. He'd sent in his men, and they'd reported back to say they had effectively razed the place, leaving behind little more than rubble within an empty building. The curious trio had escaped, but not without first understanding the reach of his power, the strength of his daring.

Smirking, Woody Simpson recalled the breathless panic of the tattoo artist who, from a safer location, had called again. With the promise of protection from the law, and a new and better location, concerns had been quieted.

And now he had DeeDee on the line.

Feet propped on the desk, shirt unbuttoned and chair tilted back, Woody listened to the final report on the day's events. Thanks to a fast-growing enterprise, he spent so much time in his office that he'd gradually turned it into a comfortable, condolike space.

He didn't cook, of course, but he had others who made use of the small kitchen to prepare his meals. He had a large-screen TV and spacious couch, and he'd brought in a king-size bed to convert a boardroom for sleeping.

Not that he ever slept during the day. Even at night, he didn't need much sleep. He'd always been high-energy, motivated and so fucking smart that others couldn't keep up.

But when he wanted an afternoon distraction—as he'd planned today before the phone started going off—the bed sometimes came in handy.

"So, you're sure they're cops?"

"I think so. They're talking with officers now, and they seem to be in charge or something."

Interesting. Maybe this would be better than killing them. It'd give him an opening, a way to infiltrate. He pondered the different plays and came to a decision. "Follow them."

A heavy pause, rife with uncertainty. "To…a police station?"

"Sure." Though he'd sent for her earlier, Woody waved off the girl responsible for unbuttoning his shirt. She moved to a chair, sat down and waited.

Like a good girl.

"But…" DeeDee tried to come up with logical arguments.

He hated being questioned—by anyone. "Wait there until they come back out, and then follow. I want to know where they live."

She hesitated. "What if they see me?"

"Make sure they don't." DeeDee had aspirations of moving up in the organization. Unlike some of the girls, she was more eager to please.

As if he'd ever give any authority or power to a bimbo.

"You blend in, Dee. It should be a piece of cake for you to stick close without being noticed." Because she wanted to stand out and be noticed, that subtle insult had her bristling.

Trying to sell him on her value, she said, "I already hit on that rough bruiser, like you asked."

"I know. You're meeting him tonight, right?" Woody glanced at his watch. "Plenty of time to do both."

"I haven't eaten since early this morning."

God, he detested whining. "If you aren't able to handle things, just say so. I can ask Michelle to take over instead."

"Michelle?"

"Yes." He looked at the trembling girl sitting across the room. "She's been anxious to gain my favor, anyway."

Michelle swallowed hard and looked away, her fear so palpable that he wondered how she functioned. She had enough sense not to run away, to perform as expected. And she did try to stay on his good side—but she was far too skittish to ever be trusted with anything important.

Anything beyond a blow job.

"I can do it," DeeDee groused.

Perfect. He could always count on DeeDee's vanity to keep her working harder. She wanted to be top girl.

She wanted to be his partner. Woody bit off a laugh at her foolishness.

"Report back after you get the info."

"Okay, but…who should I follow? I mean, I can't follow three people, can I?"

So damn stupid. Did he need to do all her thinking for her? "Don't worry about the woman." Women were always inconsequential. "You'll be meeting one guy at the bar tonight, right? So follow the other today."

"Oh, okay. Sure." DeeDee cleared her throat, then said, "I did tell you that the cop is the same guy who was here this morning, right? The one the rough guy called?"

Slowly, Woody dropped his feet and sat forward. No, she hadn't told him that. His eyes narrowed. His mouth flattened with his annoyance.

So, they were onto…something. Sniffing around *twice*. How much did they know?

Who had talked?

Seeing his dark expression, Michelle let out a whimper.

Woody ignored her. He held the phone tighter, and said to DeeDee, "Tell me now. And don't leave anything out."

It wasn't easy, doing a job bare-chested because your lieutenant needed the shirt off your back. The sun had broiled both his shoulders and his temper. This time, it would take a lot to shake off the vigilant, edgy anger. It would take Alice—but he couldn't have her, not just yet.

By the time the backup had arrived—which to Reese's way of thinking had taken longer than necessary—they'd already reached Rowdy's car without incident and had circled back around to the scene.

All had been quiet.

Instead of giving pursuit, the shooters had vacated the tattoo parlor, taking the two downed men with them.

The boys in blue, as Rowdy liked to refer to them, showed up well after that.

Reese wanted to believe that Lieutenant Peterson had scoured out the corruption, but it seemed beyond suspect to him that a five-minute ETA had taken twelve minutes instead.

Seven minutes could mean the difference between life and death. He'd been furious—but Rowdy seemed to think nothing of it.

Even dressed in his shirt, Lieutenant Peterson took over with ease, calling for several specific officers and dismissing the two who'd arrived tardy.

Once they'd secured the scene, the unis had gone from door to door, establishment to establishment, querying everyone in the area. Reese wasn't surprised that everyone had claimed not to see a damned thing.

Sometimes it was safer to play deaf, dumb and blind, especially with criminals outrageous enough to attempt murder in broad daylight.

If that had been their intent. At this point, he refused to make assumptions.

The entire day had slipped away, and still they hadn't

turned up the owner who'd fled out the back. Far as Reese was concerned, that made him guilty as hell.

Not more than an hour ago, after reminding Reese to keep her in the loop, Peterson had stormed off like a thundercloud. He'd assumed she would go home and change clothes before heading to the station. Reese didn't envy anyone who crossed her path tonight.

Not that long ago, he would have dealt with his simmering frustration and spiked temper with a long shower, a beer, a willing woman and then a good night's sleep—in that exact order.

It said something, Reese thought, that he hadn't even considered going to his own apartment. Bad as the day had been, when he thought of heading home, it meant being with Alice.

Tonight, it also meant visiting with Rowdy and Logan, Pepper and Dash, as they all congregated at Alice's place.

How did she feel about that? For a woman who'd tried so hard to close herself off from the world, it had to be disconcerting that Reese had not only bullied his way in, he'd brought a crowd.

And not just any crowd.

No longer looking so dangerous, Rowdy lounged comfortably on her couch, Cash draped over his lap to soak up attention. It was a little eerie, how Rowdy switched from lethal to carefree in such a short time.

Dash had shown up with Logan and Pepper to wait with Alice, and now they still hung around.

At least Peterson hadn't joined them, thank God. Reese knew he'd never again be able to look at her the same way.

When he'd shown up shirtless, Alice had not-soinconspicuously checked him over head to toes before going off to the kitchen to prepare coffee.

Pepper accompanied her. Reese had a million things on his mind. He easily could have died today, Peterson and Rowdy with him. The clash with the gunman left his knuckles bruised, his right knee swollen and his head throbbing.

What should have been a simple case of surveillance had sharply morphed into audacious, reckless destruction. The stakes had gone from implicit danger to attempted murder.

But he wasn't teetering off his axis because of any of that. His world had gone upside down because of Alice, because of how much he'd anticipated getting back to her. How much he'd wanted to hold and touch her after the disturbing events of the day.

Yes, he could have died; he'd faced that possibility many times in his job, and he'd always fallen to his usual routine to put the ugliness behind him.

But the usual didn't cut it anymore. Not since Alice, not since realizing that death meant never seeing her again.

He didn't even know how to function with caring that much for a woman.

Running a hand over his face, Reese rested back in the chair and tried to come to grips with her effect on him.

"Your lieutenant surprised me."

At Rowdy's lighthearted tone, Reese opened one eye and stared at him.

While still stroking the dog, Rowdy smiled.

Insane. After the violent chaos of the day, Rowdy didn't look ruffled. He showed no aftermath of a near-death experience. He didn't even look all that worried.

He smiled as if…amused.

Great. Rowdy must have a damned death wish or, at the very least, a severe lack of concern for his own life. Shortly, Rowdy planned to head to the bar for his meeting with DeeDee. But now, after what had happened, no way could Reese let him go through with it.

"You're talking about Margo?" At the other end of the couch, Dash showed blatant interest.

Who the hell was Margo? "Her name is Margaret." And to clarify further, Reese said, "Lieutenant Margaret Peterson."

Dash shrugged. "Yeah, but she goes by Margo."

Brows raised, Logan and Reese shared a look that asked, *Since when?*

"So," Dash pushed. "What did she do?"

"Not what she did, so much," Rowdy said. "But how she looked doing it." That particular, male-inspired tone said it all, but still Rowdy added, "Reese knows what I mean. I thought his eyes would fall out when he saw her."

So, Rowdy had somehow witnessed his surprise?

Both Dash and Logan turned to Reese for enlightenment.

In his defense, Reese blurted, "She has a set of breasts on her." That sounded so absurd, he rolled his shoulders, trying to loosen the growing tension.

"Who?" Logan asked, mired in confusion.

Again Rowdy helped out. "Lieutenant Peterson."

Logan pulled back. "You saw her…" And then in a choked whisper, *"Breasts?"*

"Couldn't help it," Rowdy supplied. "She showed up in this boner-inspiring outfit, and that was enough to drop Reese's eyeballs right there. But then after one of the men grabbed for her, she lost her blouse."

"Stop grinning, damn it." Reese squeezed his eyes shut. "Jesus, never in a million years did I expect…that."

Dash snorted. "What did you think? That she'd have chest hair?"

Not really, but he hadn't expected her to be so *lush*. "Chest hair, and possibly brass balls to go with it."

"Exactly," Logan agreed.

"Don't be dumb," Dash said, entertained at Reese's expense. "She *is* a woman after all."

Rowdy lifted a hand. "Noticed."

Stunned silent, Logan gaped at his soon-to-be brother-in-law.

Rowdy said, "What? She's sexy, whether you two clowns want to see it or not. But," he added, cutting off verbal reactions, "she's also a lieutenant. Sort of takes the fun out of it."

"Maybe for detectives working under her command." Dash sent a crooked grin to Rowdy. "Or someone determined to butt heads with the law." Then he held out his arms. "As it happens, I'm neither."

Well, hell, Reese thought. *Alice had nailed that one.*

Logan looked equal parts ill, alarmed and outraged, so Reese filled in the deafening silence. "It's got nothing to do with her rank in the force or any of that. It's that Peterson always dresses so…hell, I don't know. So 'official' that it's hard to see anything feminine."

In a low, appreciative murmur, Rowdy said, "Saw all kinds of feminine things today."

No kidding. "But she's actually very…" With Logan, Dash and Rowdy all waiting for his description, Reese floundered. *Hot* wasn't the right word, not for his lieutenant, not to say to his partner, not in front of Dash and Rowdy.

"I don't want to know." Logan pushed away from

his seat. "I'd as soon block all that from my brain right now."

Yeah, Reese, too. But the sight of the lieutenant's breasts would always be there now, between them.

No! God, no. Not *between* them. Just…*there.*

Peterson wasn't Alice; she didn't fire his blood and make him stupid with carnal hunger. She didn't occupy his thoughts morning, noon and night, or get him hard by her presence alone. He didn't want her sexually, therefore seeing her half-naked was more of a discomfort than anything else.

And with Logan pacing, it was time for a change of subject, and fast.

"This wasn't a random robbery or spontaneous crime. We were targeted because of the tattoo murder investigation. Someone overheard us, or knows we're on to them, and now we're a liability. Someone called the goons to get rid of us. And that same someone has the entire area locked down. No one is going to talk. That makes this whole operation bigger than we suspected."

Logan did some more pacing. "Murdering a lieutenant and a detective draws an awful lot of notice if their goal was only to protect their enterprise."

"But if they've murdered before…" Rowdy shrugged. "What do they have to lose?"

"Nothing," Reese agreed. "And that's why I want you to skip the meeting with DeeDee."

"Nope." Casual as you please, Rowdy refused him.

Stubborn, careless, macho…Reese worked his jaw. "Then Logan and I will go along to ensure you have some backup."

"They know you," Rowdy said about Reese. "If they're onto us, then we have to assume they also know you're a cop. You're out." He tipped his head toward Logan. "And he's lame."

Logan stiffened. "Lame?"

"You know what I mean." Rowdy indicated his arm. "Still handicapped."

Logan's quiet tone sounded more menacing than a shout. "The hell I am."

Undisturbed by his temper, Rowdy glanced at his watch. "I should be taking off right now. I want to go home and shower first."

Reese blocked his way. "It's too dangerous. You just said it yourself, they're onto you."

"Yeah, but that's the thing, right? I already know it." Rowdy showed little care. "They won't be taking me by surprise, no matter what they pull."

Losing his patience, Reese barked, "You could damn well be shot walking into the bar."

And suddenly, Pepper was there, her face a study in alarm. Alice fretted behind her.

Pepper looked at Logan. "Who's going to shoot at Rowdy?"

CHAPTER TWENTY-SIX

ROWDY GAVE REESE a *thanks a lot* glare. “The boys in blue are just being dramatic.”

“Actually,” Reese said, “Rowdy is being pigheaded.”

Pepper looked ready to assault him for the insult, but Logan saved him by pulling her to his side.

“Reese is right.” He kept her close as he explained the plans for the night, and the risk involved. “DeeDee—if that’s her real name—is just a lure to get Rowdy to the designated spot.”

“He can’t do it,” Pepper agreed, her voice firm. And then, directly to Rowdy, “You can’t do it.”

“You don’t have to worry, kiddo.” Rowdy moved Cash aside and pushed to his feet. “I’ll be fine. You know I can take care of myself.”

Pepper back-stepped away before Rowdy could touch her. “No.”

“And,” Rowdy added with emphasis, “it might be our best bet for finding the bastards who are tattooing girls, and maybe even murdering them.”

“No.”

He frowned. “I’m doing it.” And then to Logan, “Take care of her, will you?”

Logan held up both hands. “If you’re asking me to reassure her that you won’t be hurt, then sorry, no can do.”

Biting her bottom lip, Alice stepped into the fray before brother and sister started in on real bickering. "I'm sorry. This is my fault."

"Not even close," Rowdy said.

But Alice wasn't listening. "If I hadn't gotten involved—"

"Then no one would yet realize that those women need help." Reese held out a hand, and Alice took it. And even that, such a simple connection, meant so much. He pulled her closer and addressed Rowdy. "Logan and I will go with you. No argument. Even if he's not one-hundred percent yet, Logan is one hell of an asset."

"Thanks," Logan said, deadpan.

"And he knows how to blend in."

Pepper scowled. "Yeah, he does."

Reese continued, thinking out loud. "I can probably find a corner of the bar dark enough to hide me."

"Right," Rowdy scoffed. "Paint you green and you could be the freakin' Hulk. Hiding a guy your size isn't possible."

"Okay, fine. So maybe there's a back room, or someplace in the kitchen where I could keep watch."

In tacit agreement, Rowdy mulled over the particulars. "The kitchen is out," he said. "That'd leave you exposed, and the bar is overrun with corruption, so it's anyone's guess who's involved."

"And who might turn you out," Logan added.

"But Avery can stash you in the pantry. Hid there once myself, and it works fine."

Pepper tucked in her chin. "Avery?"

"She's a waitress at a bar I bought." Rowdy shook that off as insignificant—but no one was buying it, least of all his sister.

Jaw now loose, Pepper took a menacing step toward Rowdy. "You bought a bar?"

That soft, accusing voice made his brows come down. "I was going to tell you," Rowdy said defensively. "But today got a little busy, you know."

What an understatement. Reese cleared his throat and tried to get things back on track. "So, you trust this Avery?"

"Yeah, I do."

Logan lifted a brow. "If you just bought the bar, how well do you know her? Is she a woman you're dating?"

Pepper snorted. "Rowdy doesn't *date*. He just has sex." Her narrowed gaze held plenty of accusation for Rowdy. "And he had a really annoying double standard about it, too. It was fine for *him,* but I wasn't even supposed to look."

Tipping his head toward Logan, Rowdy indicated his hold on Pepper. "You did more than look, kiddo, so stop complaining."

"And when it comes to you," Logan said, "I'm glad he was so vigilant."

Rowdy lifted one shoulder. "But when it comes to Avery, I'm not doing either."

Dash grinned. "Is the 'no dating' part hampering the sex part?"

"Maybe. Hard to tell. But she's going to be my bartender, so it's probably best I don't go there with her, anyway."

"Spoken like a rejected man." Dash lifted his Coke in a salute. "If you can't get it, deny wanting it."

Rowdy smirked.

Because their personalities were so dissimilar, it surprised Reese that Dash and Rowdy appeared to get along so well.

"What's wrong with her?" Pepper asked.

And the men all laughed.

"Seriously, kiddo, take me off that pedestal, will you?" Full of fondness, Rowdy smiled at her. "I do get struck down every now and then, you know."

Confused by the denial, Pepper crossed her arms. "No, you don't."

"Yeah…" Rowdy slanted a look around the room, then grinned. "She's right. I usually don't."

"Then that makes Avery either really smart," Dash said, "or really special."

Maybe tonight, Rowdy would figure out which it was. "I'm willing to trust her if you are," Reese said. "I know some other good cops—officers I trust—who can blend in, as well."

"Jesus, Reese, you may as well turn on the red-and-blue lights."

Speaking over Rowdy's protests, Reese added, "Dash, do you think you can stay here with Alice and Pepper?"

"Sure, no problem." He commandeered Rowdy's place next to Cash. "We'll defend the home front, won't we, buddy?" Given how Cash's tail got started, he agreed.

Logan took over, saying to Rowdy, "You're not supposed to meet at the bar until midnight, which means it'll be a late night. I'm going to run home with Pepper so she can get some things together."

"I'm spending the night?" Pepper asked.

"I don't want you home alone." Logan cupped her jaw. "Do you mind?"

"With Alice and Dash as company? Nope, don't mind at all."

"I'll be back for you as soon as I can, but it might be

dawn before we wrap up. You just never know. I want you comfortable while you're here."

"So, I'm grabbing my pj's and a pillow, huh?"

Reese would bet his last dollar that Pepper didn't own pajamas, but he understood that they wanted some time alone. Hell, he'd love a little time alone with Alice, too. Unfortunately, he didn't see that happening, not until tomorrow at the earliest.

"I'm sorry I turned my spare bedroom into an office," Alice said. "They'd probably suggest I stay with you, since your home is so much bigger, but Cash is most comfortable here." To prove that point, she smiled at Cash, stretched out on his back over half of the couch so Dash could rub his chest. He had one soft black ear hanging off the side of the cushion.

Yeah, God knew Alice wouldn't want to inconvenience the dog. She loved him.

And without planning it, without even thinking it through, Reese said, "I'll be looking at my own house soon. Cash needs a yard where he can run around."

Startled, Alice said, "You want to buy a house?"

"The idea appeals to me, yes." Damn it. He shouldn't have just thrown that out there. It was absolutely the wrong time to go into it. "We'll talk about it later."

She held silent, but he saw the questions—and the uncertainty—in her eyes. Did she think he planned to move away from her?

"Time for us to go," Pepper said. But as she passed Reese, she said sotto voce, "I vote for a house near us, just so you know."

Reese smiled at her. "You think you could tolerate my proximity?"

"To be closer to Alice, sure."

So, she assumed Alice would be part of the deal?

What did Alice think? Reese tried to see her face, but she kept her head down.

Logan and Pepper left with the promise that they'd be back before eleven.

Rowdy and Dash hung around.

"So," Alice began. "I have an idea how we could draw out the bastards without putting Rowdy at risk."

"No," Reese and Rowdy both said at the same time.

Dash wisely stayed out of it.

"Instead of DeeDee luring Rowdy, I could lure Hickson."

"No," Reese emphasized more firmly.

"And 'bastards' sounds funny when you say it, Alice. It doesn't suit you."

She glared at Rowdy for that bit of censure. "Cheryl will be calling me. We all know she's been pulled into the scheme, that she's being used. I won't leave her to deal with that alone, and they're probably going to insist on seeing me personally. So why not—"

At her dogged persistence, Reese thought his head might explode off his body. "No, and *no*." Dear God, even hearing her speculate on such a thing made his guts twist in dread. "You're not going anywhere without me."

She folded her arms over her chest. "I need to know that Cheryl is safe!"

Reese leaned into her temper. "Trust *me* to take care of it!"

She jabbed a finger toward Rowdy. "Why doesn't *he* have to trust you to handle things?"

Dash snickered but cut the sound short when the front door opened, and a large man walked in. In a single glance, Reese took his measure, making note of everything.

A black T-shirt, bulky from a Kevlar vest underneath, was tucked into casual tan slacks. He hadn't even tried to conceal the black leather holster that held a Beretta, or the utility belt loaded with extra magazines, a stun gun, a baton and a knife.

From the corner of his eye, Reese saw Rowdy pull Alice behind him. Dash joined him, and together they protected her with a solid wall of male muscle.

Cash, unaccountably, sat up but made no move to attack.

His gun already in hand, Reese stepped in front of them all.

The big man looked from Reese's face to the gun, and back to his face with chilling indifference. "You're protecting her?" And then, looking past Reese: "Alice, he's protecting you?"

Son of a bitch. Reese kept his aim steady. He had a good idea who had just come calling. But he wasn't at all sure how he felt about the impromptu visit.

Oops, Alice thought as she recognized that whiskey-smooth voice.

New levels of testosterone throbbed in the air, along with razor sharp tension.

Rowdy tried to shrug off her hands when she gripped his shoulders and peered between him and Dash. She saw the fair, straight hair, still a little too long, and those incredible golden eyes.

Gratitude welled up anew, and a smile threatened, but Alice didn't dare. Not just yet. Not while Reese stood there, armed and dangerous.

Licking her dry lips, Alice nodded. "I believe he is, yes."

He accepted that without question, saying casually to Reese, “Put the gun away.”

“I don’t think so.” A muscle ticked in Reese’s clenched jaw. “Who the hell are you, and what do you want?”

Alice skirted around Rowdy so she could whisper to Reese, “Put it away before he puts it away for you.”

If anything, Reese became more aggressive in stance and attitude. He stepped in front of Alice again.

“Sorry, Alice, but insulting a man’s ability definitely won’t help.” Unconcerned, as if Reese, Rowdy and Dash were no threat at all, he came farther into the room, walking to the couch to sit down.

Okay, so she could see him discounting Dash. Not that Dash wasn’t big and rock solid, but he didn’t have the same level of…menace, maybe, that Reese and Rowdy exuded.

Still, Dash was an imposing male. Not as imposing as Reese, of course, but—

Cash, who’d watched the proceedings with interest, didn’t appear to mind sharing the couch. Those piercing golden-brown eyes took in the dog, scratched under his chin without a word, made a friend.

Cash thumped his tail in open welcome.

That should have put Reese at ease, but apparently he didn’t trust Cash’s judgment any more than he did Alice’s.

“You’ve got two seconds to explain,” Reese told him.

Those compelling golden eyes came back to Alice’s face.

He smiled.

And she felt more flustered.

“First a cop, and now these two.” He nodded toward Rowdy and Dash. “You’ve been getting around,

Alice." Pleasure took the threat from his compelling stare. "I like it."

A blush crawled up Alice's neck and spread out over her face. "Oh, um…" Again she tried to squeeze out from between the men, but Rowdy held her back. She gave up. "They're just friends."

"But the big one is more?"

Lord, they were *all* big, but she knew who he meant.

"Damn right I am," Reese said.

Feeling very self-conscious, Alice gave a small nod of agreement.

His smile widened into a grin. "You're allowed, you know. And you more than deserve a little fun."

The easy demeanor didn't reassure Reese at all. *"Who the fuck are you?"*

Sitting back, arms stretched out over the back of the sofa, muscled thighs relaxed, he took Reese's measure. "I'm Trace."

Finally, Alice thought, she could rid herself of the last big barrier between herself and Reese. As dangerous as the night would be, as surprised as she was by the unexpected visit, she was thrilled that Trace was here.

Now he could tell Reese anything he needed to know, and there would never again be secrets between them.

ALICE'S SAVIOR. Her knight in shining armor.

No way in hell would Reese relax his stance. "So you're the wraith."

"I've been called that, yes." He looked past Reese and frowned. "I'd appreciate it if they'd stop manhandling her."

Reese narrowed his eyes. "Turn her loose, Rowdy." But he added, "I don't want you near him, Alice."

She made a sound of exasperation. "He's not going to hurt me."

"You'll stay away from him all the same."

"Fine."

"Fine."

Trace grinned. "She was more timid when last I saw her."

Alice took immediate exception to that. "I was never timid." Moving forward a step, her thumb to her chest, she said, "*I'm* the one who—"

Reese said, "Alice, no."

She glanced back at Rowdy and Dash, both brimming with curiosity, and pinched her lips together.

"When was the last time you saw her?"

Trace's brows went up. "She hasn't told you?"

Worried, Alice shook her head. "Only as much as I had to."

Trace took that in, then made a decision. "Let's get through this, and then we can talk. I'll tell you anything you need to know."

"Yeah." Reese nodded. "You will. But for now, tell me why you're here. What do you think we have to get through?"

At the same time, Trace sat forward. "You have a problem."

"Several, in fact." Reese lowered the gun, but even when he reached out to Alice, he didn't take his gaze off the intruder.

Full of trust, maybe even relief, Alice put her hand in his and moved to his side.

"So, seriously," Dash said, without Rowdy's suspicion. "Who are you? Some type of Rambo?"

Scrutinizing first Dash and then, more thoroughly, Rowdy, Trace held silent.

Understanding his dilemma, Reese assured him, "They're trustworthy."

"You sure about that?"

As thorough as Trace appeared to be, he'd surely already done his own background checks. If he was worried about Rowdy, he needn't be. "One thousand percent."

Rowdy couldn't quite hide his discomfort with that much faith.

Mouth tipping in a barely there smile, Trace said, "Your more colorful friend seems to have doubts."

Reese didn't have to look to know who Trace meant. "He's still coming to grips with it himself. But I'd trust him with my life." He pulled Alice closer. "Or hers."

"All right then." He slid his enigmatic gaze to Reese. "Tell him whatever you like."

Alice's hand squeezed his—a silent request that he not expose Trace more than necessary.

Shit. Returning the gun to his holster, Reese flagged Rowdy and Dash forward. "We might as well sit down."

Dash wasted no time in grabbing a seat. "So, what is it? Hired mercenary? Military elite?"

Keeping the explanation short, sweet and to the point, Reese said, "He helped Alice escape after she was taken by a human trafficker."

Dash went still and silent. "No shit?"

Trace smiled. "More like Alice helped me when I made moves to shut down the whole sick enterprise. She's incredibly resilient, and she has more courage than most, along with a phenomenal amount of initiative."

As if the praise flustered her, Alice went bright red. "You know that's not true."

"I don't lie," Trace said. "And I don't exaggerate."

"Oh, well…thank you."

Warm with pride, feeling incredibly possessive, Reese kissed her temple.

"Supposedly, no one ever gets to see you." Rowdy crossed his arms over his chest. "So, what are you doing here now?"

Reese answered before Trace could. "We were followed today."

Lifting a brow, Trace showed his surprise. "You knew?"

"I'm not incompetent."

Brows now furrowed, Trace said, "Obviously not."

"Who followed us?" Rowdy shifted his gaze from Trace to Reese. "From where?"

"A woman. She was at the scene." Reese sat on the arm of the chair and patted his thigh. Cash immediately came to him. Alice stood behind him, her hands on his shoulders, silently supportive. "She followed us to the station, and though I didn't see her after we left, I'm assuming she might've followed us here, too?"

"Who is she?"

"Your date for the night." Trace sat forward, forearms on his thighs, hands loosely laced together. "It's more than probable that someone plans to come in and grab Alice while you're distracted at the bar."

That drew Rowdy back. "So, I'm not the mark?"

"Hard to tell. I wouldn't discount any danger toward you. But I think it's more likely they're after her."

"Because she saw Hickson. She's a witness." Accepting the reach of Trace's influence, Reese went cold inside.

Trace gave an affirmative nod.

Because he hadn't been privy to all the details Alice

had shared, Rowdy grew more suspicious. "You know all this, how?"

Trace looked at Reese, and Reese sighed in annoyance. "I was snooping into Trace's background—something he shut down real quick using impressive contacts—but I assume that made him curious about me."

"Given your connection to Alice, I was already curious. But, yes, I did a little more digging at that point."

"You've kept up with her?" Reese asked.

"She knows I've been watchful." Tipping his head, Trace studied Alice. "She had the means to reach me if it ever became necessary. But I haven't intruded. Alice wanted it that way."

"It wasn't necessary," Alice said, waving off his words. "You'd done enough."

"Enough being…?" All sorts of scenarios went through Reese's head.

"I cleared her of any involvement with the trafficker."

"She *wasn't* involved."

"I'm glad you understand that. But cops do like to dig around and draw their own conclusions."

Reese sawed his teeth together over that—because it was true. Without Trace's help, Alice might have undergone extensive interrogation and endless interviews.

"I got her the weapons of her choice, and the CCPs to go with them."

Dash whispered to Rowdy, and Rowdy replied not quite as softly, "Conceal and carry permits."

"Ahh."

Hands holding tight to his shoulders, Alice said, "He helped me get back to living my life."

"That was all you, Alice. Like I said, you're resilient."

It struck Reese then: he owed Trace, probably more than he could ever repay. The man had kept Alice safe, but at the same time, he'd honored her wishes, giving her the room she needed so she could stay her beautiful, wonderful self. That couldn't have been easy.

All this time, he'd resented him—the secrecy, the amount of power…Alice's gratitude toward him and her loyalty to him.

But it was exactly those things that had enabled Trace to protect her. If it hadn't been for him…

Reese swallowed hard, unable to let his mind go there. He loved her, damn it. More than he'd even known was possible.

Hell of a time for epiphanies.

He met Trace's gaze. "It's inadequate, but thank you."

Trace nodded. "My pleasure."

"I'm on it now." Reese was here, in Alice's life, and he'd never let anything happen to her. "Just so you know."

"That's how I figured it."

Astute, as well as badass. That didn't surprise Reese.

"What are you talking about?" Confused, uncertain, Alice chewed her bottom lip, looking from one man to the other. "I don't understand. You're on what?"

"You." Rowdy smiled at her. "They're talking about you."

She shook her head, still not getting it.

Reese didn't want anyone to make a declaration for him, so he said, "We're figuring out how to keep you out of this mess."

Skeptical, Alice toyed with the ends of her hair, twisting and curling it around her fingers. "The thing is, you can't keep me out of it. Cheryl called *me*. She'll want to meet with *me*."

"That's not going to happen," Reese said.

Showing a hint of her courage, Alice cut him off. "You know Cheryl is in trouble, that Hickson or some other cretin is forcing her to contact me. Why would they go to all that trouble if they know where I live?"

Trace indicated the apartment. "It's not as easy as you might think to break into an occupied building and drag out a screaming woman. And, Alice, you would scream. Right?"

She nodded. "I wouldn't go without a fight."

Oh, God. Reese wanted to rebel against that idea. A fight meant she could die in the process of being taken. But knowing Alice as he did now, she'd likely prefer that to being held captive again.

"Once I was gone," Reese said, "you'd get a desperate call from Cheryl." His muscles clenched, his heart punched hard. "If you'd taken one step out of the apartment—"

"I wouldn't let her do that," Dash said.

And Alice swatted at him. "I'm not stupid!"

Dash barely managed to dodge her.

Settling back against Reese, she muttered, "You wouldn't need to stop me, because I wouldn't do anything foolish."

Reese gave her the full force of his attention. "Define foolish." He felt irate all over again at how she'd followed Cheryl in the first place.

As if she knew his every thought, Alice said softly, "That was before I promised you that I wouldn't keep any more secrets."

Okay, so maybe that had changed things between

them. But could she really resist running to the aid of a woman she thought was being threatened?

Giving up his relaxed posture, Trace leveled a look at Reese. “You can be ruthless.”

A statement, not a question. Reese said only, “Yes.”

Alice started. “You can?”

“Hell, yeah.” Dash laughed. “Logan hasn’t told you?”

“Told me what?”

Not in the mood for nonsense, Reese shook his head. “Knock it off, Dash.”

Alice said, “No, I want to hear this.”

“Reese is a regular champion of the underdog.” Dash did little to hide his smile. “According to Logan, if Reese thinks someone’s being treated unfairly, he jumps in with both feet and to hell with the consequences. Not saying he does stuff illegally, just that he doesn’t slow down to weigh the danger.”

“Jesus,” Reese growled. “I’m a cop, it’s what we do.”

“You saved Cash.” Alice leaned against him. “That had nothing to do with being a cop.”

“That had to do with being a human being.” And not once had Reese regretted that decision, not even when Cash had eaten a shoe or marked the entire apartment as his territory.

In fact, given how Alice had bonded with the dog, he was more grateful than ever that he’d been the one to find Cash that day.

Unable to keep his hands off her, and feeling more possessive than any contemporary man should, Reese brought Alice around to his lap.

Wearing a comical look of surprise, stiff instead of relaxed, she perched on his thigh.

Trace took in the two of them with understanding. “Unfortunately, the situation is that the station still has a few bad cops running loose. Your lieutenant is doing a great job, but she's one person, and she can't do it alone."

"Meaning what?" Reese asked.

"I'm going to lend her a hand with that. I have better resources for exposing the frauds. Soon, I'll present her with a file of names and evidence." Trace didn't wait for any objections. "In the meantime, I'd like to help out with Alice, too."

Well, Reese thought, he had wanted the National Guard. But maybe one ultra-elite, super secretive wraith would do. "What do you suggest?"

As soon as he gave the implied agreement, Alice turned to him with joy. She smiled as if they weren't in the middle of a complete and total cluster fuck. "You trust him?" she asked.

Reese cupped her cheek, and gave her a solid truth. "I trust you."

"And *you,*" Trace said to Alice, "trust me." He nodded at Rowdy and Dash. "Apparently them, as well."

"Oh, and Logan," she said quickly, while still gifting Reese with that pretty smile. "They're all wonderful."

Trace did his own smiling. "I'm glad."

And damn it, now Reese even felt like smiling.

"It's more complicated than just dealing drugs, and, like it or not, Alice is in it up to her neck." All business now, Trace pushed to his feet. "Protest it all you want, but facts are facts. I can handle it—"

His arms going tight around Alice, Reese stood, too. "Hell, no."

Without missing a beat, Trace said, "Or you can handle it." His gaze never wavered. "That is, if you think you're up to it."

"I'm up."

Amused by that, Trace glanced at Alice before fixing his golden gaze back on Reese. "Of course, you did get yourself handcuffed to a bed."

Grinding his molars together, Reese eased Alice to the side and took a more aggressive stance. Trace would not push him aside, not in this.

Not with Alice.

Then Trace added, "Something similar once happened to me. Except my pants were down and a depraved bitch planned to molest me."

Dash whispered, "No shit?"

Rowdy sat forward. "So, what did you do?"

Lifting a brow in question, Trace said, "Do?"

"About having your pants around your ankles."

As if that were a fond memory, he smiled. "A woman saved me. Thanks to her, I was able to regain the upper hand." He looked at Reese. "She's now my wife."

Reese had a disturbing idea of where this little dance down memory lane might be going. "Is there a point to this story?"

"You need to let Alice help."

Doing his best to hide all emotion, Reese said simply but unequivocally, "No."

Trace ignored the denial. "This needs to be wrapped up. All of it."

"You think I needed you to tell me that?"

"No, but apparently you need me to tell you that Alice has to be there."

"Not happening."

"I can ensure her safety."

"No."

Undaunted, Trace said more firmly, "Alice has to be

available to meet Cheryl. That's the only way you'll get everyone." His voice gentled. "And you already know it."

Alice cupped Reese's face, her smile reassuring, her gaze imploring. "I can do this, Reese. I promise."

Reese knew he had little choice, but that didn't mean he liked it. He pulled her into his chest, crushed her close and muttered, "Fuck."

"Believe me," Trace said, "I understand and I sympathize. If there was any other way…"

"I know." Reese slowly blew out a breath and reached for distant control. "Okay."

They were still finalizing plans when Cheryl called and requested to meet Alice…at the same time that Rowdy would be meeting DeeDee.

Distract, divide and overwhelm. But Reese knew how he felt, and he knew Alice's determination. He saw the resolve on Rowdy's face, and the confidence in Trace's stance.

They would do this, but they'd do it Reese's way. And once it was over, he'd bind Alice to him for good.

CHAPTER TWENTY-SEVEN

ROWDY SHOWED UP an hour early in an old Falcon he'd bought for less than two hundred dollars. The car looked and sounded like a junker—that's how Rowdy liked it. Overall, it was reliable transportation and got him where he wanted to go. No one would trace it back to him.

Best of all, the truck was sturdy and locked securely.

He parked toward the back of the bar, out of the reach of a weak security light.

Something else he'd fix once he ran the place.

Cautious, he sat for a minute to make sure no one approached.

All remained quiet.

Pocketing his keys so they wouldn't make a sound, he slid over the bench seat to the passenger door and quietly opened it. He'd already disabled the lights, and the moon wasn't bright enough to give him away.

Sticking to the backs of the buildings, he went down a block, then came out to the sidewalk in front. Moving with the shadows of the night, he crossed the street and found concealing darkness under the overhang of a mom-and-pop grocer across the street from the bar. He'd barely gotten settled into the recessed doorway when he saw one of the thugs from the tattoo parlor coming down the street. Despite the heat of the muggy night, he wore a light jacket.

No doubt to hide his gun.

Rowdy saw that he sported some new bruises on his face and had his arm in a sling. Courtesy of Reese? Damn, but Rowdy hoped so.

Tracking the man with his gaze, Rowdy saw him go down the outside alley of the bar—back to the area Rowdy had just vacated.

From the other side of the building, across the open lot that Rowdy would soon lease for parking, another goon strode up. This one spoke quietly into a cell phone, and his skittish gaze continually scanned the area.

Yeah, killing us wasn't as easy as you'd hoped, was it, you bastard?

So, the men were meeting in the back. Did they plan to jump Rowdy as soon as he showed up? Had they hoped to finish what they'd started earlier?

For only a moment, Rowdy worked his jaw, then decided, *fuck it.* It wasn't in his nature to skulk around like a coward. All he'd needed to know was that Alice would be safe.

And between Reese and Trace, he trusted in that. Trace. Man, there was a mystery for the imagination. Pair him with by-the-book Reese, and Alice couldn't be more protected.

Rowdy didn't mind the adrenaline rush of danger, but he didn't want to seek it out. In fact, he looked forward to the routine, calmer life as a bar owner.

But first he needed to take out the trash.

Circling around the buildings via a different route, down an adjacent alley a block away, Rowdy returned to the back entrance of the bar. Right there, in plain sight, the two idiots stood plotting. One lit a cigarette, the red glow sending eerie shadows over his face before fading beneath a curl of smoke.

The jumpy one continued to glance around to the point that his buddy cursed him. "Damn, Phelps, relax, will you?"

"I'll relax when this is over."

"Soon." Inhaling on the cigarette again, he lounged back against the brick wall. "They got away this morning, but they won't this time."

"Shit, Lowry, you don't know that. They were fast and they knew how to fight." He rubbed the back of his neck. "I'm still in pain."

"A pain in my ass." Lowry shifted his injured arm. "They took me by surprise, that's all. This time, I'll be ready."

"You can't even know that the others will be here."

"They will. But even if they aren't, Woody will handle it."

Interesting. It never failed; the hired muscle was almost always one dimensional, meaning strong and ruthless, but too dumb to stand on their own feet. Like sheep, Lowry and Phelps needed to follow.

Apparently, Woody was the one who led.

Rowdy hunkered down, willing to wait, ready to be enlightened by anything else they might say.

"I don't trust Dee to do her part."

So that was a real name? Go figure.

Lowry laughed. "She told me she wants to fuck the guy before we kill him." Shaking his head, he muttered, "Conniving, coldhearted bitch."

Phelps didn't bother to hide his disgust. "How the hell does she think she's going to handle that in a bar?"

"Says she'll lead him out to her car and do him in her backseat." Another deep drag on the cigarette. "Ought to be easy enough to shoot him in the head soon as she finishes with him."

"To hell with that. I'm not waiting." Phelps grabbed his crotch. "If Dee wants some, I'll give it to her."

"Woody says she's off-limits to us." Finishing his cigarette, Lowry flicked away the butt. "For now."

"We should have been sent after the woman. Hickson's the one who fucked up. He should be here with the hulks, and we could just snuff that little lady who's causing all the trouble."

Rowdy thought about pulling his knife. Thought about killing them both, right here, right now.

But more info wouldn't hurt anything, so he tamped down the burning urge.

"We can't snuff her," Lowry said, "because Woody wants her. And what Woody Simpson wants, Woody Simpson gets."

"Yeah, I know." Phelps rubbed at his neck again.

Given how Rowdy had cranked on it, choking him until he'd passed out, Phelps's neck would be sore for a while. Rowdy narrowed his eyes, remembering. Satisfied.

"Woody just wants to play with her for a while, to teach her a lesson." Lowry stepped away from the wall. "I bet he'll give you a go at her afterward, as long as we don't mess this up tonight."

A fresh surge of fury curled through Rowdy, but he held it at bay with rigid willpower. Going into a rage wouldn't net him the results he wanted. For that he had to be calculating.

And as the bozos had said, fast and capable.

Dirty fighting was maybe the most valuable thing he'd learned as a street rat. He could take on two men, maybe even three, no problem.

Keeping his gaze on the men, gauging the amount of time it'd take for him to reach them, Rowdy felt around on the ground until his fingers located a jagged rock. Focused, ready to move, he threw it past the men toward a trash can. It made a clatter, and both men jerked around, searching the area, their weapons drawn.

"What the fuck?"

"What was that? Who's there?"

On the balls of his feet, Rowdy charged, plowing into both of them, taking advantage of their distraction. They all three went down, but he had the benefit of rage and momentum, while they were taken by surprise, floundering both physically and mentally.

Lowry's head hit the brick wall of the bar, and, dazed, he loosened enough to drop the gun. It skittered across the ground.

Caught under them, Phelps's face connected with the rough pavement. Cursing, he spit blood—and a tooth. He tried to haul himself free, but the combined weight of Rowdy and Lowry held him down.

Wanting this wrapped before anyone else showed up or people inside the bar were alerted to their scuffle, Rowdy hit Lowry with three rapid punches. He smashed his nose, broke his jaw, and as he cocked his meaty fist for another shot, Lowry slumped, more unconscious than not.

Rowdy shoved him to the side just as Phelps managed to crawl out from under them. The idiot turned, blood all over his face, his neck and the front of his shirt. With a guttural curse and wild eyes, Phelps took aim.

Kicking out against his legs, Rowdy tripped him, and down he went. One near-silent shot exploded, hitting the brick of the bar and ricocheting. Crying out like a girl, Phelps grabbed a mangled knee—from Rowdy's kick, not from the stray bullet—but Rowdy was quick to silence him with a boot to the face.

Phelps dropped like a stone.

Flipping him over, Rowdy put a knee in his back and bound his hands with double cuff disposable restraints that Trace had given him. Five pairs of them, Rowdy remembered, wondering if Trace expected him to take on an entire goon squad.

Phelps groaned at the uncomfortable clench of his arms behind his back.

"Make a sound," Rowdy told him, "and I'll shut you up for good. Do you understand me?"

Incoherent, Phelps babbled an affirmative.

Quickly, Rowdy checked him for other weapons and found a knife. He tossed it toward the gun Lowry had dropped, then bound Phelps's ankles, as well.

At any moment, someone could step out the back door of the bar. He had to hurry. Grabbing Lowry, he jerked a strip of material off his shirt and used it to gag Phelps. Grabbing him under his arms, he dragged Phelps over to the side of the Falcon, hidden from view.

Rushing back to Lowry, who had just started to revive, Rowdy slugged him again. He groaned. Rowdy dragged him over by Phelps and bound him the same, wrists tight behind his back, ankles squeezed together. The added pressure on his injured arm had Lowry gritting his teeth with pain.

But this man had planned to murder him. He'd laughed about the idea of using Alice. Rowdy didn't give a damn if his arm fell off.

He searched Lowry and found another, smaller pistol, along with a stun gun. With one knee in Lowry's chest, the other on his damaged shoulder, Rowdy said, "Want me to use the stun gun on you?"

Lowry stared at him with a steely-eyed gaze. But Phelps protested, gurgling behind his gag, struggling.

Without looking at him, Rowdy said, "Shut up before I shut you up."

Phelps went silent.

"Well, Lowry? How do you feel about a little jolt?" He placed the barbs of the stun gun under Lowry's chin. "Think that'll get you talking?"

A muscle ticked in his jaw. "You're a dead man. Doesn't matter what you do to us—"

"No?" Rowdy jammed the stun gun into Phelps's gut and squeezed the trigger. Phelps went rigid, his eyes bulging and a guttural growl squeezed from his throat. His body jerked, flinched…until Rowdy let up.

With Phelps now whimpering, Rowdy smiled. "He's gagged, so I knew he wouldn't yell. Guess I should really gag you, too, right?" He pressed the stun gun to Lowry's chest. "Though it might not be necessary. I hear a jolt to the heart can bring everything to a standstill."

A bead of nervous sweat trickled down Lowry's temple. *"What the fuck do you want?"*

"Answers. First of all, who's Woody Simpson?"

When Lowry hesitated, Rowdy tapped his finger to the trigger, letting the stun gun snap and sizzle.

Lowry pressed back, trying to scamper away from that threatening jolt. "Okay, okay! Jesus."

"Talk."

"He's the boss."

"Who does he answer to?"

"No one. That's what I'm telling you. Woody is it. Top of the line."

Perfect. "Where I can find him?" As encouragement, Rowdy gave another quick tap to the gun. "*Now,* Lowry."

And just like that, Lowry spilled his guts. "He's in his offices on South Street." He gave over the exact address.

"It's damn near midnight. What's he doing there now?"

"Waiting to hear how shit went."

"You mean with the ladies, right?" That was too easy for Rowdy to believe, but he played along, anyway. "Cheryl and Alice?"

Probably hoping to find common ground, Lowry nodded. "Yeah. Woody wants the bitch, that's all. You're just collateral. You can leave now, and I'll tell him we killed you. He doesn't have to know."

"He wants to kill a few cops, too."

"Because they're getting in the way! But you don't have to worry about that. You're not a cop, right?"

"It's that obvious, huh?"

"Yeah, man, it is. I mean, you don't act like any pig I know. So what do you say?"

"'Fraid not." It felt weird to say it, but Rowdy knew it was true. "They're my friends."

"Oh…shit. *Cops?* Seriously?"

Because that had once, not that long ago, been Rowdy's reaction, as well, he only shrugged.

"Well, I didn't know that, now, did I?"

He ignored the dramatic reasoning. "Anyone else planning to show up here tonight?"

When Lowry hesitated, Rowdy let out a sigh. "Do I need to kill Phelps here to let you know how serious I am?"

While Phelps gave panicked, muffled pleas, Lowry's chin went up. "How do I know you won't kill us, anyway?"

That was funny enough to make Rowdy grin. "You know, I'd like to, I really would. But those cops I mentioned? They wouldn't like it. So you can thank them for living another day. Once I get all the info I want, I'll stuff you both into the trunk and call the boys in blue to come collect you."

"You're going to have us *arrested?*"

Smirking, Rowdy said, "Yeah, I know. Unheard of, huh? But there you go. For today, that's how we're gonna roll." He nudged Lowry's chest. "Who else should I expect tonight?"

Lowry must've believed him. He didn't look thrilled over the idea, but cops were surely preferable to death in a dark alley. "Hickson will be here with Cheryl."

"Bullshit," Rowdy said. "I know that's what we were told, but no way does your boss expect Alice to make it here without getting nabbed along the way."

"True. But on the off chance she manages to pull it off, then Hickson will be here to…greet her."

"And if she doesn't show up?"

Uncaring, Lowry said, "Then Hickson will kill Cheryl, dump her body and join Woody for some…interrogation of your girlfriend."

Rowdy hit him; he couldn't help himself. It was like a reflex. Then he hit him again just for the hell of it. Swaying drunkenly, Lowry slouched to the side, his chin on his chest, his eyes dazed. "Fucking ham-fisted bastard," he muttered in a slur.

Standing, Rowdy opened the trunk and hauled Phelps to his feet. "Get in." But even as he said it, he stuffed Phelps in himself, shoving him as far back in the trunk as he could.

"Now you."

Shaking his head to clear it, Lowry used the side of the car at his back and tried to struggle up. It wasn't easy, especially considering how hard Rowdy had slugged him. "You have me tied so fucking tight—"

Rowdy grabbed the elbow of his injured arm and hauled him to his feet, shoving him near the tailgate. "Figure it out or I'll stun you and then dump you in."

Lowry more or less fell into the trunk. It was a tight fit, but Rowdy got them both in there.

He ripped away another section of Lowry's shirt to gag him. Leaning on the trunk, he asked, "How many men will be after Alice?"

"Enough." At Rowdy's narrow-eyed look, he corrected, "How the hell should I know? I'm here with you."

Again, Rowdy could tell he lied. He saw it in the shifty eyes, in the tripping pulse, the faster breathing. "Know what, Lowry? I started this without patience. Push me anymore and you're going to regret it."

"Meaning what?"

Rowdy pressed the stun gun to his crotch. "Meaning I'll make sure you never hassle another woman for the rest of your blighted life."

Lowry breathed harder...and broke. "There'll be four men. Three hired on, and..." He closed his eyes, swallowed hard.

"And?" Rowdy pressed.

"Woody's going along."

"The hell you say." Why would the boss do that? Why risk getting caught? "You're full of shit, Lowry, you know that?" Rowdy jammed the stun gun in tighter.

Lowry tried to buck away. "It's true! He likes staying in the front lines, says it keeps him sharp. He still picks out the women himself. He gets a kick out of it."

"That doesn't make any damn sense." Unless Woody Simpson was a lunatic, which...*would* make sense.

Feeling the weapon snug against his jewels, Lowry panted with fear. "Woody said he wants to see if he can get your lady friend to come along willingly."

For a second there, Rowdy thought he was joking. When he realized Lowry was serious, he barked a surprised laugh. "Old Woody must be even dumber than you."

"He's not dumb. But he does like the game."

The game of tattooing women and forcing them to be drug mules. Rowdy fought to hide his rage. "When are they supposed to grab her?"

"About five minutes ago." Around his swollen mouth and split lip, Lowry managed a smug smile. "Don't be looking for your cop buddies to back you up. Woody gave orders to kill everyone except the girl. And once they have her, they'll be coming after you. There's still time for you to make a deal with—"

Rowdy zapped him. As he watched Lowry flop and heard Phelps's freaked objections, he reassured himself that Lowry was wrong. Reese was prepared. He wouldn't be taken unawares.

They would all be okay. Damn it, they had to be.

Now that they'd gotten him to care, he didn't want to lose them. Fate couldn't be that cruel. Not even to him.

But to be on the safe side, he gagged the unconscious Lowry and slammed the trunk shut. Stalking into the bar through the back door, Rowdy decided that he'd find Reese's men and send them to help with Alice. He didn't need them now.

Handling DeeDee would be a piece of cake, and if Hickson showed up, he'd grab that bastard, too.

Unfortunately, as he stepped into the crowded barroom, he realized that Reese's men must be good, because he didn't see a single person who looked like a cop.

But he did see Hickson and Cheryl.

Damn it. For now he had to follow the plan or it just might cost that poor girl her life.

And then, just to complicate the night more, Avery came into view—and she was heading for Hickson's table.

ANXIETY KEPT ALICE'S heart beating so rapidly she felt it everywhere. Palms clammy, she popped another jelly bean into her mouth. A surreptitious glance assured her that Reese was still busy talking to Logan, bringing him up to speed.

Two more jelly beans—red, her favorite—gave her the backbone she needed to approach Trace. He was on a phone, talking low, and she hated to interrupt him, but if she waited, she might lose her opportunity.

Given the few words she overheard, Alice thought it might be his wife.

She touched his arm.

As if it surprised him, Trace looked at her hand first, then up to her face. He wrapped up the call and put the phone back in his pocket. "Everything okay?"

Stupidly, Alice offered him a jelly bean.

Brows angled, Trace said, "Thanks, no."

Regardless of what Reese thought, she didn't know Trace that well. She knew he had incomparable skill and wasn't afraid to do what needed to be done. He was smart, cunning and, luckily for her, very caring.

He had saved her life, so hopefully he wouldn't mind one more imposition. "I need you to promise me something." So that Reese wouldn't overhear, Alice kept her voice low. "Please."

Golden gaze probing, Trace looked beyond her, then leaned closer. "What's on your mind?"

"I know you have your own way of doing things, but this time, you have to do everything by the letter of the law." Wanting to make sure he understood how serious this could be, she again touched his arm. "Reese is a police detective."

His mouth quirked. "No kidding?"

Of course Trace knew that. He probably knew everything there was to know about Reese. Without thinking about it, she grabbed more jelly beans, then had to chew fast and gulp them down so she could continue.

Trace waited with nerve-racking patience.

"What I mean is..." She licked her lips. "He's an honorable man."

Those angled brows lifted.

This expression was almost more intimidating than the other. The last thing she wanted to do was insult him. "That is...you're honorable, too, of course."

"I have my moments."

He absolutely could *not* be joking with her right now. "But Reese has a code of conduct that he believes in. He lives by that code. It's important to him, so it's also important to *me*."

Folding his arms over his chest, Trace studied her. "You know I'm not going out there to slaughter people, right?"

She damn near dropped the bag of candy. "Yes, of course. You would never do that. You're...well, scary-adept with lethal skill, but you're not exactly bloodthirsty."

His mouth twisted. "Not exactly."

"You don't commit random murder." No, he only went to extremes when absolutely necessary. Alice winced, because, really, she'd done the same.

He made a small sound of exasperation—and took the bag of jelly beans away from her. "Why don't you tell me exactly what you're worried about?"

"It's just..." She needed to get it said, and fast. "You can't use deadly force—even if you really want to." Even if maybe *she* really wanted him to. "It would crush me if I was the cause of Reese being drawn into...*things* that go against his morals. As an officer of the law, he has to answer to others. He can't be put in the position of having to lie, not for me. Not ever."

"I understand."

Relief turned Alice's knees into noodles. "You do?"

He gave her a sage nod. "I'm pretty sure Reese does, too."

From behind her, Reese said, "I do."

Eyes flaring, Alice spun around. "Reese." How did a man his size go sneaking around without her noticing? "I thought you were talking to Logan."

Vaguely, Alice was aware of Trace handing her jelly beans to Reese before walking away to give them some privacy.

"I was." Reese smoothed back her hair. "But, Alice, always, at any given moment, I'm aware of you and what you're doing. You might as well understand that right now."

"Oh." She was usually aware of him, too, but she'd been so intent on having her say with Trace. "I... Good."

For her, the awareness covered more than sexual attraction, more than mere caring.

Did Reese feel the same?

He pressed his mouth to hers in a brief but firm kiss, ending it by saying, “Trace isn’t going to kill anyone that doesn’t need killing.” His gaze stayed caught in hers. “Isn’t that so, Trace?”

From the other side of the room, Trace said, “Works for me.”

Alice’s eyes widened. They were like ninjas, skulking around so silently, hearing every whispered word.

Reese brushed his thumb over her jaw. “He understands that I do things by the law, and that I’ll be held accountable for everything that goes down today.”

“I do,” Trace confirmed.

Cupping her face in both hands, Reese nodded. “Okay?”

Alice let out the breath she hadn’t even realized she was holding. “Okay.” But that wasn’t quite enough, so she threw herself against him and squeezed tight.

It felt very protective, *safe,* the way that Reese folded his strong arms around her. Laying her cheek against his chest, hooking her hands over the unyielding steel of his biceps, Alice told herself not to worry. She would play her part to a T, and Reese would see that nothing bad happened.

Trace said, “Everyone is in place. Time to move.”

After a brief, tight hug and a kiss to the top of her head, Reese handed her back the bag of candy and went to talk quietly with Trace.

And, of course, *she* couldn’t hear a single thing they said.

She knew that Reese had arranged for specific officers to be with Rowdy at the bar, with others on notice nearby for backup as needed. Lieutenant Peterson remained at the station, a central contact for everyone involved. She knew that Reese had covered every possibility, so that her safety was assured.

All other particulars were kept from her.

She watched in awe as Trace slipped silently out the sliding doors, dropped over the balcony and disappeared from sight.

In the kitchen, Logan kissed Pepper so passionately that Alice felt like a voyeur. She was about to avert her gaze when Logan ended the embrace. Abruptly, he turned and strode out of the kitchen, across to the front door and straight out of the apartment. Alice was pretty sure he hadn't even seen her as he passed.

She knew he would go to the laundry room on the ground floor and climb out through a window there. Reese would be leaving through the front door. He'd head to his car and drive out of the lot, giving the illusion that he was leaving Alice alone. And then he'd circle around and return from a different angle.

At that point, Alice would leave the dubious security of the apartment building, straight out the front doors, down the walkway and out to the parking lot.

Where men undoubtedly waited for an opportunity to grab her.

Reese would tail her, never far behind, as would Trace and Logan. They knew what they were doing. She wouldn't be out of their sight.

Eating more jelly beans, she turned her attention to Pepper, watching as she joined Dash on the couch. Dash was so sweet, teasing Pepper, trying to reassure her so she wouldn't worry.

Pepper was such a strong woman—the perfect woman for Logan. Their happiness glowed like an afternoon sun. Alice was glad for them, and she envied them what they'd found together.

God, how she wanted that with Reese.

Sitting near Alice's feet, Cash whined. She wanted to reassure him but didn't want to distract Reese, so she only stroked his head until he quieted.

Reese was in serious cop mode, focused on the task at hand.

Trace, Logan and Reese had all dressed in black. In contrast, her Capri jeans, flat-heeled sandals and rose-colored cowl-neck top looked…frivolous. Far too bright for what would happen tonight.

But she was supposed to be heading out to see Cheryl, a newfound friend now in desperate need. *Please, God, let her be okay.*

Pausing before her, Reese asked, "Ready?"

"Yes."

He searched her face, then gently took in the half-empty bag of candy. "You can still change your mind—"

"No." They needed to gather up all the players, and this was the best way. With the help of Reese's officer friends, Rowdy had things covered at the bar. She had Trace, Logan and Reese watching out for her. She would be fine. She would be fine. She would be fine.

"Alice?"

She forced her stiff lips into a smile. "I'm ready."

He didn't touch her, didn't soften or relax one iota. Confident, comforting, he said, "I'm not about to let anything happen to you."

Her heart expanded so much it hurt her chest. She swallowed back the emotion and nodded. "I know." Reese was that type of man; he'd protect with the best of his ability and, if necessary, trade his own life in the bargain. “Will you promise me that nothing will happen to you either?”

“You have my word.” He dragged the back of his fingers over her throat—and then he was gone, striding away, out the door and out of her reach.

CHAPTER TWENTY-EIGHT

DASH SAID, "THREE minutes, Alice," cuing her on the time she needed to wait before heading out.

She didn't look at Pepper or Dash, not wanting them to see her nervousness. Around men so brave, so sure of their own ability, her cowardice seemed horribly amplified.

Abruptly, she went to the kitchen to put away the candy.

"Two minutes," Dash told her.

Oh, God. Hands shaking, she opened the treat jar and got out two chews for Cash. "Come here, boy."

Dragging, his head down and his tail tucked, Cash came to her.

"Oh, now, none of that." She held his furry face and nuzzled against him. "Everything will be fine."

But Cash didn't look convinced, and even after she offered him the chews, he wanted only to lean on her.

That broke her heart. The dog was picking up on her mood, and that was so grossly unfair of her. He needed her to be strong.

He needed her to show Reese's confidence—and, by God, she would.

She straightened and said to Pepper and Dash, her voice no longer uncertain, "One more minute, right?"

Dash gave her a grave nod.

"Great. Then I have time to dig out Cash's toys." She

smiled at the dog. "What do you say, buddy? Wanna play?"

He tipped his head, studying her with his big brown eyes, his tail giving a tentative thump.

"You do!" she said with enthusiasm. "Well, come on. Let's find the toys."

Cash hunkered back on his haunches, his tongue out, his expression excited. When Alice headed into the small living area, Cash beat her to it, sticking his head under the couch and coming out with a squeak toy.

Laughing, Alice took it from him and tossed it down the hall. While Cash raced after it, she found two more toys under the couch, then another under the chair.

Pepper caught on, and, on hands and knees, she helped Alice locate the dog's many toys.

Dash tossed the squeak toy again and said, "Thirty seconds."

Her heart squeezed into her throat, but Alice hid it, piling up the toys and calling Cash over. He dove into it, scattering things everywhere.

Laughing, Pepper grabbed up a stuffed cat and played tug of war with the dog.

Dash took Alice's elbow and helped her to her feet. "Time to go, sweetheart."

"Okay." A deep breath helped only marginally. "Please keep him occupied and…and happy."

Pepper's eyes were serious, but her tone lighthearted. "Will do. Don't worry, Alice." She let Cash have the cat and reached for a knotted rope. Cash immediately lunged to get it, growling playfully.

"Thank you," Alice whispered. As quietly and unobtrusively as possible, she snatched up her purse and keys and walked out, easing the door shut so that Cash wouldn't hear.

Unwilling to risk throwing off the plans, she went down the steps and out the front door without hesitation.

As her feet hit the pavement of the parking lot, it occurred to her: If her mood had upset Cash, what had it done to Reese? Never did she want to be a distraction for him.

She put up her chin and headed for her car. With every step her pulse rushed until she almost felt lightheaded. When would they try to grab her? Would they run her car off the road? Wait until she parked near the bar? Try to grab her on the way in, or after she was already in the bar?

Imagining any of those scenarios scared her half to death. But she didn't falter, she didn't slow down or—

"Hey, Alice. How've you been?"

She froze. Oh, no. No, no, no. Slowly, feeling like the victim of a bad joke, Alice turned, and found Nikki and Pam bearing down on her.

REESE GAVE A soft curse. Even from his position at the other side of the lot, hidden inside a nondescript van, he could see Alice striving for a way out. She looked a little shell-shocked, though she quickly tried to recover. From the looks of it, Nikki and Pam were just returning from a night on the town. Decked out in tight, short dresses and high-heeled sandals, their voices too loud and their strides a little wobbly, they caged her in.

His phone gave a low buzz, and he lifted it to read a message from Rowdy. *Boss himself will grab Alice.*

Unwilling to question Rowdy's resourcefulness or let his attention waver from Alice, he sent Rowdy an acknowledgement and then forwarded the message on to Trace.

With that done, Reese scoped the area around the parking lot, but he saw no one other than Nikki, Pam and Alice.

Attempting to rush past the neighbors, Alice tried to dismiss them with a fast wave. It didn't work.

Nikki said, "Hey, hold up."

Stay cool, Alice, Reese silently encouraged her. But he could hear the voices carrying on the otherwise quiet night. Nikki was worked up, even pushier and more brazen than usual.

Blocking Alice's path, Nikki said, "So. You and Reese still doing the nasty?"

Alice opened her mouth, but Pam beat her to it, saying, "Course she is. You don't think a girl'd give that up, do you?" Pam tried to high-five Alice, but lost her balance and Alice had to practically support her.

"Tell him I'm still willing," Nikki insisted. "Anytime, anywhere. And I guarantee I can do things for him that *you've* never even heard of."

"Oh, um..." Alice struggled to right Pam, but she seemed content to lean on Alice. To get rid of her, Alice said, "Okay, sure, I'll tell him." Not.

"To hell with that," Pam insisted. "You need it more than Nik does. I swear, honey, you were about the most stuck-up, prudish woman I'd ever met. Now, since Reese has been givin' it to you regular, you're much nicer."

With a solid shove, Alice managed to peel Pam off her side. "I was never stuck up."

"Ha!" Nikki leaned into her face and almost fell off her high heels. "You were a bitch."

"Not true, Nik," Pam insisted. "She was just miserable, being so alone and all." And then in a loud aside to Alice, "We shoulda taken you out and gotten you laid sooner. But, you, clever girl, you held out and got the real prize."

"Reese?" Alice guessed.

"God, *yes.*" This time Pam fell against Nikki and they both stumbled. "He is so *hawt.*"

"Yeah," Nikki said. "So, c'mon, dish. How is he in the sack? A stud, I bet. Right?"

"None of your business," Alice admonished them both. "You should go in, maybe get some sleep."

Eyes widening, Nikki asked, "Is he in there?" She bent to take off first one sandal, then the other. "It's awful late for you to be going out. Did you two fight?"

Pam looked toward the apartment building. "If you two are fighting, maybe we should console him."

"Stay away from him."

Reese lifted his brows.

Nikki and Pam both went still.

Into the ensuing silence, Alice said, "Well." She lifted her chin, hitched her purse strap up her shoulder, and aimed a dead stare at each of the ladies. "Reese is working, and I'm on my way out to see a friend. So please, just call it a night." As she started away, she said over her shoulder, her voice still firm, "And leave. Reese. *Alone.*"

Each lady nodded.

Alice turned to continue on her way—and two shadows emerged from the darkness.

Shit. So close to home. They were counting on Reese being well and truly gone. That, or they didn't consider him a viable threat to their plans.

His phone vibrated softly again. Glancing at it, Reese saw Trace's message: *Be patient.*

Already sliding out of the van, his bare feet making

not a single sound as he crossed the parking lot, Reese dodged from car to car until he had Alice within reach.

Now, knowing he was close enough to protect her, *now* he would wait.

ALICE WAS STILL muttering about Nikki's and Pam's audacity when the men came out of nowhere—just as she'd known they would. But knowing it and experiencing it were two very different things. The shadows took shape, became ominous, and then they were right there, leering at her, intimidating with their intent.

From behind her, she heard a third man say, "Ladies," and the next thing she knew, Nikki and Pam were corralled up by her.

Alcohol dulling her discretion, Pam flirted with the stocky fellow gripping her arm. "My, aren't you a big one? Not quite as big as Reese, but—"

Alice snapped, "Shut up, Pam!" She would not have Reese's name bandied about.

The man looked Pam over. "You like them big, honey?"

"Doesn't every girl?"

Nikki pointed at Alice with impressed glee. "You naughty little slut!" She smiled and missed a step, bumping into Pam, who pitched forward and almost fell. "You've been playing the field, haven't you?"

"Yeah, she has." The guy nearest Alice showed a toothy smile. "She gets around, don't you, doll?"

Fearful for Nikki and Pam, and knowing that Reese was probably annoyed with the complication to his plans, Alice tried to defuse the situation. She needed to remove Reese's admirers from the scene. "I, ah, I was on my way to meet a friend."

"Right." The man moved closer until his body touched hers. "Us."

Pam said, "Keeping all the beefcake for yourself? Greedy, Alice. I can see not sharing Reese—"

"Reese," Nikki purred, as if savoring the thought of him.

"But no reason to hog these sweeties, too."

Alice gave a silent prayer that Pam and Nikki would shut up and go in.

They didn't.

"Never figured you for the orgy type," Nikki added. She walked her fingers up her captor's chest.

Because she doesn't realize she's been captured. Panic had Alice's vision closing in. She shook her head to clear it. "I don't know what's going on here, but I think—"

"You know exactly what's happening," the bruiser interrupted, and he settled his hands on her shoulders.

Alice lurched away but didn't get far, not with the men forming a solid wall around her.

They laughed at her impotent fear.

Alice dug in. "I'm pretty sure you plan to kidnap me."

Everyone stopped.

Nikki swayed on her feet, looking around at the men. Alarm finally started to settle in past her buzz. "What're you talkin' 'bout?"

"Who wants to kidnap you?" Pam asked.

Alice opened her mouth to speak.

And a fourth man said, "Alice is just teasing. Isn't that right, Alice?"

Shaking head to toes, Alice watched as the man left the backseat of an SUV. He was younger than the others, probably no more than his mid-twenties. Dark hair and darker eyes…he might have been attractive if he didn't scare her so badly.

Only the sure knowledge that Reese was close, keeping watch, helped her to remain calm.

The bastard behind her bumped into her again, deliberately nudging her toward the newcomer. She felt like a sacrifice, small and insignificant…just as she had so long ago, before Trace had helped her escape.

Before Reese had come into her life.

Alice tried to keep her shoulders back, her chin up, but it wasn't easy. "Where's Cheryl?"

"She's at my place, waiting for you." Hand extended, the new man walked right up to her. "You're Alice, right?"

Not taken in by his handsome face or slick demeanor, Alice ignored his offered greeting. But Pam, clearly reassured, reached out for his hand. "I'm Pam."

His cold gaze transferred off Alice's face and instead he caught Pam in his sights. As if pleased, he took her hand in his. "Very nice to meet you."

Pam smiled dreamily. "This is my friend Nikki."

Nikki wiggled her fingers in a silly hello.

"Woody Simpson, at your service."

Alice shuddered. If that was his real name, it could only mean that he didn't plan on any of them living past the next few hours.

He turned back to Alice. "Do you think your friends would like to join us?"

"No, they would not." *Please, don't make them.*

Woody didn't blink. "I think they would."

Nikki and Pam agreed.

He moved closer to Alice, his smile charming, his air cocky. "In fact, I insist." And with no more than a nod, he instructed the other men to escort Pam and Nikki to the SUV.

Damn, damn, damn. She absolutely could not let Pam and Nikki get in that car. The darkened windows would make it impossible for Reese to see them. Uncertainty would hinder his response; he couldn't leave their safety to chance when reacting.

What to do, what to do?

The other thugs treated Woody differently, with more reverence. They moved out of his orbit, ready to support him if he needed it but unwilling to get in his way.

Who was he to so easily give direction?

And suddenly Alice knew: Woody Simpson was the boss.

This was the man who had abused Cheryl, the creep who had ordered that awful tattoo on her arm.

The man who had made promises, who'd stolen a young girl's heart, only to break it so horribly.

He reached out, touching Alice's cheek, gliding his smooth fingertips along her jaw.

She no longer had a man at her back. If it came to that, she could run. Decision made, Alice demanded, *"Stop."*

Suspicious, maybe even a little worried, the men paused with the car door open. Nikki and Pam hesitated.

Surprised at her daring, Woody lifted a brow. "Problem?"

"You're the one in charge, aren't you?"

In a gesture that felt more threatening for its gentleness, Woody tucked her hair behind her ear. "I came specifically for you, Alice, did you know that? You fascinate me."

"Really?" Her heart pounded so hard it felt like

she might break a rib, but still Alice smiled. "You had Cheryl tattooed?"

"Yes."

She leaned into him, surprising him with her compliance as she rested one hand on his shoulder.

Compared to Reese, this man felt insubstantial, nowhere near as big and solid and strong. And that made him far less important.

She braced her other hand on his shoulder, too. He was taller than her, but being used to Reese's extreme height, she barely noticed. "Everyone else answers to you?"

His gaze warmed with triumph. "They do."

Looking at his mouth, leaning closer still, Alice parted her lips—and brought her knee up into his groin as hard as she could.

She put everything she had into that blow, all her rage at his brutality, his cruel mistreatment of women. Her aim proved dead-on.

Breath left him in a whoosh, his eyes bulging wide. A disbelieving, *"You bitch,"* faded into a raw groan of anguish, and he dropped to his knees, his hands holding his crotch.

Cursing with various levels of disbelief, his men jolted into action. Nikki and Pam got roughly shoved aside, Pam landing against the SUV, Nikki falling to the ground.

The ladies looked confused until they saw the guns, and then they started screaming—long, loud and shrill.

Fear got Alice's feet moving, and she stumbled back, her heart a loud drumbeat in her ears.

And suddenly Reese was there, a big, powerful, protective wall standing between her and the armed savages. He took aim as he issued orders, and unlike the weasels now dropping to their bellies, Reese's calm voice rang with undeniable command.

Trace and Logan closed in, as well, and in short order, they had disarmed and cuffed the three men.

In her peripheral vision, Alice saw Woody get to his feet. She jerked around and found him staring at her with such hatred that she felt it clear down to her bones. Her mouth opened, but nothing came out.

Eyes narrowed, posture still bowed with pain, Woody reached to the small of his back, drew out a gun and—Reese's fist connected with his face.

Alice's jaw loosened at the stunning speed of the strike. It knocked Woody back, and he landed on the ground. The gun discharged, startling a small shriek out of Alice. But seeing Woody's face, Alice knew he hadn't fired on purpose. She doubted the man was that coherent, given the look in his eyes.

Reese was already on him, taking away the gun, flipping him over, jamming a knee into the middle of his back and wrenching his arms together to fasten them with cuffs. With rough hands, Reese checked him for other weapons, ignoring Woody's moans.

Turned to look at her, Reese said, "You're okay?"

Wow. Fear receded under amazement. Reese handled him like he would a rag doll, expending little to no discernible energy.

She remembered Trace saying that Reese could be ruthless.

Now she knew why. He'd leveled that man with one punch.

She also remembered Reese saying that always, at every moment, he was aware of her.

Biting her bottom lip, she admitted that it must be true, given how quickly he'd reached her.

"Alice?"

Heck, no, she wasn't okay. Far from it.

She sucked in a breath and nodded.

With laudable ease, Reese hauled Woody none-too-gently to his feet and looked Alice over, head to toes. "Are you sure?"

Still dumbfounded by how easy he'd made it look, she nodded fast, unwilling to distract him from his work. "Yes. I'm fine."

Tenants spilled out of the apartment building. A black police van pulled up, accompanied by a squad car, lights and sirens blazing. Pam and Nikki huddled together, a steady flow of tears ruining their makeup.

Suddenly feeling weak, Alice slumped down to sit on the walkway.

"Don't move," Reese told her.

She wasn't sure she could.

Watching as he wrenched Woody toward the black van, Alice tried to catch her breath. But only for a second.

Forgetting her agreement not to move, she raced back over before Reese could get Woody into the back of that wagon. "Where is Cheryl?"

Woody looked at her, gave a mean smile and said, "Fuck you, honey."

His mocking tone and total lack of feeling pushed her over the edge. She didn't even think about it.

She just kneed him again.

"Ah, God..."

"Alice," Reese reprimanded. "Damn it." He held Woody upright with one hand, and Alice back with the other. "Honey, you can't do that."

But his mouth twitched.

Alice didn't think it was funny. She literally heaved in her anger and fear. *"Where is she?"*

"Bar," Woody gasped, curled in on himself, trying to protect his most vulnerable body part.

Using the length of his long arm, Reese backed Alice up a few steps and ordered, "Stay there."

The adrenaline rush faded, leaving her knees knocking and her eyes damp with tears. She nodded her agreement.

Reese handed Woody over to an officer. "Don't take your eyes off him. Understand me?"

The cop nodded. "Yes, sir."

Glancing over to confirm that Logan and Trace had things in hand, Reese took Alice's arm and pulled her several feet away.

Any second now, she'd be bawling like a baby, she just knew it. She could feel the sobs gathering steam, squeezing her throat and making her nose tickle.

She couldn't look at Reese, couldn't let him see her weakness.

But he just stood there, waiting, calm, *safe,* until finally she lifted her gaze to his.

"I love you, Alice."

Her knees almost gave out.

Reese caught her close, not quite smiling, but looking so warm, so…sincere.

She clutched at his shirt, her heart trying to do flips, her pulse going into overdrive.

Reese kissed her forehead. "I love your compassion and your courage."

"Courage?"

"In spades." Ignoring the way she gasped for breath, he kissed her parted lips. "I love your sweet little body, too, and how good we are together in bed."

"Reese…" She looked around, but in the commotion, no one seemed to be listening to them.

He brought her face back to his. "I especially love your temper. But from now on, please don't neuter my prisoners."

What he said seemed so silly, so unbelievable. Except for that one part… "You love me?"

"Every part of you, everything about you." He searched her face and whispered, "Very much."

Trace approached. He didn't look right at them, choosing instead to stare off to the side. "Got a message from Rowdy. Says he has it under control, but Cheryl's at the bar with Hickson. DeeDee, too." He glanced at Alice, coughed and looked away again. "I assume you want to go…?"

Reese nodded.

"I can handle it," Trace said. "And even one-armed, Logan has this under control. If you'd rather—"

"I want to finish it." Reese tipped up Alice's chin. "I don't want you to worry."

She trembled so badly, it felt like she might rattle her teeth loose. But everything would be okay.

And Reese had said he loved her.

She drew a deep breath and nodded. "Okay."

"Love that, too," Reese said with a small smile, even with Trace standing there. "How you pull it together to prioritize."

"I'll just go wait over there," Trace said, but neither Alice nor Reese acknowledged him.

She hadn't pulled anything together, but apparently she was good at faking it. "Go to the bar." Alice still clenched his shirt, fighting the urge to crawl up close to him. "Please see to it that Cheryl is okay."

"I'll take care of it."

“I know you will.” Because he was that man, the man who helped others, who did whatever he could. A hero. *Hers*.

Another second passed. Reese pried her hands from his shirt and kissed her knuckles. “Soon as I find Cheryl, I’ll let you know.”

“Thank you.”

“And Alice?” He took a step away. “When I get done with all this, you and I are going to have a nice long talk.”

Now, why did that worry her? She promised, “I’ll wait up,” and then, head and heart filled with jumbled emotions, Alice watched him go.

It wasn’t until an officer gave her a funny look that she realized she was smiling. Reese loved her.

In the middle of pandemonium, with hysterical neighbors and lights and sirens, Alice figured she just might be the happiest woman alive.

CHAPTER TWENTY-NINE

AFTER SENDING OUT the second text message, Rowdy started toward Avery, determined to keep her well away from Hickson. As it turned out, he didn't need to do a thing.

Avery was already moving off when Dougie, the bartender, slid into the booth next to Cheryl. The poor girl scooted over, pressing herself as far into the corner as she could go.

Rowdy was relieved that both men ignored her. They leaned in close for a private conversation.

Damn. So Avery had been right. Dougie and Hickson definitely knew each other.

For several minutes, Rowdy lounged in a corner, watching the exchange, wondering at what point he should intercede.

Even with his mind buzzing and his senses on alert for possible deceptions, he found himself repeatedly searching for Avery. Made sense, he told himself. Tonight would be dangerous, and he didn't want any woman hurt, most especially a woman he employed.

A woman who turned him on.

Scanning the crowd, Rowdy still didn't see DeeDee, but he spotted Avery taking an order from a trio of young men on the opposite side of the room. Avery was her usual all-business self.

The guys wanted more.

It wasn't unusual for barely legal idiots of the male persuasion to play grab-ass with waitresses at run-down bars.

The unusual part was Rowdy's urge to flatten all three of them. Rather than fight it, he moved toward her. If DeeDee showed up and saw him, well, so what? She'd know he didn't like bullies.

He was almost within reach when he heard Avery say, "Last warning, bud. You will either keep your hands to yourself, or you'll leave. Understand?"

Grinning, the idiot reached for her ass, saying, "Or we could—"

Rowdy caught his wrist and squeezed. "Or you could go home with a broken bone or two."

Wincing in pain, the guy said, "Hey, dude, let up."

"Apologize to the lady first."

"Fuck you!" He tried to swing with his other hand.

Rowdy used a grip on his wrist to twist the younger man's arm up and around behind his back. "Wrong answer."

One of his buddies charged, but he was drunk and weak. Rowdy easily moved to the side and tripped him. He wiped out on the floor, gaining grumbles from some of the other customers.

The third fool rose, chest butting Rowdy. "Asshole! Turn him loose."

"Sure. Soon as he apologizes."

"I said, let him go!" He took a short swing, punching Rowdy in the chin, and his head snapped back.

Smiling, Rowdy worked his jaw—and popped the guy. Even using his left hand, he sent the smaller man falling over a chair.

Unruffled, Avery lifted a brow. "Are you done?"

"Almost. Soon as he tells you how sorry he is for manhandling you."

"Sure, sorry, whatever." When Rowdy tightened his hold, he said more sincerely, "I'm sorry!"

Rowdy released him.

Now free, the punk said, "I'm calling the police!"

"Want me to do that for you?"

He flexed his arm, sullen. "No."

"Then get out and don't come back." Rowdy encompassed all three of them in his stare. "Any of you."

Arms folded, Avery stood silent as all three guys hustled for the door. She didn't look at all appreciative of his interference. And, really, now that he'd let off a little steam, Rowdy knew he'd overreacted.

"You can't go running off business."

But hell if he'd admit it. "I can do any damn thing I want. It's my place."

She gave him a measuring stare, then made a rude sound. "Like you'll even remember them if they come back a week from now."

Now there's where she didn't know him well. "I'll remember."

That had her propping her hands on her trim hips. "Hate to break it to you, Rowdy, but if you carry on like that with every guy who gets out of line—"

"There are more?" He searched around the bar. "Here, tonight? Where—" His gaze snagged on DeeDee as she strolled in. She wore a body-hugging black pull-on cotton dress that fit like a man's undershirt, leaving more on display than it covered.

Out of nowhere, Avery gave him a hard shove.

Because he'd been distracted with DeeDee's appearance, she took him off guard, and Rowdy actually staggered back a step. "What the hell?"

She went on tiptoe to snarl into his chin, "You should change the name of this place!"

"Yeah?" Amused by her temper, Rowdy caught her arms to keep her close. "Suggestion?"

"Yes. Call it *Getting Rowdy.*" She shoved away from his hold and said in a grumble, "That's what every attractive woman does, right?"

"Catchy. They get *rowdy* with Rowdy." Pretending to give it some thought, he nodded. "I like it."

"Ohhhh, you're…" She trailed off, clearly trying to find a word insulting enough to match her mood.

"Waiting to get *you,* Avery." He tweaked her chin. "That's what I'm doing. Waiting to get you." And with that, Rowdy walked away before he did something stupid—like kiss her with DeeDee watching.

Ten minutes later, seated in a booth, Rowdy wished for an interruption. He knew brazen women. Hell, he liked brazen women.

But not when they wanted to screw him first and then assist in his murder.

DeeDee did indeed appear to want both.

Leaning her boobs into his side, sliding a small hand over his thigh and licking his ear, she tried to convince him to go to her car.

"I want you so bad, Rowdy," she breathed.

Where the hell was Reese?

Half crawling over his lap and catching his chin, DeeDee planted a hot, wet one on him.

The second she got her tongue out of his mouth, Rowdy lifted his beer, intent on using the alcohol to sterilize things—and his gaze clashed with Avery's from across the room.

With a killing glare, she turned away.

Damn it, he needed Avery to know that it meant

nothing. Except…why should he explain himself to her? They'd be working together, so she was bound to see him hook up.

He enjoyed sexual variety.

Eventually he and Avery would get together—because he knew the chemistry was there—but she needed to understand that it was sex, and only sex. Not a commitment. Not an invitation for more.

No matter how much she intrigued him.

"Rowdy…" While straddling his lap, DeeDee rose to her knees. And right there in the bar, wedged into a booth, she tried to open his jeans.

Time to make a strategic retreat.

Rowdy caught her hands. "Hang on, honey. I'll be right back." *Fucking Reese, running late.*

He'd gotten the text from Trace that they were on their way, but another two minutes and DeeDee would molest him.

He bodily lifted her to the side, ignoring her pouts and the way she stroked his junk as he slid out of the booth seat. "Don't move."

"Hurry," she said.

Suddenly in a killing mood, Rowdy strode over to where Dougie and Hickson shared a booth. He wouldn't hurt a woman, even one as revolting as DeeDee, so he needed to find another outlet.

When he stopped beside them, both men looked up in mingled surprise and suspicion.

Itching for a little violence, Rowdy said to Dougie, "You're fired."

"What?" Dougie gave an incredulous laugh. "Who the hell are you?"

Rowdy took great pleasure in introducing himself. "I bought the bar. And since I'm not a scum-sucking bottom feeder—" *not anymore* "—I don't want your ilk hanging around. You're through here. Collect your shit and get out."

Dougie and Hickson shared a look.

"I didn't hear anything about a new owner."

"No? Guess that tells you just how important you are, doesn't it?"

Dougie clenched all over.

Try it, Rowdy thought. *Please.*

"You son of a bitch," Dougie exploded, shoving himself upright—and right into Rowdy's fist. The blow took him out, and Dougie slumped back into his seat, then slid off the booth to the floor.

"Huh," Rowdy said. "He's not only a drug-dealing worm, he has a glass jaw."

Cheryl gasped, curling tighter to the wall.

"But you," Rowdy said, turning his anger on Hickson, "are even worse. You're a coward who abuses women, a cockroach who needs to be smashed."

Half rising from his seat, Hickson said, "Now wait a goddamn minute—"

Catching Hickson by the back of his neck, Rowdy slammed his face into the thick booth top. Cartilage crunched and blood spilled. With Hickson dazed, he looked at Cheryl. "You okay?"

Frozen, she said nothing, didn't move or breathe or blink.

Rowdy tried to work up a gentle smile. "You'll be fine, I promise."

No reaction.

"Alice sent me."

She deflated on a whoosh. "Oh, thank God." Big tears filled her eyes.

Behind him, DeeDee tried to slink out. Rowdy

glanced at her over his shoulder, pinning her in place with his gaze. "Word of warning, honey. You *don't* wanna make me chase you." In his current mood, seeing the fear in Cheryl's eyes, he just might discount DeeDee's gender.

Hand to her throat, DeeDee paused.

Finally, Reese came in the front door, Trace from the back. Around the bar, several men separated from the crowd; Reese's men, now ready to assist.

Rowdy pulled Hickson out of his seat. "Here's one," he said to Reese, practically tossing the man to him. "There's another under the booth," he told Trace.

Nodding, Trace started forward.

Rowdy turned his attention to DeeDee. "It's over."

Realizing she'd been busted, DeeDee back-stepped, at first uncertainly, but then faster and faster, and suddenly she turned to flee.

She plowed right into Avery, and both women went down.

Shit. Rowdy reached them in less than a second and hauled DeeDee to her feet. One of Reese's buddies took her off his hands. Kneeling by Avery, who looked stunned, he said, "Hey." He pulled her into a sitting position. "You okay?"

She held her head in both hands. "It was a sting?"

"That's right." Rowdy brushed some dirt off her shoulder, then smoothed down her hair.

"You and DeeDee…?"

Despite what he'd told himself, Rowdy relished the opportunity to set her straight. "Just part of the setup."

Instead of relief, she looked…distraught. "So, did you actually buy the bar or not?"

"I bought it."

Now he saw relief—though she quickly hid it behind

a frown. Avoiding his gaze, she said, "Good. I was already counting on my raise as bartender."

Coming to his feet along with her, Rowdy grinned. "Then get to it. Since I just fired Dougie, you can start right now."

IT WAS DAMN near dawn when Reese got home to Alice. He should have been dead on his feet, but instead he felt energized. He'd called Alice as soon as he could, letting her know that Cheryl was shaken up, but unharmed. This time, she was more than willing to talk to the police, to ensure that Hickson and Woody Simpson got what they deserved.

Knowing what awaited him, Reese bounded up the steps and down the hall to the apartment. As he stepped inside, the first rays of sunlight slanted through the patio doors.

Logan had already picked up Pepper. Dash was crashed in a chair, staring blindly at the TV. But when the door opened, he sat forward and pulled on his shoes.

Just as she'd promised, Alice was awake, waiting for him. Both she and Cash looked bleary-eyed with fatigue, but they immediately rose to give him a proper welcome.

First things first, Reese thought, and he reached for the leash.

Alice stopped him. "Dash just had him out, soon as he knew you were on your way home."

Reese gave his attention to Logan's brother. "Thank you, Dash. For everything."

Smiling, Dash slapped Reese on the shoulder as he headed for the front door. "Anytime." He already had his keys in his hand.

"Anxious to get to bed?"

"I'll be heading for a bed," Dash agreed with a yawn. "But not my own, and not to sleep." He bobbed his eyebrows, gave a negligent wave and was gone.

Alice stared at the closed door. "He couldn't be serious."

Reese grinned.

"But he was up all night!"

Reese teased her, saying, "You should know that men consider sex a cure-all for just about everything, even exhaustion."

"Oh." Suddenly she was hugging him, and Reese breathed in the comforting scent unique to Alice. He ran his hands down her narrow back, and, yes, he wanted her.

Always.

But there'd be time for that.

"You have to be hungry," she said. "Let's eat first."

First, meaning she was amenable to lovemaking? Amazing Alice. How the hell had he gotten so lucky?

She took his hand and led him toward the kitchen. Her long nightgown nearly touched the floor. She had shadows under her eyes and rumpled hair and she was the most beautiful thing he'd ever seen in his life.

In the kitchen doorway, he pulled her around. "Alice."

"Hmm?" She looked up at him with trust and acceptance and so much more.

He kissed her, then went on kissing her—until Cash whined.

They both turned to see the dog standing by the counter where they kept the dog treats, wearing an expectant expression.

Alice bit her bottom lip. "He acts like all we do is have sex."

"He's intuitive, much like you."

Laughing, Alice gave the dog a treat, then turned to press Reese toward a chair. "Sit while I put on the coffee."

It did feel good to get off his feet. He toed off his shoes under the table, stretched and thought how nice it was to end a long day with Alice.

"Cheryl went back home to her family?"

Reese watched the sway of her hips in that fetish gown as she filled a carafe with water. "She called her mother from the station. There were some tears, but I don't think they were sad tears."

"Excess of emotion," Alice said with a nod. She gave him a shy look. "I do that sometimes, too."

"I don't want you to cry. Ever."

She laughed at that. "Sorry, but sometimes I even cry when I'm happy."

Okay, so he might have to get used to that—since he planned to keep her very happy. "Peterson got a warrant, and she's going through Woody Simpson's offices right now. She's already found tons of evidence." Quietly, because he knew how Alice would react, he told her the rest. "She also found a young lady named Michelle, who was more than willing to detail everything she'd overheard, and everything she'd seen."

Alice went still before turning in a rush. "Is she okay?"

"Peterson thinks she'll be fine." Certainly, she'd be better now than she would have been if Alice hadn't intuitively recognized that Cheryl needed help. She'd started the ball rolling on breaking a huge case of drug trafficking, kidnapping and more. "And thanks to her, we'll be able to shut down deals already in the works and ferret out buyers and distributors who'd been involved with Woody."

Alice briefly closed her eyes, but when she opened them again, she asked, "And Rowdy? How did things work out for him?"

Reese told her about the petite redheaded waitress who had occupied much of Rowdy's attention. "I have a feeling he'll be facing new challenges very soon."

Grinning, Alice said, "I'm glad." As she turned to fill the coffee cups, she asked, "What about Trace? Is he gone again already?"

It occurred to Reese that it no longer bothered him for Alice to mention the elusive wraith. "I doubt we'll see much of him after this, but I got the feeling he'd be doing some behind-the-scenes recon for the lieutenant, helping her to nail down evidence against any remaining corruption."

As if Trace's whereabouts didn't concern her all that much, Alice set the coffee on the table. "What would you like to eat?"

He smiled at her, and she blushed.

That made him laugh outright. He caught her hand and pulled her over and into his lap. "You know, if it weren't for you, both Cheryl and Michelle, and probably a lot of other women, would still be in a great deal of trouble."

"You give me too much credit." Her gaze intent on his throat, she slipped her hands under his shirt. "I'm just glad that you were able to sort it all out."

Already aroused heat filled her big brown eyes. Damn, but he loved her.

Reese traced a finger over her lips. "Looks like I'll have mandatory days off again."

"Oh?" She nuzzled into his throat, her breath gentle and warm.

He shuddered. "I was thinking we could spend that time looking at houses."

Her head came up. "You were serious about that?"

"Cash needs room to run." He tangled a hand in her silky brown hair. "And since I'm staying with you now, we need a bigger place."

She caught her breath. "Are you…staying with me?"

"I want to."

Chewing her bottom lip, she grew serious. "For how long?"

Slipping his other hand into her hair, Reese cradled her head in his palms and kissed her. "Does forever sound too long to you?"

Her eyes widened. "Forever?"

He pulled her close again, took another kiss, this one gentler still. "If you'll have us. Cash and me, I mean. We're a package deal."

"I adore Cash," she rushed to assure him. "You know that."

"And me, Alice?" He searched her face, his heart full. "How do you feel about me?"

Those happy tears she'd mentioned turned her eyes luminous and left her voice husky. "I've been in love with you since the day you said hello."

"Yeah?"

"How could you not know that, Reese? I'd done so much to protect myself that I'd shut out the whole world. But I couldn't shut you out." She gave a choked laugh. "I couldn't even stop thinking about you long enough to try."

He knew the feeling. Alice hadn't crept into his life; she'd launched a full-force attack on his heart…without even trying. "Given that I feel the same, what do you say we get married? Maybe adopt another dog or two. Have a couple of kids. That is, after we find the right house—"

Alice kissed him.

Grinning, Reese eased her back. "Should I take that as a yes?"

Nodding fast, she said, "Yes, yes to everything."

"Tell me again that you love me."

"Oh, God, Reese, I do. So much." Knotting a hand in his T-shirt, she slipped off his lap. "Now, come with me, Detective. I've decided the coffee can wait."

Perfect, he thought as he followed her toward the bedroom. His old nickname had stuck true. He'd bared it all, even his heart, and now he had Alice.

He had everything.

* * * * *

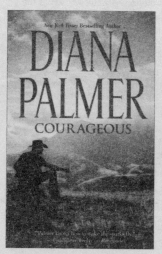

New York Times Bestselling Author

KAT MARTIN

Deep in the heart of the Louisiana bayou, a survivalist group has something that belongs to former navy SEAL Ben Slocum: his son.

That he's a father is news Ben was not expecting. But once the initial shock wears off, he takes in the rest of what social worker Claire Chastain tells him—that Sam is in the custody of an abusive degenerate, that they've disappeared... and that Ben is now the child's only hope.

Their concern for Sam draws Ben and Claire closer, each of them fighting feelings there's no time to explore. Ben's got one chance to take back what's his, and in one gunshot he could lose it all.

Available wherever books are sold.

MKM1443

New York Times bestselling author

NORA ROBERTS

will delight with these two classic tales of love meant to be!

BEST LAID PLANS

Abra Wilson had met men like Cody Johnson before—charmers who could make a woman's heart rise and fall, and smile their way out of any situation. The overconfident East Coast architect fits the bill perfectly, and Abra has no plans to fall under his spell...no matter how distracting he might become. Fortunately, Cody has plans of his own that not even Abra will be able to resist!

FROM THIS DAY

When B. J. Clark, manager of the Lakeside Inn, meets the new owner, Taylor Reynolds, she is fully prepared to dislike him. She fears that he plans to transform her lovely, sleepy old hotel into a resort for jet-setters. But when sparks fly between them, B.J. finds herself torn between her professional antagonism and her growing attraction to the man she had sworn to despise.

Available wherever books are sold!

PSNR168

LORI FOSTER

77806	ALL RILED UP	___ $7.99 U.S.	___ $9.99 CAN.
77708	THE BUCKHORN LEGACY	___ $7.99 U.S.	___ $9.99 CAN.
77695	RUN THE RISK	___ $7.99 U.S.	___ $9.99 CAN.
77656	A PERFECT STORM	___ $7.99 U.S.	___ $9.99 CAN.
77647	FOREVER BUCKHORN	___ $7.99 U.S.	___ $9.99 CAN.
77612	BUCKHORN BEGINNINGS	___ $7.99 U.S.	___ $9.99 CAN.
77582	SAVOR THE DANGER	___ $7.99 U.S.	___ $9.99 CAN.
77575	TRACE OF FEVER	___ $7.99 U.S.	___ $9.99 CAN.
77571	WHEN YOU DARE	___ $7.99 U.S.	___ $9.99 CAN.
77491	UNBELIEVABLE	___ $7.99 U.S.	___ $9.99 CAN.
77444	TEMPTED	___ $7.99 U.S.	___ $9.99 CAN.

(limited quantities available)

TOTAL AMOUNT	$________
POSTAGE & HANDLING	$________
($1.00 FOR 1 BOOK, 50¢ for each additional)	
APPLICABLE TAXES*	$________
TOTAL PAYABLE	$________

(check or money order—please do not send cash)

To order, complete this form and send it, along with a check or money order for the total above, payable to Harlequin HQN, to: **In the U.S.:** 3010 Walden Avenue, P.O. Box 9077, Buffalo, NY 14269-9077; **In Canada:** P.O. Box 636, Fort Erie, Ontario, L2A 5X3.

Name: ____
Address: ____________________ City: ____________
State/Prov.: __________________ Zip/Postal Code: ____________
Account Number (if applicable): ______________________

075 CSAS

*New York residents remit applicable sales taxes.
*Canadian residents remit applicable GST and provincial taxes.

PHLF0513BL